LINDSTRÖM

*For Emily
All the best
John*

[signature] 2018

A STONEWOOD IMPRINT

JOHN MOSS

IGUANA

Copyright © 2018 John Moss

Published by Iguana Books
720 Bathurst Street, Suite 303
Toronto, Ontario, Canada
M5S 2R4

All rights reserved. No part of this publication may be reproduced, stored in a retrieval system or transmitted, in any form or by any means, electronic, mechanical, recording or otherwise (except brief passages for purposes of review) without the prior permission of the author or a licence from The Canadian Copyright Licensing Agency (Access Copyright). For an Access Copyright licence, visit www.accesscopyright.ca or call toll free to 1-800-893-5777.

Publisher: Mary Ann J. Blair
Front cover image: Igor Stepovik/Shutterstock.com
Front cover design: Mumson Designs © 2017

A Stonewood Imprint

Library and Archives Canada Cataloguing in Publication

Moss, John, 1940-, author

   Lindstrom alone / John Moss.

Issued in print and electronic formats.

ISBN 978-1-77180-260-4 (softcover).--ISBN 978-1-77180-261-1 (EPUB).--ISBN 978-1-77180-262-8 (Kindle)

   I. Title.
PS8576.O7863L56 2018   C813'.6   C2018-900860-1
                                                                                           C2018-900861-X

This is an original print edition of *Lindstrom Alone*.

for Beverley because I love her

1 BLACK NAILS

HARRY WAS STARTLED AWAKE BY THE OPENING CHORD of Beethoven's Fifth. Calls were rare; he was always surprised. He would have preferred a riff by George Harrison but the phone came with Beethoven on default and that's how he left it. He picked up reluctantly.

"Yeah?" he mumbled.

"How are you managing?"

He didn't respond.

"I've got a client for you, Harry. I'm sending her over."

He was pleased and annoyed. Ambivalence was part of their relationship.

"Harry, are you there?"

"Yeah."

"What are you doing?"

"Sleeping."

"It's midafternoon."

"I'm looking out the window. Watching the weather."

"Is it interesting?"

"Who is she, Miranda?"

"Just talk to her."

"I'm on my way out."

"Do us a favour, Harry. You like me, remember."

"Miranda."

"Yes?"

What could he say? He disconnected. He wanted to please her. Knowing Miranda Quin was pleased made his world a little bit bigger, a little more tolerable.

He had just wrapped up a case. It was grisly, straightforward, and emotionally depleting. A distraught mother, the fury of an estranged father, the remains of a child. The woman's parents had hired him to prove the events were inevitable and there was nothing they could have done to change things. He managed to turn their unbearable remorse into sorrow, something he seemed unable to do for himself.

The first killer in Harry Lindstrom's life was himself. Three years later, torn between rage and despair, death had become his vocation. He had been a philosophy professor; now he worked as a private investigator specializing in murder. The dramatic transition from exploring the fundamental questions of existence in a lecture hall to exposing the mysteries arising from murder seemed absurd and grotesquely inevitable. A defiant, proud, and solitary man of forty-two, he held the life of the mind in highest esteem, yet lived in a world of raw feelings and haunting emotions. He abhorred brooding yet brooded; he rejected bitterness, yet grief and guilt and anger defined him. Harry endured.

He pushed his clothes along the rack in his side of the closet. Sliding his knee-length sheepskin coat from a wooden hanger, he felt a surge of sadness but looked forward to the reassurance of its heavy warmth pressed around him. Karen had the coat handmade for him their last winter together. She liked the way it was cut long enough to protect his legs in the Ontario cold. Before their final canoe trip, he had put it in storage in the cellar. When he burnt the house to the ground, it survived. The wool and leather still exuded the faint odour of smoke. Water stains blended with the patina from natural wear to make it look older than it was.

He found a flannel shirt in the bottom drawer of the dresser and drew it on over a merino wool crew neck, which was warm to his skin. While he was buttoning the shirt, he walked out into the living room and gazed at the smouldering sunset. Harry lived on the Toronto skyline. From his windows on the twenty-third floor, the world was a constantly changing distraction. He paid extra for a southern exposure. In the blur of a retreating snowstorm, the first of the season, the view across the harbour and over the islands was a painting by Turner and the city was remote. The air above Lake Ontario was infused with an eerie red glow. December snow crowding the streets behind his building would melt into slush before it could be trucked away, but from his condo aerie he could imagine it crisp and even. He preferred real winter when the snow stayed. He preferred summer, late spring, early fall. He liked the seasons clearly defined.

He sat down on the blue sofa with his coat folded over his knees. He tried to think of nothing. We're not here to enjoy ourselves, he thought. Actually, his thinking was a sort of mental plagiarism. This was Ludwig Wittgenstein's thought. Wittgenstein was his favourite philosopher—not for his ideas, which Wittgenstein's doctoral examiners at Cambridge, including Bertrand Russell, had found profoundly impenetrable, but for his irreverent wit. Whatever our purpose, I'm pretty sure it's not to have fun.

That was metaphysics Harry could relate to, even though Wittgenstein meant it ironically.

And if it cannot be spoken one must remain silent!

That was Karen, paraphrasing Wittgenstein.

Harry had missed the great man at Cambridge by a full generation but the long drawn face and lanky gait represented themselves in his mind as a ghostly presence on his forays among the nocturnal shadows of the town. Wittgenstein was still there, always just slipping from sight.

For a materialist, Harry, you're surprisingly good at experiencing ghosts.

And you, at being one.

He was not about to argue philosophical materialism. But he distinctly recalled the carved grey stone, the pale brickwork, the checkerboard marble of Trinity College echoing Wittgenstein's words, the burnished wood and worn plaster that were redolent with the convoluted clarity of his deeply serious, hesitant, intense, elusive, provocative ponderings. Wittgenstein thought in public. He did not merely issue the product of having had thoughts. You could watch him thinking! Even after he was dead. The reverberations of his mental machinations still resounded amidst the silences if you knew how to listen. And sometimes Harry did.

Yet he had no drive or desire to follow in Wittgenstein's footsteps.

Modesty, Harry!

Karen's voice was muffled. It annoyed him when she wasn't easy to hear.

Balance. I wasn't cut out for the intellectual priesthood. I wanted a life. And then.

Death happened.

Death doesn't happen; it's not an event. Life stops. There's nothing more. You cannot make an event out of nothing.

Harry.

I should be quoting Nietzsche.

I'm sure you will, you often do.

The floor shuddered and a faint rumbling echoed from the elevator shaft on the other side of the wall. Harry knew the comings and goings of his neighbours. Everyone else was home already or out for the evening. He kept a mental account of things like that. This would be his visitor direct from police headquarters. She must have slipped through the security door in the lobby.

He draped his sheepskin coat over the wingback chair he had retrieved from his great aunt's estate. It had come over from Sweden in the middle of the nineteenth century. The buzzer sounded as he approached the door. He didn't bother peeping through the spyhole. When he opened the door, she wasn't what he expected. Miranda had said nothing about her being so beautiful that he would have trouble focusing, the same way he might with someone who was terribly disfigured. His visitor was maybe twenty years older than him with radiant white hair, on the verge of old age, and stunningly, sensually attractive.

He stepped back and she walked past, straight to the window, and turned to face him with the sunset off to the side behind her so that she seemed surrounded by flames. Her features took on a light of their own, and for a moment he thought he could see the skull beneath her glistening skin.

"Lindstrom and Malone?" she said. "There's no sign."

"Can't run a business in the building."

"But you do."

"It's more of an existential diversion. Superintendent Quin knows about us, the building superintendent doesn't."

"Where's your partner?"

"Not here."

The woman glanced at his silver wedding band. Harry looked away. Images of Bergman hovered like film clips at the edge of his mind.

Ingrid or Ingmar, Harry?

"What can I do for you...?" He paused, inviting her to fill in the blank.

"Birgitta. Ghiberti." The woman spoke her name in two distinct words, as if there was a barrier between her first name and her last.

"Ghiberti. Renaissance sculptor. The bronze doors in Florence," he said. He shrugged off Karen's muted protest about being pompous. "I would have said you're Scandinavian."

"Ghiberti is my married name. My own was Shtoonk."

"Really."

"You know Yiddish?"

"No."

"It means fat, lazy, and stupid. I'm not Jewish."

"It happens."

"I kept his name after we divorced."

"And Ghiberti remarried?"

"He's dead."

"Does that mean you're a widow?"

"Once removed."

She offered a wry smile and pushed her silver-white mane back from her face. Harry thought of Ilsa in *Casablanca.* Shrewd, damaged, desperate.

Dangerous and alluring.

Birgitta Ghiberti stepped forward out of the flames. She had piercing eyes, and yet she avoided making eye contact as she surveyed the room. Apparently not dissuaded by whatever she saw, she suddenly honed in. Her eyes flashed.

"I'd like to talk to you about Bernd, my son."

Harry waited. He felt strangely on the edge of a precipice, walking in the dark beside a looming abyss.

"I believe my son will try to kill you," she said.

For a moment his mind went blank, then spiralled, grasping for meaning. He could hear the silence that followed like the roar of waves crashing against rocks on the shore below. He smiled, he rarely smiled. He smiled because he was morbidly amused. He was engaged, curious, and pleasantly aggravated at the absence of subtlety.

"I don't feel very threatened," he said.

"He intends to kill me as well. He is a serial killer."

Harry could not imagine how he and this woman fit a common pattern as potential victims.

"Normally he murders young women," she said. "Usually blondes."

In a self-mocking *femme fatale* gesture she swooped her head forward and around so that her long silver hair flared away in a pale nimbus and settled back close to her skull.

Harry shivered with revulsion but the revulsion was tempered with a tremor of apprehension.

Was she pausing for dramatic effect? He waited.

"Bernd has disappeared."

"That should be a relief to both of us," he said.

"I think he's in Sweden."

"Superintendent Quin can put you in touch with the right people. I don't do missing persons."

"You don't understand." Choosing her words with unnerving

precision, she continued, "He will execute me, he will exterminate you. He is a very dangerous man."

Birgitta Ghiberti surveyed the room again.

As a mawkish expression of pathetic fallacy, night was dropping into place behind her.

"Perhaps we should sit down," Harry said, settling into a teak and leather chair and motioning her to take the blue linen sofa. Her long legs flashed elegantly as she arranged herself in a formal design to convey poise and distress.

"Would you care to elaborate?" he asked. "If you think he's in Sweden, how are we threatened? And more to the point, why? I don't even know the man."

"I am afraid by coming here I have forged a deadly connection between you."

"Not if I don't take your case."

"He won't know that you haven't. He knows I am quite persuasive."

"How will he know that you've been here?"

"I will make sure that he does."

Harry nodded appreciatively. For a moment he might have been back in his tutor's lodgings at Trinity, prepared to debate the delusional wonders of logic over a glass of vintage port. Only this wasn't an intellectual exercise.

"Your son will murder me because you have *asked* me to save you from being murdered. Whatever my response, I am a condemned man. Seems reasonable enough."

"I'm glad you understand," she said.

The woman has no sense of irony, Harry.

"This is not about us," said Birgitta Ghiberti. "Our deaths are incidental."

Oh really.

"We must be worried about the young women," she said. "He has killed many. He will kill many more unless we stop him."

Altruism put Harry in a more sympathetic humour than extortion. Past victims were nebulous in his mind, but the passion of her plea on their behalf seemed ominously specific. Was the urgency an expression of genuine concern? She had made herself aggressively vulnerable, an anomaly he found intriguing.

Anomaly, bullsquat. She's a predatory, cannibalistic, silver-haired black widow arachnid.

He ignored the clumsy metaphor.

Simile, Harry. They're exactly alike.

"I'm listening," he said to his guest. "Explain, why do you suspect your son is a killer?"

"I know, I do not suspect, Mr. Lindstrom. Or is it Professor? Or Doctor?"

"How much did Quin tell you?"

"About you? Very little. That you were a philosophy professor and are now a detective. An intriguing vocational trajectory. I take it you didn't have tenure."

"I had tenure."

"Do you have children, Mr. Lindstrom?"

Miranda had been relatively discreet! Harry was relieved, even though the evocation of private sorrow was distressing.

"No," he said. "They've gone."

"We can't keep them forever, can we," she observed.

No, we can't keep them forever—Karen's voice, deep inside, and curiously gentle, wistful, resigned, acquiescent.

"No, not forever," Harry echoed. Miranda had not shared the details. "What kind of proof do you have?" he asked. It seemed an awkward question.

She opened her capacious and expensive handbag and took out a small tin box, the kind loose tea comes in from specialty shops. It was battered and the label was obscured by stains the colour of earth. He could make out the words *Hulda's bland*-something and *Visby Gotland*. A pair of aged and sinister eyes glowered through the smudges of dirt.

She pried open the lid and leaning forward she turned the box delicately on end over the coffee table. The contents spilled out, bracketed by a stack of newsmagazines and an unlikely bowl of artificial fruit. They appeared to be a clutter of dried fish scales, catching colourful crescents of illumination from the overhead light.

Harry sat motionless. Fingernail clippings, dozens of them, with nail polish of various hues, and oddly, all of them meticulously blackened on the inner curve. He reached out, hesitated (there was something repulsive about other people's bodily detritus), picked up a few and dropped them into the palm of his hand.

"Not the most evil fetish I could imagine."

Birgitta Ghiberti reached over and touched his open hand with her fingertips. Her enamelled nails dug into his flesh. They were a deep red, the colour of dried blood, and they were artificial.

"Trust me," she said. "These are souvenirs of death."

Harry flinched a little, and dropping his selection back onto the pile, he pulled his chair close to the table. The woman's long legs flashed across from him as she made herself comfortable again, unselfconsciously putting herself on display. He slid a lamp closer and taking up a pencil sorted through the parings.

"Obviously from many different women," he said. "I'm assuming they're all women. And Nordic, yes? Swedish. Most of them are buff or pink. Lighter complexions. A few quite garish. Prostitutes, perhaps."

Or women with bad taste, Karen offered.

"Or darker skin," he countered, playing Nick to her Nora, out loud. "Mediterranean, maybe. Is there such a thing as black nail polish?"

Goth, Harry. Of course.

Birgitta Ghiberti stared at Harry and for a startling moment he thought she was aware of his interior dialogue. But she seemed to be waiting for him to catch up.

"Let's concede for a minute these are actually evidence of murder," he said. "How do you connect them with your son?"

"I found the box hidden in a burial mound last summer."

"A burial mound?"

"In Sweden. We have a farmhouse on the island of Fårö in the Baltic Sea. There is a root cellar in a pile of rubble. Generations of children have terrified themselves playing inside it, insisting it was an ancient grave and at one time a site for human sacrifice."

"And your son played there as a child? I assume he's grown up now."

"Yes."

"Why would he save them?"

"To punish me."

"For what?"

The woman gazed across at him and smiled sadly, but made it clear she was not about to elaborate; perhaps she couldn't. Her smile was strangely unsettling. He thought for a moment, as if trying to separate the words from the thinking they expressed. He did not want to trivialize her apparent distress. "Have you considered they might be the remains of some childhood game?"

She glanced at him with scathing contempt, then gazed at the tangle of nails.

"A rather unusual game, Mr. Lindstrom."

"Did you ask him about them directly? Maybe he has an explanation."

"I did. He stormed out and I haven't seen him since."

"When was that?"

"After the worst of the snow. We were housebound for a few hours. He waited until the airport was cleared this morning, and then he left."

"But you found them last summer?"

"I did."

No further explanation. He continued, "No one noticed an accumulation of bodies."

"My son is not stupid," she snapped.

An odd reaction, Harry.

Easy, Sailor. Let's not rush to judgment.

"From this pile, I'd say there must be quite a few," said Harry. "What do the victims have in common, apart from clipped fingernails."

"They're dead."

"Yes?"

"They're mostly blondes. Swedish, a few from Norway. Girls and young women, one or two a year, maybe three, frozen in the snow; not enough to attract much interest in a northern climate, not unusual enough to suggest a pattern."

"But *you* see a pattern."

"After I found this tin, I researched. I knew what I was looking for. I have a file. Mostly sad little stories culled from the Internet."

"There must have been autopsies, investigations?"

"Cursory, at best. Deaths by misadventure, Mr. Lindstrom. No indication of laws being broken or criminal negligence, apart from stupidity on the part of the deceased for being caught out in bad weather."

"Maybe that's all it was, they were caught out in bad weather."

She gave him a withering stare. He continued, struggling for clarity.

"Surely discolouration on the fingers would have attracted attention."

"Look closely at those nails, Mr. Lindstrom. That is what you are paid to do."

Presumptuously bitchy, isn't she?

It wasn't worth quibbling about.

He poked at the nails, then picked up a small cluster again and pushed them around on his palm, examining them in the glare of a reading lamp. The sheared edges showed evidence of blackening. They had been painted after they had been cut. The corpses would have shown nothing more unusual than a recent manicure, which might or might not have been *post mortem*, there was no way of telling. Nothing to flag suspicion. And at the same time, as Harry observed these sad bits of bodily detritus that had been so meticulously altered, he felt a surge of nausea. What sort of demented artisan would pursue such ghoulish fastidious compulsive behaviour? If not evidence of homicide, the nails painted one by one, ten at a time, indicated a sickeningly disturbed psyche.

"You found a tin of fingernails, and then you researched murder?"

"It is not as strange as you seem to think, Professor. There was a death in Visby some years ago. The corpse had black smudges on her fingertips. A grisly detail that attracted little attention but it stayed in my mind."

"Visby?"

"On Gotland, Mr. Lindstrom. The large island near Fårö. Visby is a medieval Swedish town with modern amenities. No one was ever caught for that first murder, but it was like the others that followed."

"But the others didn't have blackened fingers."

"No."

"Causes of death the same?"

"In each case, the girl was not dressed properly for the cold."

Murder by design, so to speak!

"Were they sexually assaulted?" Karen was flippant; he, dead serious.

"Oh, no. Not hurt in any way."

"Apart from being dead."

"Of course."

Harry gazed out at the fading winter scene framed by the grey folds of his open drapes. He wondered how many died of exposure each winter in Canada, not counting snowmobilers who seemed to have a fatal attraction for testing the limits of thin ice and live avalanches, and how many of those were young women?

He picked up the tea box and held it so that light from the window illuminated the inside. There were still a few nails adhering to the metal. He tapped them loose on the table.

"How do you know this macabre collection belongs to your son?"

"It does."

"Mother's intuition?"

"My son has a history, Mr. Lindstrom."

"As do we all."

"Mr. Lindstrom?"

Harry could hear Karen rumbling like static.

"Are you suggesting he's killed before?"

"I am, Mr. Lindstrom. When he was a child."

"Ah," said Harry. "Who did he kill the first time around?"

"His three sisters."

Harry swallowed, and then he coughed and swallowed again.

"At the same time?"

"Separately."

"Do the police know?"

"Your friend Superintendent Quin has a report. They decided not to lay charges."

She seemed clinically detached, which seemed monstrous. But what could possibly be appropriate?

"Because they had no evidence," he offered.

"Because Bernd was very young and I was a grief-stricken single mother."

Harry was thrown by how she had displaced sorrow for the deaths of three children with bitterness toward their survivor. He was fascinated by the human need to make sense of the senseless, no matter what the cost. He wanted nothing to do with unnatural suspicions of murder and the deaths of children.

Harry, don't.

Children should not die. And yet the ambiguity of evil attracted him. Birgitta Ghiberti was not in doubt about the guilt of her son but seemed as indifferent to his motives as she was to her own in wanting to find him culpable. The real mystery, he suspected, was not in her daughters' deaths but in how their passing had shaped the lives of those left behind.

This was too close to home. As Nietzsche had cautioned, when you look too closely into the abyss, the abyss looks into you. Harry took in a deep breath. "It's all very haunting," he said, "but I'm afraid I'll have to decline. I hope you will convey my disinterest to your son."

He sat back in his chair. Karen sighed in relief.

Birgitta Ghiberti taunted. "You are afraid?"

"Not at all."

She seemed about to get up. Instead, she turned and reached deep into her handbag, pulling out a small zippered leather case. Harry reached over and took it when she handed it to him.

"You asked me why I delayed confronting Bernd until now. Perhaps this will explain. My research was driven by curiosity until I found this. I couldn't be sure. Now I am."

He turned the small case over in his hands, as if expecting it to be heavier. He recognized the Icelandic coat of arms emblazoned on the leather, loquacious with detail. Harry had holidayed in Iceland the previous summer.

"Open it carefully," she whispered imperiously. He caught the urgency and excitement in her voice.

It was a manicure kit and lodged among the scissors and tweezers and file were ten more nails painted black on the inside curves. The colourless sheen on their outer contours made them seem alarmingly fresh, as if they had just been cut.

Suddenly, the murders were as real as blood.

His gut tightened; he felt sick and his breathing constricted. This is what drew Harry to murder; the horror, the thrill, the surprise. In a flash of fresh evidence, a mother's grotesque suspicions had turned to fact. Old nails take on an opacity over the years but these were translucent. With no polish, offset by narrow bands of white, backed by black enamel, they seemed almost radiant. When he touched one, it was pliable. He could imagine the girl with the pared nails. Blonde, robust. And very dead.

But why were these ones not polished when the others were? Why were they in a manicure case from Iceland, not the old tea box? Was the killer shifting from Sweden to an equally cold and deadly venue?

Iceland? Toronto?

Harry had plunged into the story. He was suddenly caught up in the seductive ambiguities, the repulsive perversities, the nearness of death as an adversary, caught up in the challenges of an old-fashioned mystery with the horrific dimensions of a classical tragedy.

"Mr. Lindstrom?" Birgitta intruded. "You'll take the case?"

"Was Bernd in Iceland recently?" Bernd was no longer the creation of his mother's ghoulish obsession, he was real and a menace.

"He was."

"I take it he was in each place where a body was found."

"He was. He visits Sweden two or three times each winter. We have relatives there."

"On Fårö?"

"Yes. And of course he has friends in Stockholm."

"Friends?"

"He is not a rampaging fiend, Mr. Lindstrom, striding through the land wreaking havoc. He is an educated man, quite gentle and good, for the most part, but he is on an insidious quest. We must stop him by making a case for the police—or by force. To do either, we must survive. Your friend Ms. Quin said you are a survivor. She suggested you can do things and go places the authorities can't."

"Did she also suggest you should threaten me with death as an incentive."

"That was my own idea."

She's good with the unexpected answers, Harry.

Miranda described me as a *survivor*. As if surviving were an achievement.

The ghost of Margaret Atwood haunts us both.

"I'll need to see your file," he said. "I need more to go on than fingernail parings and a mother's fear."

"A mother's regret, Mr. Lindstrom. You cannot possibly know."

"I'll try."

"Good. That's very good. Then you must see what I have gathered together, of course. How much for your retainer?"

"Nothing. You pay me when you're satisfied."

"Satisfied, Mr. Lindstrom?"

"When we're done, you pay what you think it's been worth. Plus expenses."

"What it's been worth, yes of course."

The woman's face seemed devoid of emotion. He wondered what feelings were suppressed and what had died with the deaths of her children, with the conviction that her son was a killer.

Harry rose to his feet. Birgitta Ghiberti leaned forward and scooped the fingernails back into her tea box. She placed it and the black leather kit back in her purse as if they were priceless artifacts. Harry felt strangely embarrassed for her as he reached across the table to help her up, then he led her toward the door. She gave him a card with her home address in the affluent Rosedale neighbourhood.

They arranged to meet the next day at her place. Harry wanted to check in with Miranda first and take a look at the police dossier on the deaths of the three sisters.

He handed Birgitta a card of his own from the foyer table. She held it to the light. "Lindstrom and Malone, Detective Agency." She hesitated, as if trying to decipher an underlying message. Then her eyes widened and she smiled. "*Lindstromalone.com.* Your life in an email address. Malone was your wife, she is gone. You are alone."

It wasn't a question. Harry didn't respond.

"Do not be too sad, Mr. Lindstrom."

Speak for yourself, lady.

"Call me Harry," he said.

"Birgitta."

Harry could feel Karen glowering.

"I'm glad you will help me, Harry." Birgitta Ghiberti tilted her head like a young woman. "You need to understand I am genuinely afraid of my son."

Because you've spawned a monster?

Because you've uncovered his ghoulish secrets?

Because you've betrayed him?

Because you've brought Harry on-board to scuttle him?

Harry could hear Karen's words like a protracted death rattle. He found them curiously reassuring.

"Noon, then," he said.

"Noon," she repeated. "That's fine."

He ushered her out the door and closed it. He didn't wait for the elevator. The condo was his home, not the building. He listened as a soft shuddering reverberated through the walls, and then he settled onto the sofa where she had been sitting and gazed out at the evening sky.

She knows I won't ever be back, you know.

I don't imagine she cares.

He turned on the CBC. He'd given up his boycott over Barbara Budd being taken off *As It Happens* because his absence went unnoticed. Even though he was tuned to Radio One, it was only music. He turned it off.

He needed to go for the walk he'd been planning when Birgitta Ghiberti intruded. He liked walking in the dark. He and Karen used to take night-walks along the Sanctuary Line when the kids were small, towing them asleep in their sleds over furls of snow. Sometimes on his walks along the Toronto waterfront, where the city lights were obscured by the city itself, he could see the stars over Lake Ontario. He could feel himself out among them, he could see so much farther than in the daylight, he could see out to the beginnings of the universe and stroll disembodied through a provisional version of eternity.

He stopped in front of the hall mirror. His reflection glowered back at him, contemplating the deep brown eyes that stared fixedly into his own. Like cracked amber, Karen had described them. Her eyes were green and brown and golden.

Birgitta's were blue, like cornflowers.

She's very beautiful, Harry. She makes me think of the other Bergman. Ingmar, not Ingrid. Windswept islands, windswept soul. Go for a walk, I'm staying by the fire.

There was no fireplace.

He slipped on his sheepskin coat and put on the cashmere scarf that Karen had stitched into a Möbius loop and closed the front door behind him without locking it. She would have to make do with a hot bath and he would return to the lingering scent of lilacs.

He felt curiously content. He felt in no danger at all.

2 POLICE HEADQUARTERS

DURING THE NIGHT THE AIR TURNED COLD AND THE SNOW didn't melt. Harry woke up reluctantly and let his arm fall across the other side of the bed where the comforter lay undisturbed. He struggled for a moment to orient himself in the present and his dreams crumbled, leaving him anxious and confused.

He had stayed awake almost until dawn, conjuring with Birgitta Ghiberti's story, trying to turn it into a coherent narrative. Harry liked things to be coherent. As he stared out over the harbour, Aristotle and Oedipus shouldered their way into his mind. Neither was very good company. But if Aristotle could conduct a rational exploration of murder and sexuality, of suffering, revelation, betrayal and retribution, then Harry could, as well.

The difference was that Harry lived in an ironic world not an iconic one. He wasn't a dead Greek nor obsessed with illusions of objectivity. He yearned for cleansing on a personal level, an expunging of pity and fear that would purify his own damaged soul.

He was attracted to the Ghibertis to salve his wounds. Karen felt sorry for him. That made him angry.

By the first glimmer of morning, he had decided if Birgitta Ghiberti were truly in danger since confronting her son, he was ethically obliged to help her. If he were in danger himself, he was reluctantly obliged to evade being collateral damage. If young women were dying, he was morally obliged to stop a serial killer. And amidst all the depravity of the dysfunctional Ghibertis, he might find something redeeming, ennobling, cathartic.

How very Aristotelian.

We're all Greeks in the end.

Philosophers invariably take refuge from life in ancient Greece, dear Harry, among the market stalls and naked wrestlers of Athens.

Harry had never considered himself a philosopher. He had been a teacher and a thinker—philosophy was something he did, not something he was.

As Wittgenstein explained it, philosophy was an activity, a fact in itself. It was a movement toward clarity not a state of affairs to be studied.

Forget the intellectual stuff, Harry. A tea box of meticulously blackened fingernails reduces classical tragedy and high thoughts of redemption to the sordidly squalid and irreducibly ordinary.

While he was dressing, Harry paused for a moment to contemplate a box of a different sort on top of the dresser. It was a fine piece of antique Japanese lacquerware they had picked up in a flea market in England. During the dry winter before the accident, as police defined it, a fine crack had appeared on the surface and they sent it out for expert repair. The elderly man who fixed the box, a refugee from Southeast Asia, did such a good job it appeared flawless. He brought it to Harry in the hospital and refused payment. Now it held only one item, Karen's battered silver wedding band, returned to him from the mortuary.

Harry took the subway to police headquarters on College Street. He detested subways. There was something unnatural about hurtling through tunnels gouged out of the darkness that separated places they were intended to join. Whole neighbourhoods were erased from public consciousness because people travelled under them, and the shudder and screech of the rolling stock made people forget where they were. He preferred Toronto's lumbering streetcars, especially after a heavy snowfall when the world looked new and pedestrians had finally succumbed to bundling up for the season. But the lines were laid out on a lateral bias, mostly parallel to the lake, and he was going north.

Harry emerged into the cold and trudged through uncleared snow that squeaked under his boots. He gazed up at the pink granite and blue glass exterior of the police building, captivated by its monumental display of angles and planes.

The police headquarters had curb appeal; it played to the emotions with a fake flowing stream and a fractured façade. Not, perhaps, so extravagant in personality as the new extension to the Royal Ontario Museum, with the wondrous absurdity of its helter-skelter angles and vertiginous planes of glass jutting out over the pavement, but an estimable renegade, nonetheless.

"Liberating, isn't it?" He had spoken out loud.

Harry, Karen hissed.

He could hear the exasperation.

Harry stepped off the elevator at Miranda Quin's floor and made his way through groups of detectives and forensic specialists huddled in separate conspiracies over coffee and maps and broadsheets and photos. When they made eye contact through the glass wall of her office, Miranda got up and walked to her door to wave him through. Harry glanced around, fascinated by how quiet it was.

"Miranda," he said, sidling by her and sitting on the worn black leather sofa.

"You here alone, Harry?"

"As far as I know."

But you're not, Harry. I'm here.

Miranda's eyes were hazel, the same colour as Karen's. Her hair was auburn, but the grey made it lighter than Karen's. She was a very attractive woman and so was his wife, but they did not look at all alike. Miranda's features were gentle and rounded, changing with her mood from girlish to urbane, resolute to serene, while Karen's were sculptural, like stone brought to life. Miranda was handsome, Karen was beautiful.

He looked up at Miranda with a rare expression of warmth, as if what he was about to tell her was a secret. "I'm thinking of taking the case. I told her we'd look into it."

"I was afraid you might be put off."

"By the sad possibility that it's true?"

"By the deaths of her children."

Harry gazed at her, feeling rising resentment. She met his gaze without pity.

"I like your scarf," she said. "Did Karen make it?"

"She sewed the ends together."

"And a beautiful job she did."

"It has wonderfully anomalous mathematical properties. Topologically, it's a square with circular properties and a circle with rectangular properties."

"That particular one, or all of them?"

"It's a Möbius loop."

"Is it warm?"

He smiled. She had a way of subverting his pomposity by making him feel like he was in on the joke.

"So," he said. "I'm intrigued. All she's got is a Googled collection of deaths by exposure, a tea box of expendable body parts, and a mother's conviction that her son is a monster who murdered his sisters when he was a kid and may decide to kill us next. Not much to go on."

"Has he threatened you?"

"Not directly."

"I've been in touch with the National Criminal Police in Sweden about the cases she's dug up and they don't see a connection. They don't even see murder. Girls and women being careless in a cold climate. Assault doesn't seem to be an issue, but they do have things in common."

"They're dead," said Harry.

"They're female, young, blonde."

"Not surprising."

"None raped or beaten."

"Freezing to death is supposed to be gentle."

"It's horrific, Harry, no matter how gentle. I'm glad you think what she's got is worth pursuing."

"At her expense."

"Or yours if you don't find anything. I've dug up our old file on the sisters. She asked me to let you read it."

"Sounds like it's not even a cold case. There's no case at all."

"She was grieving, she still is. But it might help you understand what you're getting into."

"I'm the last person in the world to be a grief counsellor."

"You care, Harry. And it's a good read."

"I need encouragement, here."

"You're already involved."

"I need motivation."

"You want to stop people dying."

"Only God can stop people dying. That's why I'm an atheist."

"Still? You think God has forsaken you?"

"No, Miranda, I have forsaken God."

"Harry?"

"You can't understand, Miranda. You were never a believer, anyway. You were an Anglican."

Miranda winced

"Harry, you need to read her story. The woman was coping with the deaths of her children. God knows, you know, we cope with death in different ways, especially when children are involved. I think Birgitta Ghiberti was distraught. I think her mind was poisoned. She had lost three daughters in three separate incidents. She was trying to make sense of their deaths."

"So she blamed her son."

"There's a certain logic to her version of events."

"But not enough to lay charges."

"Her son was a kid, he'd lost his sisters, he was a bit weird, but he was suffering too. Morgan felt sorry for him."

"Morgan did the report?"

"In his inimitable way."

"And he concluded Bernd didn't kill anyone."

"I'm not saying that, Harry. The kid was a kid. His mother was grief stricken. Morgan left it open-ended."

"Police equivocation is not a pretty sight."

"It's quite possible the kid was the innocent victim of his mother's outrage."

"Or that she's outraged because he's a killer and got away with it."

She slid the file across her desk.

"Is Morgan still around?" he asked.

"Yeah, we make a good team. He's a lovely free spirit."

"Me too," said Harry and smiled.

As she gazed at him, sadness weighed down the corners of her eyes.

"Read it over, see what you think. It's quite eloquent."

"I'd expect nothing less."

"And Harry, be careful."

"Of course," he said. Since she wanted him to take on the case, he wondered whether she meant to be careful of the mother, the son, or himself.

Harry picked up the file and made his way through the organized chaos of the homicide department to an interrogation room. The door didn't lock from the inside but he knew he wouldn't be disturbed. He had a couple of hours, allowing for time to walk over to Birgitta Ghiberti's house in Rosedale by noon.

The room smelled of stale sweat and disinfectant.

He sat upright in the straight-backed chair and tried to read but Miranda's motivations distracted him. She was a cop but she was reaching outside the force, encouraging Harry to fan cold embers into flames.

No action is ever taken without an ulterior motive.
Yes, but whose?
Don't be obtuse, Harry.

It was Miranda Quin who had urged him to open a detective agency. She recognized that after what he had been through with the loss of his family, continuing to teach philosophy, expounding on being and non-being, life and afterlife, meaning and ultimate ends, all might seem futile, especially when he was lecturing to students who took being, life, and meaning as given, and death as a dreary abstraction. She had signed as guarantor when he applied for his P.I. registration. She knew his past, more of it than anyone still alive.

When he thought about Miranda, Karen usually stayed in the shadows.

Three decades previous, Miranda had been Harry's counsellor at a canoe tripping camp in Algonquin Park, the same camp Karen had gone to after they'd both moved on. Miranda was older than him and worlds apart. He was skinny with a massive shock of straight blond hair, and smart in a disarming way, a wry observer. And Miranda Quin could roll a canoe onto her shoulders by herself, make cinnamon rolls over an open fire, and had real breasts. With her shimmering auburn hair and hazel eyes, for the entire season she was a living version of magnetic north; every male in the camp knew precisely where she was at any given moment.

When they had met briefly on Bloor Street some years later, he was on a break from his studies in England to attend a funeral. They went for drinks. Miranda had just dropped out of the RCMP; they were on a more equal footing. She was as striking to look at, as vivacious and clever, and he was no longer a boy but a handsome young man with a furrowed brow, an aquiline nose and bold eyes, his strong features softened to a knowing scowl by his Nordic complexion. And still a wry observer, but now, as a philosopher, the wisdom of the ages weighed on his shoulders, or so he imagined. He hadn't finished his studies.

They became lovers for a few weeks. He had been happy to evade relatives clustered around the death of his beloved Aunt Beth, whom most of them resented for her having achieved so little in her life with such great élan, and Miranda was recovering from a bad affair in Ottawa. After a brief period of seclusion among familiar particulars around the family home in Waldron, not far from where Harry's own family had made and lost their modest fortune, she was in Toronto to join the police service, eventually to become Superintendent of the Homicide Division. Harry was on his way back to complete his doctoral studies at Cambridge.

For a while they stayed in touch with the occasional call or email. After he returned from Cambridge and both he and his bride began teaching at Huron College in London, Ontario, their communications were reduced to sporadic notes catching up on milestone events. After the accident, their lives again converged.

She was Harry's only living friend.

He focused on the file in front of him and began to read. A few paragraphs in, he sat back; he realized Miranda's motivation was curiosity, not forensic curiosity but intellectual curiosity. She wanted to *know*. Harry was her surrogate; she wanted him to find out the truth. Birgitta Ghiberti had rekindled her interest. She wanted Harry to fan the flames or put out the fire. Either way, to resolve the mystery—an abstract incentive appropriate to a philosopher, even if his own desire to *know* meant putting his life in jeopardy.

Morgan's version of Birgitta's account was compelling. He read the accompanying documents. There was a coroner's account of accidental death by drowning, a fire marshal's explanation for a fatal explosion from leaking gas, a medical examiner's autopsy report of death by suffocation. An hour later, he dropped the folder off on Miranda's desk.

He turned to leave, then stopped and faced her, trying to fine-tune his facial expression. She waited but he seemed stuck between taciturn and congenial.

"Well?" she said.

"Interesting. Gotta think about it. Thanks."

"You're very welcome."

"Could you call and tell her I'll be late."

"I'm not your secretary."

"Fine, keep an old lady waiting."

"She's not that old and she's rather gorgeous."

"It's all relative, isn't it."

He needed time to think. He was no more convinced of Bernd Ghiberti's guilt than his innocence, but he was enthralled by what he could only call evil that characterized the mother's story. He planned to walk up to Rosedale despite the cold.

Miranda reached into a drawer of her desk and pulled out a black woollen toque. Harry took it from her gingerly, as if he were too fastidious or too proud to countenance a used piece of clothing.

"It was my Dad's, Harry. He would have liked you to wear it."

Harry pulled the toque on and rolled up the edge. His short prematurely grey hair merged with the black wool in a jaunty corona.

"Looks good," she said.

Harry stopped in at Starbucks on the corner of College and Yonge, then headed north, shoulders hunched against the cold, with his fleece collar pulled up and the toque pulled down over his ears. Leaning into the Arctic wind that surged down Yonge Street, he walked slowly. He was wholly in the moment of his own creation. A moment at once horrifying and exhilarating. He savoured the reasons he had become a private detective.

3 BIRGITTA'S STORY

THIS IS WHAT HARRY PIECED TOGETHER FROM A BRIEF conversation with a woman who was certain her son was a killer, from an eloquent police write-up, and from speculation based on a coroner's report, a fire marshal's investigation, and a forensic autopsy. Harry's imagination was fired by the intuitive insight of his dead wife, Karen, and the confidence of Miranda Quin, an old friend who recognized that coping with sorrow gave him special insight into the sordid complexities of Birgitta Ghiberti's account. This was Birgitta's story, translated through Harry Lindstrom's mind to accommodate his fascination for ambiguity and his penchant for narrative coherence.

ON MARCH 25, 1991, Birgitta Ghiberti entered the old police headquarters on Jarvis Street just months before its postmodern granite and blue glass replacement opened on College Street. She requested an interview with someone in homicide, and with unnerving composure intensified by her blonde colouring and Nordic reserve, she informed Detective David Morgan that her thirteen-year-old son, Bernd, was responsible for the deaths of his three sisters. She had just buried the last of them on the previous Saturday. She had no proof, beyond a mother's conviction, and she had no doubts. Her son had done terrible things.

IN THE EARLY summer of 1985, when Bernd was seven, the family settled into their cottage along the Muskoka River, only twenty minutes from Port Carling. The children had been taken out of school two weeks early for the dubious pleasure of enjoying the solitude before the hordes arrived with their speedboats and jet skis. The father, Vittorio Ghiberti, generally commuted from Toronto to spend the weekends with his family, although he anticipated being tied up in the city this year with business commitments. Birgitta was happy enough with the arrangement and the four children were unabashedly relieved by his absence.

The river in front of the Muskoka cottage was broad and meandering, so that its flow seemed determined by the summer breeze. Early most mornings, because the nights were still cool, a fine mist hovered over the tiny beach in an alcove beside the Ghiberti boathouse. Sometimes the two older girls would skinny dip with the mist shielding them from the eyes of early rising cottagers nearby. Giovanna and Isabella spent most of their summers close to the water, only going up to the cottage for meals and, when their father was visiting, for compulsory board games in the evening.

The boathouse had two slips, one for the old-fashioned Muskoka launch, with its massive engine and low-profile mahogany hull, and one for the rowboat. The canoe was hauled up on the dock outside, covered by the overhang of the loft where the older girls slept while the younger children, Bernd and Sigrid, slept upstairs in the rambling white cottage with the *au pair* and their mother.

When the girls went skinny dipping, of course, everyone knew what they were doing. Giggles and splashing penetrated the grey haze that was spun to gossamer by the morning sun before fading away. The sounds reverberating along the riverbanks, echoing in boathouse slips, and rising to cottage verandahs made the old feel young and put the lascivious on edge.

Giovanna was fifteen, two years older than her sister. They were beautiful girls, both fully developed, and often taken as twins. This flattered Isabella tremendously and pleased Giovanna. On June 21, 1985, the mist was burning off from the sun by the time they woke up but they decided to swim anyway. When they went down to the sandy alcove, Giovanna dropped her towel, despite the fading mist, and waded in to her knees. Isabella hesitated, then stepped back, feeling her toes squish in the damp sand, and, grasping her towel more securely around herself, she gazed at her sister's naked body with unrestrained admiration. She was not used to her own body yet and Giovanna so casually inhabited hers, she wanted to reach out and embrace her, to absorb some of her womanliness without knowing quite what that meant.

"You are beautiful, Giovanna," she said.

"And you are beautiful, too," said her older sister.

Behind them, standing by the red canoe in the shadows of the boathouse, seven-year-old Bernd, still dressed in his Christopher Robin pyjamas, stared solemnly at Giovanna. She was just a girl when she had her clothes on but a woman with pointy breasts and golden pubic hair and strange exciting curves without them. He touched himself between the legs to be assured that he was like his father, whom he feared and admired.

Isabella whirled around at the quiet whimpering sounds and saw her little brother clutching his penis through his pyjamas. She squealed and, dropping her towel, she raced through the shallows into deep water, laughing hysterically. Giovanna sank to her knees and smiled serenely, the shallow water splashing against her rib cage, her exposed breasts, her smile, taunting him.

Bernd's eyes narrowed to a squint as he released his grip on his penis and cupped his hands in front of his stomach, rocking back and forth on his heels like an animated garden gnome. He knew he had to behave like a man but being laughed at and taunted made him angry, as it always did, so he stopped rocking and stood very still, scowling at Giovanna and ignoring Isabella, who was splashing about and giggling as she swam close enough to the boathouse dock to give him a good soaking, but she didn't, he looked so solemn.

Giovanna began to feel uncomfortable under the weight of her little brother's squint-eyed scowl. She stood up in the knee-deep water, defying him to keep looking. When he moistened his lips, then slowly drew his face into a smile, she turned away in disgust and plunged sideways toward the deeper water. The little bugger had somehow turned his humiliation into her own. Normally a graceful swimmer, she swam with a thrashing sweep of her arms, kicking a furious wake behind her, until she was almost to mid-river.

She took in a mouthful, choked and gasped for air. It was still too early for boat traffic that would build during the day to a crescendo about four in the afternoon, then taper off toward evening. But she was instinctively wary and she was beginning to feel sorry for her strange little brother. She turned and, swimming the breaststroke as she tried to catch her breath, she made her way back toward the boathouse.

Isabella was treading water close to the side of the dock, unsure of how to extricate herself from Bernd's diminutive but malignant presence, and Bernd remained motionless, enthralled by his newfound power. She was beginning to shiver and kicked her feet more vigorously, at the same time grabbing the worn cedar plank edging the dock. Giovanna was getting closer; she would chase the little bugger away, and they would emerge from the water, dignity restored.

Never had Bernd deserved more than now the nickname the girls had given him, *the little bugger*. Not, of course, in front of their father and only with caustic endearment when their mother could hear them. Sometimes they used an English accent they had picked up from reruns of *Fawlty Towers*. Then it was: *dirty rotten little bugger*. They loved him in the same way he used to love his decrepit Pooh bear, which he hauled around by a torn ear until he forgot it somewhere and it was retrieved and quietly buried.

A scream shattered the ominously quiet proceedings. Wheeling around to see where it came from, Isabella's hand slipped off the cedar and she went under, swallowing water, then gagging, sputtering, coughing, spitting bile when she surfaced. Ignoring her brother, she scrambled up the ladder, seized hold of her towel, and wrapped herself, all the while scanning the surface for her sister, waiting for her to burst into the air.

There was not a bubble, no waves, nothing.

Isabella yelled at Bernd to get help while she clambered awkwardly into a bathing suit and, yanking the lifebuoy off the side of the boathouse, she plunged back into the water and swam in the direction her brother had been staring. Bernd didn't move. She shouted, telling him to run for help. He stayed perfectly still, absolutely silent, hands cupped in front of his stomach. Frantically, Isabella swam, dove beneath the surface, peering through layers of morning sunlight aslant to the surface.

When she found her sister, doubled up on the sandy bottom, she gathered her into her arms and rose to the lifebuoy, weeping, shaking, overwhelmed with sorrow, and yet she was able to haul them both toward shore.

Her mother and the *au pair* had heard Giovanna from the wraparound verandah but they paid no attention, it was the girls playing, until something in Birgitta was stirred by the solitary scream without laughter and she looked down and saw Isabella towing the lifeless body of her older sister. She rushed to the boathouse, where Bernd was standing transfixed, and she plunged into the water fully clothed. With the help of the *au pair*, they lifted Giovanna out onto the dock and the *au pair* performed CPR but they knew it was too late. Isabella slouched against the boathouse wall, too exhausted to cry.

Bernd moved out of the way but not so far he could not survey his sister's naked body. He was fascinated by the way her nipples puckered and her breast tissue quivered as the *au pair* pounded her chest, hand over fist. His own nipples were slight in comparison. He knew about pubic hair but he had never focused on it before and at first he thought it obscured something secret but when he manoeuvred around he could see there was nothing but folds that neither repelled nor attracted him. He touched himself through his Christopher Robin pyjamas for reassurance.

He ran down the length of her legs with his eyes, intrigued by how they twitched with each thrusting lunge of the *au pair's* fist. Then slowly his gaze rose up her body, past her arms, which draped listlessly at her sides, until he reached her head, which was tilted back to accentuate the smooth arch of her neck as her mother breathed with suppressed anguish into Giovanna's mouth. He was astonished by how expressive her features were, frozen into a kind of horrified smile. It occurred to him that she was quite beautiful, dead.

Satisfied there was nothing more to see, he wandered away, looking for something to do until breakfast was ready.

WHEN HE WAS ten, Bernd discovered a passageway that ran from the back of a closet in the third-storey hall of the Ghiberti house in Rosedale, behind the sloped walls of the hip roof, all the way to the back of the closet in Isabella's room. He had known about it for years but never explored it, since it was dusty and filled with spider webs and gas pipes and water pipes to supply Isabella's bathroom, and he was quite fastidious for a ten-year-old, and more adventuresome in mind than in fact.

On December 21, 1988, Bernd lay sprawled across his bed. He was thinking about Christmas. This would be the fourth without his father. There were presents under the tree in the living room labelled Isabella, Sigrid, and Bernd, signed Papa in an unfamiliar script, but nothing for Birgitta, of course.

That's where Sigrid would be, in the living room. Her favourite pastime had recently become staring at the tree and smiling wistfully, like an old woman reminiscing. The tree was a blue spruce and he could smell its pungent scent wafting up the stairwell. He was the only kid he knew who had a real Christmas tree that only a few weeks before had been a living thing. It had been cut down in the snow and was slowly dying, but its life would be prolonged in an extravagant celebration before it was finally discarded. Other kids in his neighbourhood had expensive plastic trees and pine-scented incense, but it wasn't the same.

Suddenly he heard giggling and cringed at the possibility of humiliation. But the giggles ascended the open stairway near his door, and by leaning his head far back over the side of the bed he could see part way up the flouncing skirt of his sister's friend, Rose Ahluwalia, as they climbed to the third floor. He knew Isabella was very attractive, but Rose was pretty and wore short skirts and would sometimes flirt as if he were sixteen, which excited and puzzled him.

After the girls had reached Isabella's bedroom and closed the door, the music descended. Rush, from four years earlier, heavy on synthesizers: *Grace Under Pressure,* booming through the floor, zinging down the staircase, pounding on the walls. Bernd liked Rush but on principle despised this album.

He tried to lose himself in the din by self-consciously thinking about Rose, drawing naked pictures of her in his mind. He could do the general outline but when he tried to colour in the details he got lost.

She wasn't like his sisters, who were blonde, even the one he barely remembered who had died in Muskoka. Blonde with blue eyes, the same as their mother. Rose had dark brown hair, deep brown eyes, and a tan complexion. Not dark like his father. More like himself. His father had an almost olive cast to his skin and his hair was shimmering black. Bernd and Rose were hybrids, although he was a blend of Swedish and southern Italian while she was Greek and Bengali.

The music stopped. Bernd rolled onto his feet and slipped furtively into the hall, only to be assailed by a mounting crescendo of synthesizers, again from Rush. Instead of retreating, he smiled to himself and, under cover of "The Enemy Within," he slowly ascended the creaking stairs and moved stealthily along the corridor to the empty closet. Once inside, with the door slightly ajar for the light, he lifted away the panel at the back and crawled through into the cramped passageway, which smelled of mildew and dust. As his eyes adjusted to the darkness, he could see skeins of cobwebs. Reaching out, he swept his hand tentatively into their midst and was pleasantly surprised to find them tingle as they adhered to his flesh.

His mind focused on Rose, on the challenge ahead, he forged onward. The air in the passage was thick and tasted stale; the music was muffled into a throbbing assault; the smell was strangely exciting. The dull gleam of diffused light articulated an almost impenetrable maze of copper tubing, air ducts, insulated electrical wires, and drainage pipes.

As he edged closer to the light streaming from the back of Isabella's closet, Bernd began to breathe through his mouth. He tried to wipe away the cobwebs that had accumulated on his face but they adhered like a mask of finely spun silk. It made him feel strong.

Months ago he had ventured up to the third floor to use Isabella's bathroom. Sigrid was dawdling interminably in the one they shared on the second floor and he didn't dare use his mother's en suite. Isabella was out. After he was finished, he had slipped into Isabella's room and removed the panel at the back of her closet from its frame. He had set it upright on the floor in front of the opening so the gap across the top wouldn't draw attention to the adjustment.

Now, with the closet doors open, he could see most of the room, cloistered by the deep shadows of Isabella's clothes hanging just above eye level in front of him.

The girls were smoking furiously. The gable window was frozen shut and a blue haze swirled through the room as they danced in spastic gyrations, trying desperately to synchronize the poetry of their bodies with the cacophonous throb of the synthesizers. Every once in a while they would shout something at each other. He even heard his own name in the din, followed by laughter. Rose danced close to the closet and collapsed on the floor, giggling, reached up, and Isabella handed her a lit cigarette. Rose lolled on the hardwood, her clothing askew. By adjusting his posture and leaning low he could see up her skirt.

When she gyrated to Rush, lying prone, and rolled to the side, he could clearly see blue underwear. His favourite colour was blue sky over fresh snow. He was touching himself through his clothes. He desperately wanted her to take her underwear off but he didn't want to see anything more. He pinched the tip of his penis and shuddered.

Suddenly the music stopped. For a desperate instant he thought it was because of him. He leaned deeper into the shadows until a sharp protrusion dug into his back. He stiffened and stayed perfectly still, waiting. They didn't know he was there. They were both on their feet.

Isabella came perilously close, lifting clothes from the rack in her closet. He pursed his lips after licking them and tried to breathe through his nose but the sounds of moving air echoed in his head and he resumed breathing through his mouth, the sibilance of each quavering exhalation resounding but unheard.

He reached slowly behind him and, turning a little, his hand came to rest in the darkness on a lever attached to a copper pipe. He tried to move it but it was stiff, so he edged forward a bit, toward the light. Both girls were in their underwear. Rose was wearing a sky blue bra to match her panties. His sister's underwear was blue as well, but more like the blue of a moonlit night, silky and gleaming. They were handing each other clothing and shimmying in and out of skirts and blouses and modelling for each other, still smoking furiously.

Bernd was excited and bored. He wanted them to do something else; he didn't know what. His sister changed bras and his interest returned. He was fascinated by the gyrations, the way she did it up in front, then slid it around and leaned over, draping her breasts into the cups, standing and twitching her shoulders as she pulled her flesh up into mounds, like it belonged to somebody else.

"It was my sister's," she explained to Rose.

"Sigrid's? She's only twelve. What's she want with a push-up?"

"My older sister. Giovanna." Her voice dropped an octave. "She died, she was two years older than me. Like, she'd be a year younger than I am, now."

"I'm sorry," Rose responded, not knowing what else to say. "It's very pretty."

"It's slutty. She bought it by mail from Victoria's Secret. Vittorio would have freaked. She only wore it once. I keep it … How macabre is that?"

"Very macabre. I gotta get home."

"Okay," said Isabella without getting up. "Better put your own clothes on. Merry Christmas."

"You too."

"You celebrate Christmas?"

"No. We always have fold-up trees in our living room this time of year." She paused. "January 6th, that's when the wise men turned up on the scene. We get two Christmases, plus some neat stuff from India."

"Well, who knew!"

Rose retrieved her clothes from the tangled mess on the bed while Isabella remained on the floor, in front of the closet, not a body's length away from her trembling brother.

After Rose left, Bernd wanted desperately to escape. Isabella lit another cigarette but left the CD off, and cried softly. He was puzzled by the look on her face. He had expected pain, to accompany her weeping, but when he tipped his head to see her better, she was registering a depth of loneliness and anguish he could never have imagined.

He backed off slowly. He needed to get away from her. His sweater caught at the lever on the copper pipe. He didn't care if she heard him; he wanted to run but there was no room. He yanked at his sweater and the lever gave way. He was terrified she'd hear him. He didn't care.

Glancing back he could see her face and she was serene.

He pushed at the lever and slowly hoisted himself around and began to crawl toward the back of the hall cupboard in the gloom in the distance. Behind him, there was a small tinkling sound, like a dime dropping on a hardwood floor.

Years ago, there had been a gas fireplace in Isabella's room but it had been disconnected and removed long before the Ghibertis moved in. The gentle pressure of the flowing gas had pushed off the copper cap on the end of the pipe in the crawlway when Bernd opened the valve. Slowly, gas filled the air behind him as he crawled toward his escape. The unfamiliar smell, like hard-boiled eggs gone rancid, a sulphuric odour meant to raise an alarm, meant nothing to him. He rather liked it and felt a surge of regret as he sealed the panel and quietly closed the door to the closet before descending the stairs to his room, as strains of a Beatles tune drifted down after him.

The explosion shook the house to its foundation and lifted the roof off one end, sending shards of charred detritus through the air, but the fire was extinguished quickly, with only water damage to the lower levels. Birgitta was able to move back in, with her two remaining children, Sigrid and Bernd, by early spring.

Christmas had been ruined, of course, but Rose Ahluwalia came to the funeral on Boxing Day with her family, and when she bent close to Bernd to whisper her sympathies, he thought he could feel her right breast press into his blazer and he imagined it was covered in sky blue satin.

MARCH 21, 1991. Bernd had just turned thirteen and Sigrid was almost fifteen. Their father had died three days earlier. No one expected it. Vittorio was a handsome gregarious man, a leader in the Italian community by virtue of his business success, his attractive family, and his inclination to take charge without reference to qualifications or deference to seniority. Born in Brindisi on the heel of Italy, he arrived in Toronto in his mid teens, moved in temporarily with an aunt and uncle, lied about his age, learned a trade as a bricklayer, and thrived. As the years passed, he lost his proficiency in Italian and spoke it like an educated foreigner. That made him less intimidating to those who depended on him as his construction business prospered and more responsible to those who counted on him when he switched to finance. He was fifty-one at his death; his heart gave out. Otherwise, he was bright-eyed and robust.

Bernd and Sigrid attended the funeral service with their mother and sat in a pew near the back. Birgitta did not want to be a distraction for the widow and her children, two of them Vittorio's, and one from a previous marriage. Nor did she want to compete, for her own children were beautiful and theirs were pleasantly ordinary. She herself, while a decade older, still had her figure.

The woman had been widowed before. The Church permitted a full mass even though Vittorio was divorced. A bishop who spoke both English and Italian presided. Bernd wondered if he spoke Latin, too, or was that something people only read out loud. He would be starting high school in the fall and intended to take Latin, which was what the smartest kids did, either Latin or Chinese.

Heavy March rains resounded among the beams in the spidery heights of the cathedral. There had been a deluge of wet snow or sleet for almost a week. The burial was postponed until the following day, which the forecast promised would be cold but dry. Bernd didn't mind, he solemnly relished the trappings of death and was amused that some people apologetically explained to his mother, or to his father's widow, that they had made the visitation, signed the register, hoped the family liked their flowers, and attended the mass, but previous engagements, work, travel, or other commitments meant they would have to miss the interment. Bernd had never seen anyone buried, but, from what he imagined, that promised to be the best part.

After dinner, Bernd retired to his room. A few relatives had dropped in to express solidarity with his mother, since condolences seemed inappropriate, and she excused his rudeness for going upstairs as an adolescent expression of grief. He lay sprawled backwards on his bed with his feet propped up on the headboard, trying to see how many separate sounds he could identify.

Apart from voices rising up the stairwell and the occasional decisive trembling as the front door opened and closed, the rattle of coffee cups and the ping of crystal, there was the water running as toilets flushed, the lashing of rain against the windows, the shudder of the furnace resonating up through the joists from the basement, the sibilant hush of warm air pushed through sheet metal ductwork, and from outside a siren wailing in the distance. If he listened carefully he thought he could hear the holiday traffic on the Don Valley Parkway, the ominous squeal of tires and the occasional irritated blast of a horn.

Listening even more carefully, he was sure he could hear the whispering rush of wind through the pines that towered over the graves at Pleasantview Cemetery, and the scrabbling of ravenous squirrels searching the rain-drenched darkness to find rancid nuts buried among the gravestones the previous fall. And he could hear the wind's velocity pick up as the rain slowed to a drizzle and then stopped.

In the room next to his, Sigrid was talking on the telephone. She felt closer than ever to her odd little brother. Somehow, she had been born into a large and boisterous family and now it seemed very small. No one else in the world shared the same history, from the same perspective, and she had grown to depend on him for emotional stability.

Sigrid knew their mother was serene as a survival strategy. Her children adored her from a distance. But Bernd's unnatural composure in the face of death drew her in, as if by sheer will he could protect them both from the unimaginable pains their mother endured. He seemed to understand things Sigrid couldn't comprehend. His eerie indifference to the suffering of others she took as a measure of preternatural wisdom and spiritual calm. Still thirteen, a year and a half younger, he was her best friend and they spent solemn hours together playing Dungeons and Dragons in his room.

Tilting his head backwards over the edge of the bed, looking upside down through his doorway, he could see the steps where he'd last seen Rose Ahluwalia's legs as she flounced up the staircase with his dead sister, Isabella. He closed his eyes only for a moment to relieve the pressure of blood running from his inverted cheeks against his eyes, and when he opened them Isabella was standing in the doorway. Bernd stiffened and then with an explosive twisting he tumbled off his bed onto the floor and leapt to his feet.

Sigrid flinched but held her ground. She wasn't afraid of her brother, no matter how weird his behaviour. Being strange was part of his strength. She was wearing Isabella's black taffeta skirt with a red tartan sash and full-sleeved white blouse. On her, the outfit seemed like a costume, perhaps because it was meant for Christmas, or because Sigrid had not fully grown into a woman's body and looked like she was playing dress-up. But it made her feel good. Bernd never let her talk about Isabella and she could hardly remember Giovanna.

"You look silly," he said, regaining his composure.

"I'm just trying it on. It almost fits."

"The dead are dead, you know. Throw it away."

"No."

"Do what you want."

"Whatever. Do you think Papa suffered?"

"Do you care?"

"Of course I care. What a dumb thing to say."

"Or maybe I'm just honest, and you're not. Those people downstairs, they don't care that he's dead. They're just coming in to watch Mom, to see how she takes it. People who go to funerals and stuff are ghouls."

"The mass was nice."

"Yeah, because we're Lutheran it seemed better than it was."

She sat on the edge of his bed and smoothed the taffeta skirt over her legs. She leaned back against her hands and thrust out her chest, making her small breasts rise against the white cotton of her blouse. Looking down at herself, she felt warm inside. It didn't bother her that her brother was openly staring at the same thrusting of her breasts. She raised her legs straight and admired her ankles, then suddenly leapt to her feet.

"Let's go for a walk!"

"It's raining."

"No it's not, you know it's not, you know without looking. That's part of being a Wiccan, isn't it?"

"No, I'm not practising. I just like reading about it. You wanna play D&D?"

"No."

"Okay. Let's walk over to Pleasantview."

"The cemetery? Yuck."

"We'll find Vittorio's grave. It'll be with the rest of the Ghibertis, Aunt Terese and Uncle Tony and them. It'll be open."

"Open?"

"Yeah, they've dug it already. C'mon."

He had settled on the bed beside her but clambered over and grabbed a sweater from the floor and together they trundled down the stairs, past startled guests in the foyer, pulled jackets from the closet, and were out the door and into the dismal March gloom, on their way to the cemetery, before either had time to think much or say anything.

When they passed between the stone pillars and under the ornate wrought iron archway into the cemetery, Sigrid slipped her hand into his and trudged along so close they brushed against each other with every step. Bernd knew precisely where the Ghiberti plot was, in the part of the cemetery with lots of ornate tombstones and obelisks, angels weeping and angels ascending.

Although the rain had stopped, the air was still laden with a fine mizzle that formed halos around the streetlights. The pines loomed dark against the livid glow of the city, and the stark branches of dormant oaks and the occasional chestnut or maple stood out like fractures in the dismal sky.

Their father's grave was covered with a tarpaulin that had slipped off its supporting beams under the weight of the rain and draped into the depths of the earth. They stood close, gazing down at the darkness in front of them, fascinated by the icy glint of saturated topsoil near the top of sheer walls that descended through the murky clay into absolute black. Close to one side, an ominous mound partially covered with a mat of artificial turf admitted chunks of frozen ground to lie exposed that had been hacked out by machine. On the other side there was an awning with folding chairs stacked in the shadows.

Sigrid leaned into her brother's warmth. She knew both of her sisters lay in graves on the other side of the cemetery, Isabella in a bronze urn and Giovanna in an oak casket with brass handles, and the sky would be equally oppressive hanging over the more discreet, even reticent, tombstones and markers above and around them. She tried not to think about ashes and bone shards or mouldering flesh (or would it be desiccated, she wasn't sure). She shuddered and leaned closer against Bernd.

He twisted his neck to look at her and shrugged. He could see the horrid pale light of the city gleam a putrescent green on her forehead. He took a deep breath between pursed lips, flicked his tongue out to moisten them, and put his arm around her. They were standing very close to the edge. Suddenly, he pulled away.

"Let's clean this up," he said. "It's caving in." He moved around to the opposite side of the open grave and grasped the tilted end of a beam but couldn't move it. "Grab the tarp, we'll have to slide it out of the way."

Icy water had pooled in the canvas folds and they had to strain and tug this way and that until it came free, and then they dragged it over the mound, so it reached from the grave's edge to cover the ersatz turf. They moved around to get grips on the two beams that were tilted precariously at the edge, threatening to fall into the muck at the bottom.

"That's better," he said, once they had set the beams on the tarp, and she moved close beside him, again. He draped his arm across her shoulders. He leaned over and kissed the top of her head, tasting the damp warmth of her hair. She tilted her head to look up at him and he gave her a quick kiss on the lips. They both flinched. He released his grip on her shoulders, jerked his own shoulder in an exaggerated shrug, and she slipped down into the depths of the grave, sprawling with a gurgling splash at the bottom.

There was a roiling of muck and then silence.

As he turned to walk away he could hear her begin to cry. She didn't scream, it was more like a soft moaning. Glancing over his shoulder, an eerie apparition of the tarp, seeming to writhe as one edge was drawn suddenly into the grave, compelled him to pause. The beam near his feet teetered up onto its end as the tarp shuddered beneath it, then plunged into the darkness. The other beam tumbled after it and the unholy whimpering from the depths of the earth came to an abrupt stop.

When they retrieved her body early the next morning, Bernd was with them. After the alarm was raised that she was missing, he told them he had left her at the cemetery, where they had gone out of respect for their father, and he had become frightened when she decided to re-set the tarpaulin to keep out the rain, and he had gone home and gone to bed. There was no mystery about where she was. She was lying half-buried in muck at the bottom of the grave. When she was extricated, they saw the deep wound in her forehead. Inexplicably, she was dressed in a Christmas outfit that was soiled nearly beyond recognition. The evidence of her fingernails caked with blackened blood and frozen topsoil suggested she had died not from the beam as she tumbled into the grave but from suffocation as a slurry of frigid earth fell on top of her when she tried to claw her way out.

4 **CHRISTMAS**

COLD SEEPED IN AROUND THE EDGES OF HARRY'S sheepskin. He squinted to protect his eyes against the rush of frozen air as he picked up his speed to generate warmth. His face muscles had stiffened into an icy carapace and his nose was in the first stages of frostbite. His toes throbbed as his blood surged to keep warm. After a brief respite in Le Petit Gourmet northwest of the Rosedale subway station, where he dipped a croissant stuffed with marzipan into his third coffee of the day, he practically sprinted on the packed sidewalk until he arrived flushed and breathless at the door of the imposing three-storey Ghiberti house. When the door opened, he stood face to face with a man in his early thirties in trim condition, dressed in a thick Aran sweater, who seemed quite at home. Behind him, Birgitta was talking to a young woman who was passively blonde, as opposed to flamboyant. Birgitta nodded in Harry's direction, then walked out of his sightline. The young woman followed her.

"You must be my mother's detective," the man said, with no trace of a smile. Bernd, the missing man, was no longer missing. Harry did his best to remain expressionless. The man made no gesture toward inviting him in. Harry shuddered, clapped his gloved hands and tucked them under his armpits.

"I'd like to speak to Birgitta," he said. "Mrs. Ghiberti."

"There's no need. We've sorted things out."

"Things?"

"There are no dead bodies." He glanced down at Harry's card he had picked up from the foyer table. "Mr. Lindstrom-Malone. There are no random killings, our family skeletons are buried, my sisters were not murdered. They died. My mother has never quite come to terms with that. I'm sure you understand."

Harry knew more about arbitrary death than this man could possibly realize. Or did he know more about Harry's history than his mother did?

"It doesn't matter," said Bernd with an icy smile. "Case closed." He shut the door in Harry's face.

Fuck it, Harry. Let's go home and roast by a nice warm fire.

As they walked and for no apparent reason, she started mumbling about nihilism and the compensations of art. By the time he reached the Rosedale subway stop, she had moved on to philosophy, applauding Nietzsche and Sartre because they wrote novels that grappled with pointlessness the only way possible, in fictional terms, and admonishing Heidegger and Wittgenstein because they wrote treatises, not literary texts.

Wittgenstein and Heidegger, Harry. They weren't real writers.

They didn't pretend to be. But Wittgenstein was a poet, Harry argued. His attention to language as the limit of consciousness attracted Harry, but Heidegger, in spite of his odious politics, was more in tune with Harry's experience of death as the one and final affirmation of an authentic life. Still, he preferred Wittgenstein's company from the pantheon of beings that lurked in the labyrinth of his mind, more so than most. Of them all, he was the most poetical. He knew that poetry alone used the inherent ambiguities of language to communicate through evasions of meaning.

He wrote the most perfect poem of all time, you know.

Who? What? Harry had to scramble to keep up. She had switched from Wittgenstein to the rather odious anti-Semite, Ezra Pound. He paused in the storm to let her recite Pound's perfect poem in its entirety:

> "In a Station of the Metro"
> The apparition of these faces in the crowd;
> Petals on a wet, black bough.

When he got back to his condo, it was midafternoon. Pound's poem lingered in his mind. It was not perfect. Perfection was not what poetry tried for. But it was evocative, richly allusive, deeply haunting. It was about death and catching a glimpse of timelessness in a delicate moment of time—not so much *about* that as doing that, the words *were* themselves the images and the perfect stasis between them. Okay, perfection.

And another thing, Heidegger was more coherently focused on language than your buddy, Wittgenstein; he dwelled, as he said, in language. For myself, I prefer Saussure's semiotics, Derrida and his Derrideanisms, the expansiveness of Roland Barthes, or, more, much more, the ponderable imponderable's of Umberto Eco.

You're name-dropping, Sailor. Knowing intellectuals doesn't make you one, no more than reciting Pound makes you a poet. The poor bugger ranting in a cage in the scorching sun and the mind that wrote your perfect poem don't connect.

You guys put him in the cage and he wrote the Pisan Cantos.

Us guys? The Allied forces, your side.

I'm dead. I don't have sides.

Dusk was beginning to settle over the city but above the lake the light shimmered silver and grey. Another storm was gathering force, this time coming in over the water from the States. Harry cracked open a bottle of '61 Bordeaux and sprawled on the blue sofa. It was an exquisite claret but after a single glass he recorked the bottle and ate a snack of leftovers from the fridge. With the lights turned low, he watched the approaching snowstorm and tried not to think about dying and death.

He was relieved to be free of the Ghiberti case but uneasy. There were too many confounding variables and at the same time there were intriguing intimations of a classical paradigm—one sister had drowned, another had turned to dust in a gas explosion, and a third had suffocated under a mudslide. Earth, air, water. If there were to be a fourth, she'd be destined to die in a fire.

Patterns, Harry! We've jumped a couple of millennia from Aristotle to Lévi-Strauss.

Karen had trained as a literary and cultural theorist and had been on the same faculty in the English Department. Huron College University (*that seems redundant, Harry*), part of the University of Western Ontario (*doubly redundant*). Now, mercifully called Western University.

Harry had been hired as a specialist in British empiricism; he had written his doctoral dissertation at Cambridge on John Locke, but he was more interested during his last years teaching in the contemporary displacement of devotion by zealotry. He was still essentially an empiricist. What you see is what you get.

Who cares! That was invariably Karen's most salient argument.

Their dinner conversation was as likely to be about *Buffy the Vampire Slayer* and *Dexter* as Derrida or Claude Lévi-Strauss. Even when Harry snuck in references to his old Trinity College cohort, Ludwig Wittgenstein, it was more likely to be something about his reputation as a prophet trying to penetrate the swirling darkness of his own thoughts than to the elegant and enigmatic propositions that resulted.

Sometimes they were playful and sometimes they conversed in the abbreviated jargon couples share.

Sometimes he called her Sailor, the edge of his mouth curling slightly. After the kids were in bed, they often listened to episodes of *Bold Venture* on the net, a radio show from the early fifties starring Humphrey Bogart as Slate Shannon and Lauren Bacall as Sailor Duval. Harry's voice had become gritty from lecturing, although more like Eastwood than the smoky precancerous rasp of Bogart. Karen had been whispering like Bacall since college; it unnerved some men, who thought she was echoing Monroe, but it wasn't sensual, it was sensuous. There was a difference.

The snow clouds were closing in. Harry poured himself another Château d'Issan.

After a while, he could sense Karen's warm breath on his skin, he could smell the lilac scent of her body, he could see the sheen of her hair, feel the touch of her flesh, and hear the sweet timbre of her voice as she moved with him through the hours. Logic told him she was not there. He was not delusional; he knew she was gone. But that did not mean she was absent or ephemeral. Karen was as real and authentic to Harry as he was to himself.

They never talked about Matt and Lucy. Their children were buried in a gaping black hole inside him that sucked everything he remembered about them into itself. He simply could not bear the pain, or memories of their drowning, or his guilt for allowing it to happen. Sanity was a precarious condition, bought at the terrible cost of leaving his children behind. He imagined that he and Karen would grow older together. The children would remain children forever.

When the snow started to fall, it was flurries and the temperature rose to just below freezing. Harry bundled up casually and walked over to the bottom of Spadina. He caught a streetcar up to Little Italy. He found a nice restaurant on College and settled into a pesto pizza with a half-litre of exorbitantly priced Barolo.

Halfway through, he realized he was feeling the wine and decided to take the pizza remains home. While he struggled to put on his heavy sheepskin coat, he gazed past the glimmering candlelight into the snow flurries outside. The air was obviously still: passersby were walking upright, not huddled against the cold. It was a picturesque scene of urban winter and he was feeling a twinge of pity for people compelled to live in temperate climates, when a familiar halo of flowing white hair caught his eye. Birgitta Ghiberti. She was walking with her son, her arm linked in his.

On Bernd's far side, the same blonde woman Harry had seen for a fleeting moment in their Rosedale home leaned forward and caught his eye. They exchanged glances. She was young and blandly attractive, but when Harry looked away and then back, she had receded again into Bernd's shadow.

Were it not for the contrast with the young woman's blonde hair, which had an ethereal radiance in the candlelight flickering through the bistro window and the winter lights on the street, Birgitta's white hair might have been mistaken for blonde as well. There was nothing in the appearance or demeanour of any of them to affirm the strange sense of menace their passing conveyed. Lingering over a glass of grappa, the complimentary *eau de vie* offered by the proprietor, Harry felt reassured but strangely empty or incomplete having seen the Ghibertis together.

The next day passed and the next, and Harry was haunted by spectres of the dead Ghiberti sisters. Bernd may not have murdered them, but they died by acts of his obdurate will. Some rough beast had slouched into Bethlehem. *The Bad Seed, Damien, Rosemary's Baby.* And yet the man in the Aran sweater who confronted him at the door of the Ghiberti house had seemed less Antichrist than a righteous Lucifer, fallen from grace for bearing the light, cursed for his own survival when his sisters had perished.

Harry knew about survivor's guilt.

By the time Christmas Eve arrived, he had almost succeeded in banishing the Ghibertis, living or dead, from his mind. Young women giving up the ghost in snowdrifts seemed unreal. He called Miranda and let her know he was off the case. She was disappointed, wished him an ecumenical Season's Greetings, and told him she'd call in the New Year.

A letter turned up in the mail that he took to be a Christmas card, judging by its shape, the mauve envelope, and the writing in green ink, which was so meticulously done he thought at first it was by machine. There was no return address and no message inside, just a piece of mauve notepaper folded around a cheque for $2000. Made out to Lindstromalone; signed by B. Ghiberti.

Is it blood money?

In reverse. She's paying me to *stop* the killing.

It's to seal the deal, Harry, to say her son intercepting you at the door confirmed his guilt. If you accept this, there's no turning back.

Right. I'm thinking.

He tucked the cheque under the fruit bowl on his coffee table.

You saw the house, Harry. She can afford us. Don't look a gift horse in the mouth.

That's what the Trojans said, and look what happened to them.

But knowing Karen wanted him to take the case, understanding that he wanted her to want him to take the case, made it impossible to turn down.

Christmas Eve was special for Harry. December 24th was the anniversary of his great aunt Elizabeth Lindstrom's birth. Known universally as Aunt Beth and feared as much as revered by all who came within her reach, she was the virgin matriarch of the family. Elizabeth was the final beneficiary of Lindstrom Bros., cast-iron stove makers in Preston, Ontario, for four generations until fire burnt the uninsured foundries to cinders and the family fortunes collapsed into managed investments assigned to Aunt Beth, which lasted just long enough to see her comfortably to the grave.

The aftermath of prosperity was no help to Harry's father. He devoted his whole life to rekindling the family's small-town wealth through a series of failed business ventures, which included operating a hardware store in Nanaimo, a heating business in Neepawa, and a water-powered sawmill in Trois Rivières, as well as trying to build canoes in Fredericton, New Brunswick and Temagami, Ontario. Harry's mother was a violinist and composer with no published work or public performances to her credit. They had small, sad dreams together, large aspirations, and little money to help anyone, even their patrician and imperious Aunt Beth, had she been aware of her approaching poverty or deigned to ask.

It was Aunt Beth who sent Harry to summer camp each year. If Lindstroms of his generation were not to the manor born, he could at least be a witness to see how the privileged still played. She would have sent him to Upper Canada College as well, but his parents insisted they needed him close to help them unload when their ship came in. When Harry was ready for university, she helped with his tuition, and he got by on bursaries, loans, and summer jobs. When she died, Harry, who was her favourite and her sole heir, attended Cambridge with the deceased Aunt Beth as his sponsor. By the time he earned the scarlet gown for his Doctor of Philosophy, his inheritance had run out and his parents were dead. Although he wasn't the last of the Lindstroms, he felt very much alone in the world, until he met Karen.

Once he had a family of his own, he realized his beloved and fearsome Aunt Beth was alive in his children and she faded from his life, except on Christmas Eve. But since the imponderable horrors on the Anishnabe River, she seemed more special than ever. He settled back into his blue linen sofa, sipping a fine brandy, and let himself cry.

He had a small fresh-cut tree in the window. Its lights glowed brightly, shutting out the darkening sky.

Tears burnt, as tears do, but he let them flow.

Okay, Slate, it's time to get outta here, Karen whispered. *Time to go for a walk. Take cash, it's Christmas.*

"Yes, it is," he said, shaking himself out of melancholia, donning his sheepskin and the black toque Miranda had given him. "Come on, Sailor. Let's walk."

After he made his way up past Queen through the barren canyon of office towers, he encountered a few people, here and there, usually alone. When he saw street kids, he waited a bit to make sure they weren't smokers, then slipped a couple of twenties into shivering outstretched hands before moving on.

Such quirky largesse had become a tradition while studying at Cambridge. For five years in a row, he had celebrated Christmas on his own. The English were wonderfully jolly in the pubs and college common rooms, but notoriously loathe to have company into their homes. Had he not met Karen in his last year, when she gave a series of guest lectures during the summer, a time when Cambridge magnanimously allowed visiting scholars a go at the podium, he might have left filled with the most wonderful warm memories of a breathtakingly beautiful town with breathtakingly beautiful colleges and the most charming quarters for senior dons and the occasional professor, but no lasting friends, unless he counted the novelist E.M. Forster, who was at King's but died when Harry was five, or Wittgenstein, who like Harry was at Trinity but died before he was born.

Just below Dundas Street, he walked past a recessed doorway and nearly missed the girl sitting on folded cardboard with a neat sign propped in the light. He stopped, intrigued. The sign was decorated with Christmas stickers and read:

>   My name is Penelope
>   Spare pennies? Spare Penny
>   Please send me to Hawaii

Harry looked down at the young woman huddled for warmth into herself but gazing up at him with a kind of wounded pride. She was maybe in her late teens, early twenties; it was hard to tell. When he smiled, she smiled.

He turned for a moment to take in the Yonge Street corridor as the air filled with snow. Wiping moisture from his face, he wondered if this waif, whatever her age, had any idea how incomparably beautiful this was, with the muted neon lights glowing and the large flakes drifting. Regent Street in London, New York's Fifth Avenue were no better. Only the memory of being with Karen on a rocky promontory in the bush overlooking a frozen lake, watching the sky shake out its blanket of snow over the forest in the diffuse light of a full moon, exceeded the scene he shared with Penelope.

You're such a romantic, Karen whispered. He looked back at the girl in the doorway.

"Hawaii. You are ambitious."

"My reach exceeds my grasp," she said. "'Or what's a heaven for.'"

Given the audacity of her sign, the word play, the strategic use of punctuation he wasn't surprised to hear her quote Tennyson.

"Are you a student?" he asked.

"I dropped out."

"Me too," he said. "Why you?"

"I'm older than you think. I was in graduate school, writing my dissertation, and one day I just sat back and realized I had nothing original to say so I quit."

"Very wise," he said. "They should have given you a PhD for that."

"They didn't have the confidence," she said. "You studied Wittgenstein?"

The quip about a doctorate for the truly deserving was Ludwig's, although Socrates probably said it first.

"He's hard to avoid. But no, I studied Locke. I didn't like him very much."

"So you quit. You don't do philosophy and more?"

"We're doing it now," he said.

She shivered and nodded her head.

"Did you teach Wittgenstein?"

"No, he's unteachable."

"Unless you were his contemporary."

"Especially then. You could teach the man nothing!"

For a brief passing moment he was nostalgic for the academic world. Then all the rest he'd left behind crowded in. He reached into the sheaf of twenties in his pocket to extricate a few, then paused, and handed her his fleece-lined gloves.

"Those mitts of yours are about done for," he said. "Take these."

Her fingers were poking through the synthetic material.

"I like to have my fingers free in case I need to make change. Thanks."

"How are you doing?"

"All things considered, I'm doing."

"With the Hawaii project."

"Good."

"You'll need to have a visa or something if you plan to stay." He was not sure how literally to take her ambition.

"I'm American," she said.

"Far from home."

"Not really. Canada's been good, but the winter is, like, a bit challenging."

"It hasn't really started yet," said Harry, sadly.

"No worries, I'll get where I'm going, one way or another."

"How far, so far?"

"She reached into the folds of her worn parka and pulled out an envelope. She made eye contact, then handed it to him. He opened it. There was a bus ticket from Toronto to Seattle. He handed it back.

"So far, so good," she said.

Harry extended an arm and glanced at his watch: ten minutes to midnight.

"I'll be back," he said.

"Thanks for the gloves," she called after him. "No worries."

As he receded into the slowly swirling snowlight, he heard her final words, "Have a good Christmas. Merry Christmas."

Harry found a Royal Bank with an ATM out front. He reached awkwardly through layers of coat and sweater and retrieved the cheque from Birgitta Ghiberti in his shirt pocket, which he deposited in his account. He withdrew his maximum daily limit of $1000. Then he waited until church bells rang out, tolling in Christmas. He withdrew another $1000. He turned and walked back into the snow. She was gone. The doorway was empty. Her folded cardboard was gone.

Harry squinted into the snow, looking south. He could see an indistinct figure trudging into the whiteness. He walked rapidly through the accumulating snow and caught up to her.

"I told you I'd return."

"You and General MacArthur," she said, turning slowly and looking up at his face, saturated with melting snowflakes like her own.

"And he did," said Harry.

"I'm off my shift," she said. "Shop's closed. I'm going home."

"Which is where?"

"A very classy stairwell in a very classy building with a very classy heated garage."

"Take this with you, then."

He handed her $2000. She took the bundle of bills and examined it, then offered it back.

"I'm not for sale."

"All I want is a postcard from Hawaii. From the big island. Honolulu's too commercial."

She thrust the stack of bills at him again.

"I can't, you know."

"You can't write? Just send me a note."

Refusing to take back the money back, Harry passed her his card.

"Private investigator? I like your email address. Harry, alone. Maybe I could hire you some time, pay you back."

"I hope not. I only do murders." He leaned over and brushed his lips against her forehead. She didn't flinch, but he could tell it was a struggle. *My God, what has she been through?*

Good man, tough guy. Aunt Beth's birthday is over. Let's go home. She'll be okay.

"Bye, now," he said. "Just a postcard."

As he turned to walk away, he pulled the black toque down over his ears. He'd been tempted to give it to the girl, but she'd be basking in Hawaiian sunshine before the New Year.

He'd have to send a note to Miranda, thanking her for the Christmas present.

When he received a phone call from a midrange hotel later that night, asking about a young woman who paid cash for her room and was carrying a big wad of bills, he vouched for her, asked to have his best wishes passed on, and went back to bed with familiar voices swarming in his head, which slowly faded as he drifted off into a deep sleep.

His Aunt used to say, "The kindness of strangers is the only kindness that counts." Whether giving or receiving, it's the lack of connection that makes it authentic.

5 THE VISITOR

THE INSISTENT RATTLING OF KNUCKLES ON HIS simulated wood door awakened Harry with a start. Daylight was streaming between the partially opened pewter-grey drapes in the living room. His bedroom was still filled with the gloom of a lingering night as he scrabbled around for his dressing gown, then trudged through to the foyer that, in the north side of his apartment, was as dark as the inside of a cupboard.

Leaning to peer through the peephole, he knocked his forehead against the door and realized he wasn't fully awake. He didn't recognize his caller; the optics of the security lens suggested a man with squint eyes, no nose, and a cadaverous mouth. Although Harry wanted to retreat to his bed and try to wake up again in a more civilized manner, curiosity compelled him to identify the interloper before turning him away. He swung the door open aggressively and stood, this time on his own threshold, face to face with Bernd Ghiberti.

"Don't you people believe in the normal courtesies," Harry muttered. He could feel Karen's pleasure at being vindicated for repeatedly urging him to lock his door, which he seldom did.

Harry's visitor recovered from a brief moment of confusion. "It's Christmas, it was hard to avoid being swept in with the Yuletide hordes. I'm sorry to bother you, Professor. I see I've got you up. I need help."

"Don't we all," said Harry, stepping back to let the man in while assessing his own dishabille in the semi-darkness and running his tongue across his teeth in mild disgust. He didn't bother to switch on the light. "Come in, give me a few minutes. My God, it's eleven. Make yourself some coffee, there's a Nespresso machine on the counter."

Bernd Ghiberti was an odd intruder into what had promised to be a contemplative day. Arriving unannounced on Christmas was creepy but not threatening. He was much too polite, but that was likely an implicit apology for his previously hostile behaviour. It did strike Harry as strange that he felt comfortable with someone who could be complicit in the deaths of his sisters and might be a serial killer.

His visitor was dressed to Harry's taste. Chinos, button-down shirt over a cotton tee (Bernd's was purple while Harry tended to wear black). Buffed shoes, probably Cole Haan. Irish wool sweater. Harry's own sweater collection had been legendary at Huron. For the most part, he dressed Canadian; he liked dressing well, as opposed to being well-dressed. He wasn't very good at keeping his wardrobe replenished. Karen usually purchased his sweaters and he hadn't bought any more since being on his own.

He owned a single necktie. Trinity colours of course. He had never owned a suit and possessed only one jacket. He and Karen had indulged in impeccably tailored Armani blazers to wear with jeans for their registry office wedding. He usually kept the jacket in his office for whatever occasion the college might throw at him, but he had worn it home the night before they went on their doomed trip to Algonquin Park. Later, it had been consumed in the flames when their house burnt down.

Harry disappeared into his bedroom, closing the door behind him. He didn't know what his visitor wanted but he decided to seize the initiative by taking his time. He had a steaming hot shower, then shaved, grimacing at the ghostly distortion of his face in the fogged up mirror. By the time he emerged into the living room, he was on edge, which gave Ghiberti the advantage, especially since there were two cups of fresh espresso on the coffee table, filling the room with their congenial aroma.

Without saying anything, Harry picked up a cup and sniffed. Roma. His favourite.

The man sat on the sofa, leaving Harry his preferred teak and leather armchair. Harry put his feet up on the table, a George Jensen second-hand midcentury modern solid teak derelict he'd picked up in a Jarvis Street pawn shop. He sipped his coffee and waited. He lowered his feet to the floor and reached over to wipe imaginary marks from the teak. Finally, his guest, having finished his own coffee, asked if Harry would like another. Harry declined.

"You must wonder why I'm here?" Bernd said at last.

"Social visit?"

Harry drained his cup, got up, and made them seconds. He listened distractedly as the machine whirred and thick, rich coffee surged into each cup in turn.

"I'm worried about my mother," said his visitor.

"I'm sure you are," said Harry.

"I'm sorry about all that other business."

It seemed prudent to say as little as possible. Let the man proceed at his own pace.

"She's been rather disturbed, where I am concerned, since my sisters died."

In three separate events, Harry. It was a cumulative process.

Having worked for the last week to suppress being enthralled with the Ghiberti family, Harry bridled at finding his interest rekindled simply because this man had shown up.

Bernd Ghiberti had a curiously affable smile, shy in spite of his aura of innate condescension. He held himself stiffly and had an arch way of speaking, but he did not seem overtly sinister.

"Detective Lindstrom, this is quite awkward. My mother seems to be missing."

I would have thought he'd prefer to have her as far away as possible!

"I assume you had nothing to do with her disappearance."

"No, Detective, I did not murder my mother—although I confess it is an interesting notion. If I had I wouldn't be here."

"Cops are called 'detective.' And I'm not a professor. Call me Harry."

"Harry."

Last time I talked to your mother, you were the one who was missing."

"Well, as you can see, I'm not."

"What about the young woman, the blonde? Is she missing as well?"

"I assume she's with Birgitta."

He calls his mother by her first name. Novels have been written on less.

"How does she fit in?" Harry asked.

"She doesn't. She's just a friend. A visiting relative."

"Really. Which is it? A friend or a relative?"

"They're not mutually exclusive, are they?"

"Depends on the family."

"Birgitta enjoys having people around."

"My sense was your mother is a solitary person."

"Those are not contradictions."

"No, I don't suppose they are."

Solitude in a crowd, Harry was familiar with that. He sipped his coffee. "Would you describe yourselves as close?"

You can't be serious!

Just looking for a reaction, Sailor.

"Family is family, it's not a matter of choice. I was close to my sisters. But Birgitta has this obsession. Why would I have done them in, for God's sake?"

Innate evil. The bad seed.

"Look," said Bernd. "There's no villain here. After Sigrid died, she was the youngest and the last to go, my mother took it into her head I was responsible for all of them, Giovanna and Isabella, too. I think she held me to blame for her broken marriage as well. I don't really remember Giovanna. She drowned the same year my father moved out. I was seven, and I was ten when Isabella died in a gas explosion."

"And Sigrid?"

"I was thirteen. She fell into a hole and the earth collapsed."

"A hole?"

"My father's grave."

Harry knew the details. It was unsettling to hear the words spoken out loud, especially by Bernd.

"You were with her?"

"Not exactly. Right now, I'm concerned for my mother."

"You know she talked to the police about you?"

"When she thought I was missing? I wasn't."

"When she thought you had something to do with Sigrid's death."

"Of course. But what could the police do? She had decided I had a predisposition to murder. She did not believe in the arbitrary whims of a malevolent universe. It was easier to believe in the wickedness of a little boy who grew into a diabolical adolescent before her eyes. Heir to the sins of his father, apparently. Not to her own. When a friend of my middle sister, Rose Ahluwalia, fell from a bridge in the Don Valley a couple of years later, Birgitta blamed me. As far as I know, Rose jumped, but my mother locked me in my room for three days. I was reclusive at sixteen, I liked being alone. She wasn't cruel, she sent the girl up with meals."

"The girl?"

"Our *au pair* when Giovanna died. She came back from Guadalajara after she finished university and lived with us. Helped in exchange for expenses. She walked out one day and never returned. Probably went back to Mexico."

"Or she's dead. There seems to be a lot of death around you, Mr. Ghiberti."

"And around you, Mr. Lindstrom." There was a leaden pause in the conversation. "But then, it's your job, isn't it?"

He's not talking about your family history, Harry; not about us.

Harry gazed into the dull glow of the Christmas tree lights. He had left them on all night as a small offering in compensation for the tree having been cut down and rendered effete with coloured garlands.

"How long has she been gone?" he asked.

"My mother? A few days."

"You can't be more precise?"

"I come and go. She has an open arrangement with our housekeeping service. They look after the place whether we're there or not. I am not my mother's keeper, so to speak. We both travel and I wasn't too worried. But when she didn't turn up last night, I knew there was a problem. My sister Isabella died at home on a Christmas Eve. Birgitta would never stay away on the anniversary."

"She celebrates the anniversary of her daughter's death?"

"Observes, not celebrates, and, yes, she does. All three of them."

Harry surveyed his guest's face, and Bernd seemed unconcerned as he in turn surveyed the room. He seemed to take after his Italian father in appearance, more than his Nordic sisters who apparently had looked like Birgitta. He was an attractive man, almost handsome, although there was something a little askew about his features. They didn't match his colouring. His complexion was quite dark but his lips were thin, his long nose was narrow, his forehead full. He had dark eyes, creased at the edges; they might have been the eyes of a man twice his age. He did not smile easily, and when he did it was restrained, like he didn't want to give away too much of himself.

"Where were you when your mother thought you were missing? Were you in Sweden?"

The man unaccountably laughed.

"If I'm in Sweden, she worries. If she worries, I must be in Sweden. I'm with an NGO based in Stockholm so I'm often there."

"I thought everything in Sweden was government, even the aid organizations. What do you do?"

"You mean, what have I got to offer besides compassion? I trained as a paleoanthropologist. Old bones and guesswork. I got sidetracked."

Death was too distant in that line of work. He wanted it up close and personal.

Harry had almost forgotten his coffee. It was lukewarm but he sipped the crema off the top, which still tasted fresh, then drained the cup in a few swallows.

"It's a little hard to explain," the man said.

"Try me."

Don't be abrupt, Harry.

Bernd Ghiberti leaned forward on the sofa and gazed out over the harbour.

"Abused women."

"Blondes," said Harry, without missing a beat.

"Not at all," Bernd snapped, apparently taken aback by Harry's suggestion. "As I explained, it is a sensitive issue."

"I'm sure it is."

"I work with brutalized women. Mostly in northwest Africa, Mauritania, Mali, Niger. Places where it's impossible to keep track of the living, never mind the dead."

Harry was struck by the level of irony; he grimaced.

"Look," said Bernd. "I'm worried about Birgitta, forget me." When Harry didn't protest, he continued. "I think she's gone back to Sweden."

"She's not really missing then, is she?"

"No one has seen her."

"Then how do you know she's there?"

Bernd dismissed the question by ignoring it. "I'm sure she went via Iceland but I couldn't find an actual booking," he said. "She did a search for hotel listings in Reykjavik."

"Did she buy her flight online?"

"Perhaps on her Blackberry."

"Could she have stayed in Iceland?"

"It's a small enough place the authorities would know."

"Depends who you talk to. I've been there," said Harry. "It's not that small."

"Perhaps not." He hesitated. "I checked. She has left."

"If she was ever there."

"They are very efficient."

"And the Swedes aren't?"

"The Swedes are relaxed with their own, Mr. Lindstrom. She has dual citizenship. She would have simply walked through, especially coming in from Iceland."

"So she's in Sweden by default, since she's not in Iceland and she's not in Toronto?"

"It seems that she stepped off the plane and disappeared. She's waiting for me."

"Explain."

"I have to be in Stockholm by the end of January. She's already there, pursuing her investigation."

"To prove you are a serial killer."

"To prove someone out there is killing young women, yes."

"Then good for her, if she finds him."

"On the contrary. If she finds him, he will be forced to eliminate her."

Perhaps we should pause and discuss the ambiguity of pronouns, Harry.

Harry felt chills running down his spine.

"That sounds like a threat, Mr. Ghiberti."

"A warning."

"A rather ominous warning."

Is there another kind, Harry?

"If she is right about the carnage, and let's suppose she is wrong about me, then as she closes in on the murderer he will have no option but to stop her. By killing her, I would think. He is apparently what criminologists describe as a miscreant in the 'organized non-social category.' He is a very intelligent man, his crimes are not overtly violent, but he is viciously determined."

"Have you done research on this?"

Bernd Ghiberti acknowledged Harry's question with a nod and continued, "He will not stand for interference. Not because she will expose him. Part of him yearns to be caught. But because she will fuck up his plans."

Harry blanched at his odd choice of words.

"So long as she continues to say that I go around slaying young women, she could be in grave danger."

"She thinks you kill people, and *you're* worried about *her.*"

He is afraid of her, Harry, and for her. You love ambivalence.

I don't.

"Will you take the case?"

"Like I told your mother, we don't do missing persons."

But you like Sweden, Harry. It's midwinter. You like snow. I've never understood that about you. You like ice and snow.

Harry looked outside at the dazzling blue over the islands and the infinite colours of white.

"I think perhaps you need legal advice," he said. "You and your mother should define the limits of your relationship in a legal document."

Sometimes rational thoughts seem absurd when spoken out loud.

"Like a marriage contract. Not very likely."

"Of course."

"I avoid lawyers."

"Of course."

Harry avoided lawyers himself whenever he could. People whose profession depended on the separation of ethics from morality appalled him. It might be ethical to defend a sex-murderer like Karla Homolka but it was morally indefensible. He switched tactics.

"A couple of times you've described your mother going *back*. And you say she has dual citizenship."

"Our family owns a farmhouse on an island in the Baltic. A couple of elderly aunts still live there. Annie and Lenke."

"Their last name is Shtoonk?"

"Sviar. My mother's family on her mother's side. It's a very old name."

"Does she speak Swedish?"

"Not as well as I do. I spent summers on Fårö with my aunts after we sold the Muskoka cottage. She didn't speak English until she started school but hasn't kept up with her Swedish. Her parents were refugees from Lund and became hardscrabble farmers in northern Ontario."

"Jewish refugees?"

"They were certain the Nazi invasion would spill into Sweden, but it stopped at the Oresund, the Sound between Sweden and Denmark. They felt they were marked because they were anarchists and paranoid. Most anarchists are, don't you think? They figured their refugee status in Canada would be enhanced if they were Jews, so they co-opted a Jewish name, Shtoonk, from a Jewish acquaintance with a cruel sense of humour."

"It's an insult."

"You know Yiddish?"

"Your mother told me."

"My grandparents weren't very nice people but they got in, in spite of Canada's less than welcoming treatment of Jews. Ironically, Sweden didn't fall or capitulate. It stood aloof. That describes Birgitta, exactly. She stands aloof."

No, she does not, Harry thought. She came to see me, insisting you are a serial killer. She went to the police and made a case that you murdered your sisters sufficient that Morgan took it all down and filed a report. Composed, self-reliant, perhaps, but disinterested, aloof, not at all.

How little do offspring know their parents, he thought. But what about the other way around, does the mother know her child? That question lay at the heart of the matter.

What does he really want, Harry?

Maybe to find out how much Harry knew, before he eliminated Harry.

It seemed the case was active, again, although Harry's objectives weren't clear, or even who his client was.

"Did you always call Birgitta by her first name?" he asked.

"Since we were small, and never to their faces."

"Your father, too."

"Don Vittorio. He died when I was thirteen."

"What made you study paleoanthropology?"

"I drifted into it. I like fossils."

You can drift into serial murder, you don't drift into paleoanthropology. As a cultural theorist, that's my professional opinion, Harry.

"PhD from U of T, field work in North Africa. That's where it all started."

"Where *what* all started?"

A hint of confession? No it can't be that easy.

"Humanity, the species. Homo sapiens. To be more precise, *homo sapiens sapiens.*"

"Precision is appreciated."

"A species that knows that it knows, is conscious of being conscious. That's us. We are all descended from a single solitary female in sub-Saharan Africa. I was interested mostly in her."

"She may have been single; I doubt if she was solitary."

"That would be parthenogenesis, ha!" Bernd seemed to have forgotten the quest for his mother, old passions aroused by his fascination for the mother of all. "Virgin birth of the species. Interesting, since no intraspecific polymorphism has been found in a paternal gene—maybe that's why. Ha! Very good, Professor, Detective, Mister; sorry."

"Bernd," Harry countered, "do you kill people?"

The man smiled sadly. "No, I don't."

The curl of his thin lips, perhaps meant to undermine the gravity of Harry's question, managed to make it a sinister possibility. "I studied bones, very old bones. Then, while I was working on a post-doctoral fellowship, I discovered things in the present that I couldn't live with."

"What sort of things? About yourself?"

He seemed wary. "In Mauritania. How is this going to help find my mother?"

"Trust me."

The man gazed ingenuously into Harry's eyes, then proceeded.

"In the far country, one day, I had been walking on my own for hours and was a long way from my camp when I came across an isolated farm compound. Is this necessary?"

"It is," Harry reassured him.

"At first, the place seemed to have an austere beauty, it was unspoiled; buildings made of wattle and grasses, animals wandering free, their ribs protruding, but not like they were dying. Fires smouldered in small courtyards. The people were emaciated, which is painful to see but not unusual in the region. As a guest, I was given pride of place in a hut of my own. I rested, then went out to watch the activities of the farm. Fossilized skeletons and the original mother were far from my mind. After noticing one or two shocking displays of impoverishment, I realized not everyone in the compound was gaunt. It took me a while to comprehend. It is one thing to hear rumours of an atrocity, another to see something so undeniably real. This was a *leblouh* encampment. I had stumbled on a farm where they inflict unconscionable rites on girls the age I was when my sisters died."

"Female circumcision?"

Bernd's face had filled with horror; his eyes showed a ghastly sheen as if he saw again whatever he had seen in that remote compound.

"No, *leblouh* is not female circumcision. It is forced feeding. Some of the girls were obese literally to the point of bursting open. Literally."

"Like *foie gras*?" Harry didn't mean to trivialize the horror Ghiberti conveyed, but he had nothing else to relate to, to make it real.

"Girls being fattened for marriage. Some as young as five. Most around seven, a few as old as thirteen. You cannot imagine how drastic the methods."

Harry tried to envision the scene, but he couldn't. It was, as Ghiberti explained, unimaginable.

The man's colouring began to return. In order to continue, he seemed to become almost dispassionate. "Girls are forced to consume over two pounds of butter a day." He paused as if doing an inventory. "Forced to drink twenty litres of camel milk, eat pounds and pounds of millet. And if they throw up, they are forced to swallow their vomit." He now looked cold and angry. "It's done mostly by older women using coercion and torture. The methods are evil. Twisting of toe clamps, threats of dismemberment, and worse, much worse. On little girls, for grown men. Many, of course, literally explode from the inside out. They are discarded. But those who become suitably obese are prized possessions, passed on from the fathers who sent them there to proud husbands who buy them and take them home as proof of their manhood."

"And so your work is what? You go back."

"Not to the farms, to the families. We try, but we're up against cultural imperatives so deeply ingrained, enforced by the distortions of tradition and dogma, I sometimes suspect the struggle is a fight for our own souls; we cannot change theirs."

"Bernd, are you a religious man?"

"Because I talk about souls? It sounds less pretentious than saying 'the essential authentic humanity of the individual.' No, I am not. I am utterly secular, our organization is secular. If there were conceivably a God presiding over such things, He would be his own most damnable creation. And you?"

"No."

Harry quickly shifted the direction of their talk, not because it was invasive or distasteful, but to seize control. "Why would your mother have gone to Sweden, if you're here in Toronto?"

"She's not trying to prove I exist, Harry. She's trying to prove I should not. She's not trying to track me down but to establish my guilt. She resents me for being alive, when her daughters are dead. She's gone to find proof I should be cast into hell."

"As Pope John Paul said more than once, 'Hell is the absence of God.'"

"Then you and I, we are in hell already."

"Perhaps we are," said Harry. "And your mother's in Sweden."

Bernd Ghiberti began to smile, then thought better of it.

"I'm sure," he said.

"Not North Africa?"

"No, my work doesn't interest her."

Nor hers him.

On the contrary. He's almost too interested.

You don't want to get caught in the middle, Harry.

"Will you do it? I'll pay well."

"I'm sure you would. But I'm sorry, if I track her down, it will be on her account, not yours. Conflict of interest. She's my client."

"She hired you to prove I kill people. She fired you."

"No, you fired me. In any case, we didn't have a formal agreement. I wasn't fireable."

"Then there's no conflict!"

"And what do you propose I do if I find her? Tell her it's not you murdering those women?"

"Convince her that no one is murdering anyone. People die, Harry, surely you know that, even the young and the innocent. *(How much does he know, Harry? He's been told you were a professor and he drops hints about knowing a lot more.)* Young women freeze to death in the snow, it happens."

"I'll try to find her. Who my client is remains a moot point. The Ghiberti family, I suppose."

One way or another, Harry, you need to be paid. You're working for Bernd to prove he's innocent and for Birgitta to prove he's guilty. If he's innocent, she's a fiend. If he's guilty, then he is.

"If you're guilty," Harry continued, "your mother will pay. If you're innocent, you pay. Fair enough."

"Agreed."

Bernd Ghiberti rose to his feet and vigorously shook Harry's hand. While they walked to the door, he said, as if they were friends, "You'll like Stockholm in winter. Perhaps I'll see you there."

"Perhaps."

The fingernails, Harry!

"Do you know about a root cellar your mother described to me?"

"Of course. It's in an ancient burial tomb."

He's the authority, he should know.

Bernd continued, "We used to play there when we were small."

"We?"

"Myself, Bjorn and Inge Olafsson. They lived in the cottage next door."

"Your mother showed me a tin of human nail parings she found there. She says they belong to you."

"Not at all."

"Are you missing a manicure kit?"

Bernd Ghiberti glanced down at his perfect fingernails.

"I usually have them done professionally in Stockholm."

"Have you been to Iceland, Bernd?"

"On several occasions. We'll have to talk about it sometime."

"Yes," said Harry, "we should."

6 THE BALCONY

AFTER BERND GHIBERTI LEFT, HARRY FELT A LINGERING sense of apprehension. He wondered again if Birgitta was already dead. But then, why bring Lindstrom-Malone back into the case? Was he simply expressing a Nietzschean will to power?

Nietzsche, Harry? Really? Power over whom? If he's already disposed of her somewhere, it could simply be a matter of misdirection. Perhaps you should tell your friend, the superintendent.

Without the remains, there's no point.

Well, consider this, disappearing might be Birgitta's way of dealing with maternal dread. She's blaming herself for nurturing a serial killer. Nothing to do with existential flourishes, Nietzschean or otherwise.

Fair enough, he thought. He needed Birgitta Ghiberti to be alive. This beautiful woman, who seemed to flourish like a rose in a compost heap, he needed to connect with her, to understand how she dealt with deaths that were arbitrary and unspeakably cruel. He needed to understand whatever he could in his own life that he could neither reverse nor accept.

He tried calling his travel agent to book a flight to Sweden, but the agency was closed over Christmas. Gazing around like he was looking for help, he acknowledged the tree cowering in the window and relaxed into his armchair.

Is Bernd checking me out or trying to control my involvement? Does he want to eliminate his mother or save her? Is he a killer of young women or devoted to rescuing them? As my friend Aristotle once said, ask the right questions.

Harry considered Aristotle the patron saint of detectives, while recognizing that Francis Bacon was a more likely candidate. Understanding comes when the mind is open to wonder; when the facts are a mystery, the mystery is fact. Bacon might have said it like that. The circularity of the argument appcaled to Harry. Not for its logic, for its symmetry.

It was midafternoon on a sunny day but he was feeling restless and the temperature outside, with the wind chill, was bitterly cold. Nearly at the point where Fahrenheit and Celsius converge, it was too damned cold for a walk. Even the Inuit, he had read, stay home in their bungalows or if they're out on the land they retreat to igloos when the temperatures plummet to this extreme.

He slipped off his shoes and socks and climbed under the duvet on his bed fully clothed. He didn't sleep well; he hadn't expected to. Hovering on the verge of unconsciousness, his mind swirled with images of small bodies exploding, of drowned bodies with Botticelli eyes, bodies asphyxiated under a slurry of frozen earth, bodies shattered and charred. Female bodies, with one small boy wandering among them.

At some point the images softened into shades of drifting white, as if he had been caught up in the midst of a silent snowstorm. The bodies of young women appeared as contours in the drifting snow, with only their eyes peering through, wide open, sky blue, and lifeless. And the sound of wind whimpered through cedars, the wavering scent of black spruce filled the air. Harry woke up shivering. When he drew the duvet close around him and curled into himself, he was still cold.

He rolled over in search of warmth and when his arm draped across the empty space beside him, he woke up completely. The room was frigid. Wrapping the duvet around his shoulders, he walked barefoot out into the living room. The Persian carpet under his feet felt reassuringly snug but the air was even colder.

The balcony door had pushed wide open and swung back against the outside window ledge. The drapes were almost closed. He didn't remember doing that. He had admired the open vista of the harbour, the islands, the brilliant blue sky, before retiring for his extended nap.

Sequencing had never been Harry's strength. Instead of going for his slippers, he stepped tentatively out onto the small serrated drifts of snow, first one foot, and then, when he couldn't reach the door, the other. The snow squeaked under his weight. There was no option, to counter the weight of the door, stiff on its hinges, he had to step farther out, in small quick steps as if he were walking on coals.

The breeze sweeping across the harbour picked up. A gust lifted the duvet from his shoulders. He tried to wrap it closer with one hand while the other grasped at the door, swinging it free. Suddenly the duvet billowed and was gone. He turned to watch it slide through the air, sailing out over the water like a wounded raptor. A flash of colour by his feet caught his eye and he stopped for a moment and squatted to retrieve a ceramic orange that had unaccountably migrated from the bowl on the coffee table. It wasn't embedded in the snow but sitting on top, like it had just been placed there. As he leaned down, the door closed behind him with a bone-chilling resonant clang.

Standing up and wheeling around to face the glare of the glass, he swore. He jumped from one bare foot to the other while he tried to get a grasp on the frozen door handle. A pale shadow moved across the living room as he pressed close to see through his own empty reflection. The sad coloured lights on his diminutive Christmas tree mocked him through the glass. He tightened his grip on the door and pulled. His hand slipped off, tearing layers of skin from his palm and fingers.

Did you see someone?

Karen spoke in a clear and resonant voice to penetrate his jumping shaking shivering frenetic activity.

Focus, he remonstrated to himself. Focus, focus. He stood perfectly still. All he could hear was the moaning wind as it brushed against the building and the shuffling drone of "Silent Night" drifting from a nearby apartment.

Karen was wordless but still with him. His feet passed from burning piercing pain to an aching heaviness, like stubs of raw meat. He was afraid of collapsing. Pressing the raw flesh of his hand to the door handle, he pulled until it again tore free. He turned and grasped at the balcony rail. His hand fused with the frozen metal, he yanked it away, losing skin from his fingers of his other hand. He smashed at the glass of the door with his elbow, he smashed at the picture window with the ceramic orange, hoping the glass sheet would shatter into the room away from his exposed feet and legs but it reverberated with a dull thud, the orange broke, and the glass remained solidly fixed in place.

Karen. She was there.

Shielding his eyes from the glare, he moved close to the glass again and peered through. The grey drapes shrouded his view to the sides. He gave a last tug on the door and lost more flesh from his hand, which meant his pores were still releasing moisture, he was sweating as he began to feel warmth surge through his body, abandoning his vitals, inviting him to settle on the hard icy snow.

Where was the music coming from? I don't know, I'm tone deaf. Where is it coming from? Coming up. It's from the apartment below.

Okay. Hands too frozen to grasp anything, can't swing down onto their balcony. Shouting? Did I shout? Nobody's listening. Listen to the music.

The belt, Harry? Not long enough. Take off your pants, Harry. Get fingers going, blow on them. Pain, that's good. More pain, great, great. Good pants, Tilley Endurables. They'll hold. That's great.

With his pants absurdly around his ankles, he stepped onto them to insulate his feet while he thrust his hands up under his armpits. The pain was excruciating but soon he could move his fingers.

He retrieved his pants and standing on the icy snow again he tied one leg to the rail, tied the other leg to his wrist. Good, good, now over, swing over. Slowly, don't break, don't tear them.

And if the pants rip, it's a clear fall to the bottom. Quicker than freezing to death. Feel that wind, Harry, down we go.

Harry eased himself over the rail, holding on with stub fingers crooked over the steel, steel tearing at his flesh, then he slipped down past the edge of the cement base, and he dropped quietly into the air.

Hanging. He dangled from one arm. The wind, it was like he was falling. Pain distorted perception, displaced sense, swallowed itself up, he felt nothing at all. Only silence. He felt a melodious humming. He felt the whisper of voices. Had they left the radio on? Were they singing? Were the words in his head? There is no point to all this, that is the point. The world is all that is the case; Wittgenstein. Words thundered in his head and receded.

I'm going outside and may be some time. When they found Robert Scott his journal described his own dying and the deaths of his fellows. *We knew that poor Oates was walking to his death.* Did anyone find the frozen remains of poor Captain Oates?

Harry felt strangely at peace. He turned slowly, twisting on the end of his makeshift bindings, dangling twenty-two stories above the frozen swirling ground. The wind had picked up, stronger and stronger, slicing against his face. Captain Oates, where did you get to? Harry could see movement, the world was moving. A balcony door like his own opened slowly. Muffled voices. Then a man's arms. *Get a knife, cut him down, damned material is tough, get him in.* Harry passed out.

HE WAS AWARE of the horrific pain before he fully regained consciousness. It seemed if he could only wake up, it would go away, but as he entered the light it became worse.

"Harry?" said a voice. "Mr. Lindstrom, can you hear me?"

Perché me ne rimuneri cosi? Perché, perché, Signor?

"His eyelids are fluttering."

Was faith in the absence of God superstition?

His head swarmed with the philosophers he had taught who tested the limits of God in their minds. God, but the pain was unbearable.

"Mr. Lindstrom, do you know where you are?"

In a hospital, what hospital? His life started to come back to him, penetrating the pain.

"Yes," he said.

"Can we call someone?"

"No."

"Family? Friends?"

"It's okay."

"You need someone."

Karen.

A young woman smiled. She was wearing a loose blouse with an annoying teddy bear pattern. The other woman she had been talking to left the room.

Harry tried to isolate the source of his pain.

Harry, they're pumping morphine into you.

Then why does it hurt so much, Sailor?

"My toes!" Harry mumbled through clenched teeth, his head pivoting back and forth on the pillow. He was shivering, convulsing in small rapid twitching.

The nurse placed her hand over his arm, just above the IV needle, and moved her fingers in a gentle rhythmic motion, in time with his heartbeat.

He shivered and felt hot and cold, like warm streams of liquid were running through frozen tissue inside. He could hear the sound of ice-cubes crackling in a glass of cold water, he could feel the sound. He could hear himself breathing.

When he woke up again, another nurse was on duty, an older woman in a floral blouse. The room was a different colour. It was night. Harry wept from the pain until he was fully aware, and then he choked it back, but his temples pounded under her gently massaging hands.

"How are you doing, sport? We thought we'd lost you."

"Me too."

"Can you feel the warmth?"

Harry shuddered. He could feel her ministering touch, he could feel warm tremulations.

"Your insides have been washed with warm fluids, Harry. It's called *lavage*. You're on a thermal drip. Plus morphine."

"Okay," said Harry. The pain shooting up his left leg was unbearable.

"We can up the dose. When you're a little stronger, you can self-administer. For now, let us do it, okay."

"Okay."

"Your heart stopped. You're a lucky man."

Harry couldn't assimilate the two parts of her statement.

"Those people tried CPR, they were trying to help. Cracked some ribs. Nothing that bandages and bed-rest won't cure."

For the first time, Harry realized some of the pain was not coming from his foot. He drew in a deep breath and briefly the pain in his chest superseded the pain from his toes.

God, Harry, breathe gently, breath slowly.

"We had you on a cardiopulmonary bypass until you warmed up and we could get your heart pumping on its own, that's when you had your innards in a warm rinse."

"Was I dead?"

"Not brain dead, you're talking to me now."

Harry could feel himself slipping away. She was Jamaican; he was slipping into the sounds of her voice, bathed in tropical sunshine.

When he awakened, it was light again and the room was no longer the cadaverous green from the night-sky of the city glaring at the window. It was a gentle beige and the nurse with the teddy bear blouse was back.

Don't get sentimental on me, Slate.

His left foot was still excruciating. He couldn't differentiate one toe from another, but at least he knew where the agony came from; he could concentrate on its source, try to make the pain tolerable.

Willpower and morphine, Harry.

"I'm going to have to change your dressing, Mr. Lindstrom. The doctor will be in after lunch. Can you just lie back?"

"And think of England?"

"I beg your pardon?"

"Nothing. Yeah, have at it. They bloody well hurt. I think somebody sold you a fake: your morphine's a placebo. My toes are throbbing like they're going to fall off."

"Mr. Lindstrom. Harry. A couple of them are very damaged. The nerves are dead. They've turned black."

"They bloody well hurt."

"Phantom pain."

"The pain's not phantom, for Christ's sake."

"The nerves have been destroyed, the pain's in your head. You'll have to be careful."

"Still hurts."

Harry realized he could not feel the injured toes while she cleaned away the wound, yet the phantom pain was so intense he thrust his head hard against the pillows and fought back tears. If pain were a colour, this was white, subsuming all others. He shut his eyes, sheet lightning flashed, and he could see inside his brain: it looked like a turbulent sky in the dead of a midwinter night.

"There, all done. You can get some rest."

"My hands?"

"I'm sure they hurt. You lost some skin, surface flesh; you're wearing gloves filled with a gel."

"Thanks. What's your name?"

"Adrienne."

"Thanks, Adrienne."

"Which hospital? Toronto General?"

"TGH, yes." She rested a hand lightly on his and leaned close, trying to see through the pain in his eyes. "There must be somebody we can call."

"Thanks. I'm okay."

"I'll up the sedative. You need rest."

Harry hovered on the dark edge of unconsciousness. His mind swarmed with words as if they were images. The Devil's Cauldron, Anishnabe River, Algonquin Park. The words shattered into fragments that wheeled though his mind. Thundering torrents. Wilderness surging. A river collapsing. Eyes filled with terror. Limbs flailing. Mouths screaming water. Foam streaked with blood, swirling with viscera. Absolute blackness, absolute silence. Then flames, the stone house in Granton, the consuming fire. Close to where the legendary Donnellys were murdered. Their own house burnt to the ground. Sometimes the horror of that story seemed to merge with his own.

Harry dreamed his terrifying memories of emptiness. He was in a different hospital room. The blinds were drawn. From a great distance he could hear the words of Psalm 22, the words of Christ's roaring from the cross. Someone was praying, reading scripture, someone was singing Puccini. *Perché me ne rimuneri cosi? Perché, perché, Signor?*

After two weeks in a military hospital near Algonquin Park and six weeks in the hospital in London, Harry had been declared recovered. (As if you can recover from death.) He was discharged in the evening and went home and everything was in place but nothing was the same. The old stone house on Sanctuary Line that he and Karen had lovingly restored stood proud in the rural landscape and, now, unutterably incomplete.

They had taught themselves carpentry and plumbing, wiring and drywalling and stone masonry. For a decade the house was their passion, and as it came alive they were in its thrall, and the children were part of what they had made. For Harry, it was a permanent place that would outlive them, and they were its guardians for a generation or two. It was the home his parents had never provided. It was the Lindstrom home in Preston that had sustained his Aunt Beth long after she moved to Toronto. It was the only home Harry had ever known, and now it was empty, as only the homes of the dead can be.

The Black Donnellys had lived not three miles away, and their story of murder and vengeance a century before had become part of the heritage that Karen and Matt and Lucy and Harry felt was as real as their own historical past. They had taken on the identity of this small corner of Canada, inseparable, they thought, from its past or its future. It gave them a place to stand on.

He entered through the porch at the side. The wisteria flourishing on the trellis cast more shadow this late in the summer, this late in the day. The Muskoka chairs inherited from Karen's family, the blue play table with two small benches, the table set with tiny cups and saucers for four, waited for the family's return.

He pulled the door closed after him, swallowed up by the hollowness inside. He rummaged through the house the whole night long, opening and closing every door, checking cupboards and drawers, shifting furniture, rolling back carpets, shaking out linen, spilling books and clothing and toys across floors, desperate to find some impossible remnant of their lives that would twist time around and bring them back. He could smell the scent of lilacs that seemed to emanate from Karen, whether she was wearing perfume or not. He could smell the scent of the children. The dead were everywhere around him and he could not connect.

In the morning, he found a five-gallon container in the garage, filled with gasoline for the lawn mower. (Karen had wanted to go canoeing in the wilderness.) He retrieved vise-grips from the basement to get the top off. (Matt was excited about sleeping in a tent and cooking meals over a fire and listening to wolves. Lucy marvelled at being in a park she had seen in a painting.) He emptied the gasoline over the living room furniture. He could not think where Karen kept the matches. (It was him: he missed the hidden rapids.) He found matches in the kitchen string drawer buried under a nest of elastic bands, surrounded by half-used packages of birthday candles.

Seated resolutely on his front stoop, while the flames leapt over his shoulders and smoke billowed into the sky, Harry listened to sirens wail out their lament through the crackling air. Memories of summers long past crowded his mind: the scent of cedars, of campfires, the brushing of air through pines, the liquid murmur of hulls as they slipped though the waves; the plaintive howl of wolves at night, the distressed cry of loons echoing across black water. Algonquin Park was a summer experience. Winter was another country entirely. He imagined swirling snow and searing winds and ignored the outstretched arms of the volunteer firemen. As sparks became embedded in his clothing and scorched his hair and flames seared his flesh and clouds of smoke swirled down to engulf him, they hauled him away from the inferno's embrace.

Time passed. He was given Matt and Lucy's ashes. Karen's body had been absorbed into the wilderness. Possibly it had drifted downriver and lodged irretrievably under the islets of floating swamp in the marshlands along the northerly side of Long Pine Lake. He placed the ashes of the kids in a common urn and buried it in the Catholic cemetery near Lucan on the Roman Line, although Harry and Karen were not Catholics and the children were heathens. He buried it with no marker in the dead of night, close by the tombstone signifying the nearby remains of the Donnelly clan, who may, or may not, have earned their heinous fate. The grass there grows a rich emerald green. Karen loved irony.

Harry did not go back to teaching philosophy, although Huron College graciously invited him to return. He moved to a small furnished apartment in London and watched through closed windows as southwestern Ontario slowly turned into autumn. When his friend Miranda Quin came for him, he took her advice and moved to Nanaimo, a continent away, before finally resettling in Toronto. Karen followed his progress over the next three years.

And Harry endured.

7 POURRITURE NOBLE

HARRY SAT WITH ONE FOOT PROPPED ON THE OTTOMAN that the super retrieved from his locker in the basement. It had come with his teak and leather chair. He leaned forward to adjust a cushion, then slouched back from the effort. TGH had discharged him after a week, and he was healing but he still hurt like hell. His injured toes were throbbing with pain, yet when he tried to wiggle them, he felt nothing. If he wasn't looking, he would have sworn they were moving.

The fractured ribs were tolerable as long as he avoided coughing. He avoided coughing. His fingers and palms were tender but healing, the tips were okay, his nails were intact.

He had been home a couple of days before he emailed Miranda Quin. When Beethoven's Fifth played on his phone, he knew who it was.

"Is that *lindstromalone.com*?" she asked when he answered. "Harry, what the hell is going on? Your message was cryptic, really weird. You dangled from a balcony, pantless, your heart stopped, you froze to death? What's happening? There wasn't any report. Why didn't you call me?"

She listened sympathetically while he described the disembodied pain from the toes of his left foot.

"How do you know it's from your toes if they have no feeling?"

"In my head. When I touch them, they're virtually dead. But they hurt like a son of a bitch. It's not a pretty sight," he told her. "But I was lucky."

"Oh, for sure."

"I was. The little toe was nearly a goner but they managed to save it. Looks kind of mangled but it works. Which is a good thing. You need it for balance. The big toe lost a chunk from the knuckle to the end. It looks as bad as it feels."

"That must be gratifying," Miranda exclaimed. "Can you walk?"

"Right now, I can hobble. It hurts, which they tell me is a good thing. Whatever that means. The ribs are almost better."

"The ribs!"

"I cracked a couple. They tell me I should be getting around in no time with hardly a limp, except when I run. And the phantom pain might stay for life."

"That is a complex figure of speech," she said.

"A phantom for life? I suppose it is."

"So how in God's name did you end up locking yourself out with a wind chill of forty below, and dangling from a pair of pants by the wrist? I'll say this: you're very inventive. Eccentric, but inventive."

"I think someone was trying to kill me."

"Kill you?"

"Yes."

"Seriously. On your balcony. Barefoot and pantless."

"The door was wide open when I woke up from a nap. There was an orange outside in the snow."

"A what?"

"An orange."

"For goodness sake, Harry. A clockwork orange?"

"When I bent down to pick it up, the door closed behind me. And locked. It didn't do that on its own."

"You sure it wasn't an apple?"

"No, it was a ceramic lure and I bit."

"Ouch, but it worked, apparently."

"And when I looked in, I thought I saw someone moving. It was hard to see through the glare. I'm sure someone was in there."

"And why are you telling me *now*? Why didn't you report this, Harry? I'm homicide, remember. You were dead. That makes it murder."

"I resurrected?"

"A technicality. Dead is dead."

"Apparently not."

"Didn't this strike you as worth pursuing?"

"I wasn't dead for all that long."

"So who was it?"

"Miranda, I have no idea."

"It could have been the notorious serial killer Bernd Ghiberti."

"Not as funny as you think. He had just tried to hire me to find his mother."

"Really. Nothing surprises me anymore. Who else, then?"

"I haven't made any friends in Toronto, but I've made a few enemies."

"I'm your friend, Harry."

"Don't come over."

"Takeout? Thai or Italian?"

"Surprise me."

"I'll bring a friend of my own."

Harry scowled. He surveyed his living room. Everything seemed new, even his antique Persian carpet. Things had not worked out relationships with each other, the way they do over time. The spaces between them were empty. His eyes stopped at the blue-black depths of his Blackwood etchings, each brooding with energy in the afternoon light.

He had three David Blackwoods. He preferred original works and abhorred commercial prints, especially by Tom Thomson or Turner or the ubiquitous van Gogh, unless they were authentic posters for an exhibition. He had a framed poster of a sultry nude with flaming red hair by Gustav Klimt hanging in his bathroom. It was a detail from a larger picture. He picked it up in a junk shop on lower Jarvis St. as a time-warped souvenir of having seen the original with Karen in Vienna, twenty years earlier. Near the end of his career as a philosopher, he had published an article in an obscure journal on the curious relationship between art and value, after the original of that same Klimt had sold for $135,000,000.

He and Karen had owned a fine copy of "Fire Down the Labrador," Blackwood's most famous work. The burning ship, the crew fleeing into the night in a small boat, the monolithic iceberg, and the huge grinning whale twisting beneath them, aroused a curiously unsettling *schadenfreude*, pleasure in response to what Schopenhauer might have called the horrific sublime. Their original copy was lost in the fire but he had tracked down another and bought it, along with the haunting "Brian and Martin Winsor," which showed an abandoned dory at sea, the oars still set, jammed in an ice-flow far from the shore, and a nostalgic triptych called "Notes from Bragg's Island" that made him feel like a secret watcher, exposed to the details of Newfoundland life. The three pictures spoke to each other, held conversations that echoed his own troubled world. The mythic drama, the allusive emptiness, the melancholy secrets. As his eyes drifted away, he could hear the voices of the dead.

He wandered inside his head and the voices became quite distinct, although only Karen's was familiar. He seemed to be walking with Wittgenstein through the familiar passages of Trinity College. The great man was talking to himself. Then Karen intruded to discredit whatever his argument was by declaring him a Nazi.

No, said Harry, Ludwig was like Italy, only the opposite. During World War I he was on their side. In World War II, he was on ours. It was Heidegger who was the Nazi. Harry was alarmed that she didn't know better. He stirred restlessly on his chair. Wittgenstein was an Austrian Jew who abjured his vast family fortune to think. Hardly a fan of *der Führer* (whom he had known at school in Linz).

But Heidegger slept with Jews.

With Hannah Arendt, yes, so she said. And with Elisabeth Blochmann. But he was a signed-up member of the National Socialist Party and devoted to Hitler.

And yet so important a thinker!

Ezra Pound was "important," and he was a rabid anti-Semite.

That's different.

He dozed restlessly, and a couple of hours later, following the trembling sensation of the elevator, there was a knock on the door. *My God*, Karen murmured. *Doesn't anyone use the buzzer? Don't people get what a security system is for?*

She's a cop.

People shouldn't be walking through like there's a revolving door.

Harry shouted to come in. He was surprised when it wasn't Miranda.

"Detective Morgan."

"How are you doing?" Morgan seemed a bit sheepish, as if he'd wandered into the wrong party. "I hear you've had some trouble."

"A little. Help yourself to a glass of wine. If you prefer white, there's an unoaked chardonnay in the fridge."

"Right beside the Château d'Yquem, I see."

"You know wines?"

"Yes, I do," said Morgan. "The better ones."

"We'll have that one for dessert, after the spicy Thai."

"It's a '67. Perhaps you should hold onto it."

"Perhaps I should."

Harry. That bottle cost me a fortune.

Conversational *hors d'oeuvres*, Sailor. Exchanging hockey scores. Talking baseball. That bottle's forever.

And so it should be.

The d'Yquem had been in their makeshift wine cellar during the fire, along with a prized '45 Mouton Rothschild. The water-stained label exuded a smoky aroma. He kept it in the fridge for safekeeping. He had sold the Château. Mouton, but not the d'Yquem which had been Karen's present to him when Lucy was born. She had a colleague pick it up in England and smuggle it home. 1967 was the best year in the history of sauternes, someone told her. She looked it up. D'Yquem was the best of the best.

Morgan admired the view, then settled on the sofa.

"So," Morgan said at last. "Someone tried to throw you over." He got up again and peered through the door, then rattled it and tested the latch.

"The going over was my idea. Someone tried to freeze me to death."

"And nearly succeeded, I hear. How're the toes?"

"It's all in my head."

"Phantom pain?"

"Apparently."

"So, what happened?"

Morgan seemed fascinated by Harry's account of how he had rescued himself, but dubious about the conspiracy theory.

"What theory? I was locked out."

"I'm just suggesting: if the door slammed shut in the wind, at minus twenty the humidity from the room might have frozen the latch solid almost instantly."

Harry glowered. This guy wasn't here for the dinner.

"Was it locked when you got back from the hospital?"

Harry continued to glower. Anyone might have unlocked it again. The super, the neighbours downstairs who rescued him.

Morgan smiled. He wasn't buying it.

Harry's piercing eyes, grey hair cut short, resolute set to his mouth, his posture erect, even with his injured foot propped up on an ottoman, affirmed his presence as a naturally strong, proud, and quiet man who could never imagine having nearly brought about his own death, locking himself out in the cold on Christmas Day.

"I took a look at your file," said Harry to distract Morgan from his CSI trajectory. "On Birgitta Ghiberti."

"On her son, yeah, Miranda told me. That was from twenty years ago, before we were partners." For a moment Harry thought he was talking about Birgitta. "You knew her before I did," said Morgan. "I never went to camp."

Since that observation evoked no response in Harry, he continued, "Birgitta Ghiberti was a troubled woman. Astonishingly beautiful. An

Ingrid Bergman blonde. Dark eyebrows, an amazing mouth. I imagine her hair is grey by now, or dyed."

"She'd be the same age as Bergman when she died." Her hair was all the colours of white, Harry thought. Until he had seen her, he didn't understand what that expression meant.

Harry gazed at Morgan who was staring out over Toronto Island. This unkempt man with the furrowed brow and crooked smile, with whom Miranda had shared so much of her life, clearly he had a good mind, unruly, perhaps, but.

But what, your own mind is unruly, Harry, it's naturally chaotic, that's why you were drawn to philosophy as a discipline, bankrupt as it was. It forced you to think, not just have thoughts. So you could emulate your intellectual soul-mate—

It was Heidegger who declared philosophy dead, displaced by what he oddly enough called *thinking*. But back in my Trinity days I was struggling with Locke and the primacy of human experience, I wasn't thinking about thinking.

What a shame.

Harry turned to Morgan. "Do you remember the details?"

"Hard to forget. It was inspired depravity."

"The son's behaviour?"

"The mother's story. She made it so vivid; it was difficult not to believe. I think the contrast with her icy composure made it more convincing."

"But you were inclined to doubt it, just the same?"

"There was no proof. An exceptionally compelling version of personal tragedies, each more unbearable than anything I could imagine." Morgan stopped, then added, "What happened was terrible, but people find ways to endure."

They do, don't they, Harry.

"I figured it was her rendition to account for the unaccountable."

"To create what you might call cosmic balance," said Harry.

"You might."

He wouldn't, apparently.

"So," Morgan went on, "I did believe that she believed it herself. I talked to the kid. Then I wrote it up. You're probably the only person who's read the report right through, except maybe Superintendent Quin. And do *you* think young Bernd did what she says?"

"There's no proof that he didn't."

There's no proof God doesn't exist.
"There's no proof that he did," Morgan countered.
There's no proof that God does.
"You think it was Ghiberti who locked you out in the cold," Morgan noted.
"You don't think anyone did."
"True."
"And what about part two?"
"That he's a serial killer? You don't take that seriously, do you?"
"In the 'organized non-social' category. That was his own designation."
"He confessed!" Morgan was obviously amused.
"He implied. He came here looking for his missing mother. We talked. He wanted to hire me."
"To find his mother? Killers don't usually hire investigators and then try to eliminate them, especially by weather. A bit of a double irony there."
He doesn't talk like a cop! But then, you don't talk like a professor.
I split infinitives and avoid the word Heidegger whenever I can.
Harry offered Morgan a wry smile.
"I think he was here to find out how much I knew."
"Presumably too much." Morgan shrugged. "Any idea where she is?"
"Sweden, apparently."
"Apparently? It shouldn't be hard to check. Are you still working for her?"
"I suppose I am. To prove her son is a killer and to rescue her, if he is, or to rescue her from the real killer, if he isn't."
"An interesting family."
"All families are interesting, especially when there's murder involved."
"You sound like a Russian novelist."
"Thank you."
"I'd walk away from this one, Harry. While you still have a few good toes."
Amused by his own sordid wit, it was Morgan's turn to offer a wry smile. Harry stared out the window, gratified that the city was behind him, out of sight.
He looked down at his hands. They were nearly healed, the pain was gone but the skin crackled when he moved them.

The buzzer from the lobby sounded in the foyer. Harry started to get up.

"Stay where you are," Morgan said. "I'll let her in."

THEY DECLARED DINNER a Ghiberti-free zone and chatted about the weather. Morgan left early. Miranda and Harry sipped sauternes in chilled champagne flutes that he kept in the freezer. A Château d'Yquem, but not the '67.

"I don't usually like sweet wines," she observed.

"*Pourriture noble*," he enunciated in execrable French.

"What on earth are you talking about?" She sat on the blue sofa with her legs tucked under her and grinned. She might have been twenty-two.

"Noble rot," he explained, adjusting an imaginary monocle in his best imitation of Lord Peter Wimsey. "Botrytis afflicts the grapes and they turn sweet. It's like ice-wine, only each grape rots in its own time. At Château d'Yquem, they're picked individually, grape by grape, at the height of decomposing perfection. There's so much sugar left over when the alcohol kills off the fermenting process you get this! Nectar of the gods."

"To coin a cliché. It's delicious."

"From rot comes perfection."

"From manure come mushrooms," she said.

"Have you ever read *Lord of the Flies*?"

"Pardon? I'm not sure, maybe I did."

"What about *The Bad Seed*?"

"Saw the movie," she said.

"Some day we should talk about evil. You know, the kind we're born with."

"Okay."

"But not now," he said. "Tell me about being a cop."

Now that's a non sequitur, Harry.

"It's not a good time. I guess you know after Christmas we buried one of our own. The first in over a decade. Twelve thousand came to the funeral. Phalanxes of mourning cops from every part of the country, hundreds and hundreds up from the States, streaming into the Convention Centre. It was heartbreaking and it made you proud."

"Did you know the guy?"

"No."

"Proud, to belong?"

"Yeah. Let's talk music, your favourite subject. John Lennon? A poet-philosopher."

"Aren't they all," he said.

"The best ones."

"Have you ever seen Puccini's *Tosca*?"

She liked opera.

Harry began to sing in his terrible nonmusical voice: *"Nell'ora del dolore, perché, perché, Signor … dum dum … perché me ne rimuneri cosi?"*

"Which means?"

"It doesn't have to mean anything. 'In my hour of grief and tribulation … why hast thou forsaken me?'"

"Harry?"

"It's not about me. You might think there is no solace in knowing we're all going to die, but there is. I feel cheated because death didn't take me at the same time. Now I'm impatient."

"Harry, are you okay? You're not going to do something stupid?"

Working in homicide, she had watched parents bludgeoned by the imponderable shock of a child's death. She had learned there was no consolation, not ever, only different ways of coping. Some parents were enraged, some were consumed by grief, some lost their minds. Some retreated into the delirium of religious cant. One thing survivors all had in common: a terrible and suffocating sense of guilt. It should have been them who died.

She slid forward and perched on the edge of his ottoman. She reached out and let her fingers rest on the back of his hand.

"Well?" he said.

She squeezed his hand.

He tried to smile.

"Harry, it wasn't your fault."

"I was warned about the rapids. I missed them. Did you ever paddle the Anishnabe?"

"A lifetime ago. What about the fire? Were you trying to kill yourself, then?"

"The house was too empty." He paused. "I didn't want to die. I didn't want to live."

"And now you do?"

"Which?"

"You need to be their witness. They deserve that."

Miranda drew in a deep breath.

"Are you still having focused hallucinations?" She asked tentatively.

"That's an oxymoron," he responded. "You're referring to my occasional conversations with Karen. I wouldn't call them hallucinations. We just like to talk."

"Do you see her, Harry?"

"If I look away right now I see you. Not with my eyes but you're here. My other senses, memory, imagination, the desire to know, all this assures me you're here. That's how it is with Karen, I know she's around, when she is. We're the sum of our experience, Miranda. Like Sartre said, and Camus. As long as I'm aware of myself, Karen is here."

"You think like a philosophy professor, Harry. I'm not sure that's a good thing."

"No, it's not a good thing, but it's unavoidable. Six years at Cambridge and twelve teaching at Huron will do that."

"Do you ever think of going back?"

"To professoring! Never. To thinking rationally? Possibly."

"What about the children, Harry?"

"What about them?"

"Are they ever with Karen?"

"They're dead. Of course they are."

"When she visits?"

"She doesn't *visit*, Miranda."

Tremors of pain crossed his face. The cost of his guilt was the banishment of his children, their memory driven out of his mind. He wanted to try and explain but swallowed the words and remained silent.

Miranda Quin's eyes watered as she peered at him. She dabbed at her face with the backs of her fingers. Then she took a deep, steadying breath. "Goddammit, Harry."

He looked at her sympathetically. He knew that genetics, John Calvin, and years of confronting atrocity kept her from openly weeping. They had known each other since he was a child. He understood only too well the constrained sensibility at the heart of her reticence. He struggled to change the subject. "Karen used to teach mysteries, you know. As a theorist, she could justify anything. She came up with a course on the murder mystery, where the authors are Canadians who use Canadian settings and express a Canadian sensibility. Louise Penny, Giles Blunt, John Moss, people like that."

"I didn't know there was such a thing as a Canadian mystery," said Miranda.

"That's part of the Canadian sensibility, not knowing."

"I thought you were going to say, 'the biggest mystery is that we have a Conservative government!'"

He gazed at her with confused affection.

"Sometimes I tell her I love her."

"And what does she tell you?"

"She says, 'I love you.'"

"Of course she does, Harry."

"She never says 'I love you, *too.*'"

AFTER MIRANDA LEFT and feeling emotionally reckless from sharing fine wine with a genuine friend, Harry let his mind wander unfettered. Before long it took him where he never wanted to go and held him transfixed. For a while, the past became more real than the present.

The red canoe on the grey cedar trestle glistened with morning dew. It was not red like the sun-bleached canoes of childhood but the colour of flowing blood when it hits open air, the colour of life or of life slipping away. Harry grimaced, then smiled. He and the old man hoisted the canoe onto the roof of his Volvo wagon. His memory was vivid. The blood-red colour was already congealing to crimson as the white light of dawn turned azure and the sky opened with the promise of a perfect day.

It was spring. They wanted to get into the bush after the worst of the blackflies and before the tourists. At eight and five, the kids were old enough for a wilderness adventure. The family had their own gear but Karen tracked down Virgil's Outfitting Emporium on the phone, and Virgil assured her he could rent them a brand new canoe, then pick them up Sunday afternoon at the foot of Long Pine Lake, and shuttle them back to their car.

For a few days he could leave behind Wittgenstein, Nietzsche, and Kant; he could forget about fate and irony and the will to power. He didn't pay much attention to Virgil's rambling description of the river.

8 TO STOCKHOLM

HARRY OPENED HIS LAPTOP AND RE-READ MORGAN'S NOTE. A stewardess brushed against him and he instinctively made himself smaller, drawing his arm in and tightening his shoulders. She apparently didn't notice and he slowly relaxed. He had not touched a woman's body in over three years. He returned his attention to his email.

The bad news: Scandinavian Airlines had no record of Birgitta Ghiberti on any flight from Reykjavik to Stockholm. The good news: Morgan's contact in the NCP, the Swedish National Criminal Police, reported Birgitta having been seen at a New Year's Eve party celebrating the opening of the Hotel Skeppsholmen, an event made prominent because the building itself dated from 1699. The Stockholm County Police, who checked the guest list supplied by the hotel, confirmed this sighting. The intriguing confusion: Bernd had insisted no one had seen her in Sweden, yet there she was, at a public reception.

When the SAS Airbus landed in Keflavik, Harry disembarked. He had chosen to follow Birgitta's route and was planning on spending a couple of days in Iceland. By breaking the journey, according to the doctors at TGH, he lowered his risk of embolisms from his injuries.

Harry had been to Iceland the previous summer for no reason at all. He had wanted a change, to go where he wouldn't meet anyone he knew but still felt a familial connection. The Lindstrom side of his family was originally from central Sweden, but a brief stint in Iceland played to his affinity for the Nordic, and the place was cool and serene with warm and affable people who wouldn't press him too closely. After a week he had gone home, not rejuvenated, but no worse for the wear. Given his general state of mind, this seemed the mark of a successful break from the ordinary.

Getting onto the bus for Reykjavik under brilliant airport floodlights, he hardly noticed that it was dark at midafternoon, and he dozed fitfully until a frozen pothole sent him lurching against the seat. He buckled sideways to relieve the pain in his ribs, he blinked, trying to get oriented, and leaning down to see through the front window, he gasped. The horizon was on fire with the lights of the town, which glared into a dark blue sky flecked with pinpoints of starlight, and across the whole blue vista was a swirl of dazzling green, as if the spirit of van Gogh had drawn a light wand through the firmament in an abstract expression of pure intense breathtaking beauty.

Looking out to the side, Harry could only see glimmering shadows blotched with patches of darkness. He had expected more snow, but what little there was lay in frozen sheets, skimming the rocky ground like a cover tossed casually to keep the land safe through the long winter.

As he stepped off the bus to the side of the Icelandic Parliament House—the oldest democratic institution in the world, with the vaguely allusive name, the Althingi—Harry felt comforted. The salt-sea air on his face was crisp, but not as cold as Toronto. There was a village quality to the surrounding buildings, an eeriness to the streetlights glowing against the midday darkness. Trying to get his bearings before making his way to his hotel, Harry rotated slowly around to take in the entire scene when he suddenly found a large bearded man who had not been there a moment before blocking his view.

The man grasped his bag, with Harry resisting, until the man smiled.

"Mr. Lindstrom."

And he knows my name. Harry relinquished his bag.

"Would you come with me?"

"You are?"

"Rikislögreglan, the Iceland Police. David Arnason. Chief Constable."

"I'd be honoured," said Harry as they removed their gloves and shook hands. He was not sure if he was about to be fêted or placed under arrest.

Instead of going to the police station, they walked to his hotel, the same one he had stayed in the previous summer, a flat-faced three-storey building sheathed in narrow clapboard painted off-white, its small-paned windows beckoning with the promise of congenial warmth inside. Chief Constable Arnason dropped Harry's bag at reception but insisted they go straight to the bar, where he ordered two pints of Guinness Extra Stout.

"Now then," said Harry's host, once they had settled into chairs at a small table close to the fire. "You do not have a cell phone, I believe?"

"How would you know that?"

The other man smiled.

"I left it at home," said Harry. "I abhor the damned thing."

"You are what they call a Luddite, perhaps."

"Simply a man who does not offer the world easy access. And who would I call?"

"For business? Your wife?"

"I work alone, Chief Constable." Harry paused. He was probably the only Canadian in his early forties who did not drive a car. He had a licence but he never drove; there was no need, living in downtown Toronto. And while he owned a cell phone, he did not treat it as a bodily appendage. "My wife and I stay in touch, she knows how to reach me."

In fact, his original cell phone was lost with Karen's in the fire. They used to text each other through the day from adjoining offices at Huron College and while sitting side by side in their living room on the Sanctuary Line, indulging in word play, role play, even foreplay. And now, while having a replacement had been low on Harry's priority list, Miranda insisted he buy one. He usually left it in the string drawer among elastic bands and used corks in his kitchen.

"Well then," said the other man affably as he presented Harry with his own phone. "You will use mine. We received an important call for you from Canada. You are to call back."

An important call. But only after they had their drinks in hand. In front of an open fire.

We could like it here, Harry. They have their priorities right.

Arnason tapped in a number on his phone with his thumb, listened, then handed it over to Harry. It could only be one person trying to reach him from Toronto, from anywhere, and using the police to make contact. And who knew he wouldn't be carrying his cell.

"Harry," she started right in. "Morgan told me you were back on the case."

"Apparently I am."

"Good. Be careful. You could have let me know."

"I could have. But I'm really not certain what my case is, apart from unravelling the sordid complexities of a very strange family."

"You could have let someone know where you were staying?"

"It's where I stayed last summer. I'm there now."

"I had to lean on the good graces of Detective Arnason."

"Chief Constable."

"There's been a murder that might interest you."

Harry's mind raced, anticipating what Miranda would say.

"Are you there, Harry?"

"I'm listening."

Arnason was talking in loud whispers to the couple at the next table. He had shifted around so that his back was toward Harry, creating a barrier of relative privacy. An expressionless man from reception had walked over and set Harry's registration form down in front of the chief constable for his signature. He laughed and slid it around to Harry, who signed it and slid it back.

"We found the body of a young woman, a blonde. She was frozen to death in the snow. Naked, but wrapped up. No sign of sexual assault. Sound vaguely familiar? Can you give us any leads, Harry? Morgan says your Birgitta Ghiberti is in Sweden. And her son is on his way, today or tomorrow. We called on him after we found the girl and he offered to come down to the station. He acknowledged that his mother had given us cause for concern. He was very co-operative, but of course he knew nothing to help our inquiry. He seemed worried about Birgitta. When we told him she had turned up at a party in Stockholm, he didn't seem relieved. That was the strange thing. Then when I told him you were already on your way, he did. Seem relieved."

"Sounds like my job's redundant. They can connect without me."

"Too late, Harry. You're in the middle. If he is a killer, she's gravely at risk and so are you. You need to stop the killing. If he's not a killer, you're still vulnerable—did it ever occur to you she may take revenge on you for proving him innocent. Her consolation for being wrong. And remember, his concern for her may be genuine, even if he is—"

"The killer."

"After all, she's his mother. And if it is someone else, not him, that person may also decide to eliminate you for jeopardizing his criminous enterprise. Or if Bernd killed his sisters, but someone else killed—"

"Enough, Miranda! It may seem *Grand-Guignol* from the cheap seats, but I'm part of the horror show on stage."

"Do the characters know they're in a play?"

"Not the play they're in. Oh, for God's sake, Miranda. We're on long distance."

"Nobody calls it that anymore. So who are you working for, exactly?"

"Depends on what I find."

"No conflict there, Harry."

"When did the girl die? You called me about a murder."

"You called me."

"When did you find her?"

"January's been a very cold month, even for January. No thaws. That would have helped. She was discovered under the snow in a cedar maze. A bunch of kids were digging a fort in the drifts. They didn't call us until they'd recruited a few of their friends to help dig her out."

"So much for a pristine crime scene."

"Well, they churned up the snow quite a lot but..." For a moment he thought the line went dead.

Lines don't go dead any more, Harry.

Miranda continued. "They found something very disturbing beside the corpse." She paused again. "Your Möbius loop, Harry. They found your cashmere scarf."

"They what?"

"They did."

Harry, that was careless.

To lose it, yes. Not to leave it there. I didn't.

Convince your buddy, not me.

"I didn't notice it was missing, Miranda. I hadn't been going out for the last few weeks."

"So, you think the person who tumbled you over the balcony planted the scarf?"

"I tumbled myself, but yes, whoever shut me out in blizzard conditions took the bloody scarf, killed your girl, and wants to set me up, or at least force a connection between me and the crime."

"You believe it was Bernd?"

"I do."

"He'll come back to us, then. He doesn't think we suspect him."

"At least now your ex-partner will get that I wasn't the victim of a frozen lock."

"I think Morgan's on your side, Harry."

"Well, you know it couldn't have been me doing the killing. I was in Toronto General, having my toes amputated."

"Bits of your toes, Harry, and they fell off, they weren't cut off."

"A matter of semantics. I still have the pain as reminders."

"She was probably dead before you went into the hospital, Harry. From reading the accumulated snow layers, it seems likely she died before Christmas. We'll know more after the autopsy."

"And no one reported her missing?"

"Not until mid-January. She was basically a street kid, scrounging to make ends meet, estranged from her family."

"And she ended up among the Rosedale elite. If she was in a garden maze, it must have been Rosedale. Was she naked when she died?"

"Explain?"

"Was she in the blanket already, or bundled up after she was dead?"

"I'm not sure. I'll get back to you on that." For a moment neither said anything, and then Miranda continued, "So, do you have an address for Bernd, can you talk to him in Stockholm?"

"And say what? Did you kill a girl in Toronto before you left home? I can reach him through his NGO. What was the girl's name?"

"Ilsa Jóhannesdóttir, if I've got the pronunciation right. Seventeen years old. Her family had just moved to the city last fall."

"Jóhannesdóttir. They were probably from Gimli."

"And you know that because?"

"The Icelandic name. Gimli is on the shores of Lake Winnipeg; the people are mostly Icelandic, with a few Swedes and Ukrainians thrown in for excitement. I've got relatives there. You can't seriously be asking if I killed her." Since Miranda said nothing, he continued defensively, "Some of my Swedish forbearers emigrated north from Minnesota about the same time as the mass immigration from Iceland in 1875." He paused. "So, Ilsa Jóhannesdóttir; no rape, no torture. But naked. That's different. How did she die?"

"So far, it seems from exposure. And one more thing. Her fingernails had been bitten to the quick; they weren't cut. But there was blackening on her fingertips, black nail polish."

"Oh, Jesus."

Harry glanced at Arnason who was laughing and joking with the couple at the next table and still managing to take in every word on Harry's end of the conversation. "Her family, how're they doing?"

"Torn to shreds. They're taking her back to Manitoba when we release the body."

"Can you send me a full report?"

"Unofficially."

"I'm staying at Bentleys Hotel in Stockholm; it's on Drottninggatan Street, not far from the station. Do you want to make a note of that?"

"I'm recording us, Harry. I've got it. I can email the file."

"I'd like a hard copy, including pictures. I don't want to use a printing service; it's a little too grisly. I'll talk to both Ghibertis if I can track them down."

"Isn't that why you're going?"

"Yeah, and everyone lives happily ever after, unless someone else dies."

"If there aren't more murders, you've got a dead end. You can come home."

"There are only dead ends, Miranda. You said your girl was naked. The bodies in Sweden have been fully clothed, without coats, but indistinguishable from random deaths by misadventure in winter. So, apart from the fingernails, what connects them?"

"At this point, you."

Harry said nothing.

"I'll talk to you soon, Harry. I just thought you needed to know. And Harry—" For a moment he expected her to pass on her regards to Karen. She didn't. "You take care," she said and clicked off.

Harry handed the phone back to Chief Constable Arnason, who spoke unabashedly about overhearing the conversation.

"I know the name, Jóhannesdóttir. A young woman, yes. Death by snow. It happens. Naked, not so often." He looked sad for a moment, then rallied. "Would you like me to arrange a tour for you? Seljalandfoss Waterfall is just south of here; it falls two hundred feet from an overhanging cliff. Spectacular at dusk. We do have a few hours of daylight, you know. Iceland hangs like a jewel from the Arctic Circle. We only have full darkness one night of the year. I can go on, if you wish. Like a tourist brochure. What about a thermal plunge in the Blue Lagoon? But, Harry, you're tired. Perhaps you would like to retire and join me for dinner, say at 8:30, here."

The big man stood up before Harry could respond and once Harry was on his feet, gave him a huge bear hug, his bushy beard scratching insistently at Harry's ear like it had a life of its own, and walked out into the strangely luminescent twilight of the late afternoon.

At the door, Harry thought to ask him about Birgitta.

"Birgitta Ghiberti? No, I don't think so. Is she Italian?"

"Swedish." Harry described her.

"Was she travelling alone?"

It had not occurred to Harry she wasn't.

The next morning, Chief Constable Arnason reported back that there was no record of a Mrs. Ghiberti landing in Iceland, and no one answering her description had stood out as a guest at any of the larger hotels in Reykjavik—which was not surprising, given her Nordic features.

The chief constable drove Harry out to Seljalandfoss. Higher than the Horseshoe Falls with a fraction of the volume, the water billowed like shaken silk and pooled at the base, not crashing through rock like Niagara. He had already seen the falls on an episode of *The Amazing Race*, but as they approached it seemed unfamiliar.

Harry had an abiding appreciation for the sublime, Schopenhauer's blend of beauty and dread that moved him to awe, but when he stood behind the cascading curtain of water at the base of the falls, he felt sick at heart. Karen had been curiously absent on the drive out along Route 1. For some reason he couldn't comprehend, Harry had not connected a natural tourist attraction in Iceland with the murderous waters of the Devil's Cauldron on the Anishnabe River in Algonquin Park. Not until he got there. And then the horror of his memories sent waves of shock and remorse coursing through him so that he had to grasp Arnason's arm to steady himself.

While they drove from the falls to Sólheimajökull Glacier, Chief Constable Arnason didn't intrude on his silence with questions. Harry admired him for that. For all his garrulous bonhomie, he was a sensitive man.

The glacial tongue was intriguing but Harry felt emotionally bruised from his experience at Seljalandfoss Falls and declined Arnason's offer to take him on a private tour of the more accessible reaches of ice illuminated by the midday sun. He opted to return to the hotel for a Guinness or two.

The policeman obliged, and they drove back in companionable silence. The big Icelander, however, excused himself at the hotel entrance, having police business to attend to, and Harry didn't see him again before his departure the following day.

CHIEF CONSTABLE ARNASON'S cousin was to meet Harry at Arlanda Airport and drive him to his hotel in the heart of Stockholm. He insisted it would be no trouble at all.

Coming into the arrivals area, Harry looked for a replica of Arnason. A woman blocking his way smiled warmly. She was well over six feet tall and quietly beautiful, if beauty were sound and quietude a measure of perfection. He tried to step around her. As he moved to his left, she moved to her right. He assumed she was smiling at someone behind him and sidestepped again, and she did the same.

"Either you are Chief Constable Arnason's cousin or I am exceptionally awkward," he said, assuming she understood English.

"You are, and I am," she said, turning her smile up to full volume. "Hannah Arnason, yes." She reached out and shook his hand, then took his bag, which he relinquished without a fuss. He was tired and his toes hurt. She was undoubtedly stronger than him and a good two inches taller. Four in heels.

And, Karen admonished, *she's a good deal better looking than you are, Harry. You're an attractive man, my darling, but she's so outrageously perfect, it could be classed as a disability. There's no future in it, Harry. Everyone, including yourself, would wonder why she bothered. Although, I repeat, you are attractive, but you're only a mortal. Be nice, but be wary.*

They walked to the car without talking and for the first time in over three years Harry wondered where Karen's voice was coming from. Her description of him as attractive amused him. Her warning about another woman, based on his limitations, unnerved him.

"You will like Sweden very much," the woman said as they drove toward the city. "You have been here before many times?"

"No," said Harry. "Only once, with my wife."

"Ah, you have a wife. That is good."

Harry gazed out the window as they drove along an embankment beside a frozen river. His toes hurt. He hadn't taken his shoes off on the flight, afraid he might not get them back on. Finally, after they circled through side streets and pulled up in front of Bentleys, he turned to her and explained, "My wife is dead."

"I am so sorry. Was she a good wife?" Her question was awkward but without condescension or malice.

Yes, Harry thought, she was. She is. He got out, retrieved his bag from the back seat, thanked Hannah Arnason, and walked a little painfully up the steps, through the outer door, up more steps, and turned to the small reception desk tucked off to the side.

Bentleys was a small hotel with a curiously Britannic name where Harry and Karen had stayed for a few days after an academic conference during their first year at Huron. He had booked there because he remembered the name; it was not about reliving the past.

After registering, he took the open elevator that ascended behind a mesh screen up the middle of the circular stairwell to the fifth floor and hobbled along to his room, a small and charmingly minimal garret with a tiny balcony and a spacious bathroom. He said nothing to Karen, but he knew exactly where she was in the room, dressed in her signature jeans and Armani blazer, the wedding outfit she had worn on their earlier visit.

He unpacked and hung up his few clothes and put away his sweaters and small things in dresser drawers.

"Karen?" he said in a soft voice.

Yes, she responded. He liked when she seemed to be talking out loud.

"This is silly."

What?

"We're having our first posthumous quarrel."

You are, I'm not.

"I'll never see her again."

That would be stupid; she could be useful.

"Not if it upsets you."

Harry, how could it upset me? I'm not even here.

"Yes, you are."

No, I'm not.

"We sound like a Rogers and Hammerstein musical."

Please, for God's sake, Harry, don't break into song.

"Let's have a nap, then we'll go out and explore."

Harry, it's dark, it's cold. I'm staying here. You go without me.

"See, you're annoyed."

No, I'm not.

"Yes, you are."

No, I am not, I am not, I am not.

"Go to sleep. I love you."

And I love you, Harry. Sleep tight.

When he felt himself beginning to wake up, Harry caught a subtle scent of lilacs, but he was disoriented. Before opening his eyes he scanned through his mind, trying to sort out where he was, while an unfinished dream urged him to fall back into a deep and comforting sleep. He could hear muffled sounds of the city drifting up from the street. He had smelled snow in the air when he came in, and he was sure it was snowing. Big flakes, because it wasn't all that cold and there was no wind in the eaves outside his window. With his eyes still closed, he could tell it was daylight. He had slept right through. Despite his stopover in Iceland, he was jet lagged.

A horn honked warily on the street below, someone shouted. The Drottninggatan was open for business, allowing limited access for delivery vans and service vehicles. A few blocks south, the street was a pedestrian walkway, running right through to the old town. Harry opened his eyes to confirm he was in a room at Bentleys.

The bedside telephone jangled and he grabbed at it, trying to choke off the noise.

"Mr. Lindstrom. There is a visitor for you. Please come downstairs to the dining facilities."

Harry hung up without asking who it was. He loved the precision of so many Swedes when they spoke English. He thought of lyrics by ABBA but couldn't remember anything other than a throbbing "mama mia," which kept resounding through his skull while he shaved.

It would be Bernd Ghiberti. Miranda had said he was on his way. Obviously, he was already there. Eating breakfast, no doubt. Harry was enthralled with the rich generosity of Scandinavian breakfasts. He assumed Bernd would indulge.

Harry walked down the stairs to get his blood flowing, but when he swung around past the reception desk into the breakfast room, he discovered Hannah Arnason sitting by herself in the window overlooking the street. She was a stunning apparition, sipping coffee. Beyond her, outside, snow filled the air.

9 A DEAD WOMAN IN THE PARK

SHE'S NOT MUCH OVER THIRTY, KAREN WHISPERED.

Ah, said Harry to himself, then she's older than I thought.

"Ms. Arnason. Good to see you. Don't get up. I'll just grab a coffee. Can I get you a refill?" When Harry slipped into the comfortable chair opposite, he started to offer an apology for his cold behaviour coming in from the airport.

"It is Inspector Arnason," she said. "No, you were not so cold. We do not know each other. For the present moment, I am here on police business."

"Police," said Harry with surprise. "I hadn't realized. National or County? I understand your two forces overlap."

"NCP," she said. "National. I work closely with the Stockholm police on criminal cases that extend beyond their jurisdiction."

"Ah," he said, eyeing the plates of cold cuts and cheese, breads and yoghurt, sweet buns and cereal being removed from the buffet table and taken back to the kitchen. "I appreciate the offer, but for the time being, I'll just poke around a bit and see what I come up with. It's far too soon to get the police involved."

"You are already involved with the police, Mr. Lindstrom."

Harry looked at her, trying to decipher the impenetrable blue of her eyes.

"Really? How involved?"

"I am in need of clarification. Your credentials are *suspect.* Is that the word?"

"Possibly it is. I'm not sure what you mean."

"You were a private investigator in British Columbia, yes?"

"Yes, briefly. Several years ago."

"In a place called Nanaimo, yes? It is very beautiful, I understand."

"It is and it isn't."

"And you had some trouble there, am I correct?"

"Not really," said Harry. "I didn't pay much attention."

Hannah Arnason ducked her head to the side and looked over at him through a veil of hair the colour of moonlight. Her features were relaxed.

Express the unexpected, Harry. Beautiful women learn that from birth.

"Who told you about this?" he asked, ignoring Karen.

"I would not be permitted to say."

Harry turned to gaze out the window. The air was filled with snow but the pavement was nearly bare. Either Stockholm was exceptionally efficient with snow removal or it received relatively little precipitation. He looked back into the room, surveying the worn floor. Two men at the far side of the room began unrolling a Heriz carpet of astonishing beauty that reached almost from wall to wall. An ornate field of madder red floating on a sea of midnight blue filled the room with warmth. He had a Heriz in his living room but this one was better, although not so old. Neither he nor Inspector Arnason said anything as the men manoeuvred tables and chairs until the final roll of the carpet was at their feet.

They stood up and moved aside. The workmen said nothing but rearranged their chairs on the cleaned carpet, then motioned for them to sit down again, which they did. Hannah Arnason offered a generous smile. A fine carpet in the restaurant of a small hotel: this was Sweden, gracious to a fault.

Harry sat back abruptly and stared out the low-slung arched window that created the illusion of an intimate alcove, although from street level they appeared to be under its heavy curve, bearing up the weight of the building. Tall blonde women walked by, each wearing a garnish of snow, each dressed immaculately in a wrap-around coat with a fur collar, stepping through the fresh snow in high boots with fur trim. In fact, most of the women on the Drottninggatan, and the men as well, might have been walking along Bloor St. in Toronto. People in more temperate climates always looked surprised by winter. Not in Stockholm. And not all of the women were blonde, or tall. But they were all dressed for the cold.

He turned to address Hannah Arnason but fell quiet when she smiled again. He realized he was scowling. He did his best to smile in return as he recalled lines from a Yeats poem he'd studied years ago: "Like a long-legged fly upon the stream, Her mind moves upon silence." He found the description unnerving.

He said, "As far as I know, only a handful of people are aware I'm in Stockholm. Two of them are cops, one in Toronto, one in Reykjavik. Another is my travel agent. And then there's Bernd Ghiberti."

"And myself, of course." Her smile was unnerving. "I know you are here, Mr. Lindstrom."

"I'm here as a private citizen, a Canadian in good standing."

"And you are Swedish, also?"

"A long way back. A Canadian smorgasbord: Swedish, Scottish, German, English, Mennonite from Switzerland."

"You are religious?"

"After fleeing the American Revolution to protect their faith, my Mennonite ancestors settled in Canada and lost it."

"Québécois? You have French?"

"No. I lived there for a couple of years when I was a kid."

"And from Sweden? Where?"

"The central lake district, I think."

"And why, exactly, are you here?"

That is not an existential question, Harry.

As her smile faded, he felt a chill. He was about to explain when a woman from reception approached their table and handed him a manila envelope. A copy of Miranda's file had reached the Bentley before he did.

"Do you mind?" he asked before opening it.

"Not at all. I see it is from the police in Canada. From Toronto. It is a nice place?"

"Yes, it is," said Harry. "A nice place. Look, are you going to arrest me?"

"What for? You are on private business, yes? But police business, as well, I believe."

"I should get something to eat. I hate to be rude but what I'm *on* is nobody's business."

"Do not worry, Mr. Lindstrom. It is not so confusing." She pressed her lips together and sighed. "It *is* confusing, yes?"

Okay, Harry. Enough of this.

Harry opened the envelope and set out photographs of a frozen corpse on the table between them.

Well done, Harry. Nothing sets the opposition at ease like pictures of a naked dead woman.

Inspector Arnason picked up the pictures and examined them carefully, tilting each to the natural light coming in under the window archway. Her facial expression hardened without changing. She had seen it all before.

"You are a licenced investigator in Toronto?" she asked, setting down the photographs. "What about Nanaimo? Please you explain."

Ha, a grammatical error.

"Simple," said Harry, ignoring Karen. "I spent part of my growing up on Vancouver Island."

You'd better clarify, Harry.

"Later, as an undergraduate, I studied at the University of Victoria for a couple of years. My parents were living in New Brunswick at the time, on the other side of the country. When I was a student, I took a bus trip up to Nanaimo, but my childhood friends had moved on. It's a beautiful town. Coastal bushland, mainland mountains in the distance, and semi-depressed. That attracted me when I wanted to set up as a private investigator; it seemed like a good place to start. Semi-depressed. Not many murders. I was only interested in murder. Familiar but strange. I was an outsider in a place I knew well."

She was listening as if what he said was important.

"You went to jail."

"They let me out."

"Then, you left."

"Yeah."

"Why?"

"My friend who had encouraged me to locate there, then urged me to relocate in Toronto. More anonymity, useful in my line of work, and more murders. She's a police superintendent in homicide." He tapped the return address printed on the top of the manila envelope.

"Were you trained for police work?"

"No, I was a philosopher."

"You are joking."

"Cambridge PhD, professor of philosophy at Huron College, south-western Ontario. And I suppose that accounts for why they put me in jail."

"You go to jail in British Columbia for the practice of philosophy."

Harry was charmed by her precision. He was sure her English was learned second-hand, not on location. Her accent was perfect, her syntax too perfect.

Not always.

"I had a disagreement with a judge."

"That is not a good thing in Sweden."

"He insisted I answer a question from the witness stand the way he wanted me to."

"Really! How extraordinary."

"'*Yes or no*,' he asked. '*Neither*,' I replied. I was a witness for the prosecution and they already had a good case. But I was asked if, in my professional opinion—"

"As a philosopher?"

"As a private eye, trained mostly by Dashiell Hammett and Elmore Leonard."

"They are famous detectives in your country?"

"No. Well, possibly. Anyway, I was asked, 'Do you see the man who was holding the gun in this courtroom?' I tried to explain that I saw a man who looked like the accused and he had been holding something in his hand that might have been a gun. But the eyes play tricks, they fill in details."

"So you are a philosopher but not a disciple of John Locke?"

"Uh? Not really."

"You do not accept Locke and Berkeley, that knowledge arises from the experience of the senses."

"Uh, well, yes and no. In this case, no. I refused to state unequivocally that the accused was, or indeed, was not, the culprit. I was more in a Nietzschean frame of mind at the time. I was sent to jail for a week, for contempt of court. That seemed absurd since it was the court that held me in contempt and not the other way around. My friend suggested I relocate to Toronto, which I did. And how do you know about the empiricists, Inspector Arnason?"

"I am sure you do not mean that to be a patronizing question, Dr. Lindstrom. Yes? We have a very good educational system in Sweden, very good universities. I went to Lund, myself, where I read philosophy. That was before I decided to be a policeperson and went into extensive training."

"Oh," he said.

Harry. Be careful. She's very young.

"And I do know who Elmore Leonard is, and Dashiell Hammett. John Travolta, *Get Shorty*, Humphrey Bogart, Sam Spade. We know these things, even in Sweden."

"Of course." Harry felt like a bit of a fool and changed the subject. "Bernd Ghiberti told you about Nanaimo," he stated, as if clarifying something they both understood. "I wonder why."

"Mr. Ghiberti? No. It does not matter. I am satisfied."

Don't count on it, Harry.

"It was Ghiberti. He's dug into my past."

"We have met, Mr. Ghiberti and I. I have met also his mother, Birgitta. Stockholm is not so big."

"You know about his mother's accusations, then."

"Yes, we do. And we have been talking to your superintendent."

"Not mine. I'm not a cop."

"Ms. Miranda Quin. She is your friend."

"She is."

"I am puzzled though. Why you are here?"

"Are you in charge of the Ghiberti file, Inspector?"

"There is no Ghiberti file, Mr. Lindstrom. But, yes, if there was, I would be in charge."

He nodded, appreciatively.

"And you?" she continued in a sociable tone. "You are here, doing what, Mr. Lindstrom? Would you prefer Dr. Lindstrom or Professor?"

"I'd prefer Harry. I like Sweden. I've never been here in winter."

"You are rather mature to be coy, Mr. Lindstrom."

Ouch. Harry, work with her. She could be useful. And even if she's not, she's preposterously attractive.

Harry explained as clearly as he could why he was there.

When he finished, she said, "You are here, then, for your friend, Ms. Quin."

Not really, he thought. He looked out the window. Large flakes of snow drifting downward filled the air. He could hardly see across the narrow street.

She tried again. "You are here in case the Swedish police are not very good." Harry looked back at her and let a wry smile pull his mouth slightly askew. "Well, then," she summarized, "you are here in the service of evil, so to speak. If no one actually hires you until the job is done, neither the mother nor the son are your clients unless things turn out for the worse."

Holy perdition, Harry. Don't get into an argument about evil.

It's just one of those words people use.

Inspector Arnason leaned forward across the table. Being so tall, when Harry moved forward in his chair to accommodate her gesture, their heads almost touched. Then she tilted her head to the side and whispered, "You are here because there is much confusion and you are a man who likes clarity. There is an equal possibility of heinous crimes or of no crimes at all. You are a philosopher, Professor Lindstrom. You are intrigued by what you do *not* know even more than by what you do. It will be a pleasure working with you."

"Are we working together?" he whispered. "Why are we whispering?"

"Unofficially, of course," she said in a full voice, sitting back. "I have recruited you and you may use me as you wish."

Harry!

But Harry felt old. Hannah Arnason made Harry feel old. It wasn't intentional, there was no malice involved, nor was it because she was one of those people who seems to exist inside a photo shoot, perfectly lit, no matter what the light, and groomed to perfection. He felt any response was a betrayal; that Karen deserved better.

Don't be absurd, Harry. I'm dead. You're hung up on guilt, not love.

I haven't done anything yet.

And it's unlikely you will. Not until you stop confusing what you miss for remorse.

His reverie ended suddenly with the insistent jangle of her cell phone. It was a popular tune, the beginning of a song by the Beatles. He tried not to follow her side of the conversation by getting up and finding a sweet bun on the breakfast table that had unaccountably been left behind by the staff who presumably feasted on whatever the guests didn't eat. He managed to devour most of the bun when she beckoned him back to the table. Before he got there, she stood up, ducking her head to miss the arch looming over their alcove.

"We must go now. You would like to come, I think. There has been a naked body found in Hagaparken. She is covered in snow, perhaps murdered."

"Unless she wandered away from a sauna."

"No, there is no sauna in Hagaparken."

Harry retrieved the photographs from the table and slipped them back into the manila envelope with the copies of the police report. Hannah had taken a good look at the pictures, but when he had offered her the report itself, she had pushed it to the side. Either she was disinterested or she already knew what it said.

He dropped the envelope off at the desk and asked for it to be delivered to his room. He would go over it later.

As they drove north through the thick falling snow along the E4 toward Uppsala, Harry remarked that her Volvo wagon was much like one he used to own.

"This is not my car," she said. "I drive a Saab. It is also Swedish."

"But you're not."

"I am Swedish, yes. But my father is Icelandic. He studied in Sweden and tried to take home a Swedish wife."

"Tried?"

"My mother did not want to be married. She refused to go. She has never been to Iceland. I used to visit my father every year, and all my cousins. The chief constable is my favourite, of course."

"Of course."

The air was absolutely still as they entered the south gate. The snow had dwindled to a few flurries and then stopped as the sky filled with brilliant blue, and there was a hush over the landscape that Harry could sense, even before they passed the visitors' parking lot and came to a stop near several official vehicles, including an ambulance and a police cruiser.

The park was not at all what he expected. The new snow lying heavy on the bare branches of the hardwood trees was magical, but the discipline of the trees' placement in columns and clusters among pavilions and broad open spaces accentuated the ways nature had been carefully organized, like an eighteenth-century English park, to make wilderness seem tame and accessible. The natural world, designed by a landscape architect to charm the human eye. As they trudged through the fresh snow, following a line of footprints toward a cluster of people in the distance, Harry marvelled at the patient conviction it would take to plant saplings and mound earth into contours for generations ahead.

There were ski tracks here and there intersecting their progress. He followed them with his eye as they cut across broad swards of meadow, through the ghost-white trees and around strange buildings, over ponds and past ruins. Harry caught sight of the famed Copper Tents, originally stables built to look like an Arabian palace, striped blue and yellow, standing forlorn in the drifting snow.

It had been a skier who found the body. The Haga Park was a very public place, even in winter, despite its relatively vast size and distance from the city. Harry preferred Nordic skiing through bushland and wilderness but had to concede there was a special charm to following trails set by skiers among pavilions and follies, greenhouses, a butterfly house, and a Chinese pagoda. All this was contrived by King Gustav III and his progeny for their people's amusement, and their own. It was not like skiing in Algonquin Park, which Harry and Karen had always planned to do.

In the shadows cast by the grand, sprawling pavilion, with its pale yellow walls and columns of white Gothic windows rising like a spectre out of the snow, a knot of people was gathered around the body. They were chatting, shuffling to keep warm although temperatures had risen with the snowfall far above what they had been during the night. They were waiting, apparently, for Inspector Arnason to appear on the scene.

Harry was reassured. She had clout.

The girl looked realistic rather than real. The falling snow had melted on contact with her flesh, until her temperature dropped to match the atmosphere, covering her with an opaque glaze. The covering glittered in the sunlight like a crystal shroud, accentuating her nakedness and at the same time allowing her a pathetic semblance of modesty.

Inspector Arnason left him on his own while she spoke to various people, including an elderly man wearing old-style cross-country ski clothes made before synthetics. Harry noticed that his skis, which had been stuck upright in a snowdrift, were wood. And, inevitably, the poles were bamboo. The man looked like one of those annoying ads taunting North Americans for being less fit than a seventy-year-old Swede.

Harry looked down at the girl. The sun was warming her icy carapace and it was melting, sliding off contours of her body, exposing her skin. Harry watched in horror as she turned from what might have been an artist's mannequin or a grisly sculpture into a frozen corpse.

She was young, still in her teens. She was blonde. There did not appear to have been a struggle. There were minor scrapes around her ankles, nothing severe enough to suggest she had been shackled. The surface skin on the bottoms of her feet was finely lacerated, but not enough to draw blood.

Harry ran his eyes along the length of her body. Her eyelashes had been the last part of her to release their burden of frozen snow; they looked unnaturally white and full. Their weight drew down her eyelids, but what he could see of her eyes indicated they had been brown, although now they were almost colourless, opaque, reflecting the blue of the sky.

"She was pretty," said Hannah Arnason, who had moved up beside him and was watching him think. "There is no blanket wrapping, Harry. I doubt she is connected to your Toronto murder."

Harry bent down and because the ice covering on the girl's fingers had melted, he was able to examine her nails. They didn't appear to have been cut recently but they were painted with black matte polish on the inside curves.

10 **OLD TOWN**

ON HER INVITATION, HARRY AND HANNAH ARNASON MET for a candlelit dinner in a cozy cellar restaurant off Vasterlanggatan in Gamla Stan, the oldest part of the city. He had been to the old town before, but in the summertime. Passing in winter among canyons of office buildings and chain stores, through the bleak archways on Helgeandsholmen, and across a busy street channelling gusts of ice-laden snow and furious eddies of exhaust from passing traffic, he was relieved by the sudden transition that placed him in a blazing maze of cobblestone passageways and well-lit alleys. Gamla Stan offered warmth and intimacy to counter the frozen darkness. The haunting medley of stone work and brick and wood from different eras, sometimes all in a single façade, created an ambience that was even more inviting in the illuminated night than in the long twilight of summer.

Harry appreciated the Swedish genius for making winter habitable. He looked around their underground cavern as they sipped postprandial liqueurs and, for a moment, he was almost content. Karen had been with him the whole evening, and yet in no discernable way did she intrude through a sumptuous dinner and the free-flowing discussion that circled again and again, always coming back to the Ghibertis.

Harry could see that Hannah was puzzled by him. Tiny lights glinting off stemware and cutlery from the myriad candles around them shimmered in her hair and sparkled in her eyes. But Harry talked to her like a normal person, an experience her profound good looks had probably prevented since puberty. There was no hostility in his restraint. He wasn't wary, resentful, or struggling with a stifled libido. He was enjoying her company.

While they briefly extolled Birgitta Ghiberti's capacity for aging gracefully, an elderly man with a face like a satchel approached their table. He was sporting a bad dye job but his pitch-black hair was cut mercifully short.

You don't often see someone that old so obviously suffering the ravages of nicotine, Karen whispered. *They're usually dead by his age.*

Harry smiled. His gesture caught Hannah's eye as she glanced up at the man who came to a stop by her shoulder.

The man leaned down and said something to her in Swedish. He handed her a small paper envelope that she peered into, then folded into a square and tucked into the palm of one hand.

Harry could smell the stench of stale tobacco from across the table. Somewhere in the back of his head, a balance was moving toward equilibrium, with the hyper-fit septuagenarian of that morning being countered by this man, of the same age, hovering on the brink of self-induced annihilation.

Inspector Arnason said something to the man and he answered, and then he stepped back and stared at Harry until she waved him away. He shambled off into the gloom of their candlelit crypt and she looked at Harry with a mixture of amusement and disappointment, the way a mother might, at her own delinquent child.

"Is there a problem?" said Harry, addressing the self-evident when an explanation did not appear to be forthcoming.

"There is." She seemed uncomfortable, as if he had let her down. "Professor Lindstrom, where did you go last night after I dropped you off at Bentleys?"

"Why?"

"Please tell me."

"I went to bloody sleep. What's going on?"

Bloody was an ancestral memory, a genetic expletive. Harry didn't swear very often, but sometimes that particular word burst through from his querulous English forbearers, who were normally subdued by the Swedish and Scottish and German chromosomes running in his blood.

Armason seemed in no hurry for an answer, as if the sinister implications of her query needed time to take effect. Harry felt trapped, not sure if he should get up and walk out, laugh, or roundly protest the absurdity of this disconcerting twist in the evening's events.

Easy, Harry. Just because the messenger looked like a smoked cadaver, doesn't mean he's the angel of death. No one accused you of murder. Not directly.

Bloody hell, Harry mumbled to himself, with the subliminal trace of a Northumbrian accent. Lost somewhere in his DNA was the capacity to swear in Swedish. And despite six years living in England, he had not picked up the Cambridge vernacular, in contrast to university associates who returned from a summer session at Oxford sporting an Oxonian lisp that stayed with them for life.

He tried to read the expression in Hannah Arnason's eyes, but they gleamed with myriad flames. He leaned back, she leaned away. The softened light on contours of her cashmere sweater undulated like moonlight as her body moved beneath the material.

Focus, Harry, something is seriously happening here.

"We seem to have a problem. My constable has brought me certain information that compromises our situation."

"Our situation?"

"We could go down to my office. Or we could be civilized and order another brandy. At state expense, of course. Nothing you say will be held against you in a court of law, not until you sign a statement of confession."

"Well, we should be civilized, for sure. And what would you like me to confess to?"

"My colleague says—"

"Your colleague looks like he should retire before he gets buried alive by mistake."

Shut up, Harry.

"He is only fifty. He smokes."

"I noticed that."

"No, you could not notice. Not in a restaurant, not in Sweden."

The man exudes nicotine. As for being fifty, who knew.

"And what does your *colleague* say about my *case*."

"Perhaps if I ask the questions, it would be better."

She waved to a waiter and signalled for two more brandies. Cognac, good quality. Neither of them spoke until it came, and it was almost as if her smoke-drenched cohort had never intruded. Swirling the amber liquid in her glass, she gazed into its depths.

Then, without looking up she asked him, "What did you say is your wife's name?"

"I didn't," Harry responded.

"It is Karen, I believe. You said she is dead. It *was* Karen." She was not chatting, she was conducting an inquiry by candlelight.

"Yes, it is Karen. I'm not sure what business that is of the National Criminal Police."

"You wear a wedding band, yes?" She gestured toward his left hand. "There is a mark on your finger, but no ring."

Harry waited.

She unclenched her fist and the small white envelope slipped onto the table.

"Would you open it, please?"

Harry reached out with his left hand and picked up the folded envelope. He turned its contents into the palm of his right hand. He flinched, as if the ring were white hot. He closed his fist around it, defiantly, then opened it slowly.

"And where did you get this?" he asked, keeping his voice at an even timbre.

She reached out to take it. "May I?"

He held his palm open and she took the silver band and held it up, aslant to the closest candle, as if she were admiring the lustre of a fine wine in its flickering light.

"You, of course, have no idea where we found it?" she said.

"I'm afraid to guess."

"It was under the dead girl at Hagaparken. Embedded in the frozen snow-water that had melted from her body heat and re-froze after she died."

She toyed with the ring in her fingers.

"What about prints?" he asked with inane logic.

"Yours and mine, Dr. Lindstrom. It was wiped absolutely clean."

"What about chain of evidence?"

"It has not been out of our possession since morning." She turned the silver band in the flickering light. "A few dints. A jeweller's mark. A sterling hallmark. And a message, *h and k forever*."

"My wife died in an accident," said Harry, his voice indicating no emotion.

"Yes?"

"The ring was found at the scene, her body was never recovered."

"I am sorry."

"Yes," Harry said.

"It is difficult to bury the past under such circumstances."

Was that mordant wit or careless cruelty?

"I have no desire to bury the past."

"I imagine you do."

"Perhaps. This whole dinner was a set-up. Your weasel friend, he was part of it."

"But it was very enjoyable."

"It seems to have taken an unpleasant turn."

"Murder is unpleasant, Harry." She offered this as a truism, not likely to be disputed.

"But why on earth? You already had the ring. You knew it belonged to me. Did you think I'd confess over dessert?"

"You seemed a man more responsive to congenial company than intimidation, given all you've been through."

"And how do you know what I've been through?"

"We have been very busy today."

"You and the weasel."

"Yes."

"Jesus." Harry couldn't think of anything else to say.

A prayer and a curse, Karen whispered.

It's neither if you don't believe.

"And how do you think I managed to get the victim under my power, take her out to Hagaparken, kill her, and get back for a good night's sleep. The poor girl deserved better."

"Deserves better, that is interesting. And did you get a good night's sleep? And how do you know she died at the Haga Park, not before? How could you know that, Professor Lindstrom?"

She set the ring down on the table between them.

Harry squinted, trying to see into her eyes. She was unnervingly pleasant and deadly serious.

He grimaced. "Don't be bloody ridiculous, Inspector. The abrasions on her feet and ankles, they were minor. Just enough damage to show she'd been walking barefoot in fresh snow, breaking through the crusty layer every few steps. She couldn't have walked very far. If you check the heels of her palms, I'm sure you'll find shallow lacerations from where she occasionally fell. She was forced, probably at gunpoint, into a death march. When she was sufficiently weakened by the cold, the killer left her to die, which she curled up and did. The killer's footprints filled in with new-fallen snow. I imagine you found evidence of frozen tears on the girl's cheeks. Her upper eyelashes were heavy with unmelted snow but her lower lashes were frozen clear, from weeping as she died an unspeakably pitiable death."

"That could almost be taken as a confession," Hannah Arnason observed, swirling her cognac and inhaling the aroma.

"Or what I like to call 'thinking out loud.'"

"I'm sorry, Mr. Lindstrom, Harry, but there's also the rental car."

"The what!"

"A car was rented in your name. Picked up after closing hours."

"Not by me. Check the credit card."

"Prepayment by cash. Actually, you have a rebate coming to you."

"How much?"

"I, I'm really not sure."

You've got her, Harry. Her case just collapsed. It was built on conviction and you raised the element of doubt by being a smartass. Well done. Really.

He reached into his pocket, awkwardly slithering around on his chair to get to the bottom. Damned Tilley pants, he thought with affection, as he slipped open the hidden Velcro pocket and fished out a silver band, which he placed on the table, side by side with the one from the crime scene.

"I never wear it when I fly," he said. "Observe, they're a pair, but mine is bigger. My fingers swell. Your smaller one is Karen's. And I have no idea." He stopped.

"You have no idea, what?"

"How it got under the body, how it even got to Sweden. I'd hardly carry it around with me, but if I did, you don't think I'd drop it! If you like I'll take off my pants right here and show you the damned secret pocket. It's the apex of Canadian ingenuity. Nothing falls out; I guarantee it. And presumably so do the Tilleys."

"The Tilleys?"

"They make the pants."

"You have a relationship with your pantmaker?"

"No, with the pants."

He picked up Karen's ring. It felt cool and then warm from his reflected heat. "Actually, I think I do know how it got here without me." He set it down again. "There was an incident in my apartment."

"An incident?"

"Someone broke into my home. I was there but I didn't see who it was. The intruder locked me out in the bitter cold. On the balcony. Sounds funny. It wasn't. This person must have taken a scarf my wife made for me and, apparently, the ring. The scarf ended up beside a girl's frozen corpse in Toronto. She was murdered while I was in hospital recovering from exposure after the balcony scene." (This wasn't strictly true, but he was not about to risk being accused of murdering that girl, too.)

"And you didn't notice?"

"What, that my things were missing?"

"The ring. I will look into the incriminating scarf," she said. "Would you say incriminating or compromising?"

"Neither. And no, I didn't notice the ring was missing. I miss my wife, I grieve, but I don't do a regular inventory, I don't celebrate anniversaries, I do not obsess about tokens and talismans kept in her jewellery box."

"And the person who locked you out of your home killed the girl in Hagaparken?"

"Apparently, yes."

"Do you know who that person would be?"

Harry was sure of nothing, but the appearance of Karen's ring suggested Morgan's cynicism about how he had been locked out was unfounded. There had without question been someone there.

Hannah Arnason looked puzzled for a moment, then leaned forward across the table, careful not to incinerate the contours of her cashmere sweater in the candle flame that flickered between them. Her eyes were a deep blue, the colour of night. She smiled. She picked up the larger ring and delicately slipped it on his finger. She took the other ring from him and returned to the envelope, which she refolded carefully before tucking it into her purse.

She took his hand again, with the silver band gleaming in the candlelight, and held it palm up in both of hers.

"That is all I will need for now," she said. "You see, in Sweden we are not so unsophisticated. Our methods are perhaps designed for the personality under scrutiny. Thank you for a lovely and enlightening dinner. And yes, the state will pay for us both."

"I'm free?"

"As much as anyone is."

He sighed, audibly relieved. It had been more of a strain than he wanted to admit but an excellent dinner.

"May I ask you one last question, Harry? Why silver? Usually wedding bands are gold."

"We liked silver."

"Ah," she said. "The moon, not the sun."

"Something like that."

11 BEER AND FIRELIGHT

IN THE MORNING, HARRY TRUDGED THROUGH THE NEW snow, avoiding icy patches, until he reached a small residential hotel farther north in the city, the address Hannah had given him for Birgitta Ghiberti. The proprietor had never heard of her. Harry described the beautiful woman who looked like Ingrid Bergman with pure white hair. The proprietor giggled. He had no idea who Ingrid Bergman was, but the woman with white hair was probably Birgitta Shtoonk. The proprietor giggled again. Shtoonk was an unusual name, apparently in Sweden as well. Yes, she had left that morning. With a young couple, he thought. They didn't come in. No, she didn't leave under duress.

By midday, the air had turned bone chilling and the snow squeaked under his boots as he walked. His toes were so cold he hardly felt them. He wrapped his sheepskin coat tightly around his body, cursed the intruder for stealing his scarf, and pulled his toque down over his ears. He had no desire to take a taxi or bus, and a subway under a city of islands left Harry cold, although he had heard it was a tourist attraction.

He eventually reached the office of the NGO that Bernd Ghiberti worked with, loitering in the tiny lobby long enough to warm up after they told him Dr. Ghiberti wasn't due back for another week. If he had been seen in Stockholm, he was there on personal matters.

Harry reluctantly spent the rest of the day exploring the Tunnelbana. Overcoming his aversion to subways, he retreated from the weather into Stockholm's buried labyrinth and was so awestruck that he simply wandered, getting off trains at will and back on when he wished. For a few hours, he was utterly distracted from murder.

Underground stations carved into the solid rock astonished him. Escalators at Radhuset descended among billowing red walls through the substrata into a vast cavern with a polished stone floor. Rising from it, penetrating the rock overhead, was the lower portion of a huge column. Harry slouched down on the floor and conjured a vision of a fiery flood of molten lava burying the column from the top down, hardening to leave a bubble around its base that allowed passersby a hint of its former grandeur.

He had been in constructed ruins before, most notably at the summer home of a Canadian prime minister, now open so the public could marvel at the man's ghoulish obsessions. But this was neither defiant nor macabre. It was a celebration of the improbable.

Harry could relate to that. An existential confrontation with the absurdities that define us. Time and consciousness, logic and imagination, deconstructionism at work.

It's time to move on, Harry. You'll get hemorrhoids sitting on marble.

In other stations, as he moved through the afternoon, he discovered rock that was carved and painted to look like an overhead lily pond, a flaming sky at sunset, a waterfall, an excavation site, providing complementary backdrops for paintings and sculpture from classic to abstract, awesome to droll. But at the same time, it was always rock, deep under the surface of the earth. It thrilled him that all this was done for the people of Stockholm themselves.

When he finally emerged from the T-Centralen onto Vasagaten in the lingering twilight, a gentle snowfall had warmed the air and he walked over to Bentleys in a very good mood. He picked up a sweet bun and a decaf along the way to tide him over until breakfast. He didn't feel like dining alone.

Inside the front door of the hotel, a small foyer opened onto the staircase leading up to the reception desk. On the stairs, wrapped in a thick coat to ward off drafts as arriving guests pushed through the doors, Bernd Ghiberti sat hunched over, with his knees together, waiting for Harry. He seemed to be dozing and didn't look up.

It wasn't until Harry was inside the doors that he saw another man slouched in the shadows close to the elevator, out of the concierge's line of vision. The second man sucked on a lit cigarette and was blowing pale clouds of spent smoke up into the open elevator shaft. It was a futile gesture to avoid compliance with the laws he was paid to enforce. Flicking his cigarette in a flurry of sparks onto the marble floor, he stepped out into the light. His face was creased and cross-hatched like a weather-beaten satchel. He nodded toward the man sitting between them, then nodded at Harry and grinned.

"Your friend, Mr. Lindstrom, I have brought him to you." His yellow teeth made his grin look feral, his eye teeth glinted like fangs.

Bernd slowly rose to his feet and moved down a step to avoid putting Harry at a disadvantage.

"It is good to see you, Harry," said Bernd Ghiberti, holding out his hand. "Do you like Stockholm in winter? I hope so; it is the Scandinavian version of a hot fudge sundae, cold as ice cream and deliciously warm."

"Very poetic. I was looking for you."

"And for my mother. I take it she is not hiding, except from me."

"I'm here in spite of certain untoward obstacles."

"Ah, the balcony incident."

"You've heard?"

"From Superintendent Quin."

The stench of stale tobacco swirled around them as the elevator descended and opened to disgorge a couple chattering in English and dressed in polar exploration gear. Americans, probably. Canadians take winter more casually. No accent. Probably from southern California.

When the weasel came down to the same level, Harry was surprised he was roughly his own height. The man gave the impression of being diminutive.

"I will leave, now," he said. "Inspector Arnason sent me to bring him to the Bentleys Hotel. He is here. Good night."

As an afterthought, he addressed Harry directly, "I am Sverdrup. We did not meet at the restaurant." He turned away and took out a fresh cigarette from a crumpled pack, scraped a wooden match on the wall and lit up before stepping out into the night. Surprising a man like that didn't carry a lighter.

"Well, then," said Harry. "We'd better go for a drink. Aquavit?"

"Akvavit," said Bernd, amending the proposal. "Fermented potatoes and herbs at 40 percent. Perhaps we will have something more subtle."

Harry set his decaf and the bag with his sweet bun off to the side on a step. Together, like old friends, the two men pushed through the snow-filled night air to the closest bar.

Harry ordered a beer and Bernd Ghiberti ordered cognac.

"So," said Harry, as they settled in close to a roaring grate fire. "I'm guessing you had an alibi."

"An alibi? For which occasion?"

"The night before last."

"God, that woman is amazing. She and the old guy with the bad dye job came to my hotel an hour ago. We had drinks in the bar, we talked, then she left. Somehow her associate ended up escorting me to your hotel. I knew where Bentleys was, but he tagged along just in case."

The woman was amazing, indeed. She conducted interrogations by stealth. Harry wondered if this was Swedish protocol or her own peculiar way of doing business. Intriguing and very effective. And wily and manipulative. By delivering Ghiberti to Harry, Harry's ill-defined quest was subsumed into her own inquiry. He was, in effect, working for her.

"And she asked you where you had been two nights ago?" Harry said, trying to seem casual.

"Among other things, yes. We were just making conversation. My God, she's good looking, but larger than life if you know what I mean."

"No," said Harry. "Explain."

Bernd Ghiberti flashed a grimace of annoyance, then shrugged. He swirled his brandy in the oversize bowl of his glass and inhaled the aroma. "I was with friends, Bjorn and Inge Olafsson," he said.

"All night?"

"Until midnight. Then I went back to my hotel. I either stay there or with the Olafssons when I'm in Stockholm." He wrote down the hotel address on a slip of paper and handed it to Harry. "You can always leave a message if I'm out." He took back the note and added the phone number of his friends. "I've known them since childhood, a brother and sister. They have the house next to ours on the island of Fårö. Have you ever been there?"

Harry shook his head.

"Where Ingmar Bergman lived. Windswept and haunting."

"Of course," said Harry.

Bergman was always a good topic of conversation between Swedes and outsiders. Swedes were fiercely proud of the filmmaker's fusion of landscape and the tortured human psyche, but righteously defensive about gloomy stereotypes. When in Sweden, however, Bernd Ghiberti seemed to identify as an outsider, an Italianate Canadian who spoke Swedish and summered in the Baltic. Bergman didn't appear to interest him.

"You used to go there after Giovanna drowned."

"Vittorio held on to the Muskoka cottage until he died, but after Giovanna I never went back. I was a boarding student at Upper Canada College—my sisters went to Branksome Hall but they lived at home. In the summers I was sent to stay with my aunties on Fårö. Free to wander among stone walls and giant boulders on the north end of the island. Birgitta would sometimes visit while I was there."

What an odd way of putting it.

"She knew Bergman," he continued. "That was during what she called his 'dark interlude' between film-making and death."

"Do you have a car?"

"Of course."

"Rental?"

"No, I keep it for when I'm in Sweden. My friends look after the old thing; they drive it when I'm not here and store it in their garage. Is this an interrogation?"

"Conversation," said Harry.

"I realize why I was being asked for an alibi," Bernd offered. "I read about the girl in Hagaparken. She froze to death like the girl in Toronto—I talked to your friend Superintendent Quin about her. It seems my mother's sordid suspicions are contagious."

"It doesn't help that you were in the same city when both murders occurred."

"I was. And during that same period there were a thousand other murders in the world. It is a statistical probability that some were young women, some of those were found naked, a few of them died of exposure, and even a few were in places I happened to be, when they expired."

"Which only proves that your guilt is a statistical possibility."

"Then I am guilty of bad math, but not murder. And here I thought serial killers were exceptionally bright."

"Only the organized, non-social variety, as you've said yourself. The disorganized asocial offenders are usually quite stupid."

Bernd seemed amused. "My work in Africa should be proof that I'm neither."

Or he found a place to kill women with relative impunity.

While he seemed to find something droll about their conversation, Bernd Ghiberti did not smile. His dark eyes, creased at the edges like a much older man or someone too much exposed to the sun, glinted in the light from the open fire that bled the colour from his lips and highlighted the length of his nose.

Then Bernd said in a quiet voice, "Professor Lindstrom, you also were in both places at the time of the murders."

Harry ordered another beer. Ghiberti nursed his cognac. They both stared into the fire. When the beer arrived, Harry sat back and appraised his situation. He was across from a man whose own mother wanted Harry to prove he was a serial killer, and who appeared to be mildly amused by the attention this brought him from the police and from the investigator he had more or less hired to prove his innocence and because he was concerned for his mother. He seemed almost content, gazing into the flames. His eyes reflected the pulsing glow of embers in the grate.

Harry tried to imagine what horrors those eyes might have witnessed? And strangely, he conjured images of girls in North Africa enduring the most grisly brutalities because of their sex, and not blonde girls and young women drowning, or incinerating, or being suffocated by earth collapsing on top of them. Or dying exposed to the frigid air.

For a moment, it seemed to Harry his mind merged with Ghiberti's, and he could see into its darkest recesses with chilling clarity. This man may have killed and would kill again, to create order out of chaos, to impose an elemental structure on a universe reeling out of control.

"The women." Harry said, not as a question but with a leading intonation, as if he expected Ghiberti to finish his thought.

"The women, yes."

"The young women, here and in Toronto, they weren't sexually assaulted."

"Weren't they?"

"Doesn't that strike you as odd? They were stripped naked, but left in pristine condition."

"Perhaps their killer was not interested in sex."

"Perhaps he was incapable of sex. There's a difference, isn't there?"

"I wouldn't know," Ghiberti answered. "My expertise is with the dead, not the dying." Warming to this wry summary of his abandoned career, he continued, "The dead can sometimes tell us a great deal about ourselves."

"I'm sure they can," said Harry. "And what about all those other girls?"

"What other girls?"

"The corpses your mother has tallied up who seem to appear from time to time, punctuating the winter landscape. And always in places you have just been, apparently."

"What about them?"

"I understand they were not naked."

"Is that significant, Professor Lindstrom?" He was irritated. Hardly an admission of guilt, but it was a start, a chink in the proverbial armour. "My mother," he said, his voice softening as he shifted the direction of their conversation. "You have not managed to contact her?"

"Have you?"

"No, of course not. I was told she attended a public reception at the Hotel Skeppsholmen. I was not in the country at the time. I only arrived a couple of days ago, just before you did. As I suspected, she made it through Swedish customs from Iceland without anyone noticing. And now she has disappeared again."

"Perhaps she's avoiding you."

"I'm certain she is. Oh, you're joking, stating the obvious. I had hoped you might have had better luck."

"If you're asking, do I know where she is? No. Am I concerned for her well-being? Not really. Am I searching for her? Good question."

"But isn't that why you're in Sweden?"

"No, I like Sweden, I like Sweden in winter."

"You must find her, you know. It is very important."

"Have you tried your aunts on Fårö? She could be out there in the Baltic, on the family farm."

"It is only a farmhouse. And yes, I contacted my aunts and they haven't heard from Birgitta in months. I checked with the girl. They don't have a telephone. They're very old and prefer to live in the past. Or watch television. They have a TV."

"The girl?"

"A young islander who works in Visby. She attends Gotland University."

"Sounds like Fårö is isolated even from Gotland. It would make a good place for your mother to hide."

"The aunties would never be able to keep a secret."

"Depends on the secret. All old people keep secrets, Bernd."

"I'll have to remember that, should I ever grow old."

"Is it in doubt?"

"My growing old? Yes, of course it is in doubt. Not so much as for my mother, however. She is teetering on the cusp of senescence, Harry. You think that unkind? Not so unkind as imminent death. She is in grave danger."

"From who? Whom?" Harry winced. He usually avoided pedantic flourishes. They had once enhanced his authority in the lecture hall and among former colleagues who knew he had graduated from Cambridge.

Mid-sixties is hardly senescent, Harry.

"From whom?" Bernd said with a rhetorical flourish. He scowled and the flames flickered against the contours of his face like a cheap metaphor. "From me."

Harry sank back into his leather chair.

The other man sank back into his, swirled his cognac so vigorously the aroma wafted through the air between them. The low ceiling glistened and the plaster walls cast an eerie sheen. Other patrons drank and chattered as if nothing in the world had changed.

"You?" said Harry at last, acknowledging the dramatic shift in strategy. "You've told me you were afraid if she closed in on the killer he'd have no choice but to do her in. Now you're saying it's you she should fear. That's a bold admission."

"It is all quite Darwinian, if you think about it. Survival of the offspring, nature red in tooth and claw."

"Might I ask how you would kill her?" Harry posed the question as blandly as possible, on the premise that the more detail he was offered, the less likely the crime, which he knew to be the opposite with potential suicides, but this was about murder.

"It doesn't matter."

"*To whom* doesn't it matter? Look, Bernd, why not go to the police?"

"For what? If every case of matricidal fantasy were turned over to the police, there'd be no time for traffic tickets."

"But I take it, conflicted as you appear to be, your intentions are more substantive."

"That is why I need you to intervene, Harry. I want you to save her life."

Or to track her down for him, to make his job easier.

Harry took a deep draft of beer and set his glass back on the table in the exact place it had been sitting, and turned the glass in the circular pool of condensation, slowly spreading the moisture into a thin shapeless smear.

"Are you saying you want to kill your mother because she thinks you're a killer? You can see there's a circularity to the argument. It's fascinating."

"I'm glad you're amused."

"No, I'm appalled. Well, intrigued, that might be more accurate. And alarmed. And perhaps a little depressed at finding myself in the middle of it all when I could be touring the T-bana, or back at home, brooding with a view."

"Understand this," said Ghiberti. "My mother wants to destroy me. There is nothing frivolous about that. Whether I am a serial killer or not is irrelevant."

"Not to the girls who died in the snow, not to their grieving families."

"Of course. But this, right now, is between my mother and me. She means to destroy me. And I will resist."

"By destroying her first."

"If I have no choice."

"But you do. There's always a choice."

No, Harry. You don't believe that.

"I am asking you," Bernd continued. "Save her life. I promise, without your intervention, she will die."

"Or she *is* already dead and you're planning to use me as, what? A scapegoat, an alibi, a witness after the fact?"

The last time you saw him in Toronto, you thought he might have already killed her. Now you're wondering the same thing! Patterns of suspicion, Harry?

"No, she is alive." Bernd said this with a suppressed snarl that startled them both.

"Then for God's sake man, you don't need me to intervene. Walk away from it."

"Please find her." Bernd's voice was eerily controlled. "You're staring at me, Harry. What are you seeing? Stay out of my mind; I promise you, it is not a comfortable place to be."

You always want to understand, even when there's no explanation.

Mystery and the rational mind are not always incompatible.

Exactly, she whispered, *they feed off each other's limitations.*

Easy, Sailor, you're talking like me.

"Trust me," he said out loud. "I have enough going on in my own head."

"Find her before I do, Harry."

"And do what?"

"Wait."

"Until."

"It will not be a long wait."

"And then?"

"Do whatever is necessary."

Abruptly, Bernd rose to his feet, tossed a bunch of bills on the table, and grabbing his coat from a peg on the wall strode out into the night, leaving Harry to finish his beer on his own.

12 **SUMMONED**

HARRY WALKED BACK ALONG DROTTNINGGATAN TO Bentleys. He pulled his toque down, warmed by Miranda's thoughtfulness, and huddled into his smoky sheepskin, holding the collar snug with a gloved hand so that he peered furtively over it like an animal in distress. Not until he was halfway up the exterior steps to the hotel did he sense the presence of Sverdrup, standing in the shadows, his leathery face illuminated by the sustained glow of a cigarette as he inhaled its smoke into the depths of his lungs, or what was left of them. He was outside, this time, but there was no question: he was waiting for Harry.

"If you would please to come with me," Sverdrup said, flicking his cigarette like a bit of stage business into the snow on the sidewalk below. He stepped down to street level and started walking south. Harry hesitated. He could see his cold decaf through the glass, beside the stale sweet roll in its bag on the step. He was tired and he felt oppressed. But he was curious, and in no doubt that the weaselly man with a face like a satchel intended on leading him to a rendezvous with his boss.

They found Hannah Arnason in a bistro down a narrow passageway just inside the old town, eating a late dinner on her own.

When they approached her table, she stood up, welcomed Harry with a handshake, and dismissed Sverdrup for the night.

She motioned to a chair, inviting Harry to join her. It seemed her office was wherever she happened to be.

She was wearing what looked like lace-up hiking boots but with pointed toes and three inch heels. A marvel of absurdist design, which gave her sufficient height that Harry felt momentarily diminished, a response reinforced by a dramatic sweater that swooped over her shoulders in a scarlet wave, shielding her from drafts while she ate. He drew himself up to his full height and sat down.

"You have met with Bernd Ghiberti," she declared.

"I have."

"And you think he murdered the girl in Hagaparken."

"In all probability. And the Icelandic girl in Toronto."

"I have been in touch with your friend, the superintendent. She asked me to watch for you."

"To watch for me?"

"Yes, I have met her, you know."

He didn't.

"When I was a student. She had a nice partner, a man who was very sexy." Hannah Arnason said "sexy" like she was complimenting Miranda on her wardrobe. "I was in Toronto, training to be a policeperson. You would say a policewoman, but I do not like that word."

Harry wasn't about to argue with her on the limitations of English in relation to gender.

"We went to your headquarters and they lectured us."

"Not *my* headquarters. And what did she say?"

"Oh, I do not remember. It was almost ten years ago."

"No, now. When you talked to her."

"Oh, yes. She agrees."

"With what?"

"With you. With me. Mr. Ghiberti kills women, yes. It seems probable. Would you like some dinner? I know you have eaten nothing. I have ordered for you."

Before Harry could protest or consent, a waiter appeared and set a blue and white plate in front of him with sautéed beet slices, sauerkraut, mashed potatoes, three sausage links, and a sprig of fresh parsley. He had not realized how hungry he was.

"I will pay," she said. "Please enjoy."

Hannah Arnason watched him eat and he felt strangely at ease. When he finished, he told her about his conversation with Bernd Ghiberti.

"And you believe him?"

"That he might murder his mother?" said Harry. "Yes, it seems reasonable that a pathological psychotic with homicidal propensities and a sordid childhood should aspire to matricide."

"Isn't a psychotic by definition pathological? And a pathological killer by definition psychotic?"

"Possibly."

"Then it appears you must be her saviour, Harry."

Harry flinched.

"Unless we can find other crimes to arrest Mr. Ghiberti for before he does it, which seems unlikely at the moment. You appear to be all that stands between his mother and death."

Nicely ambiguous.

"Can't you protect her?"

"From what, a bad life, a difficult son? There is nothing we can do; there's nothing to be done. There's nothing to be done." She seemed for a moment to be humming to herself, but Harry had no idea what it was. "Not until after it happens. That's the worst part of police work: clearing up the mess you were powerless to prevent."

"And what would your official position be, if I were to kill the man, as he seems to want? I don't go around killing people, you know."

"Not unless you have to, I'm sure. In anticipation of a crime, as a preventative measure, that would be justifiable perhaps, but homicide, nevertheless. In self-defence, or to save a life, possibly acceptable, if the mitigating circumstances are truly that."

"What?"

"Mitigating."

Harry ate quietly while Hannah Arnason watched.

As a philosopher, he had been fascinated by the conflict between being a free agent in the world and witnessing life shaped by factors beyond his control. Here he was in a Stockholm bistro, with a woman of stunning beauty and inspiring presence, who seemed to play him like a puppet on invisible strings, but only after he had been played by a woman who looked like Ingrid Bergman and by her son who apparently killed young women to watch them die.

Until now, as a P.I. dealing with murder, Harry had felt like a priest at a wedding who officiates over matters he knows nothing about. He was attracted to murder because it turned the morbidity that haunted him inside out, so he could deal with it as an abstraction. Sometimes this seemed like a betrayal, using crime as a shield from reality.

Forget free will, mortality is stacked against you. But if the end is already known, everything else is a terrifying illusion. So…

In the instant that passed while he and Karen argued theology, Harry suppressed a surge of panic from the invading memory of a smashed canoe on a perilous river. And when he did, the conceit of being a puppet or a celibate collapsed.

He knew exactly what he was being asked to do.

He was being sponsored by this woman across from him to take a life, if necessary, to save a life. And, at the same time, being warned that it must be a rational act.

"Harry, do you carry a weapon?"

"No."

"Good, it is safer if you do not."

"For whom?"

She smiled ambivalently.

"Do you carry a gun?" he asked her.

"Possibly I do. It is not so important for me. My work begins after the crime has been committed. You are not so lucky, I think."

They stared at each other across the table. He could see a distorted image of himself in the depths of her eyes. Odd, they had turned almost obsidian in the ambient light.

"Birgitta is likely to find me before I find her," Harry said. "I'm assuming she still wants me to help make her case that her son is a monster."

"You're not sure? *Possibly employed*, that is a new demographic."

"Possibly paid. That's an old one."

"Harry, if the son does not get to her before you do, he will be there soon after. The question is: does he want you as his witness when he kills her, or does he want you to stop him before he does it? Or is arranging your presence meant to ease his conscience, before killing you both? Be careful, my friend."

She leaned over and took his hand in hers, slowly turning the silver band on his finger. "Any man who invites you to kill *him* is prepared to kill *you*."

"Do you happen to know where she is?" he asked.

"More to the point, does he?"

Is that an evasion or a warning? Harry wondered, but expecting no answer said nothing.

She let go of his hand, but he left it poised on the table between them while he gazed at the ring, then into the darkness in her eyes, and then he smiled a sad smile and they talked of other things.

Karen was unhappy with the unorthodox approach to investigative procedure. *Police follow protocol for a reason,* she whispered. *It protects them from their own worst impulses.*

But Harry was intrigued by Hannah's eccentricity, he liked that she hovered on the edge of convention. Dangerous and alluring, an effective illusion.

Gradually, the evening dissolved and Harry found himself back at Bentleys. He slept fitfully and woke midmorning, disoriented because the day had moved on while he slept.

He reluctantly struggled to extricate himself from the warmth of the down-filled duvet. Despite images swarming through his head of clandestine meetings and furtive encounters, subterranean columns and snow-blown passageways, he found himself strangely at home. It was as if his Swedish genes had finally connected with the world around him. His bed in Bentleys seemed inevitable. Stockholm in winter felt familiar at a visceral level.

It brings out your inner Viking, Harry.

What does? he wondered as he pivoted and rolled onto his feet.

Her words seemed to be coming from deep under the duvet.

Being here, it's a good place to be.

He turned to look in the direction where her voice might have been and noticed the corner of a small mauve envelope sticking out from under the door.

Even before opening it, he knew whom it was from. The mysterious delivery, the mechanically elegant inscription of his name in green ink, the absence of postage or an address; who else but Birgitta moved with such stealth at the edge of his life, an ambiguously threatened and ominous presence most notable for being elusive.

The signature inside confirmed it was from Birgitta Sviar. Not Ghiberti or Shtoonk. He wondered if she had variant personalities to go with her different names. Above the signature was an address:

Hotel St. Clemens
Smedjegatan 3
Visby, Gotland

There was no salutation, no plea for help or assistance, just a brief note suggesting he take the ferry from Nynashämn. The note was neither an invitation nor an explanation. Terse to the point of being imperious, it was a summons based on the assumption that he would come to the island of Gotland because he had no choice.

Harry was perplexed. While he should have been feeling relief to know she was safe for the moment, he was annoyed that she hadn't simply knocked on his door. They could have worked out survival strategies together.

Harry couldn't quite reconcile the grim hauteur to the note with the curious blend of incipient paranoia and gracious composure when Birgitta had first approached him. There had to have been a major shift in how she perceived her relationship with her son, and consequently with Harry. From being the pursuer, she had become the pursued.

If her back's to the wall, she'll be dangerous. I'd rather have him as an enemy than her. At least he's out in the open, and she's shrouded in shadows.

I have no reason to fear Birgitta.

You have no reason not to.

He called the front desk. A male voice answered. "Yes, Mr. Lindstrom?"

"Did a woman come in during the night, asking for me?"

"A young woman, yes. About two in the morning."

"A young woman? Are you sure?"

"I think she was blonde. There are so many blonde women in Sweden, Mr. Lindstrom. Perhaps she was not so young. It was late. I told her she could not go up to your room unless I called first, but she did not want me to call. She left a letter, and I put it under your door so as not to awaken you."

He is a man, Harry. A woman would notice another woman's age. A man only if she is attractive or not.

"Was she attractive?" he asked.

There was a dull pause on the other end of the line, and then the voice said, "I am sorry, I did not think you would want to be disturbed."

Meaning "yes, she was attractive." He's feeling guilty for ruining a midnight tryst.

While he showered, Harry puzzled out the implications of insisting they meet in Visby. Was she on her way to Fårö? Was she safer on Gotland than in Toronto or Stockholm? Was she closing in on Bernd— the pursuer pursued again in pursuit? Was Fårö where the dark purposes of this very strange family converged?

Then why didn't we go there in the first place?

Because something has changed in the family dynamics. Whatever brought her to Stockholm has driven her away.

The same could be said for you, Harry. Whatever brought you to Stockholm is now compelling your departure. You have no moral alternative but to go to Gotland. And you're curious. You're dying to know what you've got yourself into.

He chuckled.

When he finished dressing, he picked up the large manila envelope Miranda had couriered to him and thumbed through the pages, setting the photographs off to the side. He was not sure what he was looking for until he found it, a paragraph about the girl from Gimli, noting that her skin and the blanket weren't fused by the cold, indicating her flesh had been frozen before the blanket was draped around her. Was this an awkward expression of delayed remorse? Or a means of wrapping the body to make it less repellent while transporting it to the cedar maze?

Perhaps both. Or for some other reason, Harry.

Yeah, Harry agreed. Disgust and remorse weren't generally in a serial killer's vocabulary.

Looking at Birgitta's note again, he suspected she was casting herself as a lure to bring him in from the edges. And he was biting. Either she had discovered new and irrefutable evidence against Bernd or she knew Bernd was determined to kill her. Or both.

Either way, Harry, protector or witness, you're an indispensable part of the plot. She needs you to convict her son, or as a guardian to mediate the consequences of her own convictions.

He telephoned the number on Hannah Arnason's card. She wasn't in. He left a message: "Onto something interesting. Heading off to Gotland. I'll be in touch."

Not heartwarming, Harry. And annoyingly vague. Just enough mystery to pique her interest? Do we go by ferry or fly?

13 VISBY

BIRGITTA HAD DIRECTED HIM TO TAKE THE FERRY FROM Nynashämn. At this time of year, that could only mean she intended to create a delay. It would be bitterly cold on the open Baltic and the approach to Gotland could be obscured by weather or whitewashed with snow. She had probably flown early in the morning and wanted him there, but not too soon. He decided to fly.

As it turned out, the weather was perfect. The infinite shades of grey in the Baltic exaggerated the limitless expanse of an azure sky, as if the whole universe were in daylight. However, by the time Gotland loomed from below and his plane had begun a broad circling pattern before landing, a vague sense of apprehension had crept through Harry and displaced his pleasure at observing the world from a celestial perspective. Something he had noticed in Arlanda Airport had been working away at him.

While scanning the departures board for his Skyways Express flight to Visby, a flashing on the arrivals side caught his eye. Two flights from Reykjavik were listed in close proximity, one with SAS and another with Air Iceland.

Birgitta Ghiberti had flown to Iceland and disappeared, according to her son. Then she turned up in Stockholm at a public reception before vanishing again.

And?

What if she doubled back? he wondered. Two airlines, dual citizenship, two passports under different names. Very hard to keep track. She could have returned to Toronto after Bernd paid me a visit on Christmas Day, then flown directly to Stockholm. Bernd and I were both in the cities where the murders happened, when they happened, but there's a reasonable chance that Birgitta was too.

Murders don't happen, Harry. But so what if she was there? You're not suggesting?

Anything's possible.

That's doesn't mean everything *is.*

He gazed down at the wind turbines that were spread across Gotland as far as he could see, reaching skyward like quills on a startled porcupine. The image made him smile. As the plane swooped low, the town of Visby loomed like a magnificent miniature, too perfect to be real. On the western slope to the sea, in the heart of the modern city, a medieval town contained by a high wall stood largely intact from the fourteenth century when it had been a pirate redoubt. Red tile roofs floated over snow in the midday sun and everywhere inside the walls the standing ruins of church towers soared awkwardly upward, stone claws slowly releasing their grasp on heaven after various wars for the island's possession.

Harry closed his eyes. The town became Birgitta in his mind, a complex trope for a woman he had met only briefly. She carried her age like a beautiful façade, with its intimations of conflict and compromise, intrigue and survival. But what secrets, he wondered, what terrors and horrors and unholy memories, lay buried within?

The plane jolted as it touched the earth and rolled to a stop. He opened his eyes, disembarked, caught a taxi. They drove through the northern gate, and he had the cab drop him at the modest entry to the Hotel St. Clemens that opened off Smedjegatan, a narrow and unassuming street, into a small courtyard fronted by buildings of different vintages.

At the reception desk he was treated like family, a distant relative who hadn't been seen in years. The woman was surprised, though, that he was there already. Harry was surprised she knew anything about him.

"We have been expecting you, yes. Tomorrow, Dr. Lindstrom. But you are not to worry, we will accommodate you. Ms. Sviar will be delighted to see you, I am very sure, but surprised you are here too soon."

Harry settled into his room in an outbuilding that opened directly onto the street. He discovered in the brochure by the bed that every room was different and the price ranges varied considerably. His room was quaint and cozy, and he loved that it was not like a hotel. He felt as if he were a guest in a country estate that had somehow become enclosed within the stone walls and narrow spaces of a bustling town.

After soaking his injured foot in ice-cold water until it was numbed, he walked over the shovelled cobblestones of the courtyard to reception and was disconcerted to find Birgitta had gone out, but not so unsettled as the concierge, who clearly felt it inappropriate behaviour. The woman had booked Harry's room and therefore in some respects qualified as his host.

The concierge called a taxi, not because the distances within the walled town were great but because it was cold and her guest was unfamiliar with the layout of the medieval streets, which, she assured him, would be confusing to a stranger like himself. He was wondering how he differed from strangers *unlike* himself when a cab pulled into the courtyard and the kind woman stepped out into the cold to give directions without first asking Harry where he wanted to go.

He watched carefully, in lieu of dropping breadcrumbs, as the driver took him along the Murgatan, just inside the eastern wall, up past Österport, the Gate at the top of the old town, before dropping him off at the Skafferiet Café on Adelsgatan, which the driver assured him was a very good choice. For what, Harry wasn't sure, since he hadn't been consulted.

For a moment before entering, it occurred to him that Birgitta had set up a rendezvous, but once inside he quickly realized this was unlikely. She was a woman who would choose her setting to best advantage. The Skafferiet celebrated its age, its rustic charm, its worn and battered authenticity, with a casual panache that would be inimical to Birgitta's languid elegance.

Picking up a coffee at the gourmet shop counter, he moved through an arch into the first of two low-ceilinged rooms filled with the dancing flames of candles in wall sconces and tea lights on tables, surrounded by walls of thick painted boards washed in pale blue. The depths of the candlelight caught in the textures of age-weathered wood created a magical sanctuary. He passed by the crackling fire and settled into a small table with a clear view of the elevated hearth and of the adjoining room with its ancient benches and larger tables for rendezvousing mothers with babies and clusters of kids learning to drink coffee and be worldly-wise.

Sipping his latte, he gazed at the quiet hubbub as people around him bought pastries, drank coffees, and chatted amiably where for centuries, it seemed, they had been doing the same thing.

Stay in the present, Harry.

His own presence wasn't in doubt. But why he was on Gotland seemed more obscure than ever in the Skafferiet Café. Karen had argued it was out of curiosity, or following a moral imperative. He was inclined to think it had something to do with professional pride or, at the other extreme, with innate morbidity, whatever had led him into philosophy as a career and shaped his more recent fascination with arbitrary death, whether accidental, self-inflicted, or through malicious intent.

He walked over to the counter and ordered another latte.

Resuming his place with a good sightline to the fire, he purposefully avoided self-inquiry in favour of dealing with the Ghiberti anomalies.

Anomalies, Harry? People are dying.

The last two—they don't fit the pattern.

Well, since I'm inclined to believe the case against you in the Haga Park was fabricated, that leaves Bernd—

Who had alibis.

More like plausible explanations.

Which Miranda Quin and Hannah Arnason both seemed willing to buy.

Taking the word of a serial killer—

—if he is—

—over yours.

They haven't arrested me.

Not yet. They know where you are. Perhaps you're more useful under the illusion you're free.

The same could apply to Bernd.

It could.

He toyed with the dregs of his coffee, swilling them gently to reveal patterns in the grounds at the bottom of the cup. He looked round. The fire was blazing. Everyone seemed to be with someone else in the ancient café. He felt hollow inside and very alone.

It was a familiar feeling, like he was a little in everyone's way. Harry had grown up as an only child, but without the advantages of being firstborn. His older brother died when Harry was seven, drowned playing pond hockey while they were living in Trois Rivières. Harry remembered him vividly, in the last three years merging him with his son Matt in his anguished memories. His parents never recovered from Bobbie's death but they closed ranks and were mutually supportive. Isolated in their grief they held Harry awkwardly close, but without intimacy or affection. He could not take the place of his lost brother but was a continual reminder of his absence. He lived with his brother's ghost until the day he left home, when Bobby apparently decided to stay with their parents. Harry went off to the University of Victoria on Vancouver Island for his first two years, then Victoria University in Toronto for the next five, switching from business to honours philosophy, followed by a master's and almost forgetting he had once had a brother, had once had a family.

During those Toronto years, he spent a number of happy weekends with his venerable Aunt Beth, trying to recover his misplaced childhood in the warmth she reserved only for him. She was ancient by then but survived long enough to watch him graduate. He did not bother informing his parents about convocation, although he let them know he was heading off to Cambridge the following year. They didn't respond to his letter and both died before he returned.

Harry got up and walked out into the afternoon twilight. Following a map he had picked up at the café counter, he made his way over cobbled streets smoothed by the winter snow and through passageways between buildings that pressed close on either side. He stopped in a little shop and tried on a nubuck sports jacket from Finland. He had noticed it in the window from the taxi on his way to the Skafferiet Café. The jacket was a perfect fit. Like the Armani he'd destroyed, it moulded to his body with gracious opulence. It made him feel good. He didn't notice the price until he paid, but shrugged off the pain as a necessary evil.

When he put his sheepskin on overtop, he realized the leather would take on the same smoky aroma. He found this strangely reassuring. The two of them together, the coat and the jacket, were a little too bulky for comfort. He'd pack the jacket up in his carry-on bag, but for now, it felt good.

When he began to walk again, his toes throbbed, and after a while the moisture from his opened wounds bathed them with sickening warmth. He passed safely into the courtyard of the St. Clemens Hotel. He had hardly noticed when he checked in but the hotel was nestled snugly at the back against the walls of a ruined church, cloistered in shadow and stone.

Sanctuary, he thought. But from what or for whom, he wasn't certain.

After cleaning and dressing his toes, he hobbled over to the main desk. Birgitta had been back and gone out again, much to the embarrassment of the motherly concierge. Harry crossed the courtyard back to his room and settled in for a nap, but his mind roiled with a sense of foreboding, centred around this unusual woman who was obsessed with her son as a serial killer and courted his hatred like a spider, a fly.

For someone who had requested Harry's presence, she was strangely elusive. Was it fear, indifference, or a power play to establish control?

Drifting into sleep, he entered a shadowy world of medieval

fortifications under siege, eighteenth-century coffee houses as the refuge of sages and scoundrels, and snowscapes with wind turbines rumbling above the bodies of two naked women, frozen with eyes open, gazing into a blank future. He was aware of himself only as an absence.

When he woke up, he had to grasp for a moment to find who he was. Identity re-established, he got up and phoned the concierge to connect with Birgitta Sviar. It didn't surprise him to find she had not yet returned.

"She will be at one of the restaurants on the Stora Torget, the big square farther up the hill. Perhaps she did not understand you are here in your room."

"Did you tell her?"

"I am so sorry, Dr. Lindstrom. I thought you were together already. I will call you a taxi."

"No, thanks. Thank you, I'll walk."

"I saw you are injured."

"The walk will do me good. I just need to loosen up a bit."

The big square was actually quite intimate, with the lights of half a dozen restaurants gleaming off the snow piled neatly in rows. Harry walked by each of the restaurants very slowly and the smell of roast lamb filled the air as he passed. He could not see Birgitta Ghiberti. He did another round, this time going in and explaining that he was looking for a friend. When he had no luck, he stood under a street lamp, feeling absurdly forlorn.

A young woman wrapped in furs walked toward him, moving very carefully in high-heeled boots over the icy pavement.

"Excuse me," said Harry in his most non-threatening voice.

"Yes," said the woman in perfect English, smiling graciously and not in the least intimidated. "Can I help you?"

Harry grinned. "If you were a visitor, where would you find the best place in all of Visby to eat?"

She gestured around her in a sweeping motion.

"There are so many good places," she said. "And always the Gotland lamb is superb."

"But somewhere special?"

"A hotel down by the harbour, the Lindgarden. It has very good food and very nice atmosphere. Perhaps you should try there."

She gave him directions, and Harry made his way downhill on cobbled streets and past medieval walls toward the Lindgarden. His toes thrust hard against the front of his boots. He tried to distract himself by admiring his surroundings. Stockholm was a city of bricks and mortar, Visby of timber and stones. Both favoured warm pastels on stucco and plaster. As he descended toward the harbour, the roofs of the walled town below him gleamed vermilion in the moonlight. The walk itself was an adventure through time.

Ms. Sviar was sitting in a corner. The table was set for two. When he approached her she looked up, smiled. They might have been lovers, meeting by candlelight, or old friends getting together to reminisce.

"Mrs. Ghiberti," he said. "I seem to have found you."

"And I, you, Dr. Lindstrom."

She motioned to a chair and a waiter held it for Harry as he draped his heavy sheepskin over the back and slid into place at the table. The waiter tugged at his coat, which Harry relinquished, and took it off into the shadows.

"It is a pleasure, once again," said Birgitta. "May I recommend the roast lamb. It is from Gotland sheep and there is nothing better. But you must have it blood red, of course. Or the rack, but then a little more cooked so the meat will strip easily from the bones."

Harry grimaced and decided on salmon fillet, with a side order of coleslaw, which somehow in Sweden was a gourmet treat.

He noticed the Lindgarden's extensive wine list included the 1945 Ch. Mouton Rothschild among its selection of Premier Grand Cru Bordeaux. The price was not given. If you had to ask, you couldn't afford it. He couldn't.

They ate quietly and after they were finished, Harry observed that he had been asked by Bernd to find her.

"Why? I'm not missing."

"He seems very afraid for you."

"*For* me or *of* me."

"Both, I suppose."

"Am I so formidable?"

"Apparently you are. Given your shared history, his fear does not seem entirely arbitrary."

"Are you afraid of me?"

"Should I be?"

"Possibly you should."

"I'm not. Puzzled perhaps, but not afraid."

"Puzzled? By what?"

"By your connections with the dead young women."

Her eyes widened, as if he were being indiscreet.

"Which ones? You don't imagine that I killed somebody, do you?"

"It hadn't occurred to me that you had," he responded. It had occurred to him. He wasn't shocked that she seemed entertained by the possibility of being a suspect. Considering the ominous play of intimacy and icy detachment in their relationship, nothing would surprise. She wore paradox like *haute couture.*

"Would you like a liqueur, perhaps?" she offered.

In the glimmering light of the dining room, Birgitta Ghiberti radiated a kind of beauty he had seen in paintings of the early Renaissance, combining a saintly glow with an earthiness that made her desirable without being accessible.

She ordered Xante for them both, and when their drinks arrived they quietly sipped as they savoured the taste and aroma, which suggested baked pears infused with cognac. It was a new drink to Harry and he was pleasantly surprised by its complexity. Most liqueurs left him less than happy with their cloying sweetness and the contrived intensity of their flavour.

"Do you know I am named for a saint?" she said, as if the statement were relevant.

"No," said Harry. "But I'm not surprised. There are lots to go around."

"Saints?"

"Saints' names."

"Saint Birgitta's great vision, in the fourteenth century, was a number."

"A number? How many angels can dance on the head of a pin, a question with profound implications among clerics at the time."

"No, no. The number of Christ's wounds as he made his way to the cross."

"Is that significant?"

"In her vision, it is. He claimed to have received 5475 blows. Her Lord told Saint Birgitta that if she were to recite fifteen Hail Marys and Our Fathers each day for a year, she would honour each wound on its own, and He would be very well pleased."

"You are telling me this because?"

"Because I am. Do you know your Hail Marys and Our Fathers?"

"I do, but they're not mine."

"Not Catholic?"

"Not Christian."

"Agnostic?"

"Antagonistic." He shrugged. Shrugging was the best possible way to avoid a discussion of religion. If it wasn't leading to enlightenment in relation to murder, he was happy to forgo the theological chatter.

She gazed at him over her glass. Her long fingernails looked almost real in the burning light that filled the room from the fire and candles, dancing off the walls in patterns suggesting Gustave Doré's chiaroscuro version of Dante's Inferno.

"I didn't expect you until tomorrow."

"But you did expect me."

"Oh yes. I knew you couldn't resist the possibility of another young body."

"Another?"

She lowered her head and smiled discreetly.

"Are you saying?"

She is, Harry.

"That I might kill again? Yes, of course. I thought you had it all figured out."

I told you.

Harry was at a loss for words. This woman so horrified by her son as a killer, was she spontaneously confessing to murder? He waited for Karen to comment but she chose to remain silent for the moment.

"The two young women?" he asked with as much coherence as he could muster. "You're saying…?"

"In the cedar maze, yes, and in Hagaparken."

She was enjoying his discomfort.

"Not Bernd?"

"And not you, Dr. Lindstrom."

Of all the questions he wanted to ask, the first that came to mind seemed perhaps the most trivial: "The girl in the blanket, was it revulsion or remorse?"

"Was what, I'm not sure what you mean."

"Why did you cover her?"

"Oh that. Well, I took her north to Muskoka. She was outside a part-time agency on Eglinton Avenue. I told her to hop in; we'd skip the commission. I needed help with preparing our cottage for winter guests. She was a pretty little thing, a bit nervous, a nail-chewer. By the time we got to Port Carling, she was relaxed; we were old friends. When it seemed we were locked out, I told her I'd pay her anyway. I suggested we compensate for the trip with a wood-fired sauna down by the boathouse. I built a low fire in the stove that was fed from outside; we stripped to the buff in the little vestibule. And you know, Harry, my body stood up pretty well by comparison. Eventually, I stepped out, locked the door, got dressed, heaped snow on the fire, and when I was sure it was out, I went for a late lunch at a diner in Port. Nothing to it, really. I spent a few hours at the library and after dark when I returned she had passed away. She froze to death in a sauna. Isn't that ironic? It must have been a gentle death—not even scratch marks on the walls. I wrapped her in a blanket before I put her in the trunk so she wouldn't thaw."

The waiter approached and asked if they wanted another Xante. They both nodded, yes. Harry hoped it would calm his churning gut, and Birgitta, apparently, to celebrate arousing his revulsion.

"So there you are. Is that what you wanted to hear? The girl in Stockholm was a variation on the same theme. This time I had a gun. It wasn't real but it was effective. I picked it up at an antique shop in the old town. It looked very authentic."

"And you planted my wife's wedding band under her corpse."

"Your wife's wedding band?"

Harry waited.

"Yes, yes I did."

There didn't seem to be any explanation to account for her lapse in memory, so Harry continued, "You stole it from my condo."

"From that beautiful jewellery box. I love Japanese lacquerware."

"And you tried to kill me. Why?"

"Oh no, you're wrong about that."

"Well, you got my attention. I lost bits of a couple of toes and died for an unpleasant period of time from hypothermia."

"Poor you, but you don't remember it, do you? The being dead part. People only think they do. And the toes, do they still hurt?"

"They do. And the orange, that was to get my attention, as well."

"The orange? Oh yes, I remember. It struck me as odd that you'd have ceramic fruit; you don't seem the type. It clashed with your lovely carpet. The clockwork orange."

"In the snow."

"Yes, in case you thought the door had blown open by itself. I wanted you to know someone had been there. I didn't want you to know why."

She seemed to be reciting the details as if she had gone over them, perseverating, trying to inscribe them in memory.

"You assumed I'd think it was Bernd?" And he had.

"If I took the ring and your scarf and just disappeared, you might never have known. I needed you to make the connection."

"With Bernd. You thought an orange in the snow would do that?"

"Very Dadaist, don't you think? It did work, didn't it?"

"And you planted the scarf and the ring because?"

"To keep you involved." She offered a condescending smile.

"You do not believe in natural justice?"

"Ah, but I do. I do not believe in police."

"You do not believe in the law."

"Law should never be a matter of faith, Harry. What I do believe in is the capacity of the desperate to endure." She sighed. "I'm surprised you didn't wake up. If you'd ever had children, you would have."

He was about to protest but he stopped himself. The less she knew about him, the more comfortable he felt.

"And if I had wakened?"

"What, you would have captured me? But you didn't."

"You were still there when I came out of the bedroom? You locked me outside. I saw you through the window."

"Whatever you saw, you never imagined it was me."

"You knew I'd freeze to death."

"No, Harry, I knew you were resourceful. That's why I hired you, or, if you'd rather, since you refuse to be paid in advance, why I enlisted your aid. I needed you. I still do."

"Then I'm glad I survived," he responded, with a caustic absence of expression.

"You think you've caught me, now, of course?"

"I do."

"Unless I've caught you, Harry."

How can she be so smug, Karen hissed? *What's she up to?*

Damned if I know.

And damned if you don't. We have the answer now; we just need the right questions.

"Are we at an awkward impasse, Harry?" Birgitta's eyes widened again. "I do not expect absolution, you are not my priest. And more to my benefit, you are not the police." Her lips curled at the edges. Far from appearing to be cornered, she seemed empowered by his presence. And by her confession.

Birgitta Ghiberti tilted her head low, looked up at him through her lashes, and her lips parted into a seductive curve. This was evil incarnate and her beauty was enhanced by her crimes. Harry reached across the table to put his hand on hers in a futile gesture of suppression, in a morbid attempt to connect, but she pulled coyly away.

Why connect, Harry? Connect with what? You want to understand, don't you? You can't.

"I'll tell you what," the woman said, sitting upright again. "Let us suppose I have taken up my son's curious pastime—"

"It seems you have."

"But by choice, Harry. Not under compulsion."

"An interesting distinction."

"I will make a deal with you. Your pact with the devil, if you'd like. I will not do another while you're here. So, good for you, Harry, you have prolonged a human life. Of course, you can't stay forever. I can."

She's taunting you, Harry. But why?

"And if I find your victim first?"

"Perhaps you can save her life."

Maybe you did connect, Harry. You've always had a way with beautiful women. Or maybe your professorial convictions about our fundamental humanity are still as contagious. Maybe she's not as bad as she wants to be.

Believe it, this woman wants to be bad.

Birgitta stood up and smoothed the front of her long skirt over her thighs, then leaned down and whispered, "In spite of all that you know, Harry, there's nothing you can do. Have a nice walk back."

He tried to settle the bill, only to find she had paid for both of them on her way out. By the time he retrieved his coat, she was gone. Outside, he saw her slip into a small blue sedan parked across from the Lindgarden and drive off toward their hotel.

Harry pulled on his black toque and drew his sheepskin close. His toes seemed a banal distraction. He ignored the pain and as he walked he wondered, did this strange woman really kill those girls or was this another delusion? Bernd now seemed more the victim of his mother's malevolent obsessions than a villain.

In the morning, Harry would try to reach Hannah Arnason. He wondered if she knew any of this. They needed to talk.

14 THE RUINS OF ST. CLEMENS

HARRY WALKED PAST AN ANCIENT LOG BUILDING AND along the deserted Strandgatan toward his hotel. A small blue car parked in the shadows caught his attention, and he approached it warily. No one was in the car but it was poised across the end of a cobbled passage leading away from the harbour, as if the driver meant to return shortly. The lights of a tiny souvenir shop not far above the main street flickered from people moving about inside. He moved up the snowy incline and walked slowly past, keeping to the darkness as much as he could.

Birgitta was having an animated conversation with the clerk. Harry backtracked to peer in, realizing they would not be able to see him through the reflection of the shop interior. Birgitta's back was to him but he could see the other woman clearly, although it was impossible to read her expression. She was young, a blonde with flushed cheeks, an attractively upturned nose, and with pale eyebrows that made her eyes seem bland. She was listening attentively and then shrugged as the older woman leaned forward and kissed her in the French custom on both cheeks and turned to face Harry directly.

Rendered invisible by the reflection, Harry turned down the passageway and walked back along Strandgatan until he heard Birgitta's car start up and pull away. Then he returned to stand in the shadows just down from the little shop, close enough he could observe the girl inside making preparations to close for the night.

She moved around purposefully in a cozy sphere of light, oblivious to monsters waiting in the darkness. She thinks she can be pretty and young with impunity, Harry thought, but these are a killer's invitation to murder. He wanted to warn her, but how and of what. He slunk back farther into the shadows as the shop lights went out, and he watched her exit into the lane, wearing a long coat and a fur hat much like Birgitta's. She bent to lock the door before turning casually to enter the gloom of snow-streaked streets without another soul in sight.

He followed her at a distance as she turned up onto Mellangatan and passed under a low arch that spanned the street, making it seem even narrower than it was. She seemed almost to glide through the sinister web of shadows and light that draped along walls of stucco and stone and drooped across piles of snow and cobbled pavement. As they moved through the night he caught brief glimpses down side streets of ramparts and battlements illuminated by the waxing moon in an eerie piecemeal tableau. Suddenly she veered off and he thought he had lost her, but she had taken a short cut and appeared back in the open around the corner. She passed a small group of people laughing and singing, and Harry instinctively averted his head when they crowded by him.

Not until she had turned in through a gateway and Harry caught up did he realize they had approached Smedjegatan from below and he was in front of the Hotel St. Clemens. He retreated back down the street to the separate entrance that led to his room. At the far end of the short corridor, he was able to peer into the courtyard. The girl was at the main entrance. She hesitated, then entered, and Harry lost sight of her.

By moving into his own room, which overlooked the courtyard, he had a better view of the reception area. The blonde girl was asking something at the desk. Then Birgitta appeared. From where Harry was, they looked the same age, with the same colouring. They might have been sisters. They talked off to the side so the concierge couldn't hear, and then they kissed perfunctorily on both cheeks and the younger woman went out the door and stood within the pale walls of the courtyard, looking directly at Harry's window.

He trusted she could see only the reflection of the ruined medieval church behind her. Still, he flinched and moved back into the darkness.

When he looked out again, she was gone.

Harry still had on his sheepskin coat over the nubuck jacket. He hurried out the door and along the corridor into the street. She was nowhere in sight. Good, that was a good thing. She was safe for the time being.

He went back to his window, holding the curtains back to give him a broader view. The girl was there again, she had only slipped into the shadows beside an outbuilding. He couldn't tell if she was looking in his direction.

Eventually Birgitta came out. She was dressed in the same long coat and fur hat she had worn when she left the Lindgarden. She squinted through the glare of the exterior light, then walked directly over to the girl.

The two women leaned close and conversed with an urgency

conveyed in the silence of Harry's room by their postures, before again kissing on both cheeks and stepping back from each other. The blonde girl turned and hurried away and Birgitta arranged herself, poised in the shadows, close by the little blue Fiesta she had been driving earlier in the evening, and waited.

Harry watched for about ten minutes. Birgitta was obviously getting cold. She stamped her feet and wrapped her arms around herself and took off her gloves and blew warm air onto her fingertips.

The blonde girl reappeared. Harry perked up, leaning close to the glass as if he might be able to hear what they said. The window fogged from his breath, blinding him and threatening to betray his hidden location. He didn't dare clear it off. The two women were now ghostly spectres. When he changed his position to a clearer portion of the window they were out of his sightline. Shifting a little, he could see they had moved around while they talked and he couldn't tell one from the other.

Then, one of them left and the other walked right by Harry's window, glancing in his direction. For a moment, she was less than a body's-length away. It was Birgitta. She moved on, around the opposite side of the main building, and disappeared down a passageway that led directly into the church ruins.

Harry was sweating from being overdressed in his room. He took off his coat and jacket.

That's it then, is it? Aren't you curious?

I'm curious about a lot of things.

About Birgitta Ghiberti, aka Shtoonk, aka Sviar, aka Ilsa Lund.

Come again?

Ilsa, Ingrid Bergman, Casablanca. Come on, Bogie, get with it. Where did she go? It's a little creepy to be touring ruins by moonlight. Let's check it out.

Harry knew that sometimes there was no point in arguing. He put his coat back on and stepped out into the cold on the street end of the corridor. He had decided to approach the remains of the church by stealth, assuming Birgitta hadn't simply cut through to another destination. He was less likely to be observed if the girl from the convenience store had arranged an assignation.

He walked briskly around the irregular block to the north side of the ruins and moved out from the shadows of buildings and trees into the nearly full moonlight, which exposed him completely. The walkway to the main entrance had not been shovelled and his boots crunched with each step. He had the sense of himself as a silvered apparition making enough racket to wake the dead. When he stopped, he could hear himself breathe.

Passing between buttresses that shouldered what remained of the outer walls, he surveyed the interior. There was no sign of Birgitta. At first he saw only emptiness, but when he stepped inside, the gleaming columns and intersecting arcs, the curves of crumbling vaults, the finely carved tracery of Gothic windows, and the stolid Romanesque arches left over from an earlier age, all moved him to distraction. For a moment he forgot why he was there.

The very notion of death seemed obscured by the awesome beauties of destruction. Harry took off a glove and touched the back of an index finger to his eyes, to press away the moisture and clear his vision.

Among the mysteries evoked by the ruins, he sensed the absence of music. He could almost hear the drone of a medieval choir lifting above the silvered snow in the nave. He stood motionless, listening, but he could only hear the hush of the night in the dark centre of an ancient city.

A faint rustling stirred the air. Harry lowered his hood. By turning slowly he determined the sounds came from the farthest end of the nave, where an interior wall had crumbled into a rough and menacing hollow among the shadows. He approached slowly until he could see a human figure hunched over, kneeling with head bowed. He stopped to catch his breath and then moved closer, and he could see that what he had taken as devotional posture was an expression of ghoulish engagement.

The indelible image of Nosferatu, toying with a victim, turned into Sverdrup. With his jet-black hair and demonic pose, the man seemed more like one of the damned than film could ever imagine. In front of him, the body of Birgitta Ghiberti lay sprawled across snowy rubble with her head split open. Blood from the wound formed a black pool on the ice that reflected Sverdrup's distorted figure in shimmering layers of moonlight.

Harry trembled with an overwhelming sense of remorse. Her death diminished him, as all deaths do, but more so, it was a judgment. She had come to him for protection from her son, her son had urged him to protect his mother from him, and Harry had let them both down. Deep inside he heard voices declare his failure, voices quivering with sorrow and fear, small voices scratching on the inside of his skull.

Sverdrup shifted his position, and from Harry's perspective his ghastly complexion flared into a leathery sheen as he lit a cigarette, then subsided into a putrescent glow, pulsing brighter when he inhaled. Sverdrup finally stood up; his fingers gleamed black in the moonlight from blood still warm on his hands. He turned and nodded at Harry, who until that moment was not sure if his presence had been detected or if he had been nothing more than the flutter of a moving thing in the dappled night.

"She's dead," said Sverdrup.

Harry backed away a little. Death must have taken her by surprise. He wondered if she had time to recognize her assailant. Sverdrup seemed an unlikely killer. In spite of the matte black hair, his sickly pallor, and the squinty eyes sunk deep into his head, he was a constable in the National Criminal Police.

Sverdrup must have followed her through from the hotel courtyard. He moved closer to Harry and blew smoke into the air between them. Even turning his head to the side, Harry could not avoid the sweet warm tobacco aroma that enveloped them both. Harry stood his ground.

Sverdrup had blood on his hands. If "Ockham's razor"—the principle held sacred by philosophers that the simplest explanation was best—then Sverdrup had just murdered Birgitta Ghiberti. But Harry knew he had not; sometimes gut feelings trumped logic. Sverdrup and his boss were strange but surely not deadly. They thrived on complexity. Whatever had brought Sverdrup to Visby, Ockham and his razor didn't apply.

Whomever the dead woman had been intending to meet had bashed in her skull and fled only seconds before Sverdrup and Harry arrived.

Harry shuffled a bit to the side, so that he was standing directly over the corpse. As he did so, Sverdrup moved back a little to give him room. They were being polite with each other in that stilted way enemies have when they are forced by circumstances to be congenial. Sverdrup coughed and spat but said nothing. Harry hunkered down and Sverdrup dropped to his haunches beside him.

Very limber, Harry, but too close.

Birgitta Ghiberti's fur hat lay on the frozen snow, just outside the shadowy crypt that was formed by shade from the moon. The fur riffled in the slight breeze. Beside it a boulder the size of a pineapple, its jagged contours streaked with cerebral tissue and blood, left no doubt it was the instrument of her brutal demise. There was no blood on the hat. She had removed it before she was struck. Or someone else had.

As Harry stood up, a hand clutched him firmly through his sheepskin from behind, sinking long fingers into his shoulder. He was startled; he had not sensed her arrival.

He tried to shrug free as he turned slowly to face Hannah Arnason, but the more he struggled, the more firm and unwavering her grip. He was not prepared to make a scene, so he assumed a relaxed posture, close enough to her that he could feel her warm breath breach the dark cold between them.

"Inspector Arnason, it's Harry Lindstrom."

"Yes, Mr. Lindstrom, I know it's you. And you have found Mrs. Ghiberti, I see."

"I'm afraid she's dead."

"You have a gift for stating the obvious, Mr. Lindstrom." She released her talon-like grip from his shoulder and brushed the outside of his coat to smooth out the indentations left by her fingers. "We seem to have got here a little too late."

"Apparently we did," said Harry.

She doesn't mean you.

"Inspector Arnason," he said. "I saw this woman ten minutes ago. She came through the passageway from the hotel. I followed her the long way around."

"I'm sure you did, Mr. Lindstrom."

"She was dead when I got here. Your man, Sverdrup, was already with her. I didn't see anyone leave."

"Perhaps we'll find footprints in the snow."

Harry looked at her quizzically. The ground surface inside the ruins was icy or crusted over. There wouldn't be any footprints.

"You don't imagine I killed her, for God's sake?"

As he spoke, she manoeuvred him to the side, and Sverdrup slipped on the cuffs over Harry's gloved wrists.

Sverdrup wiped his bloodied hands on his pants, then took out a cell phone from his coat pocket and poked in a number. He said something in Swedish, surprisingly brief, then snapped the phone shut and put his gloves on.

"You see, Harry," said Hannah Arnason. "It's pretty straightforward. The constable came one way and I came another, and there you were in the middle. You and the corpse of Birgitta Ghiberti."

"But Sverdrup got here before me."

"Apparently not. Too bad, really. It is unfortunate."

"Yes, it is," said Harry. He was incredulous. Why would Sverdrup lie?

"We will have an opportunity now to talk about the other murders."

"The other what?" Harry was alarmed.

"We have much to discuss," said the woman who in her high boots towered over him.

The three of them moved like ghostly shades out through the open space past the entry, where the breeze was beginning to build, and headed up the deserted street to a parked car. As they climbed in, it occurred to Harry he would be relieved when they got to the Gotland County police station. This weird woman, like a Valkyrie and her shadow, gave all the appearance of leading a slain warrior to his final resting place. The police station would be infinitely preferable.

But when the car pulled forward to an intersection, it turned down a small side street and cut across several more, before plunging through the shadows of the Norderport and speeding off into the darkness. Twisting his head, Harry watched through the back window as the lights of the town were swallowed up in the night.

He cleared his throat to speak, but he could find no words adequate to protest his apparent abduction. He was alone in the back seat. No one had bothered to do up his seat belt, although theirs were secured. He leaned forward.

In a firm but conciliatory tone, he said, "Inspector Arnason?" He offered his words as a litmus test, trying to read the forces at play.

There was a brief pause before Sverdrup shifted slowly around from the passenger seat to stare at him, eye to eye, and suddenly his gloved hand flashed through the air and crashed against the side of Harry's skull. Harry saw it coming, and then the world disappeared.

15 IN A KITCHEN SOMEWHERE

HARRY LAY SPRAWLED ACROSS THE BACK SEAT AS HE slipped in and out of consciousness. He couldn't distinguish between muffled sounds of the road jangling in his head and shards of light that lacerated the swarming darkness or the penetrating throbbing in his right temple. It all seemed a jumble of painful sensations.

He knew he was on the island of Gotland. He knew he was a prisoner in the back of a police car, driving north from Visby. He suspected he had a concussion; he must have smashed against the side window from the force of the blow. He assumed that he was in grave danger, but what bothered him more was the feeling that he was misunderstood.

Only you, Harry! You'd rather be tortured to death than not be "understood." Karen whispered the word with a vehemence that he thought was funny as he slipped into oblivion. When he returned, she was still there, whispering. *You don't give a damn if you die, Harry. You think that gives you an advantage but it doesn't. Because I don't want you dead. You've got to live with that.*

He felt the car wheel onto a rough side road and after a few minutes come to a stop. He was aware of being hoisted onto his feet but his mind was disengaged from his body. He observed himself stumbling with his arms around his captors' shoulders. It was someone else, someone he didn't know, and he was having trouble sustaining his interest in the whole scenario.

They entered a room through a side porch and when the lights flared he saw they were in a kitchen, probably in a deserted farmhouse. It seemed almost as cold inside as out, but it was warm enough that the dank smell of mildew penetrated his hazy awareness with a restorative pungency, and he was suddenly and painfully alert.

Sverdrup lit a fire in the woodstove, and Hannah Arnason, after cuffing Harry to a chair, brought together the makings for tea. Sverdrup kneeled almost solicitously and removed Harry's boots.

"No cream or milk," she announced. Since she was speaking English, Harry assumed she was directing her congenial observation at him.

"That's okay," he said. "I take it black."

She filled a kettle from the kitchen faucet and placed it on the stove, and then she dampened a tea towel and proceeded to dab blood from Harry's forehead. She offered no apology. Sverdrup observed the proceedings with casual indifference. The room began to warm up. The central heating must have been turned down but was sufficient to stop the pipes from freezing. By the time the tea was ready, the room was almost cozy, although tinged with the aroma of stale tobacco emanating from Sverdrup's clothes. Clearly, though, he did not smoke in his superior's presence.

"Sugar?" It was Sverdrup who asked.

"Sure," said Harry, who seldom drank tea and never with sugar, but felt he might need the sustenance for whatever lay ahead.

Sverdrup removed Harry's cuffs long enough to help him off with his coat, which he hung with the other two on pegs by the door. Then they sat down at the kitchen table and sipped their tea in silence. If one of them had not been in handcuffs, with a trickle of blood seeping from a slit in his right temple, while another picked absently at flecks of dried blood on his hands, and the third seemed ominously serene, they might have been old friends so at ease with each other; language was superfluous.

Harry could hear Karen whispering, but he couldn't make out what she said. He looked around the room. It was pleasantly nondescript. He looked down at the little tea canister on the table. For a brief interlude, Harry was amused by its familiarity. The label read: *Farmer Hulda's blandning, Kränku, Visby Gotland.* He thought immediately of Birgitta. It was the same kind of tea box in which Bernd stored his cache of fingernail parings.

The photograph of Hulda, staring out from an oval frame, was pure genius as a parody of ersatz sentimentality. She unequivocally scowled, perhaps at herself in the mirror, but certainly at the tea connoisseur. She looked authentic, with the wattles, jowls, folds, creases, and glowering eyes of a real person.

"You like the tea?" Hannah Arnason asked, seeing his gaze fixed on the canister. "It is very good."

Harry grimaced. He did like the tea; it tasted like Earl Grey with a hint of orange. He wondered if the woman beside him saw Hulda as a parody or simply as someone who had lived a demanding life and was unhappy approaching its inevitable end?

So much from a tea label, Harry. Why don't you try reading the leaves?

"It is from a shop in Visby," said Hannah Arnason, catching his line of vision. "Kränku. They have very nice things for sale. Teapots and dishes. No woollens. Have you seen Gotland sheep? They have black faces, yes. In the snow, sometimes you can only see their expressions. It is very comical."

"I just arrived this afternoon. Yesterday, by now. I haven't had a chance to tour the countryside." He paused, then added, "Not in daylight."

"So, Mr. Lindstrom. I need to ask you some questions. It would be to your benefit to give me good answers."

Harry smiled at the subtlety. He wondered if *good* answers were the answers she wanted to hear? Or honest answers to the questions she needed to ask?

The woman shifted her chair around so that she could look Harry directly in the eye. At the same time, Sverdrup slid his chair back on the linoleum, stood up, and arranged himself ominously in the shadows at the farthest edge of Harry's vision. Hannah Arnason leaned forward so that he caught the scent of her body and felt the warmth of her breath.

"Harry," she said. "I want you to tell us," she paused for effect. "Apart from Birgitta Ghiberti, how many people have you killed?"

Harry stared into her eyes. The lustre in their steely blue depths had turned black. He knew he was a puzzlement to the National Criminal Police, or at least to Inspector Arnason and her odiferous shadow. But Hannah Arnason was inviting him to confess to multiple murders. He had a choice, either to protest vehemently or to wait until she revealed more, giving him something to refute or dispute or ridicule. Hannah toyed with her cup and gazed back at him with her head lowered in a gesture of feigned intimacy.

"Harry, it is your turn to speak."

She sat back a little and the air stirred between them in a subtle flourish of bodily scent and the aroma of controlled hostility. For the first time, Harry felt the cool edge of fear cut through his gut.

Perhaps he wasn't afraid of death. He and Karen were not in agreement on that. But as Karen had put it with caustic understatement, he definitely feared being *misunderstood*. Almost as much as not understanding. To be abducted, even annihilated, in the midst of confusion, as a rational, moral, and responsible being in the world, struck Harry as bloody horrific.

"What would you like me to say? Where do I start?"

She unexpectedly smiled.

"Wherever you wish."

This is a very strange interrogation, and it's not over a bistro dinner. Be wary, Harry. She's too cool for comfort.

Harry searched in his mind for a line from William Blake. Or was it Emily Dickinson? He tried to focus.

Good for you, Harry. You're living proof of the bicameral mind.

"Let's work backwards," he said. He listened to himself, to make sure he was speaking out loud. "Inspector, start with the most recent corpse. I can explain why I was at St. Clemens. But I have no idea how *you* turned up just minutes too late. Or Mr. Sverdrup, minutes before me."

"Exactly. We followed you and we were too late."

"I did not kill Birgitta Ghiberti. Look at me: the only blood on my clothes is my own. If we weren't sequestered like fugitives, you could check it against the blood on Sverdrup's hands. Or on the bloody cadaver."

Hannah Arnason nodded amiably. "You think we are fugitives?"

"I'm not sure what to think. We are not at a police station, we seem to have fled the scene of a very unpleasant crime, and I have been smacked on the side of the head." He glanced around and realized his assailant had slipped out for a smoke. He and the woman occupied the room on their own, filling it the way a condemned man and his executioner occupy the space in a death chamber.

"In fact," he continued, "I was planning on contacting you in the morning. Birgitta told me she murdered the girl in the park and the one in Toronto."

"Really? She confessed! How unexpected. How convenient for you that she is dead."

She's not being ironic, Harry.

"She was quite open about it."

"That is most interesting. She does not have a reputation for murder, of course, only for making unpleasant accusations. We have circumstantial evidence connecting you to the girl in Stockholm, not her. Remember your wife's ring. And what if I were to tell you we can prove it was you who killed Ilsa Jóhannesdóttir."

"Ilsa, the girl from Gimli—don't be absurd. Call Toronto, Miranda Quin can clear this up."

"Mr. Lindstrom, apparently this will come as a surprise, but it was Superintendent Quin who contacted us. It was her idea that you were involved with the girl's death. I was told she came from Gimli; it is famous as a settlement during the Icelandic diaspora."

Harry took a deep breath. Miranda Quin was his only real friend in the world. He could think of nothing to say beyond a forlorn and meaningless expletive: "For God's sake."

"She has proof," Hannah Arnason explained without emotion.

He drew in a deep breath. "Circumstantial," he said.

"A brown scarf, yes. It is yours."

Harry exhaled through clenched teeth. Birgitta was still a force to be reckoned with. He was being swept into some looming disaster by the machinations of a dead woman.

"It was a plant," he said. He took a breath so deep his ribs ached. "Miranda talked to you about this?"

"Yes."

"Damn bloody hell."

Hearing his own voice so strongly uncertain made him shudder. Images of powerlessness swarmed through his head, images of water that turned violent and coalesced around the deaths of his children. He felt like he was losing everything all over again.

He reached out to touch the woman's hand. She moved it away.

He swallowed, his ribs ached miserably.

"You can't really believe I murdered those girls. Does Miranda believe I murdered them?"

"Yes."

"For the sake of God almighty, I didn't."

She leaned forward again, into his personal space as a challenge, not to connect. "I am disappointed, Harry. I thought you would make this easier. Let us move our discussion to the third victim."

"She's still alive," he protested, but at this point nothing was certain. "She was with Birgitta before she died."

Inspector Arnason glanced away then back with a penetrating glare.

"I do not know who you mean. I'm talking about the girl from last summer."

Harry slumped in his chair. The cuffs bit into his wrist, the pain felt good. It was a reminder there was a real world that made sense, even if it seemed to be slipping away. He twisted against the steel until he could feel blood spurt through the opened wound. He tried to focus on the warm blood draining down his wrist into the palm of his hand.

"Harry, pay attention." For a moment, he thought it was Karen, reeling him in, but the voice belonged to the policewoman leaning so close the warm scent of tea on her breath washed over his face before he passed out from the pain, from his concussion, from the terrible absurdity of his entire life.

Gradually he seemed to emerge out of blackness. Karen was with him. They were in a different kitchen, exploring an abandoned farmhouse on the Sanctuary Line near Granton. He knew he was somewhere else at the same time. He couldn't think where or when.

The Granton house was structurally sound. The floors were broad pine planks, filthy but in good repair. The plaster had pulled away from the lath in places, exposing rough-cut joists and jigsaw views from the kitchen into the living room with its massive fieldstone fireplace. The ceiling plaster had collapsed and lay in rubble under foot. The exposed beams were hand-hewn and solid. He and Karen had driven out to Lucan in search of St. Patrick's cemetery on the Roman Line. They had taken faculty positions at Huron College in London and wanted to explore the territory. In those parts, that meant searching out the tombstone of the Black Donnellys. Disappointed to find the original pink granite obelisk erected by William, the surviving son, had been replaced because it featured the word "murdered" five times over and attracted tourists, they drove out of the Irish settlements and into Scottish country around Granton. An abandoned farmhouse on the Sanctuary Line caught their eye. Neither of them was experienced in building; they were both academics, and Karen had grown up as a wife-in-training in the Niagara region before rebelling and pursuing her doctorate. But they bought the dilapidated ruins and a couple of acres, and over the next decade, through the births of two children, they restored the house to rustic beauty.

When the kitchen in Gotland swam into view again, it was distorted. He was spread-eagled face-up on the linoleum. The handcuffs were off. Sverdrup was kneeling over him, applying a damp towel to his right temple. The man seemed to notice that Harry's eyes were open, but he ignored him as he proceeded to bandage his lacerated wrist. Sverdrup rose to his feet and disappeared out the door into the shadows, returning with a small chunk of ice, which he wrapped in the blood-soaked towel and applied to Harry's forearm.

Harry realized he must have strained his arm when he collapsed off the chair onto the floor. He couldn't move his fingers through the pain.

Hannah Arnason remained seated at the table, watching Sverdrup's activities with apparent disinterest. Their roles had reversed. Patience gradually turned to annoyance. Her assistant had strung out his ministrations long enough, and she began to breathe stiffly though flared nostrils. Sverdrup was clearly accustomed to reading her signals and helped lift Harry to his feet and back onto a chair. He didn't bother trying to secure him. Harry wasn't going anywhere.

"Now, then, welcome back," said Hannah Arnason. "Let's start with the girl on the glacier."

"What bloody girl on what bloody glacier?"

"You were in Iceland?"

"Last week."

"Last year."

"In the summer," he mumbled. "Yes." He could see where this was going.

"And you toured a glacier."

"I toured several. With guides."

"Always with guides?"

"When I was on the glaciers. Otherwise, I trekked around on my own."

"Think back, Harry. Think about visiting Sólheimajökull Glacier."

"I was there last week with your cousin, Chief Constable Arnason. He took me to Seljalandfoss Waterfall, then to the glacier. We got out of the car to smell the scent of snow drifting down from the ice field, but we didn't go up onto the slopes."

"Not last week. But in August you did."

"No, that wasn't one of the glaciers I toured. You can check."

"We already have, Harry."

"And while you were trekking, the girl disappeared."

"And later you found her dead."

"So you admit that?"

"I didn't think you were making up corpses."

He looked at Hannah like she was one of his former students who had just come up with a familiar idea as if it were brand spanking new. He proceeded to clarify:

"I admit to knowing where you're going with this. I certainly do not admit to abduction or murder. I don't even recall any fuss over a missing girl while I was in Iceland."

"Do you read Icelandic?"

"No."

"And you do not speak Icelandic."

"No."

"And she was only missing, not dead. She was found in a crevasse. She was not discovered until after you left."

"Chief Constable Arnason would have had no reason to suspect me."

"Perhaps not until Miranda Quin called when you landed in Reykjavik. Perhaps then he made the connection with Ilsa Jóhannesdóttir from Gimli."

"But if Miranda thinks I'm a killer, why would she call me at all?"

"To prevent you from killing again? It is possible. It is not my concern."

"The chief constable gave no indication I was in trouble."

In trouble, Harry!

"My cousin *suspected* you did *not* kill the girl on the glacier. Suspicion is open-ended, Harry, it leaves room to be affirmed or refuted."

"Your cousin conducted an investigation over Guinness and interrogated me during a tour of the geographic wonders of Iceland. He found me innocent."

"He found you 'not guilty.' We both know that only means a substantive case could not be made. Now it is different, perhaps. I informed him about the girl in the Haga Park with your silver ring."

Harry raised himself in the chair. He said, "I think I'd rather be in Toronto, dealing with Quin. You and your cousin, it must be a family thing—his methods are almost as devious as your firelight chats."

"There was no fire at the bistro."

"Candlelight, there were candles."

"Yes."

"And Superintendent Quin asked you to look out for me. Literally, as it turns out. That's why you're here on Gotland."

"It is more complicated than that."

She looked ominously inscrutable. He decided to seize the initiative.

"The girl in Hagaparken had black on her fingertips. What about the body in the glacier? Did she have manicured nails? Were they cut very short? Were they blackened?"

"It would have been difficult to tell. She died very slowly, in excruciating stages. Her fingers were frozen before she expired. She'd tried to claw her way out. The flesh was shredded and caked with blood, the nails had been torn away, some of the finger bones were exposed."

"She must have been frantic."

"Desperate, frozen to insensibility."

"Was she naked?"

"No, of course not. She was found in a glacial crevasse."

"And yet her fingernail parings turned up in Toronto. Did you know that? No, well they did. That means they were cut off before she plunged into the crevasse. Painted black after, apparently. She didn't just slip. It wasn't an accident; she wasn't pushed on a vicious whim. It was all planned out."

"That could be taken as a confession, Mr. Lindstrom."

Slate, you're tired, you're in pain, you're fed up and confused. Do us both a favour, be humble, stop talking.

But Harry ignored the advice.

"It seems that I've been refining my *modus operandi*: first, bodies clothed, gentle deaths, then a violent push, then wrapped in a blanket, then stark naked."

"The girl in the glacier, she was my cousin Judith."

"Oh, I'm sorry, I really am." Suddenly the dead girl was real. "Not the chief constable's daughter, I hope?"

"No, he is alone. He has had three wives but no children. I did not know her well, not since we were small."

"She was your age?"

"She was like me, in her early thirties. Very old for your victims, Harry. But it was Judith's death that connected you to us. And now we have caught you in the act."

"The brutality of Birgitta's death doesn't fit anyone's pattern."

"No, it does not."

"Does it occur to you that forensic patterns are like constellations; they exist entirely in the eye of the beholder?"

"Constellations exist because there are humans to observe them. What is your point, Harry?"

"That *is* my point! They're how we describe what we see, and we end up thinking they're real. Those small points of light, some are stars and some are galaxies filled with a billion stars. We draw lines between them and say they are the hunter, Orion, or Ursa, the bear. We do that, sometimes, we connect the dots with flyspecks and think we've seen the truth, when all we're seeing is flyspecks and dots."

Hannah Arnason listened. She seemed fascinated with how a man so apparently absurd could be a killer.

"Do you know where you are?" she asked.

"No, not really."

"Do you have any idea why we have brought you here?"

"None at all. I'd feel more comfortable in a Visby jail."

"And does your mysterious situation not make you afraid?"

"Vulnerable, not afraid."

"You are very inconsistent, Harry."

"Real people are."

16 ROGUE JUSTICE

IN THE LAST FEW HOURS, HARRY HAD BEEN HORRIFIED, anxious, baffled, intrigued, frustrated, angry, defiant, and proud. He had been wounded, insulted, and taken prisoner, apparently as a victim of rogue justice. He had been fearful, at times, but never afraid. That's what he told himself. Fear was a survival mechanism, a visceral response demanding resolution through action or a change in attitude. To be afraid, however, was a debilitating state of mind. He intuitively shifted his attitude to counter the fear of being afraid. It was about the only thing he could do that was under his own control.

He was inconsistent, as Hannah Arnason explained. That was both disconcerting and gave him comfort. Cold comfort; reassuring distress. Word games. A compound oxymoron.

Get it together, Harry! She's more inconsistent than you are. She's warm, she's cold, she's passive, then aggressive. A friend one minute, an adversary the next. What's she got to be afraid of?

He scrutinized his abductor. She watched him watching her. Suddenly, she got up and motioned Sverdrup to follow her. She strode out onto the porch, letting in a rush of cold air before the door swung shut behind them.

Harry surveyed the room. Two doors led into the rest of the house. Not promising avenues of escape. Escape to where? He knew the farmhouse was isolated by the diminishing number of lights flashing against the car windows when he had been sprawled semi-conscious in the back seat.

They had taken his sheepskin coat and his gloves. His toque was in the coat pocket. Where were his boots? His scarf was in Toronto. I can't escape without being properly dressed for the occasion, he thought. Damn, damn, damn. I'm damned.

He wondered if they were alright out in the cold. He felt a strange sympathy for his captors. They seemed as confused as he was. Captain Oates, he's not coming back.

The Stockholm syndrome, Harry. Get it together. Forget it. Not in Sweden, okay?

Harry was worried Karen would begin speaking out loud, and he'd have to answer. And then there'd be no possibility of a rational outcome.

You don't really think there is one, now?

Harry grimaced. He realized that absolute candour might be the only way to force Inspector Arnason to sort out what she was up to. If he could only be rational, perhaps she would respond in kind.

He felt Karen's pity. For his naiveté. Before he could protest, Hannah Arnason burst back into the room with her henchman close behind. Whatever the topic of their confab, within minutes they had turned the deserted farmhouse kitchen into an interrogation room, rearranging the chairs and moving a floor lamp with a moth-eaten shade closer to the table before turning out the overhead lights.

Harry was illuminated, the inspector was in shadow, and Sverdrup faded into the darkness at the musky edge of the room.

Harry was apprehensive. He didn't know where that fell, between fear and being afraid, but it was unpleasant.

"Now then, Mr. Lindstrom." She spoke in a businesslike tone that utterly denied the sinister absurdity of their situation. "Let us suppose you are not telling me lies."

"Fair enough."

"Your friend the superintendent thinks you murdered the girl in Canada; Chief Constable Arnason suspects you did *not* kill my cousin Judith in Iceland, which leaves open the possibility that you did; there was evidence at the death scene in Hagaparken that you were there when that girl died in the snow; and Constable Sverdrup found the corpse of Birgitta Ghiberti and you were there in the shadows before the blood had stopped flowing from the hole in her skull. Yes?"

"No."

Suddenly Harry's neck snapped to the side and his vision shattered into coronas of dazzling light. Sverdrup had walloped him on the back of his head.

"Yes," Harry murmured.

He waited until the room resolved into coherent images.

"What you have said is correct, as far as it goes." He shook his head slowly. "May I speak without your goon giving me another concussion?"

"Of course," she said, leaning forward into the cone of light, so that the glare shimmered in her eyes with an amiable glow. "Now that we agree on the facts."

"But there are other ways of reading them." He braced himself for a blow from the darkness behind him, but she looked up with a flickering change in expression, and Harry could sense that Sverdrup had backed deeper into the shadows.

"Please, you explain everything. I will listen."

"There's no point in asking about procedural abnormalities, I suppose?" He could feel Sverdrup looming behind him, but Hannah Arnason leaned even closer, the way she had that first evening at dinner, when he saw the night sky in the depths of her eyes. She nodded her permission for him to continue.

She shifted back from the light again, leaving Harry ominously on his own.

He tried to gather his thoughts.

Hannah Arnason spoke from the shadows, "Please, you may talk. Think of me as the judge, my colleague the jury."

He wasn't sure if the slight stilted nuances in her speech were because she was speaking an unfamiliar language or if they were somehow an affectation to make herself more dangerously alluring.

Oh for God's sake, Harry.

Inhaling deeply, he proceeded to explain how Birgitta Ghiberti had probably doubled back to Canada from Iceland at Christmas, travelling under her Swedish passport, and with a pathological deference to irony had murdered an Icelandic-Canadian girl in a sub-zero sauna in Ontario. Leaving the evidence of Harry's scarf to prove the villain was a man she had recruited to prove her own son a serial killer.

"Why?" asked the woman in shadows.

"Why did she tell me all this, or why did she try to frame me? I don't know. I do not know. But she seems to have abandoned irony in Stockholm. She simply force-marched a naked girl through the snow in the Haga Park until the girl dropped from exposure."

Simply!

"Again, framing you."

"Yes."

"Why naked?"

"I have no idea."

"And what about the blackened fingers, Dr. Lindstrom? Why would she imitate the primary marker of the killings she ascribed to her son, if she was trying to blame you? Doesn't it seem far more likely that you would do that, yourself, trying to shift the blame to him?"

"It does seem more likely. But that's the beauty of it. That's exactly what she assumed you would think."

"You realize, Harry, you have just provided motivation for murdering this woman, including the rage you must have felt to end her life with such brutality."

Deep breath, Harry.

"Not rage, revulsion. She horrified me."

"By being so calm about murder?"

"We had dinner together at a place called the Lindgarden. In spite of her grisly confessions, we had an absurdly sociable time. Lamb, salmon, followed by Xante, two of them, it tastes like pears and cognac."

"I know what it tastes like. So you had dinner together. Is that not an odd thing to do with a person you suspect of murder?"

"You also had dinner with me! Several times."

Her smile from the shadows broadened, then collapsed as Harry continued, "I'm not sure bashing someone's brains out isn't kinder than killing them slowly in the natural conditions of a northern winter."

Murder by geography! Harry, you're not a witness for the prosecution.

But he was convinced the best way through was to expose the truth, not matter how compromising it seemed.

Let the chips fall where they may, eh.

"Let's suppose for a minute that I'm *not* a monster. Who else might fit the description? The victim's son, right? Let's suppose he actually is a serial killer, let's suppose he was legitimately implicated in the deaths of his sisters, and let's not forget that he tried to enlist me to prevent him from killing his mother, something I dutifully reported back to you over sauerkraut and sausages. By candlelight. Obviously, in the case of Birgitta, he was emotionally involved. It stands to reason, if he felt compelled to kill her, he would need to do it in a fit of passion, using the only weapon at hand, a boulder among the ruins."

"Harry, you are from a winter country?"

"Yes."

Mon pays c'est l'hiver.

"Then, tell me. How do you pick up a boulder from the frozen ground? It is almost impossible. It would be iced into place."

She has a point, Harry. You should have anticipated this.

"Perhaps it was from one of the walls."

"In Sweden our ruins are not crumbling."

Harry didn't need Karen to tell him to take another tack.

"The blonde girl who met Birgitta at the Hotel St. Clemens can vouch for me."

"Really, you talked to her."

"No, I followed her from the shop where she works."

You can see how that looks, Harry.

"In a souvenir shop off the Strandgatan. I wanted to make sure she got home okay. But strangely enough, she went right to our hotel. I watched her meet with Birgitta."

"You were spying?"

This isn't getting any better.

"I did. I was. She went away, apparently to arrange some sort of meeting between Birgitta and someone else, presumably Bernd."

"You don't know for sure?"

"No, I was inside, watching through my window."

"How convenient. And neither of them saw you?"

Good point, Harry. Either of them might have.

"Birgitta left and went down the passageway into the ruins."

"And the girl?"

"She disappeared."

"Again, how convenient for you. And what does this prove?"

"Birgitta had implied the girl would be her next victim."

"Implied? Over dinner and a Xante cordial?"

"Two of them."

"Just like her son told you he was going to kill Birgitta. Harry, for a man who is troubled by patterns, you seem to be trapped in quite a few."

Harry didn't respond.

"And Birgitta announced that she would blame the girl's death on you. But instead she met with this same girl, where? In the courtyard of the St. Clemens Hotel, where she was a registered guest. Not a clandestine plot, I think. No. But it is a lovely hotel. I have stayed there myself. We will look for this girl. We will also check you out of the hotel. The concierge might become worried."

That's ominous, Harry. You'd better start seriously thinking about an exit strategy.

"Assuming this girl exists and is still alive," Hannah continued, "just what can she tell us?"

"I'm not sure, but whoever she arranged to have Birgitta meet, that's your killer."

"Of course." Hannah stifled a yawn. "I'm afraid this girl is one blonde too many, Harry. A dead end."

So to speak.

"Before we conclude," Hannah Arnason said, leaning again into the light, "let us return to the matter of *why* Birgitta Ghiberti would go to such monstrous extremes as you have described? Maybe you have a theory, Professor."

"Perhaps, and this may sound strange…"

Are you sure about this?

"Perhaps," he continued, after a long pause, "it was all about love."

"For you? My goodness."

"For her son."

As soon as he said it, Harry knew he was on the right track, as grotesque as it seemed. Sometimes murder is a family affair.

"Once she became absolutely convinced he was a serial killer, it was a way to get closer to him. Having betrayed him, she could make amends by emulating his crimes, with variations to suggest I was the culprit."

Harry, even I'm not convinced.

"And do you think the son murdered his mother as an act of love, as well."

"Quite possibly, yes."

My God, Harry.

There's no use trying to explain this one, Harry thought. It has to do with the perversity of the bond between them, rooted in horrific violations of natural affection. They were compelled by so much death to protect and punish each other.

Explain that to the jury. Give it your best shot, Harry.

But Harry said nothing. He was contemplating the horrific relationship between love and death that defined the Ghibertis. It was as easy to imagine one of them killing for love as dying for it. Bernd's desperate need for his mother's affection could have led to unspeakable acts.

Hannah Arnason stood up and walked around the room, circling Harry who tried to follow her with his eyes but kept losing her in the shadows. She sat down again and with a small cough offered Harry what seemed a throw-away question, "Before we conclude, do you have anything to add about the murder of Judith Arnason?"

"In the glacier? What more can I say? Perhaps she slipped in."

"After painting the inside edges of her fingernails with black polish?"

Which doesn't prove anything except the murders are connected. It doesn't even prove the same person did them.

Suddenly he understood why Birgitta Ghiberti had chosen the Iceland route back to Sweden. To get Harry there. To implicate him in this murder, too.

Miranda Quin must have mentioned to Birgitta that he'd been to Iceland the previous August. It was the kind of gossip people offer, when they're trying to anticipate a bond between strangers.

In that innocuous moment, Birgitta's plot was born.

Harry had been in Iceland at roughly the same time as Bernd must have been there, a visit that coincided with the disappearance of a young woman whose body turned up in a glacial crevasse.

Lure Harry back to Iceland, force a connection in the minds of police between Harry and the frozen corpse.

Why bother, Harry? They can't make it stick.

I don't know. I do not know.

Perhaps Birgitta knew how Hannah Arnason thinks.

Meaning what?

She seems willing to proceed with the prosecution with insufficient evidence.

Yeah.

They had met, you know that. Birgitta could be tapping into the pathology of a rogue cop.

I don't think Birgitta could have anticipated all that's happened.

You have doubts?

I always have doubts. It's called critical thinking.

Then how about this? Your being in Iceland was just a coincidence.

Part of Harry wanted to retreat into a corner of his mind where he could debate the absurdities of free will, but he knew Karen would block him.

"Try checking on Bernd Ghiberti's exact whereabouts when your cousin was murdered," he said. As an afterthought, he added, "And his mother's, as well."

Hannah Arnason slid her chair away from the cone of light and stood up, looming over him. Her movement stirred the odours of wood smoke and mildew and stale tobacco, mixed with the fresh winter scent of her body and his own salt-sweet smell from the strain of confinement.

The overhead lights flashed on. Evidently, the trial was over.

Sverdrup moved around into Harry's line of vision. He was squinting and fidgety, shuffling as if his feet were frozen, although several times over the past few hours he had stoked up the woodstove and the room was warm.

Harry tried to make eye contact but the man was nervous and glanced away. Hannah Arnason turned to look down at her cohort. She said something Harry couldn't make out and Sverdrup stiffened. She cast a fleeting look at Harry then back at Sverdrup, then retrieving her coat, she walked out into the night, closing the door behind her with a decisive thud.

Harry had the horrible feeling Sverdrup had been given the job of executioner. From the anguished look on his weasely face he wasn't too happy about it. Harry started to get up but Sverdrup pushed him back, catching him off balance. Harry was in no shape to fight.

The man leaned down close to Harry and whispered, "Horatio. My name is Horatio Sverdrup."

Nothing more.

The car outside coughed and turned over. The engine revved and then slowly faded until it was out of range.

Harry looked up into the other man's face, which still reminded him of a worn leather satchel, and Horatio Sverdrup had tears in his eyes.

Oh God, Harry, this doesn't look good.

Sverdrup reached into the depths of his coat pocket. Harry realized the man had never taken it off, even when the kitchen warmed to a comfortable temperature. He eyed his own coat on the peg by the door, doubting he'd ever wear it again.

Was Sverdrup digging around for a knife or a gun? Whatever, it seemed reluctant to leave the confines of his pocket.

Harry decided to flail out, try to take the man down. It would be a desperation move, since although the other man gave the appearance of being decrepit, he was not suffering from a possible concussion, or gouges cut into his wrist and a sprained arm, or fractured ribs and wounded toes. But as Harry began to ease his chair stealthily away from the table, ready to spring, Sverdrup's hand emerged with a jerk from his pocket.

Clutched in his fist was a squashed chocolate bar, furred at the edges of the torn wrapper with lint and whatever detritus had been nesting in the man's pocket. Triumphant, Sverdrup held his prize up and blew on it vigorously, under the misapprehension that it had now been sanitized. He then plunked it down on the table in front of Harry.

"You eat," he grunted.

"I'm not really hungry."

"You take it."

Harry's expression of bewilderment seemed to amuse the other man, who almost smiled.

"You will go away. Please, it is better."

Harry stood up tentatively. He placed the weird token of civility into his pocket, but lurched as he moved forward and had to grasp the edge of the table to stabilize.

"Please, Inspector Arnason, she has gone to Visby. She will ask questions about Mrs. Ghiberti, and about the blonde woman in the hotel courtyard, and about you. She will return in two hours, maybe not so long."

"Then, perhaps this will be over once she checks out my story."

"Yes," he responded with a doleful countenance. "When she comes back, she will kill you."

17 WINTER LANDSCAPE

HARRY TRUDGED THROUGH THE RUTS OF SNOW ALONG the laneway. He was surprised how far the farmhouse was set back from the main road. The wind had died in the stillness before dawn and the air was bitterly cold. The night sky was swathed by the magical brightness of a parhelion, formed by the refraction of moonlight through ice crystals high in the atmosphere. The snow glistened with a billion points of light, and Harry felt an unsettling happiness seep through before slipping away.

He was wearing Sverdrup's fur-lined hat over his toque and Sverdrup's thick sheepskin gloves over his own. The man had insisted he take them.

Sverdrup had practically pushed him out of the door, having tried to explain the situation in brief while Harry laced up his boots.

"You must understand," he said. "Inspector Arnason is very good police. It is in my honour to work by her. But she is not herself. That is a good expression, I think. Not herself, but she is not someone else. You need to know, please hurry, it is for her I want you to go, so she will not do some very bad thing."

Harry had risen to his feet and donned his heavy coat but stood resolute, making it clear he needed further clarification. Sverdrup shrugged, as if giving up something under duress.

"The dead girl on Sólheimajökull Glacier, you know, that was Inspector Hannah's half sister, yes." He paused to let Harry assimilate the implications. "They were very close, yes. The father was the same, but not the mother."

Harry was stunned. "Why didn't she say?"

"Because that is not how she is. She is great policeperson. Very unusual, yes, but in National Criminal Police she has good results, so that is okay. We are partners, yes. It is okay. You must hit me now, so I will bleed."

Harry understood.

He took a deep breath and punched the other man square in the face with enough force that he thought he could hear the cartilage in his nose crack. It was hard to separate hearing from feeling; his sense responses flowed together in the ongoing rush of adrenalin. Blood spurted from Sverdrup's nostrils as he staggered back against the table.

"Very good," the man sniffled. "Now you take these, and you go." He handed Harry his gloves and hat, then reached into a pocket and took out his wallet. After removing his police identification, he handed the wallet to Harry. There is money but do not use credit cards or we will find you too soon. You must go quickly now, away from Visby."

Harry reached out and grasped the man's hand.

"Thank you, Constable Horatio Sverdrup. You know I am innocent?"

Sverdrup turned and spat into the open door of the wood stove. "It does not matter."

AT THE HIGHWAY, Harry turned north, away from Visby. He had only the vaguest sense of Gotland geography but he knew there was a ferry to the island of Fårö at the far end, and he was certain that's where Bernd would be, taking sanctuary on Fårö with his maiden aunts, finding perverse redemption for killing his mother—he would have convinced himself that her death was a family obligation.

The family that slays together stays together.

Not if they're killing each other.

When Hannah finds out you're missing, there'll be hell to pay. She'll call in the Gotland Police.

I doubt it. If she suspects her shadow set me free and I think she will, despite the bloodied nose, she'll be pissed off but not inclined to go legit. She's a rogue cop; she likes it that way. And she'll know Sverdrup did it for her. They'll come after me on their own.

Either way, she wins. This is a vendetta, Harry. Whether Bernd kills you or she does, she'll have avenged her half sister—and at the same time enhanced her reputation as an eccentric cop. I wouldn't want to be in your boots, Harry.

He thought he could hear the sounds of her laughter drifting over the moonlit snow.

When he reached an intersection, he hunkered down at the side of the road, drawing his long sheepskin coat close around him, finding an odd comfort in the smoky emanations it gave off as he settled into its warmth. It was light when a bus came along. Harry clambered aboard, nearly frozen. He used Sverdrup's money to pay and settled back on a seat directly over a heater. When he woke up, they were at the ferry terminus.

He bought a ticket in the tiny kiosk and walked on board, but he didn't relax until the ferry pulled away from the wharf. He watched through the layers of ice on the cabin window as Gotland slipped from view and Fårö loomed in the offing. And then, once again, he felt an unsettling happiness.

A man in one of the small shops at the Fårö terminus agreed to drive Harry to the Sviar farm.

Harry wasn't trying to cover his tracks. The authorities would arrive and either he or Bernd would be charged with murder, or Hannah and her shadow would turn up, and Bernd's presence would protect him. He gazed out the car window. His head throbbed and he tried to focus on the scenery.

Fårö was flat and snow covered but not at all bleak. From Bergman movies, Harry had anticipated a featureless and forbidding landscape, with weatherworn trees, windblown grasses, and haunting old houses clinging to the rocky shoreline. It was all this, but they also passed cheerful roadside cafés, a few gift shops, and low-slung cottages here and there between pale farmhouses with bright painted doors, conjoined by an endless lacework of stone walls, some revealed only as ridges in the drifts and others blown clean. If churches and wind turbines dominated the little he had seen of Gotland, their absence characterized what he could see of Fårö. He was enthralled with the emptiness, possibly the way Bergman had been when he first came to the island sixty years ago. It was a place that invited him to pour out his soul, knowing it would never be fully depleted.

Although they had not said a word to each other for the entire forty minutes it took to drive the length of the island on snowy roads, when the driver pulled up at the Sviar farmhouse, he smiled, shook Harry's hand, and refused the offer of money.

Harry surveyed the weathered old house. Despite a steep tile roof and small gabled window on the second story, it hunkered stolidly into the landscape. The pale stucco walls and frameless mullioned windows gave it a ghostly appearance against the low foliage and snow-scaled fields. A turquoise door set over a low stoop was the only concession to joy.

Harry pushed through the gate in the stone wall. The walkway hadn't been shovelled since the last snowfall. There were echoes of footprints where snow had drifted into the depressions.

Before knocking at the door, he turned to gaze out over the open sea, which seemed wind-whipped into sullen submission, the waves choppy but small, with veils of blown spume sweeping away from their ragged crests. The clouds were sullen and low, threatening with squalls of driving sleet. It was breathtakingly beautiful, like a Blackwood etching, a vital blend of silvers and pewter grey, blue-black, and the infinite colours of white.

Between the sea and the house, beyond the wall and the road, a ramshackle wooden shed stood off to the side, perched among boulders on the shore. The shed was coated on its weather side with layers of ice from the spray of the sea beating against the rocks.

He wondered if the stone walls of Fårö were continuous segments of a single long and intricate thread stitched deliberately over the island, holding the land and the people together. Off in the distance, a towering lighthouse rose out of the whiteness, piercing the sullen grey sky like a needle. Was that where the stone walls converged?

As soon as he had clambered from the car into the morning cold, Harry had pulled the fur flaps of Sverdrup's hat down over his ears. He was effectively deaf, although his other senses had sorted themselves out over the last couple of hours. Images of his captivity seemed strangely a blur. He reached a gloved hand to his right temple. It was sore, but the throbbing ache had faded away. The pain in his arm had subsided to a tolerable level, and the excruciating tenderness of his toes had dispersed into the general mélange of discomfort.

As he stared out over the seascape, he became aware that stale warm odours of uncirculated air had begun to wrap around him from behind. His muscles tightened defensively as he turned to face an open door. Standing in the doorway was a diminutive blonde, a young woman with an upturned nose and pale blue eyes. Not what he had expected.

"Mr. Harry Lindstrom?" said the woman, and in those three words he could tell her English was nearly perfect. Of course, it was the girl in the courtyard, Birgitta's intended next victim, the blonde messenger who arranged for Birgitta's deadly assignation among the ruins of St. Clemens.

"Please come in." She surveyed the weather horizon. A storm was building offshore.

He stepped into the warmth. She took his sheepskin and Sverdrup's gloves and hat and arranged them on pegs on the hallway wall. He tucked his black toque and his own gloves into his coat pocket.

Sitting across the living room, side by side on a deeply stuffed sofa, two elderly ladies looked up from watching television and nodded in his direction. One was lean and severe, the other was portly. The lines on their faces had taken different directions as they had aged, but they had obviously originated in the same genetic pool.

Annie and Lenke, the maiden aunts, did not smile.

The young woman introduced Harry. They seemed to have been expecting him, or at least were not surprised by his visit. Annie, the thin one, looked vaguely interested. The heftier one seemed annoyed by the intrusion. They were both nibbling on biscuits and drinking tea. *Farmer Hulda's blandning* from *Kränku*, Harry imagined. They might have been Hulda's blood relatives.

"I am Skadi," the young woman explained, as she motioned Harry to follow her through to the kitchen. "Bernd told me you were coming."

Harry recalled there was no telephone in the farmhouse.

He stared into her eyes and saw his own distorted reflection in their bland cheerfulness. There was no indication she knew anything about Birgitta's death.

She poured Harry a cup of tea and slid a plate of dry biscuits across the table, taking one for herself. She did not offer him milk. Was it because she didn't take it herself? What on earth had Bernd told her, to make her so guileless? He sipped and smiled when she slurped. She was very young. If she was a student at the university in Visby as Bernd had suggested, she must be in her first year. She was quietly affable.

"When did you get here?" he asked.

"We came on the first ferry, this morning. It was still dark. You must have arrived on the next."

"Where is he now?"

"Bernd? At the Olafsson cottage. Our friends, Inge and Bjorn, he saw them in Stockholm and said he would drop in to check on winter-damage. I told him it was okay, I was there last week. But he insisted, so we stopped and I walked on by foot. It is not so far, just down the road. Then I made my aunties some tea."

Her aunties. She's family.

Harry noticed there was another cup and saucer set out, in expectation of Bernd's arrival.

Should he tell her Birgitta was murdered? Might the knowledge put her and her aunts in jeopardy? He said nothing.

Bernd appeared in the kitchen doorway. They had not heard him come in and apparently his aunties had only nodded, the same way as they had greeted Harry.

Bernd was flushed from the cold but quite cheerful.

"Harry," he said, ignoring Skadi, "you look like hell."

"With good reason," said Harry. He offered nothing more. It was up to the other man to clarify the situation. Not because he had the power, but Harry felt comfortable, with witnesses present and his adversary out in the open where he could see him.

Bernd did not look like someone who only hours before had smashed in his mother's skull with a rock. If there had been any doubt in Harry's mind about this man's capacity for evil, it was dispelled by Bernd's preternatural composure. Harry was certain now of the possibility.

Circular argument, Harry.

"Perhaps we should talk," Harry suggested without urgency, trying not to alarm Skadi, but indicating they needed privacy.

"Yes, of course," said Bernd. "After you have rested. Skadi will show you the guest room. There's a new traveller's toilet kit on the dresser, courtesy of Air Iceland. You can shave, brush your teeth, wash up, and have a nap, then we'll talk."

"Very civilized," said Harry.

Skadi got up and walked over to Bernd, kissing him in a perfunctory way on both cheeks.

"You're cold," she said.

After Skadi led Harry to the room, he noticed the door locked on the inside. Wallpaper from the 1950s above thickly varnished wainscoting. Amateur oil paintings had been hung during the past few generations without deference to aesthetics, and several pieces of driftwood affixed to the walls cast skeletal shadows from the overhead light. The flesh-toned curtains looked like they hadn't been opened in years, but they were sufficiently sheer that a diffuse natural light filtered through, struggling vainly to enliven the pallor that spread out from the incandescent bulb in the ceiling fixture.

There was a cramped en suite bathroom.

Harry locked the door quietly, then performed his ablutions and collapsed on the bed. He could hear Skadi and Bernd talking in low voices in the kitchen. Neither had commented about the wound on the side of Harry's head nor inquired as to why he was there. The television mumbled to the aunts in the living room and Harry fell into a restless sleep.

ACCORDING TO THE old man what made the Anishnabe so good for a family trip was, paradoxically, the rapids were too dangerous to shoot. There was a lovely swift current but a lot of big water crashing through gorges that you had no choice but to portage around. With proper respect, the river was safe and exciting, even this early in the season, and the terrifying beauty its violence had worked on the terrain was sublime—in Schopenhauer's sense, awesome and turbulent with the power to destroy.

"You'll have a straightforward paddle, the first three-four hours. You can't get lost, you know, it's all downhill." The old man chuckled at his own joke. "When you get to Roll-Away Rapids you keep hard right. Then real soon after that you cross to river-left and take the portage around Devil's Cauldron. You'll want your feet on the solid for that one. Hang on to your kids, so's they don't get too close to the edge. After that, it's flat-water all the way. If there's whitecaps on Long Pine, sit tight, there's a campsite just down from the falls. I'll come up by motor and get yez."

He described Roll-Away Rapids as a riffling on the surface and easy to run. Virgil knew the country so well he could not imagine misreading the signs, the vast slopes gathering into tumultuous crags, the twisting gorge, pines giving way to tenacious cedars on the battered shore. Virgil would decipher all this at a visceral level, knowing exactly where the rapids would be, even this early in the season when they were not really visible, so deep was the melt-water flooding.

18 THE SHED BY THE SEA

HARRY WOKE UP WITH A START FROM THE STABBING PAIN in his toes. As soon as it had his attention, the pain subsided. His thoughts shifted to a gut-wrenching ache in the pit of his stomach. He took a few deep breaths. His ribs hurt. He tried to relax, tried to erase tumultuous images of water. He thought he had been dreaming about his brother, about Bobby's drowning in Trois Rivières. He could hear rattling of dishes in the kitchen and the television still rumbled from the living room. It might have been a pleasant domestic scene, but for the causes of death that converged in this farmhouse on the edge of the world.

Harry the philosopher had earlier been considering the various implications of his predicament as an intellectual exercise. But when he woke up fully, he was in the suffocating grip of powerful, if jumbled, emotions. His gut responded to his being only a partition away from a serial killer sipping tea in the adjoining room, but even more because the congenial killer's mother had planned it that way.

Harry walked into the bathroom and splashed water on his face. He was still half asleep. The pipes shuddered when he turned off the taps. They knew he was up.

He glanced over at himself in the dresser mirror. He wasn't there. The brief sense of shock that ran through him set off an alarm. Just because the world doesn't make sense, that didn't mean he couldn't make sense of the world. He reached out and tilted the mirror downward and watched the ceiling swing back and his own image rise into view.

So, what was Birgitta's motive, getting you mired in the muck?

It's not like I haven't been trying to figure that out.

Getting bitchy won't help. You're not going to find answers in a mirror.

Only by proclaiming her guilt for murdering those girls and promising to kill another could she be sure I'd follow her back to the hotel.

And that is important why?

I'm not sure, but it is. I think she saw me watching her in the courtyard from my window.

When she was with Skadi.

Yeah.

Harry gazed into the depths of his eyes. It was the same as when he was a child, searching for his soul, for some revelation that would let him know who he was. He couldn't believe he was nothing more than a boy looking into a mirror. He had trouble now believing he was the man the boy had become.

Don't get maudlin, Harry. Stay focused.

Harry turned his back to the mirror. He waited for Karen to continue.

She was after your innocence, Harry.

Harry's lips formed a thin smile. He waited.

It's about innocence, Harry, not guilt.

Harry waited.

It's a powerful motive.

Innocence?

She had enough confidence in you to believe you'd fight, and fight fiercely, to prove your innocence. She knew, backed into a corner, you'd be driven to expose Bernd for the killer he is. At whatever the cost. She counted on that. And here you are.

Fiercely, eh. With my hosts rattling dishes in the next room.

You're not a guest, Harry. You're a prisoner.

Harry did not think he was fierce. He envisioned himself a gentle contemplative man.

We'll see about that. You'll do what it takes to get us out of here.

There was knock on the door, followed by Skadi's small voice inviting him to join them for lunch.

The table was set for three.

The aunties apparently ate in the living room in front of the TV. No phone but satellite television. They obviously wanted to limit communication to an inward flow. He wondered if they ever watched the news.

Harry and Bernd dug into healthy portions of cold lamb and boiled potatoes, sautéed in butter and garlic, garnished with a sprig of parsley. Skadi ate more modestly. Harry wondered where the food had come from? How far were they from a store that sold fresh produce? Driving out, he had been absorbed in the austere beauties of the Fårö landscape. And in suppressing pain from his head, his forearm, his wrist, and of course, his toes. Even parsley could help get his bearings. He needed to start paying attention.

He hadn't heard sounds of traffic, but vehicles move quietly on packed snow. There must be mail delivery. Not necessarily. There must be neighbours. There were only six hundred residents spread across the entire island. Tourists, not likely. Friends? Aunts Annie and Lenke, ensconced on their plush sofa, appeared to be socially self-sufficient.

Coffee was offered to finish things off.

They drank quietly. Harry tried to read the relationship between Bernd and Skadi, but it was impenetrable. They both seemed to belong there, but somehow not at the same time, not together.

Bernd appeared preoccupied but relaxed. Skadi was more distant, as if trying to hear voices from a long way off, and occasionally she permitted herself a small smile, as if the occasional message was getting through.

It was time to force things to a crisis.

"Bernd, your mother—"

"Not here," Bernd snapped. His dark eyes flashed a warning.

Skadi still didn't know Birgitta was dead!

Check.

Bernd did.

Check.

And Bernd knew that Harry knew.

Now that seems unlikely.

But he does.

Checkmate.

"Shall we go for a walk? I'd like to show you something." Bernd spoke with no suggestion of malevolence or panic in his voice, but with an underlying force that made it clear this was more than a social invitation.

No way, Harry. Stay where you have witnesses.

Harry glanced at Skadi and then looked at Bernd, who had risen to his feet.

If it's one to one, I can look after myself.

Tough guy, Bogie. I thought you were a gentle, contemplative man.

Fiercely, remember.

"Let's go, then," Harry said, also rising.

"Good," said Bernd. "We'll walk along the shoreline."

Bernd moved out through the living room into the hallway. Harry followed but had to stand back to allow the other man room. Aunt Annie glanced up with a look of recognition and immediately let her eyes wander back to the flickering screen. Aunt Lenke didn't look up.

Unexpectedly, Skadi appeared behind Harry and helped with his coat, both pairs of gloves, and his toque. It struck him that she had cast herself as his second in a duel that was about to take place. And yet her facial expression was neutral. He couldn't tell whether she was oblivious or just didn't care which of the two men survived.

Harry trudged in Bernd's footsteps, head down against the force of the onshore wind. Once they crossed the road, it was easier going, even though they were more exposed. The snow had blown clear in large patches of frozen shale, but drifted in the lee of the boulders like mounded shadows.

They made their way to the weather-beaten board and batten shed. An old fishing dory leaned up against it. Its bottom looked worn but sound. Patches of yellow paint were chipped away and the lapstrake planks were furred, but there were no cracks. It had clearly been displaced years ago from its rightful refuge inside the shelter. A couple of red plastic fuel containers were set into the dory's lea; a curious anomaly since there was no engine. A pair of old oars protruded from the shadowed space between the boat and the shed.

At the top of a low ice-glazed ramp on the seaward side, Bernd lifted a wooden bar from its slots and set it aside, then fiddled with a broken padlock holding the double-hung doors closed to the elements.

Harry hesitated for a moment, then followed Bernd inside.

He might clobber you from behind and kill you, Harry. Taking down a dangerous fugitive and eliminating his worst enemy, all at the same time.

Or he might simply want to know how much I know.

Harry sat stone-faced on a bench with his back to a wall while Bernd split some kindling and started a fire in the rusty pot-bellied stove. When he set down the axe, Harry was tempted to reach for it, but the other man was closer, and there could be an extremely bloody battle for possession. If the other man ignored him, then he would be stuck with an axe in his hands for no apparent reason.

The inside of the shed began to tremble like a gigantic ember from firelight seeping through the copious cracks and open seams in the cast iron. The walls were lined with cardboard boxes that had been slit open and tacked to the studs. Graphics and print at odd angles shimmered as the warmth from the stove displaced the cold. Both men took off their outer apparel.

There was no sign of fishing gear, apart from an ancient coil of rope, but there were tattered comic books on the plank floor and a few coverless copies of *Playboy* on a workbench that spanned the onshore side of the shed. The centrefolds appeared to be intact.

Harry could tell by the way Bernd settled so comfortably into the space that this had been his boyhood hangout.

Bernd sat on the bench opposite.

"Now we wait," he said, in a voice that seemed congenial and yet threatening.

"Interesting," Harry responded, looking the man straight in the eye.

"You know my mother is dead, of course."

"Apparently I killed her," said Harry.

"Yes, that is how it appears. That's how the inspector sees it."

"You've talked to Inspector Arnason?"

"In the early hours of the morning. She came to my hotel in Visby to tell me Birgitta had been murdered."

"And she told you I bashed in her skull?"

Harry thought he saw a tremor of emotion sweep across the man's face.

"Interesting, isn't it?" said Harry. "You warned me you would do it, you asked me to stop you. Was that just to keep me close to the action? You planned to frame me from the get-go."

A sliver of firelight glinted in the other man's eyes.

"No," Bernd said. "That was Birgitta's idea."

Harry leaned back against the cardboard wall and half-closed his eyes.

We were right, Harry. The brutal blow was kind. It seems they were in it together.

"You killed your mother with her consent. At her request, her insistence, perhaps. She left you no option."

Bernd looked down at the rough planks of the floor and the firelight fell from his eyes. His head bowed slightly, and his long nose cast a flickering shadow across his cheek that looked like the edge of a deep and bloodless wound.

The crackling of the fire against the din of the gusts hurling pellets of spray against the doors muffled but didn't erase the sounds of their heavy breathing.

"Perhaps she discovered she liked it," Bernd said.

"Killing?"

"Yes."

"But it horrified her?" Harry hoped for at least that much.

"She asked me to stop her. Once you have killed in cold blood, there are no moral imperatives left. It is difficult to resist doing it again."

"You know this."

"I know this."

He raised his head, and the light through the cracks in the cast iron glinted in his deep-set eyes.

"But killing your mother was different."

"You can love and fear and hate the same person." Bernd paused, as if taking stock.

She knew she was going to die, Harry. That's why the confessional revelations over dinner. Pleasure from the power of knowing what you, the pawn, couldn't see coming, what you didn't have the moves to prevent.

"You kept to the shadows," said Harry.

"She died painlessly."

"You slipped away."

"By moonlight. When Inspector Arnason showed up in the small hours, I was actually surprised to learn she thought you had done it. But it all fit. My mother was still in charge. She framed you for the murders she committed, so why not for her own execution? She knew that you would follow her into the ruins."

She saw you watching, Harry.

"Was Skadi a part of all this? How much did she know?"

"We told each other everything."

"Everything!"

"I'm sure we lied here and there. Out of love, not squeamishness."

"But you didn't tell her Birgitta was dead."

"I would have, eventually."

"When Inspector Arnason arrived at your hotel, were the Gotland Police with her?"

"She was on her own."

"And after she left, you picked up Skadi and came here. Why?"

"Why bring Skadi? Skadi lives with the aunties when she's not in Visby. Why come? To find you. And you came to find me. And here we are, in a fisherman's shed on the bleak and blessed coast of Fårö."

"Inspector Arnason told you I'd be on Fårö?"

For the briefest instant, Harry was skeptical. If Hannah Arnason knew where Harry would be, then his escape was a set-up. Hannah and Sverdrup had stage-managed the whole thing. Sverdrup took one on the nose to ensure authenticity, not to fool his boss but to fool Harry. And it worked.

Harry had headed north to confront Bernd Ghiberti, the serial killer. Bernd was their primary target. It was a calculated risk, given they seemed convinced by Birgitta's scheming that Harry had killed at least two young women, and the jury was out on which of the two men had caved in the back of Birgitta's head.

"You had to come, Harry, you had no choice. I'm the only person who can prove your innocence. You knew I had nowhere else to go."

"And I may be the only person able to prove your guilt."

"But I doubt that you can, Harry. It is your word against mine. And you were found with my mother's blood on your hands."

"Not literally. It was on Sverdrup's."

"Inspector Arnason's assistant. An unpleasant man, isn't he? Some people are innately unpleasant. It's a genetic trait."

"When you said we're waiting, are we waiting for Hannah Arnason?"

"The police, yes."

"But she will come without the police, Bernd. She is hell bent for vengeance and Sverdrup is her accomplice. It's just hard to say whether she's after you or me."

"Maybe both."

Bernd Ghiberti slouched on his bench, then straightened and sat back, leaning against the wall. The two men eyed each other warily.

The wind howled against the walls. At last the other man spoke, "I do not believe Hannah Arnason is an outlaw."

Virtue is where you find it, Harry.

"She's certainly a renegade," Harry said. "And highly motivated. She wants revenge. You murdered her sister, the young woman in Iceland last August. You dropped her down a ravine and the girl died an ungodly miserable lonely death."

"Arnason's sister! I didn't know. But you'll get blamed for that one, too, Harry. I know you were in Iceland last summer, as well as in Toronto and Stockholm when the murders occurred. If you die, I am exonerated."

A heavy price to pay to prove a guilty man innocent, Harry.

"So you have a moral obligation to kill me," Bernd declared.

"So it seems."

"I wonder if Birgitta knew you were such a righteous man? She must have, to play you so well."

"Righteous, perhaps; not self-righteous, I hope."

"All good works are self-righteous, Harry. And my mother counted on you being a good man. Myself, I also have a capacity for good."

Also, Harry!

"My project in Africa is to honour my sisters. A form of self-righteousness, I accept that. I have never done harm in Africa."

"Ah," said Harry. "*Noblesse oblige.*"

"If I die, you will never establish your innocence."

"And if you live?"

"You will never establish your innocence."

The sides of the pot-bellied stove glowed molten red. The air had become stifling, both men were sweating, the wind howled against the board and batten siding, and the old shed shuddered on its meagre foundation.

Harry knew he had nowhere to go. If he was not literally a prisoner of the man across from him in the shed, he was certainly a captive of the windswept landscape, the sparse population, and the pitiless weather.

He could understand Bernd wanting to bring him to the shed. Whatever was going down between them, it had nothing to do with the aunts. Or with Skadi. It was a place where Bernd was comfortable, a refuge in childhood, a secluded retreat, and a sanctuary, now, from the insults assailing him, thrown up by his sadistic mother and a collapsing world.

Harry was reluctant to break the silence. Taken out of context, this was a companionable interlude. If he had been expected to rage against Bernd, it wasn't going to happen. Hannah Arnason had hoped to unleash a fury that would flush the serial killer into the open. Why else set up Harry's escape? Birgitta Ghiberti had been motivated by exactly the same desire: force Harry to expose Bernd in order to establish his own innocence. She wanted Bernd caught, no matter what the cost. Birgitta wasn't trying to protect her son but to stop him from killing again.

What if Bernd did the last three, as well? What if Birgitta didn't murder those girls? And you didn't, we're fairly certain of that.

His mind was swirling in a galaxy of possibilities.

Birgitta had described the lacquered jewel box? She had seen the ceramic fruit on his coffee table. From where she had been sitting on the blue sofa, she had had a vantage through his bedroom door; she could have seen the box during their interview. She didn't necessarily take anything from it, and she wasn't necessarily the intruder who locked him out on the balcony. It could have been Bernd, after all. She knew the wedding band had been found with the frozen body in the Haga Park. This only proved that she and her son had been in contact since the murders. And she knew about the Möbius scarf in Toronto!

If she had killed no one, why would she arrange her own execution?

When his mind had been shattered by emotion after the accident, Harry had fallen apart. Too much thought and he was like a dry stick in the wind, too much feeling and he was threatened with perpetual grief. It wasn't always easy being Harry. But when a logical challenge presented itself, brought sharply into focus by danger, the fusion of battered intellect and charged emotion was a lovely distraction. He was almost happy.

Bernd Ghiberti stood up and paced. There were no windows and no lights, except for the dancing strands of fiery illumination from the blaze in the pot-bellied stove. The double doors rattled in the wind. Harry watched the man closely, wondering if he shouldn't take the initiative. The axe was within reach. If he picked it up, there was no turning back. He might be able to stop Bernd from killing again, something the police and Bernd's mother were unable to do, by driving an axe through his skull. Hannah Arnason had virtually sanctioned such extreme action.

Not your style, Harry.

He glanced at Bernd who was looming over him. The axe was within his reach, as well. He addressed Karen: not my style, either, to be crushed by a psychopath in the blink of an eye.

Don't blink.

Harry thought about that, then addressed his adversary in a conspiratorial whisper, "They won't be in a hurry, you know. No one's going to be here anytime soon."

Bernd looked at him quizzically. Harry improbably patted the space on the bench beside him. Instead, the other man pulled up an empty crate and settled onto it at an angle, so they both were washed in a sheen of firelight.

It was time to talk.

"Why did you bring me here?" Harry asked. "You said you had something to show me."

"Only this place."

"Really."

"It is the one place in the world I feel safe. I wanted you to see it."

That was a startling admission, apparently for both of them. Harry tried not to show his surprise but Bernd Ghiberti seemed thrown by what he had said. He rose abruptly, on the pretense of checking that the doors were securely shut. He gave them a good shake, then returned to his crate.

"It seems to have fallen on you to be my witness, Harry."

"To what?"

"My life."

Harry waited.

"When I was small, we came here on short visits to see the aunts, all of us, except my father. My sisters Giovanna and Isabella and Sigrid, my mother, and myself. And Skadi. We were a family. After Sigrid died I was sent here every summer for two or three months."

Harry gave him time to gather his emotions, then asked, "Skadi? She couldn't have been here back then?"

Bernd seemed to have been caught off guard. Harry could tell he was taking a brief tour through his storehouse of memories, trying to arrange them in a logical sequence. Bernd circumvented Harry's question.

"Skadi and I played together, sometimes we did puzzles. I taught her chess but she would usually beat me. She didn't like that so we stopped. She never came here, to my shed, though. This was my private place. She had her own up the road."

"Bernd, she's far too young. She's a student."

"She is completing her PhD in Nordic studies. Her doctorate."

Harry was incredulous.

"She is twenty-eight," said Bernd.

"Skadi?"

As a great judge of women, Harry, you are quite inconsistent.

Harry struggled to process the new information about Skadi. Could there be any significance beyond an adjustment to accommodate a shift in his perception of the empirical world?

Don't be pompous, Harry.

I'm not, he responded, pompously.

"How is she related? Is she a Sviar?" he asked out loud.

Bernd looked at him and said nothing, and in that instant Harry knew.

Skadi appeared young because her complexion was pallid and her features bland. Her blue eyes were pale, her nose slightly upturned in the Scandinavian way, and her hair was the colour of lemons. Her smile was kind and gentle and knowing. She might have been an adolescent Ingrid

Bergman. Or the actress at thirty, but out of focus.

"She's your sister, isn't she?"

Bernd nodded assent with forbearance, suggesting it wasn't something either to be ashamed of or talked about. It was just what it was.

"What's her special interest?" asked Harry. With his residual set of mind as an academic, it was more important for Harry to situate Skadi in an intellectual world than to sort out her parentage or the strange circumstances of her isolation.

Bernd Ghiberti took a moment to comprehend the question, then shrugged as he answered. He too was an academic.

"Her dissertation is on the correlation in Nordic countries between aesthetic expression and the conditions of winter."

"Winter?"

"Perpetual darkness, bitter cold, social isolation."

"What about robust constitutions, warm fires, congenial dispositions?"

"All that, and more. She looks at the bright flowers in embroidery, sleek design in furniture, violence and vengeance in the sagas."

"An expansive project."

"An important project. She's been working on it for years. She travels, does research, writes. She's made a couple of forays to Greece and Italy for comparative purposes. Once recently to Canada. But, mostly, she works closer to home. She speaks the Scandinavian languages, Suomi, and Icelandic. She is in some ways a simple soul. She supports herself as a clerk in a shop, or spends her time with our aunties. Eventually, she'll reach an end."

"You're very fond of her?" His own observation puzzled Harry, since Bernd and Skadi had seemed to occupy different dimensions when they were in the kitchen together. He hadn't detected animosity, but there had been no affection, either. The kiss on both cheeks in the French manner didn't count.

Bernd responded with a slight scowl. Harry tried another tack, again voicing his question as a statement of fact: "She was very close to your mother."

Bernd seemed to equivocate for a moment, then answered, "They were close."

"And Skadi shares your mother's ambivalence about you?"

"That is a tactful way of putting it, yes: my mother's *ambivalence*."

"You must have been about five when she was born, right? But not in Canada, I assume."

Bernd seemed relieved by the possibility of candour. "My parents separated after Giovanna died. Three summers before that, my mother was on Fårö for a few weeks. It was kind of a retreat, she explained. She came back again for a long visit the next winter."

"Birgitta had a summer affair, then returned to have her baby." Since Bernd did not demur, Harry went on, "Who was the father?"

"I don't know."

"I find that hard to believe."

"My interests are focused on the dead, not the living. I don't really care who he was."

"Does Skadi know?"

"We never talked about it. Skadi was here when we visited in the summer of '83. We were all our mother's children on Fårö. I thought Skadi was the lucky one, staying with Aunt Annie and Aunt Lenke. After Sigrid died, I came every summer on my own. My mother would visit, occasionally, but we seldom saw her. She had friends on the island."

Obviously.

"Skadi is her mother's daughter. She's named after Scandinavia, the goddess of winter and the hunt."

Bernd got up and stoked the fire. Blazing light flashed out from the roiled embers and broke into streaks across the cardboard tacked to the walls, as if the two men were trapped in a fiery inferno. Bernd left the iron door open while he picked up the axe and split more lengths of wood, which he stuffed into the flames. Then he closed the door, turned to address Harry, thought better of it, and returned to his crate, where he sat, leaning forward. The dry sweet smell of wood smoke filled the space between them.

Harry waited. What Bernd was going to tell him would be important to their mutual understanding, perhaps to their mutual survival.

"I don't remember my sister Giovanna until she was dead."

Bernd spoke in the way people do when they're beginning a lengthy narrative. He took in a few deep breaths, as if he might run out of air. His enunciation was deliberate but his words flowed together. His eyes were fixed on the eyes of his listener. Opposite each other in the smoky, fire-flecked shanty, Harry was doubly a captive.

19 A STORY RE-TOLD

"THE DEATHS OF MY SISTERS BECAME A SINGLE EVENT IN my mother's mind, Harry, episodes in a story about me. You, the police, whomever she talked to, you don't understand me at all. I see myself through a glass darkly. You see only reflections in the glass of yourselves."

"'But face to face we shall know each other.'"

"First Corinthians. A bit distorted, I believe. But no, I was thinking of Bergman's film where the protagonist comes face to face with God."

"She was schizophrenic."

"Yes. And I am neither the creator nor the protagonist. In *my story*, as we are calling it, there are three stories, a trinity of sorts, and I am fifth business in all three, an engaged observer despite what you and your Toronto detectives have divined from my mother's account."

Harry could see in his eyes, hear in the timbre of his voice, that gathering memories were taking inexorable shape in Bernd's troubled soul, as if he had told himself so many versions he was desperate this time to get it right.

You don't believe in souls, Harry.

"When Giovanna drowned, I watched," Bernd continued. "When Isabella died, I survived. When Sigrid tumbled into an open grave," he paused. "I walked away. I was the common factor in each death. This is not solipsism, Harry. The only thing known for sure was my presence. This to my mother was the cumulative proof of my guilt."

Harry listened to the muffled sounds of the wind and the sea, to the crackling of the fire in the pot-bellied stove, to the laboured sounds of their breathing.

Some of his tension eased when Bernd began talking again.

"The summer I turned seven, that's where the story begins. That's when the rituals of summer ended. Everything changed.

"Giovanna and Isabella used to sleep in the loft over the boathouse. Sigrid and I slept up in the cottage with our parents and the *au pair*. We missed out on the morning swims but saunas at night were a family affair. Even Vittorio would join us. I used to imagine the *au pair* was envious and homesick when she watched, but she would have been too shy to join in, had we asked.

"On June twenty-first, 1985, I wandered down to the boathouse early in the morning while the mist was still rising off the water. My older sisters rushed by. Both dropped their towels and waded, bare-naked, up to their knees. I watched. I was sad. It was probably that summer I first became aware I was not like them. I ached to be included in their circle of open affection, the way even Sigrid was, who was less than two years older than me. But the circle had closed, and I was a boy, on the outside. When our father came on the weekends, I was even more on my own.

"Their splashing in the shallows made me desperately need to pee. I didn't want to leave. I pinched myself through my Christopher Robin pyjamas. I had to go badly, but if I released my grip I'd have an accident. It's still very vivid in my mind, Harry. I stood resolute like a toy soldier, and very confused.

"Isabella thrashed through the water toward the boathouse where I was standing by the upturned canoe. She threatened to soak me. She knew what I was doing. She knew I'd wet my pants if I tried to retreat.

"Giovanna yelled, 'Leave him alone.' She stood tall and her breasts seemed to float on sunlight reflected from the water splashing around her legs. Isabella slapped the water in my direction. I let go of myself. A sudden warm stain spread across the front of my pyjamas.

"Giovanna whooped and dived toward the deep water, surfaced and swam away from the scene of my humiliation. Trying to choke back the laughter, she must have inhaled a mouthful. She doubled over and turned back for shore. She sputtered for air. She screamed. A surge of water flooded her mouth, convulsed her throat, and her lungs spasmed as the warm thought of her small brother filled her with love and she slowly spiralled to the sandy bottom."

"How can you know what she thought?"

"When you think enough about something, the details become real."

Harry regretted interrupting. He rose to his feet, stooped and picked up the axe. Bernd gazed at the throbbing red of the pot-bellied stove that reflected in the sheen on his face. Harry shuffled through the mottled light toward the double door. He stopped and swung the axe hard into the chopping block, sending spasms of pain across his shoulders and down his arms. When he tried to wrench the blade free, it had sunk so deeply into the wood it refused to yield. Fine. He left the axe there. He tried to open the doors for more air. They resisted from the force of the wind.

Sit down and listen, Harry. The most important thing on his mind is to have you hear his story.

Why?

That troubled him. The apparent urgency, the reliance on hearsay, on Bernd's need to rework the facts unaccountably made him feel claustrophobic. He edged his way back to his bench, feeling winded as he sat down. Still staring at the stove, Bernd began talking again.

"I stared at my dead sister lying on the dock. She was strong and kind and clever, and I couldn't understand why she refused to rise up and make me feel better. I remember standing transfixed with my hands clasped in front of me to hide my shame, and I clearly recall my eyes drifting from her long toes up her legs, past the golden pubic hair, her trembling stomach, her breasts distended under the *au pair's* pounding fist doing CPR, and along her elegant neck tilted back so my mother could blow air into her lungs, finally to her limpid blonde hair spread across the grey cedar planks.

"This is what is important, Harry. She was more beautiful at that moment than anything in the world. Beauty and horror merged in my mind, forever inseparable. Beauty and horror…" His voice trailed off.

"Bernd?"

"Sorry. So there I was. Seven years old. Gaping in pissy pyjamas at my dead sister, Giovanna. I turned away. I needed to change before anyone noticed."

"What about Isabella?"

"Oh, she noticed but she wouldn't tell. That would have implicated her in the crime. Or perhaps she had already forgotten. She had a sister to grieve, sorrow to wash her memories away."

Yet sorrow made his own memories more vivid, Harry thought. "Why is it so important to tell me this?" he asked.

"I used the word 'crime' just now. In my mother's story, there was one crime in which three girls died."

His crime was being there, Harry. For God's sake, he was seven.

Or was it for becoming aroused, Harry thought to himself, to Karen. Check out Freud on juvenile depravity.

Fuck Freud.

Death has not made you genteel, he silently countered.

"Are you comfortable talking about sex, Harry?"

No, he isn't, not always. About intimacy, yes. About the mechanics, not so much.

"That depends," Harry answered, a little nonplussed by the awkward segue. "Are you?"

Bernd smiled. "I am a Swedish-Canadian. I can be quite open about such things. There is a saying, you know: 'Never trust a Swede who avoids talking about sex.'"

"And never trust a Canadian who talks about it." Harry suspected Bernd's aphorism was no more authentic than his.

He wondered if Bernd was trying to alert him to the importance of what he was about to say or just the opposite, to play down its significance?

"Despite my mother's strange allegations, I only became aware of sex as a personal experience around the age of ten. Sadly, the good feelings I discovered were undermined by haunting shame, a sense of transgression that had been instilled so deeply it seemed innate. I avoided touching my penis when I peed, standing against the toilet to drip dry rather than giving it a good shake. I refrained from soaping my penis when I bathed. I thought of it as *it*, with a will of its own. *It* was capable of rearing up on a vibrating bus or in school when I was called to the board or while reading a comic strip where voluptuous pen-strokes teased my imagination. I had become the 'little man of the family' and was mortified that a rogue erection might betray my unsuitability for the role. It was all very awkward.

"Then early in the autumn of my eleventh year, alone in my room, trying to think of nothing at all, I had an orgasm. Do you remember your first, Harry? Surely, every man remembers his first. It was the greatest, most frightening, and terrible feeling I had ever experienced. After a week to recover, I tried it again, and thereafter managed once a day. I associated the explosive ecstasy with guilt more than shame. Guilt, I understood. Guilt was what held our family together.

"Four days before Christmas, I was sprawled on my bed in the middle of the day, singing to the ceiling. *O Tannenbaum*, I think it was. Of course it was. I remember perfectly. I was quite precocious, you know. I knew the words in German. *Wie treu sind deine Blätter ... O Tannenbaum ... Du grünst nicht nur zur Sommerzeit ... Nein, auch im Winter, wenn es schneit.* By the last stanza I was caught up in the conflicting imagery of tree branches still green after being cut down in the dead of winter, aflame with candlelight in the stifling warmth. The lyrics were highly arousing."

It's not the most sensual song I can think of!
You were never a ten-year-old boy.

"Isabella and her friend," Bernd continued. "Rose Ahluwalia, they flounced past my open door on their way upstairs to Issie's room. Before long, the pulsing music of Rush descended from above. I followed the mounting crescendo up to the third floor on a devious project, fraught with the possibility of humiliation, but filled with the promise of unspeakable excitement. I crept through the back of a closet in the hall, the child in me playing out the plot of *The Lion, the Witch, and the Wardrobe,* the adolescent envisioning images from the stolen issue of *Playboy* hidden under my mattress.

"By the time I reached the back of Isabella's closet and could peer through into her room, I was desperately trying to stifle the laboured sounds of my breathing. Asphyxia and euphoria together as I watched them dance. Provocatively. Childishly. Giggling and swooning. Smoking furiously as they stripped and dressed up. At one point I gasped. The music stopped. I drew in a deep slow breath. The music started again. If they knew I was there, they didn't let on. My attention shifted from Rose to Isabella. I was confused. My sister in her underwear, silky and gleaming like a moonlit night. Isabella shimmying, Isabella dropping her bra and gyrating as she put on another that squashed her breasts upwards, Isabella laughing. It belonged to her dead sister, she announced theatrically. Isabella crying. Tears and laughter together. Rose, no longer a player. After a while, Rose put on her own clothes and left."

Bernd stood up and stoked the fire. The flames blazed molten on his face. He turned away and tried to wrench the axe free from the chopping block. The handle broke, leaving him clutching the shaft like an artifact from the distant past. Bracing the handle between two split logs, he stamped on it. The first time his leg recoiled. He winced and did it again. The shaft broke. He stuffed both pieces into the stove and sat down, grimacing, as Harry supposed, with pained satisfaction.

"Well then," he said. "That was a moment chock full of meaning."

Harry addressed Karen. "Meaning what? Symbolism is your department."

I have no idea. That's probably the point. A broken axe? It means what you will. Or nothing at all. A diversion, a distraction to obscure the sexual intensity.

Or to relieve it, Harry thought, as Bernd continued.

"I watched as my sister collapsed on the floor in front of me and wept softly against her arm. My entire body shook with a sense of violation inseparable from arousal. She lifted her head, rolled sideways to retrieve a cigarette from a pack on the bed, lit it, and sank down in front of me again, softly caressing herself, her whole body, her breasts, between her legs, her long neck, as smoke circled in soft clouds around her.

"I exploded. I lurched in surprise, quivered from head to toe. I pushed sharply away from the back of the cupboard, forcing the copper-pipe lever behind me to the side. I leaned forward. Isabella's face was contorted with pleasure and yet eerily serene. Frightened, confused, I scrambled toward the empty closet where I had entered. I was overtaken by the unfamiliar sulphuric smell of Easter eggs gone rancid.

"Emerging into the hallway, I descended the stairs to my own room. Strains of a Beatles tune drifted down, I couldn't be sure which it was.

"After the explosion and the fire, after Christmas and the funeral, I struggled to assimilate what had happened. Christmas, of course, had been ruined. Water damage destroyed most of the presents and the few that survived the flames and the frozen water from the fire hoses were thrown out when contractors moved in and cleared the wreckage. Isabella's urn at the funeral was nearly empty.

"Rose Ahluwalia attended the service on Boxing Day with her family. When she bent close to whisper her sympathies, I thought I could feel a breast pressing against my arm. I imagined it was covered in sky blue satin."

Harry peered at the speaker through the shimmering gloom. Sweat streaked Bernd's face, distorting the lines and contours. It was almost as if he were wearing a mask.

"The point is," said Bernd. He stopped abruptly, as if the point were obvious.

Shadenfreude, Harry. Pleasure from another's misfortune.

In spite of another's misfortune, Harry responded. The sensuality of shame. The fusion of sexuality and death.

"Fire marshals determined the gas valve had been forced open. It was clear what had happened. They didn't name me as a voyeur. I was ten and there was no proof. My mother was cautioned to keep an eye on me. Which she did. Assiduously. And to take me for therapy, which she didn't."

Harry?

I hear you.

He's using you, Harry.

He needs to connect. He's connecting.

To atone for his sins. You know your Bible, Harry. Sins are transferred to a goat who is then cast into the desert. You're the goat.

Isn't there a Nordic equivalent?

Possibly it's him. He's his mother's scapegoat. You don't want to be his. Remember, for scapegoats to be effective, they die.

Harry shook his head and moved into the flashing shadows between the stove and the workbench. He grasped the edge of the bench and squeezed the worn wood until his fingers hurt. He took a few deep breaths from the swirling vortex of air near a crack in the boards.

Okay, Sailor. I'm back.

He returned to his place, which Bernd took as a signal to continue.

"What about Sigrid's death?" he asked.

"We're coming to that. It was another equinox, the spring this time. March 1991. It was the day my father's funeral got cancelled. I was almost fourteen and well-embarked on an introspective, aloof, and cheerless adolescence."

Those same traits in an adult make him seem interesting, self-reliant, and serious, yes?

"Actually, it was only the burial that got postponed because of heavy spring rains. The funeral itself went ahead on schedule and it provided me with a chance to observe my father's other family, which until then had been essentially a myth. I wasn't impressed.

"The service was in a cathedral. I had grown up Lutheran, despite Vittorio's occasional genuflections in the direction of Rome. In death, he was a Catholic. So, inevitably, we knew my mother would haul Sigrid and me off to celebrate a requiem mass for the repose of her despised former husband's pathetic soul, if only to annoy his widow with our piety. Birgitta enjoyed triumph and irony in equal portions.

"I actually enjoyed the funeral service. While I had serious doubts about the existence of God or an immortal soul, I'd come to believe in death as an object of supreme interest. This led, eventually, to my becoming a paleoanthropologist."

And possibly a serial killer.

"At this stage, my ongoing inquiries into God's being as well as my own were of the same high seriousness as the games of Dungeons and Dragons I played with Sigrid. Her room was next to mine. I often heard her chattering on her phone to friends, but she didn't go out much. The two of us hung around together, listening to music, talking inanely, sometimes just reading.

"In the evening after the church service, I was lying across my bed with my head hanging over the edge, staring at nothing. I could hear my sister in our shared bathroom and then only the sounds of the house. Suddenly, my dead sister Isabella walked into my line of vision. My God, Harry, can you imagine it? I leapt to my feet and whirled around. If it was a ghost, I wanted to see her for sure, before she faded or fled. But it was Sigrid, dressed absurdly in a Christmas outfit Isabella had worn only once. The black taffeta skirt hung a little limply on her adolescent hips and the full-sleeved white blouse accentuated the slightness of her figure. The red tartan sash gave her a carnivalesque appearance.

"'Where'd you get that stuff?' I demanded. The last time I'd seen those clothes they were splattered in cranberry smoothie. I'd made one as a surprise and tried to hand it to her over her shoulder from behind the sofa. I assumed the entire outfit had been shredded and burnt in the explosion the next day, but Sigrid explained Isabella had dumped it down the laundry chute, even the sash. After the fire, Birgitta sent it out to be cleaned. It was returned immaculate, free-of-charge, and stored in the bottom drawer of Sigrid's dresser.

"'You look silly,' I told her. I was irritated, as if she were violating my connection with Isabella.

"'I look gorgeous,' she said and then added, closing the discussion, 'The mass was nice.'

"'Yeah,' I said. 'Because we're Lutheran it seemed better than it was.'

"She sat on the edge of the bed and smoothed the taffeta skirt over her legs. She raised her legs straight and seemed to admire her ankles. Then suddenly she jumped to her feet.

"'Let's go for a walk!' she declared.

"'It's raining,' I said.

"'Not very much.'

"'Okay,' I said. 'Let's walk over to Pleasantview Cemetery. The grave is open.'

"'What do you mean, *open*?' she said.

"'They haven't filled it up yet.'

"'Of course not, Vittorio's not in it.'"

Empty graves give me the creeps, Harry.

Harry closed his eyes and massaged his temples. Was that Karen or was it him? He was haunted by the knowledge that her body had never been recovered. Her absence was gnawing, and persistent, like the pain of a phantom limb after amputation.

After dismemberment would be more appropriate.

He sat back and gazed into the fiery depths of Bernd's eyes. I'm debating with myself, he thought. Empty graves are both symbolic and actual, an image of death with no death in sight.

Bernd was clarifying his relationship with Sigrid. Harry noted his descriptions were more elaborate than in the earlier episodes. He recalled dialogue, he remembered what seemed extraneous details.

To you, maybe. Not to him. Don't forget, he's older with each death.

But the same age, retelling.

"We liked hanging around together," Bernd was saying. "As Birgitta grew increasingly distant, we learned to depend on each other. We were close in age and shared the same memories. That was an illusion, of course, but an illusion that bound us together in a hostile world. To Sigrid, Giovanna remained serene and ethereal and eternally still, lying beatific in an oak casket with her head on a satin cushion, surrounded by music and flowers. In my mind, she was beauty and horror, inextricably bound. Sigrid envisioned Isabella being forever a stunning young rebel, while in my mind the shattering of her body was inseparable from an explosive moment of ecstasy.

"So, we trudged through the bleak evening without speaking. A fine drizzle saturated the air. When we reached the cemetery, it spread out before us like a garden of the dead. The landscape had been shaped into small rolling hills with avenues of trees and clusters of shrubbery."

Bernd paused, then moved to eloquence by his memories, he continued.

"Looming out of the earth like so many clutching fingers, innumerable tombstones seemed luminescent, creating their own low-lustre sheen. It was eerie and strangely inviting.

"We moved through the gloom to the area where weeping or ascending angels were the dominant motif. Towering pines brushed against the soft wet breeze with whispering murmurs, and the occasional dormant oak grasped at the lowering sky. We kept a firm grip on each other until we arrived at the Ghiberti plot.

"A tarpaulin meant to protect our father's grave from the elements had slunk low under the weight of the rain pooled between supporting beams. When we stood close to the edge, a gust of wind rippled the water surface. We both gazed in the direction of our sisters' graves, where the tombstones were modest and stolid and death was reduced in its grandeur from the pathos of angels to terse notations of lifespans inscribed on flat faces of stone.

"Sigrid leaned into me for warmth. I leaned my head down and breathed the scent of my sister's warm damp hair. I was younger but in the past year had grown taller. She gazed up at me. I knew we were cast in the same eerie light of the wet city sky. It was like death had washed over us.

"Unnerved, I broke our embrace.

"Without a word, we set to work repairing our father's grave. We dragged the tarpaulin up and over the mounded earth. The pooled water slid off and splashed into the depths. The ends of the two beams plunged into the muck at the bottom. We hauled them this way and that to work them free, then together we dragged them out of the hole and leaned them across the tarp to hold it in place.

"I was sweating from the effort. She was chilled. I wrapped my arms around her and drew her deep into the warmth of my open coat. She shivered, and we rocked back and forth on the grave's edge. I could feel her thighs against mine and her breasts burning into my flesh. I felt myself becoming aroused.

"She leaned a little away and tilted her head up and with both hands drew my head toward hers until our lips touched and our breathing merged. I could feel my body rising against her as she pressed closer. The rocking stopped and a slow gyration of our bodies together filled us with overwhelming sensations of terror and lust."

Harry, he's doing it again. He's remembering his victim's memories as well as his own.

His victims, plural? You accept his mother's version?

And you accept his?

The facts support either.

Or neither. Listen.

"Our lips felt swollen and dry and, as we moistened them, our tongues touched and we drew in our breaths in unison, sucking the air and the moisture from each other's mouths."

"Bernd." Harry felt intrusive, an unhappy voyeur.

"She turned fully into me, Harry. The night sky whirled and the earth quivered and suddenly I exploded and soared and crashed against my trembling sister, and our shared encounter subsided into the tenderness of a long and innocent embrace.

"I remember I turned away shyly. She remained close by the grave. In a few moments, I knew we would settle back into our separate selves and this would never be talked about, not ever again. Our bond would be secret, its meaning impenetrable, and its strength enduring, for as long as we lived.

"As I walked away from my father's grave and away from my sister, I heard a gurgling splash, a roiling of muck, and then silence. She must have kicked a clod of earth into the grave, I thought. Glancing back, I couldn't distinguish her from the shadows. The sounds of whimpering drew me toward her, then made me stop. I wanted to hold her but I knew she needed more time. With sadness and joy, I turned and walked slowly toward home. She would catch up if she wanted.

"Walking out the gates and down the long street through the rain-drenched chill, I could not hear her fingers clawing at the frozen earth as she drew a suffocating slurry down on top of her in the bottom of the grave. I could not hear her final fleeting thoughts as her love flickered warmly and faded and everything ceased. I could not feel the beginning of loneliness that will stay with me until the moment I die."

20 **FIRE AND ICE**

WISPS OF SMOKE ESCAPING THROUGH CRACKS IN THE pot-bellied stove had accumulated into a grey vapour. Harry's eyes were watering. His nostrils were seared and his lips were parched. Harry inscribed the story in his mind, not exactly as Bernd had told it, but as he had received it. He recorded, edited, modified, clarified, and intercut with fragments of the earlier report to create from the raw materials of Bernd's confession a disturbing narrative that he felt to the quick.

He had listened attentively even when Bernd's mind wandered into the past and lost him there and he lapsed into moments of silence, trying to get his emotional bearings. Harry knew he had never before attempted or dared to put the deaths of his sisters into a coherent account. Nor had he ever revealed such intimate details, even to himself.

"So that's it, Harry," said the man opposite. "Should take me a lifetime of Our Fathers and Hail Marys." He stopped. "The last time I was in a church was for my father's requiem mass. Do you know the Lord's Prayer?"

"And my Hail Marys."

"You're not Catholic?"

"God, no. I was a philosopher. Had to know arcane chants and rituals. The history of ideas follows a giddy line."

"Give me a Hail Mary, Professor Lindstrom."

At first Harry thought Bernd was joking with an unlikely football allusion, but he was serious. Harry leaned back against the cardboard tacked to the wall behind him. The other man leaned forward. Harry began:

> Hail Mary, full of grace,
> The Lord is with Thee,
> Blessed art thou among women,
> Blessed is the fruit of Thy womb, Jesus.

It made him uneasy, reciting a prayer so laden with meaning that he found utterly meaningless. He had no doubt that God had fled from the world. He was less certain about the nature of his own presence in the world God left behind.

>Holy Mary, Mother of God,
>Pray for us sinners
>Now and in the hour of our death.
>Amen.

"Amen, yes. Thank you."

"Why?"

"Because you are my confessor, Harry."

Witness, perhaps, but confessor? Confession was supposed to lead to absolution.

Absolve yourself, Harry. Start closer to home.

Karen had slipped back into his mind.

I've never been away. I've been listening. The nuances are intriguing.

They are. The same story could provide a sound basis for deviant behaviour, shaping the pathology of a serial killer, or a horrific account of innocence lost, suffering and shame endured.

Harry had grown to like this man. Candour and pathos were conceivably instruments of a malevolent mind, but there was much in Bernd's narrative that he connected with. The man had offered a story of growing sexual awareness from childhood into adolescence not unlike the experience of most boys as they struggle toward maturity. But Bernd's journey was marked by crisis at every stage. Beauty and death were inextricably linked; pleasure and death were inseparable; the connection between affection and death was inexorable.

And from the sidelines, his mother tormented him with insidious accusations and taunting judgments. Perhaps Bernd had killed no one.

He admitted to killing his mother.

No, he just didn't deny it.

Too much sympathy, Harry. You're this guy's prisoner.

Harry wasn't sure about that.

The thickest smoke layer had expanded down from the rafters and was becoming unbearable.

"Bernd," he asked, "did you kill your mother?"

Bernd answered with what seemed almost a benign silence.

"Did you kill the Mexican girl?" Harry said. "Your *au pair*."

"No."

"Did you push Rose Ahluwalia from the bridge into the Don Valley."

"No."

Harry was inclined to believe him.

"Did you murder the Icelandic girl?"

"Which one? The girl in the maze or the girl in the crevasse?"

Harry grimaced. "Either of them?"

Bernd Ghiberti stood up and smoke swirled around him. He seemed to be listening to something. Harry heard it too. A scraping behind him and a banging on the wall outside. He felt a brief series of thumps against his back. The wind must have caught the yellow dory that had been upturned against the shed and sent it skidding away.

As Bernd began moving toward the double door at the seaward end of the shed, Harry heard a thud of wood on wood coming from outside. Bernd rattled the door. Someone had dropped the lock bar into the upright slots.

Harry remained seated. Bernd toured the interior perimeter of the shed, banging on walls that echoed with disheartening resilience. The chopping block had dried and he wrenched the broken axe free. He surveyed the interior again, then he flung the axe into a wall. The old boards were thick, dry, and weathered like iron. The rusted head of the axe careened through the thick air and landed at Harry's feet. Bernd dropped the broken handle onto the plank floor in disgust.

Harry opened the stove and using the broken axe handle he spread the embers out, but that only increased the smoke, so he pushed them all to the centre and they burnt in a fiery pile, forcing the heat to draw the smoke up the chimney.

Both men sat down where they had been, Harry on the bench, leaning against the exterior wall, and Bernd on the crate.

"Surprised?" said Harry.

"It must be Inspector Arnason and Constable Sverdrup. Which begs the question, why lock us in?"

"You mean 'invites the question.' Begs means beggars, it means to avoid the question."

For God's sake, Harry! This is no time for pedantry. Let's get out of this God-forsaken inferno.

But Harry was in no hurry.

"What about Skadi," he said. "Could it be her?"

"Locking us in? God, no. Why? It makes no sense."

Does anything ever make sense? When you get up too close, things fall apart. When you spin out too far in the widening gyre, things fall apart.

Shades of Yeats. Who's the pedant, now?

Harry wanted to use their incarceration to his best advantage. He said, "Let's suppose your mother set up her own execution."

"Yes."

"To make a case, not against me but against you!"

"Why would she do that?"

"She had already offered you up as a serial killer."

"Which I'm not, but go on. I'm listening."

"Let's suppose that's what she was doing. She needed more than circumstantial evidence. She offered herself as *habeas corpus*, in its original meaning—'the court shall have the body.' So, she invited Arnason and Sverdrup to witness her death. She used Skadi to lure you to the ruins of St. Clemens with murder in mind—"

"How could she be so sure I'd kill her, Harry?"

"That's something between you and your mother and Skadi that I haven't quite figured out. You were prepared to do it, though. You told me as much."

Bernd seemed more amused than apprehensive. Harry's explanation had too many gaps to be credible. He wiped away smoke from the corners of his eyes.

"Of course," Harry admitted, "she did her damnedest to push me into being implicated, as well. Insurance, I suppose. And here we are. The police have the corpse as material evidence."

"And Inspector Arnason has us."

"Or Skadi."

"I didn't tell Skadi that Birgitta is dead. And she wouldn't hurt me, Harry. You, maybe, but not me."

Bernd coughed on smoke inhalation, and his eyes watered until tears slid down his cheeks, gathering at the stubbled creases at the sides of his mouth.

"Bernd, did you kill Birgitta?"

The other man smiled enigmatically. "There's killing and there's killing."

"Yeah," said Harry. "And there's blaming and there's framing. If that is Hannah Arnason out there, she thinks she's locked up a killer."

"Perhaps. But which one of us, Harry?"

"Maybe she doesn't care."

"Faulty syllogism, Harry."

"Hers, not mine."

"If it isn't you, it must be me."

"Yeah," said Harry. He was distracted by the smell of gasoline. Both men sniffed the air and shock registered on their faces simultaneously. Together, they rushed to the leeward end of the shanty where the fumes were seeping through from outside.

"This is not good," said Harry. He placed the palm of his hand on the wall above the workbench and moved it around until he found a hot spot and recoiled. The cardboard turned a charred brown as they watched. Fissures began to form on the surface and then a few delicate flames popped up like tiny flares, and suddenly, with a whoosh, the entire wall burst into a sheet of fire.

They scrambled back to the far end of the shed, closest to the sea. The true horror of their situation registered in their eyes as Bernd turned to Harry and announced in a strained voice, "Angry litigants locked in a burning cage."

Is he quoting?

I think it's his way of summarizing, without confessing.

Death confers guilt on the guilty, honour on the innocent.

Thanks for that, but it doesn't help.

The two men dropped to their knees. Bernd choked, wheezing as he tried to replenish air expended from his last observation.

Harry struggled to think rationally. He looked around with mounting desperation. "If we both die," he said, as much to himself as to Bernd, "Hannah has avenged her sister. No matter which of us she thinks it is, the killer is dead."

He fell forward onto his hands, finding breathable air closer to the floor.

Bernd gasped, coughing and spitting, determined, like Harry, to remain rational to the end. These were men whose academic training had instilled in them the primacy of thought, above all, until the moment of death.

Harry, get us out of here.

Yeah.

Harry, when there's no retreat, you attack. We can do this.

Behind them were the barred doors made of thick boards. Harry crouched low and peered under the layers of swirling smoke that descended almost to floor level. The blaze roared gold and vermilion, licking the side walls in giant tongues of flame, like a monstrous beast of fire was about to consume them.

At the far end, he thought he saw shards of daylight above the workbench as it collapsed into fiery embers. It must have had generations of motor oil and paint soaked into the wood, and it burnt faster than the surrounding walls.

Suddenly, Harry stood up, grabbing both coats from the pegs by the door. He hauled Bernd to his feet. The other man staggered, Harry braced him, wrapped his coat around him, wrapped his own coat over their heads.

He shouted unintelligibly into Bernd's ear. They started to move. The other man stumbled and fell to the floor. Harry lifted him, struggled to hoist him over his shoulders in a fireman's carry, got him up, winced from the searing pain in his sprained forearm, choked, resisted coughing by holding his breath, grasped his coat which had slipped down to expose their heads, and lunged directly into the flames, leaning, almost falling, so their combined weight carried them forward. He scrambled to maintain momentum, and reaching the fiery wall over the workbench, he sprang upward and plunged directly into it. They crashed through the weakened wood and rolled out onto the snow. Coughing, gasping for air, deafened by the roar of the fire as the entire inside of the shed burst into an inferno from the influx of oxygen and flames shot through the roof where the onshore wind swept them into smokeless shreds of pure heat. Harry's bespoke sheepskin smouldered on the snow beside them.

Crawling away from their funeral pyre, hauling Bernd over rocks and snow, Harry reached a small haven formed by iced-over shrubbery where they were safe from the searing flames and protected from the lashing ice-laden wind. Sitting sprawled on the frozen ground and slouched against a boulder, cradling Bernd across his legs, Harry's mind was swarming with the physical sensation of being in the present moment. With no thoughts at all.

The stench of singed hair assailed his nostrils. His face felt like it was on fire, and he scooped up snow to cool the flames, but the snow was crystalline and lacerated his skin. Gently he held a handful of snow against Bernd's livid cheeks. They weren't blistered but he was peeling, so Harry assumed his were the same.

How much are we the same? he wondered, rocking the man gently, realizing he was thinking again.

You're not a killer, Harry.
I don't think he is, either.
He crushed his mother's skull with a rock from a church wall.
Is that different from other rocks?
Harry. You've survived an ordeal together. That doesn't make you alike.
In some people's eyes, I *am* a killer.
Don't you believe it! (She was thinking about the Devil's Cauldron.)
I don't, I don't. But I could be. Birgitta arranged the facts, didn't she?
Facts aren't truth, Harry. (Was she thinking about their current relationship?)
I'm glad we survived.
I'm glad too, Harry. I love you.
"I love you too," he mumbled into the wind-chilled air.

Bernd squirmed around, trying to sit up. Harry gave him a gentle push and he settled back against the gnarled trunk of an ancient shrub. Bernd squinted to bring Harry into focus.

"Harry," he mumbled, "You didn't say—"

"I love you? No."

"Thank you." Bernd's breathing was laboured.

"Once they find out we're alive, Hannah and her accomplice have no choice but to finish the job."

"It's us or them, Harry. We fight back."

Bernd and Harry as unlikely allies. Bernd started coughing and rolled across Harry's legs onto his stomach, retched, rolled back. And seemed to pass out.

Yup. Harry summoned his interior John Wayne. We'll fight 'em to the death, partner.

Harry, for God's sake. Your new best friend is a monster.

Right now, that's a good thing. I need a killer on my side.

Our side, Harry. I suppose the mark of a successful serial killer is he doesn't seem like a serial killer. But this guy is deadly.

He's likeable.

He's unconscious.

Harry reached up, trying to scrape a crisp fragment of skin from the bridge of his nose. His fingers were too numb for the job, and his face was burning, too tender to touch.

In Norse mythology, Midgard or Middle Earth was created from fire and ice. Harry felt like he was caught up in the moment of creation.

Movement along the shore caught his attention. At first he thought it was ground cover whipped up by the growing storm, working itself into a frenzy. A figure slowly came into focus, moving in their direction. She was pushing against the wind with her head tilted away from them, taking the force of the icy squalls full in the face. She stopped close to the fire, by the upturned yellow boat, and stared into the flames.

Beside her were two red fuel containers, one lying empty on its side, and what looked like an open box of signal flares.

The shanty shimmered against the sea. The roar had died to a whimper, punctuated by the slumping noise of burning boards as they crashed inward, sending up spirals of sparks that the wind swept away.

There was enough of the back wall standing that Harry could make out the unnatural gap where he and Bernd had burst through.

The woman gazed at the hole, then glanced down and noticed Harry's sheepskin coat. She picked it up and shook out the wisps of smoke. She suddenly turned in their direction as if she had had a revelation. When she pulled back the hood of her parka, he saw it wasn't the beautiful and treacherous Hannah Arnason. It was Skadi, standing perfectly still.

21 **ANGELS**

THE YOUNG WOMAN STOOD RESOLUTE. THE WIND BLEW her hair wildly forward into a luminous halo framing her face. In contrast, her bland features in the glare from a turbulent sky caught her stillness like a black and white photograph. She was beautiful, haunted, haunting, inscrutable. Ingrid Bergman. Birgitta Ghiberti. Angel of mercy, angel of death?

Harry stared at her, waiting to see which way her appearance would go when she stepped out of her freeze-frame posture.

Suddenly she scrambled toward them, her face filled with concern.

"My goodness," she exclaimed, speaking her perfect version of English. "Were you in there? Bernd, Professor Lindstrom!" She repeated their names several times, as if doing an inventory. "Come, we will get you into the house. Please, let me." She ran her bare hands tenderly over Bernd's injured face. He opened his eyes and squinted in recognition. She touched the back of one hand to Harry's cheek. "Come, please. We must go inside."

Why is she speaking English, Harry? It's an odd time for courtesy. And where'd the "professor" thing come from?

She wrapped their coats over their shoulders. With Bernd supported between the two of them, they made their way through the swirling snow to the house. When they got inside, the aunts looked up. Annie smiled briefly, Lenke nodded.

Skadi led them directly into the kitchen and tossed their coats out the back door onto the floor of a summer porch.

"They're scorched," she explained. "They smell. You smell, both of you." She directed Harry to a kitchen chair. "Sit down here, please." She guided Bernd to the settee against the wall by the back window. Harry got up and helped stretch him out. The man was conscious but passive, recovering from oxygen deprivation or in shock. He had been briefly coherent before Skadi arrived to help them but seemed to have collapsed into himself. His breathing was coarse but steady; his deeply creased eyes were open. He watched them but made no effort to communicate.

Skadi took a plastic tub of yoghurt from the refrigerator. Turning to Bernd, she dabbed yoghurt directly onto his face, over the grime of smoke and the peeling surface layers of skin. He winced but did not protest. Next, she applied her home remedy to Harry. The yoghurt felt cool. Then as he sat quietly watching her brew up a pot of coffee, it began to sting. That must be the therapeutic effect, he thought.

Who the hell ever heard of putting yoghurt on a burn? If it hurts, rinse it off. We need to work on our strategy, Harry.

He excused himself to go to the bathroom off the room he had been in before, with the familiar driftwood sculpture and several generations of amateur paintings on the walls. Bernd's room. And whose, before that? It was a room curiously free of gender or personality. Skadi's room must be on the second floor, with the small gabled window overlooking the sea.

He leaned across the sink and tamped handfuls of cool water onto his face until the drying yoghurt was washed away.

Standing straight, he squinted, trying to come to terms with the image of himself in the mirror. He looked like a stranger. His grey hair was seared at the front. He touched it and strands crumbled beneath his fingers. His eyes seemed darker under a furrowed brow that was scorched with livid streaks and his aquiline nose was creased with patches of peeling and exposed raw skin. His jaw, which he liked to think of as strong, was embedded with soot.

Not bad, Bogie. You find yourself quite handsome, don't you, battered and burnt? Whoever said, "Vanity, thy name is woman"?

Nobody, actually. Hamlet said, "*Frailty*, thy name is woman." He was talking about his mother.

An appropriate allusion in the present circumstances.

Birgitta was the polar opposite.

To Gertrude? Possibly.

If anything, she was Claudius. Murder is an instrument, not an end.

Think about that, Harry.

The way the ceiling light refracted from the mirror into his eyes and gleamed out from his reflection sent shivers racing down his spine. Karen was standing so close he could feel her breath on the back of his neck.

Murder is an instrument, not an end.

Sometimes and sometimes not. The deaths accumulating around the Ghibertis over the last decade could be divided that way. The serial killings that Birgitta researched and catalogued could have been ends in themselves. Death was the intended outcome fulfilling the desires of a psychopath, someone who functioned normally in the world because of the release available through murder. By contrast, Birgitta's death was instrumental. Barbaric as it was, it was meant to serve a purpose beyond itself.

Throwing the blame on you, Harry.

Possibly. Or Bernd.

What about the others?

The girls in Toronto and Hagaparken? Their deaths certainly weren't ends in themselves.

They were for the women who died, Harry. And all to blame you. That's a loathsome responsibility.

I wasn't being framed for murders committed; the murders were committed to frame me. Loathsome barely begins to cover it.

Harry shuddered and looked past his image in the mirror, into the bedroom behind him. To one side of the window there was a large picture he'd hardly noticed before because it was so much a romantic cliché. A castle with drawbridge down set on a small mountain in a dense forest under a vast blue sky. What drew his attention, now, were not the hackneyed graphics but the fact that it was an incredibly intricate jigsaw puzzle and someone had varnished and framed it. Someone determinedly proud of the work and indifferent to good taste or the judgment of others.

That last bit could describe your Inspector Arnason and her demonic familiar.

Harry nodded assent to himself in the mirror.

She's determined, Harry. When she turned up and nothing was resolved, she tried to cremate you alive. You had already got away from her once. She wasn't going to let it happen again.

Immolate, not cremate. I wasn't dead yet.

Have it your way. One way or another, she'd get her man. And where is she now?

Good question. Maybe she couldn't stand to hear the sizzling and popping of burning cadavers. Like Sam McGee, she didn't want to risk peering into the furnace roar. Her job was done. She packed up and went home.

She'll be back.

Harry walked out into the kitchen. For the briefest moment, he thought he saw Birgitta Ghiberti slouched elegantly over her coffee.

Skadi gazed up at him through a veil of long blonde hair and the illusion was reinforced. Yet when she sat back and shook her hair away from her face, she looked so young and bland and innocent, with her pale blue eyes and crinkled smile, the connection collapsed.

Before he sat down to savour the proffered coffee, Harry glanced over at Bernd lying inert on the settee. "So Skadi," he said, "when did Inspector Arnason get here?"

The young woman looked startled. It was as if Harry had asked her a question so unexpected she had to struggle to get her bearings before answering. "I sent her away. I'm sorry."

"Sorry? You couldn't have known."

"That I, that she—"

"Skadi, did she light the fire?" It had not occurred to Harry she hadn't. He had suspected Skadi of locking them in, but not of trying to burn them alive.

"She must have. Unless it was Constable Sverdrup."

"You know his name?"

"I asked to see their identification."

Really? That seemed uncharacteristically assertive. Bernd moved on the settee as if pain was rising from deep within, then subsided into silence, listening.

The wind raked against the shingles, and the rafters and joists groaned overhead. The windows rattled and the lights flickered. Skadi dug out some candles from a drawer but the power didn't go out.

"We're in the midst of a storm," Harry said, stating the obvious.

"Yes, we are," she answered cheerfully, apparently back on solid ground. "I love winter storms, don't you?"

Storms in southern Ontario were seldom raging. Violent weather in Toronto, from his snug vantage high over the harbour, was a spectator sport.

He could taste the salt in the sea-laden air seeping through the farmhouse imperfections, through little cracks in the ancient framing, creases in the mortar between stucco and stone, tiny gaps in the eaves. He could feel the entire building wrapped in a fury of snow and sleet. And he felt strangely comfortable.

Skadi did not seem at all perturbed. The aunts in the front room had turned up the volume to hear over the storm, the serial killer who had bashed in his mother's skull slept noisily on the settee, and Harry's principal adversary had departed with her accomplice, having failed in her efforts to burn him alive, although she probably didn't know that she'd failed. The coffee was good, and he detected no malevolence in the howling winter surrounding them.

Life was interesting, but their brief interlude of illusory innocence wouldn't last. He hoped Hannah Arnason would not make an appearance, but he needed to know where she was.

"Did Inspector Arnason say what she wanted?" He wondered if Skadi knew her mother was dead. Surely Hannah had told her. Could she have torched the shed in retribution? "Where did you say we were?"

"I didn't. I told her you had gone out. I didn't say where."

"Bernd's car is parked in front."

"I told her you'd gone for a walk."

"With a storm gathering offshore? Didn't that strike her as unlikely?"

"It didn't seem unlikely to me, so why her? You and my brother had things to attend to."

"What sort of things?"

"Why ask me, Professor Lindstrom? That was between you and my brother, things Bernd didn't want me to hear. You had secrets, so you went out. For a walk to the old boatshed, to the barn, to the Olafsson cottage."

She had become quite animated as she explained herself, gesturing with a sweep of her open hand across the front of the house to indicate their possible walk as the storm closed in. She pointed in the direction of the shed then to the small barn out back, which Harry could just make out in the gusting snow through the kitchen window over Bernd's settee, and then toward the east, in the direction of the ferry, to indicate their neighbour's deserted cottage.

"So she just left?"

"They both did. I don't think they wanted to get caught out by the weather."

"But you had quite a chat, didn't you?"

"Not really. Just at the door. We did not have a lot to chat about."

"Weren't you curious why she was here?"

"I am not a curious person, Professor Lindstrom."

She's writing a doctoral dissertation on aesthetic expression and the conditions of winter in Scandinavia, Harry.

Nordic, not Scandinavian. She includes Finland, Iceland, the Faroe Islands, possibly Greenland. With side trips to Italy, Greece, and Canada.

You're a pedant. She's curious.

Skadi seemed to connect with Harry as a *professor*. Just how much information had she exchanged with Arnason and Sverdrup?

"Were other police with them?" he asked. "Police from Gotland?"

"Why?"

"Were they alone?"

"Yes."

"Skadi."

"Yes?"

"Did you start the fire?"

"Which fire?"

"The shed."

"Yes."

The question was intuitive, the answer spontaneous. Skadi's reprieve had collapsed. Bernd groaned again.

Everything changed. Harry gazed into Skadi's eyes. Their eyes locked. She offered a beguiling smile but no further explanation. As if nothing had changed at all.

"More coffee?"

"No," said Harry. Her smile slowly collapsed into sadness as he watched. "No, thank you."

She fidgeted in her chair, got up, and went over to the settee. She pulled a blanket over Bernd, tucking it around his shoulders. He wrapped his arms around himself under the blanket. She returned to the table. She sat down, staring at the surface.

"Skadi." Harry spoke in a conciliatory voice. Almost conspiratorial. "You love your brother, don't you?"

"Yes." She stared at the dregs of her coffee, picked up the cup and swirled it. "Very much."

"You wanted to protect him, didn't you?"

Leading question, Harry. Let her speak for herself.

She's not exactly bubbling with candour.

"But you also wanted him to die, didn't you?"

She looked alarmed.

He realized his mistake. He amended his statement.

"You *needed* him to die. It was necessary. Something you had to do. You weren't trying to kill me. It was him."

She raised her eyes to his.

"No," she said, "I was not trying to kill you, Professor Lindstrom."

"I was collateral damage?"

"But you didn't die. Neither did Bernd. Everything is like it was."
No, not really.
"Skadi, tell me why you set the shed on fire."
"I was afraid that Bernd was in trouble."
"Was it something Inspector Arnason said? Skadi?"
"Yes."
"Did she tell you about your mother?"
"What about her?"

Bernd said he hadn't told her. They drove up from Visby together, and he didn't tell her their mother was dead, and certainly not that he'd killed her. Perhaps Hannah Arnason told her, assuming Hannah and her demonic familiar had been there at all.

She seems remarkably calm.

Remarkably.

Maybe Birgitta's death seemed justifiable, measured against the pitiless murders she'd committed, if she did them, and if Skadi knew.

Then why punish Bernd?

Bloodguilt, Harry.

She has to know about the other murders, the earlier ones as well.

And?

Maybe that's why she tried to kill Bernd.

To save him from himself.

She's a very strange girl.

Almost thirty, Harry. Hardly a girl, but strange, yes. There's a definite disconnect with reality.

"Skadi, you and I need to talk."

She smiled demurely, as if he had just asked her to dance.

"Of course, Professor. What shall we talk about?"

Innocence contrived in the face of depravity is not to be trusted, Harry.

With the storm howling outside, the day fading into afternoon twilight, and the smell of burnt human flesh vying in the air with the scent of coffee, there was no reason to expect this strange young woman across from him would not sprout fangs and cry havoc.

"Cry havoc," he muttered.

Harry, you're speaking out loud. Say something sensible.

Skadi stared at him, bewildered. The television had fallen silent.

"Cry havoc?" Skadi repeated in a loud voice. "What's that?"

"'Cry 'Havoc,' And let slip the dogs of war!'" declaimed Aunt Annie, who had appeared unnoticed in the kitchen doorway.

She rolled her head to indicate the rousing impact of the storm all around them. Aunt Lenke, who was as plump as Annie was slender, leaned close against her.

"*Julius Caesar*, Marc Antony," said the thin stooped woman in sonorous English, "For myself, for the dramatic expression of hopelessness, I prefer the Scottish play.

> Tomorrow, and tomorrow, and tomorrow,
> Creeps in this petty pace from day to day…"

She pulled away from her sister, who was helping her to maintain equilibrium.

> "Out, out, brief candle!
> Life's but a walking shadow, a poor player,
> That struts and frets upon the stage,
> And then is heard no more.

"And this is the best part," she declared, as if her own words were coming from the mouth of Macbeth, himself. "Listen, the words rise, they resonate, and then they collapse; the music falls.

> It is a tale
> Told by an idiot, full of sound and fury,
> Signifying nothing.

"Nothing, nothing, nothing, nothing. Amen. Good night, sweet children. Lenke and I are going in for our naps."

The two old ladies disappeared down the dark hallway, brushing noisily against the walls, and Harry heard first one door shut and lock and then another.

He looked at Skadi for a reaction, but Skadi seemed not to have noticed anything unusual.

22 FAMILY SECRETS

HARRY PEERED OVER AT BERND THROUGH THE GLOOM. THE barn out back had been displaced in the window by the reflection of the kitchen as the overhead light struggled to counter encroaching darkness. Bernd's eyes were wide open. His face registered a sort of startled disbelief, but he gazed at the ceiling and made no effort to speak.

When Harry looked back at Skadi, she had transformed. What had seemed a fey unawareness of her aunt's declamation had been the initial stages of shock. A shadow slowly descended over her face as an appearance of profound horror set in. She looked as if she had seen Banquo's ghost.

Harry observed her with as empty and open a mind as it was possible to sustain.

Skadi turned in her chair and said something to Bernd in Swedish. Surprisingly, Bernd answered.

She turned back to Harry.

"We did not know she speaks English," Skadi said in a plaintive voice.

This family never ceases to amaze me.

Harry addressed Skadi, "You've lived with her all your life. Bernd's known her all of his. She never spoke English before?"

"Not ever. Bernd and I used English in front of the aunts when we wanted to talk privately. It was our secret language." Her eyes darted around the room, trying to see invisible things. "My God, they know everything."

"Skadi, what do you mean, *everything*?"

"Our secrets."

She looked over at Bernd. He seemed to have lapsed into a comatose state.

"Skadi, have your aunts always been here on Fårö?"

"In this house, yes. Except during the war. Aunt Annie went away. She was an actress."

Of course she was. Harry calculated, if Annie were eighty-five now, give or take, she would have been in her late teens, early twenties.

"In Stockholm?" he asked.

"Helsingborg. They sometimes played to Nazis who came over the channel from Denmark, but mostly to Swedes. I knew they did Shakespeare. I always assumed in translation. She never, not ever, not once, told us she spoke English. Never."

"She played Lady Macbeth."

"She spied on us. All her life, she spied on us. On Birgitta, too. The three of us spoke English so the aunts wouldn't understand." Her face contorted like a portrait by Edvard Munch. "She knows all about us."

"Skadi, why do you think she waited until now? She could have gone to her grave without letting on."

She gazed at him helplessly, hopefully, as if he might penetrate the unfathomable. He tried:

"I imagine it reached a point early on, long before you were born, where it would have been far too compromising to admit that she understood. After years of being a voyeur, she couldn't suddenly appear naked herself. And yet, Skadi, she's done just that. She's stripped away the disguise. She knows. And Skadi, she wants *me* to know."

This isn't about you, Harry.

This time, it is!

"Skadi, Annie has been silent for sixty years. And now she's revealed herself. What is it she wants me to know? Tell me, what secrets?"

The young woman glowered at him. Her pale eyes were as cold as ice, her complexion was ashen, her lips were pulled into a grimace, and her teeth gleamed in the dull light. He thought of his previous allusion to fangs, but she looked less like the undead than the damned. A soul in torment.

"Tell me," he repeated. He reached across the table in what seemed a habitual gesture and took one of her hands in his. It was cold.

He waited.

Skadi's eyes seemed to focus on some invisible spectre between them. "She came home after the war."

"Your Aunt Annie?"

"Yes. She had a baby. Here, on Fårö. In this house."

Harry tilted his head, trying to draw Skadi's eyes back to his.

She spoke softly, "Her baby's father was a German officer. He and Annie were in love. At the end of the war, he was shot. In Denmark. Executed, perhaps. Unofficially. The baby was sent to Canada."

"To relatives?"

"Yes."

"Emigrants, anarchists from Lund."

"Yes. My mother was born Birgitta Sviar. She became Birgitta Shtoonk—they were refugees, they foolishly thought a Jewish name would gain them sympathy in Canada. I knew all this from when I was very small, but I did not know Aunt Annie spoke English. I wonder if Auntie Lenke does, too."

"She doesn't need to."

"Why would Annie betray us?"

"Was it betrayal? Can't you imagine it gave her a kind of magical power? She knew things that nobody imagined she knew. I think it was the only real power she had left in the world. It made her special."

"Lenke never went away; she's never been to Stockholm. She visited Visby a few times when she was younger."

"And the two of them shared secrets. That's how they survived, that's how they endured. Just like you and Bernd. Your secret lives kept them going."

"There really were no secrets, were there?"

"Did you ever talk to Annie about your mother?"

"No, but about her lover, yes. Bernd and I, when we were small and fearless, we asked her about him and she said, 'Ach, he was just a man. You expect a villain with horns or a hero who lived in a castle like Bernd's puzzle. He was killed in reprisal for his country's mistakes, and I came home to Fårö. It was not a time to keep souvenirs; we sent your mother away. That is all the story you need to know.' She was not angry with us, but we never asked her again."

"And your mother came back to visit and had you."

"Yes, when she grew up. She came back often."

"After she was married? Her own family were poor."

"Her adopting family called her their Aryan bastard. She was their little Nazi reject with perfect blonde hair and perfect blue eyes. They despised her for being perfect."

"Skadi, did you ever meet her parents?"

"The Shtoonks, no, never. When she was seventeen, she ran away."

"Did you ever meet your father?"

"My father? I don't know. If I did, it doesn't matter. I am a Sviar. We are an ancient family. My father is Sweden. That's what I liked to think when I was small. And it is true."

"How do you know so much about your mother?"

"Birgitta told me herself. We would sit on the boathouse ramp and watch the sunset at the end of each summer, and she would tell me her story. She would tell me how much she loved me and how much she wanted to keep me safe on Fårö. She said I would stay all my life with my aunties. She would rock me in her arms and tell me how special I was. Then, the next morning, she would leave."

"Why didn't she take you back to Toronto?"

Skadi looked puzzled.

"After she and Vittorio separated? Did you ever ask?"

Skadi shyly responded, "Birgitta told me I was like her. I did not belong in Canada."

"Was she ashamed of you?"

"Of course not! She wanted to protect me."

"From Bernd?"

"From things that could happen. As each of my sisters died, she treasured me more—those were her words, *she treasured me*. But I needed to stay here."

"For protection?"

The young woman paused to gather herself, then continued, "Every year, Bernd would come. Even after we were grownups, he came two and three times each winter and every summer. He spent more time with me than anyone else except my aunties. I remember Isabella and Sigrid quite well. Giovanna has always been a ghost. And when Birgitta came to visit us she was my mother, and she would tell me terrible things about Bernd in secret. This was the bond between us, that Bernd had murdered my sisters. It was our secret."

"And yet she sent him off to stay with you, alone."

"My aunties were here."

"But Birgitta wasn't."

"Sometimes she was. She believed I was in danger in Toronto, but here I was safe."

"Why?"

Skadi tilted her head in a fey gesture that might have been condescending or simply expressing disinterest. Either way, Harry felt the chill.

"Did you believe Bernd was a killer?"

"It didn't matter."

"Were you frightened?"

"No. I wasn't a Ghiberti."

Harry sucked in his breath.

"Is that why she thinks Bernd killed them, because they were their father's daughters?"

"It is hard to say. Birgitta was very definite in her opinions, but she was often obscure."

"Do you think she wanted them dead?"

"Oh, that is horrible. Of course not."

"And you and your mother were close."

"The three of us, yes."

"Including Bernd?"

"Birgitta was his mother. She was my mother. He is my brother. We loved Bernd. I love Bernd, now."

"But you tried to kill him."

Her face opened into a sweet and guileless smile. If she had felt any guilt for setting the fire, she had forgiven herself.

"You know about your mother's research?"

"About those dead girls? Yes."

"One or two, sometimes three a year, for the last ten years."

"Not so many, I think. But yes, I know about them. They died very peacefully. They fell asleep in the snow."

"Do you know who killed them?"

"Nobody killed them. They lay down in the arms of winter. They gave up their lives to the natural world. Imagine, imagine how gently they slipped away."

She might have been talking about a mythical cult, about death as a sacred rite of passage.

"Before they expire, you know, a warmth seeps through their bodies, and their minds are flooded with memories, and their souls turn into celestial music, which only the dead can hear. They are very happy."

"Bernd told you this?"

"I study such things. I travel for my research."

"Skadi, have you been to each place where these girls died?"

Her smile turned almost beatific and her eyes widened, and then her features buckled into a sullen mask. She stood and walked to the window, peering out into the storm.

"It's letting up." She spoke in a voice devoid of personality. It was as if she were trying to obliterate the cheerfully morbid young woman she had been only a few moments earlier.

Harry wasn't ready to move on but when he asked about why the dead girls were blonde she demurred. When he asked if she associated them in her mind with her sisters, the bland lustre for an instant left her eyes, but she recovered and smiled. When he asked if she were jealous of them, she responded, "Not after they were dead. Of course not. They were my sisters. I loved them. They were very pretty. My mother is pretty."

In Harry's perception, the storm had not abated.

The winds still beat against the house and wailed in the eaves. Snow caught by the light of the kitchen window streaked horizontally, obscuring the night in a swirl of reflected particles too frenzied for the eye to sort out from the blur.

He heard the click and rattle of a door opening down the hall.

Aunt Annie appeared in the kitchen doorway, framed in darkness but her face washed in the harsh illumination from the overhead light so that every crease and furrow looked like scratch marks on velvet.

The young woman and the old woman stared at each other, caught up in a moment of incomprehension. Then there was another click and rattle, followed by the shuffling sounds of another old woman making her way down the corridor. Aunt Lenke appeared in Annie's frail shadow, peering around her sister until the light caught her eyes.

Harry rose, even Bernd stirred on the settee, but the tension between Annie and Skadi sucked the air from the room and left the others suffocated and feeling extraneous. Skadi stood up and moved away from the table, arresting any gesture to get closer to the old woman. She wavered on the balls of her feet.

Harry, Karen whispered, *say nothing.*

But there was no risk of Harry intruding.

"Skadi, darling, I can't sleep," said Annie. She might have been Vanessa Redgrave. She was speaking in perfect stage English. "Skadi, it is over, now, dear."

"I'm sorry," said Skadi. She turned to Harry. She seemed to be recapitulating in her mind, working out where they were in her narrative.

Harry looked to Aunt Annie, but the old woman's watery eyes were fixed on her pretty, unworldly granddaughter.

"Skadi, tell Professor Lindstrom."

Harry turned back to face Skadi. The young woman looked into his eyes, searching.

What does she want, Harry. Absolution? Understanding?

Affection.

"Skadi," he said, reaching out and guiding her back to a chair. The aunts remained in the doorway.

She gazed up at him with an empty face. He glanced over at Annie. The old woman smiled. It was a genuine, warm, embracing smile. It was meant to take in the world. It was a forgiving smile, meant to forgive the world.

"Skadi," he said, reaching down and holding her hands in his, in what was becoming his characteristic gesture among these mysterious blonde women of Sweden. "Were you in Iceland last August?"

She nodded in the affirmative.

"And you went hiking on the Sólheimajökull Glacier with a young woman."

"Yes." Her eyes turned so pale the irises disappeared, leaving her pupils a glaring black. "I mostly travel in winter so I can spend the summertime with my aunties."

Harry took a deep breath. "Did your mother suspect?"

"She told me Bernd was responsible."

"For the murders?"

"They were not murders. The girls died like beautiful maidens in a saga."

"Your own saga."

"I watched them, I stayed with them, they never died alone, not before Judith. She made me sad."

"Judith, the girl in Iceland?"

"My mother loved Bernd in spite of his flaws. What she called his moral deficiencies."

What a curious family, Karen whispered.

"Skadi," said Annie from her doorway. Harry looked over at her. Her skin had turned grey. Her sister was bracing her to keep her from slipping to the floor.

Harry, she can't just decide to die. Help the old woman.

Yes, she can. She's very old and her story is over. She's been waiting for this for a long time.

"Tell the professor where Inspector Arnason and her constable are," said Annie, and as she began to topple, Harry stepped forward. He helped Lenke move her into the living room. He settled them both on the sofa.

Annie slouched down against her plump and quiet sister. They whispered to each other as he adjusted their pillows. They were a singular dark creature of secrets. He glanced at the flickering television screen, then turned and walked back to the kitchen. Bernd was sitting up on the settee, with eyes wide open, and Skadi sat leaning on her elbows at the table.

"Skadi," Harry said, "what did your Aunt Annie mean? Where is Hannah Arnason?"

Skadi glanced up, caught his eye, gave him a sweet bland smile, and spoke in Swedish.

"Bernd," he said, turning slowly around on his chair, "what did she say?"

Bernd closed his eyes.

Harry got up, went over, and shook him. Bernd's eyes flashed open. He spoke a few words in Swedish.

Harry walked back to the table. He sat down opposite the young woman. She smiled and with no outward coercion she announced, "They are locked inside the Olafsson root cellar. It is a burial mound. They will have passed on by now. Fårö is very cold in winter. Sweden is a very cold country. But it is very beautiful, don't you think?"

23 THE ROOT CELLAR

HARRY LEANED INTO THE SQUALLING SNOW WITH HIS head turned so the wind couldn't suck the breath from his mouth. With Sverdrup's fur-lined hat pulled down to his ears over Miranda's father's toque, he still needed to clutch his gloved hands against the sides of his head. His toes throbbed as he slipped among the ruts and ridges of the road, pushing sometimes through drifts where the snow was up to his knees. His injured ribs ached as he heaved to catch his breath. On his right, the low stone wall rose up from the landscape and moved along with him, and on his left, the storm howled across the open shoreline, sealing sparse clumps of shrubbery in layers of icy spray. Just behind him on his leeward side, Bernd was valiantly struggling to keep up.

Skadi had not tried to interfere as Harry prepared to go out. She had even offered him a flashlight and warned him the batteries were low. At first Bernd watched from the settee. He had inhaled more smoke from the fire than Harry. He tried several times to get onto his feet but subsided when he couldn't process sufficient air. And finally, with a mighty heave, he rose and commanded Skadi to bring his scorched coat from the porch. Skadi bristled but got his coat, while imploring him to let Harry go it alone. Harry tried to discourage him, as well, but Bernd was like a man possessed; he was not going to be left behind.

Only a few hundred metres down the road, Bernd tugged at Harry's coat. He bent low and spit grey bile into the snow, then shouted something and Harry leaned away from the wind, trying to hear.

Bernd shouted again, "In here." He pulled Harry toward a break in the wall where a gate might have been in the past. "The Olafsson root cellar. Over there."

Once through the wall, Harry became aware of a mound looming in the storm-swept scene behind a gnarled ancient oak. As they trudged closer around to the lee side, it became apparent the mound consisted of boulders piled so high the top disappeared in the weather. Harry turned on the flashlight. A cone of brightness protruded from his hand and faded at its outer edge. He turned it off. The ambient light in the thickness of swirling snow indicated a full moon above the storm, casting a pale luminescence over everything.

Bernd leaned close and, grasping his arm, led him into a shadow on the side of the mound that proved to be a cavity set into the stones about the size of two men standing upright.

"Full moon!" Bernd, spat noisily out into the wind, then spoke in a remarkably strong voice. "That's better. I can breathe. Do you know this is the night of the Midwinter Sacrifice? I'm sure there's no connection."

"Bernd, is this really a burial mound?"

Protected from the wind, they didn't have to shout.

"Neolithic."

"And the root cellar?"

"It's all the same." Bernd nodded toward the depths of stone and darkness. "We cannibalized our past, Harry. Tell me a culture that didn't." He paused to catch his breath. "Steel from the Twin Towers ended up in an American battleship. Roman roads became cathedral walls. Our communal grave became the family root cellar."

His words sounded with surprising clarity and a slight echoing resonance. Harry turned his fading light into the depths of the cavern. Less than a body's length away, it picked up the details of an ancient oak door, studded with iron protrusions. There was a simple slide bolt at waist level holding it closed.

He moved close to the door, touching the primitive lock with his bared hand. It moved. He turned to Bernd, who formed a grim silhouette against the blur outside. He slid the bolt back and pulled on the door, prepared for the worst.

A sudden burst of candlelight flared and guttered to absolute darkness. But in the brief moment of illumination, he had seen the glowing faces and glittering eyes of Hannah Arnason and Horatio Sverdrup, both of them looking pleasantly startled.

"Come in, come in, come in," said Sverdrup in English. "Close the door, you will let in the storm."

Harry shone his flashlight around but the room swallowed the dying beam. As soon as they pulled the door closed, however, he was blinded by the flare of a match, then comforted by the smell of burnt sulphur as Sverdrup re-lit four candles that were poised on jar lids on a decrepit old table.

"Welcome," said the man whose leathery face seemed even more ancient in the flickering light. Sverdrup moved away from the table and the top of his head disappeared as his black dye-job merged with the enveloping darkness.

"It is the night of the Great Midwinter Sacrifice," said Hannah Arnason. "It is good you are here, thank you."

She rose to her feet, towering over them in the confined space. The entire chamber was no bigger than a tomb for four, if they were laid out in state, with room for a few ragged shadows around the edges. She shook their hands heartily.

She might have been a pagan goddess, the way she glowed in the candlelight, with her long blonde hair burnished to spun gold and her blue eyes burning obsidian black. She seemed huge, and Harry realized both he and Bernd were still huddled low from battling the bitter winds and bent under the stone ceiling, which seemed to rise above her, where she stood in the centre of the chamber.

"Sit down, gentlemen. Warm yourselves." She indicated some empty crates on the floor by the table. The candles had taken the chill off the chamber quite nicely. Sverdrup helped both men loosen their coats. Harry set his borrowed gloves and hat down on the rubble floor beside Sverdrup.

Hannah acknowledged this affirmation of Sverdrup's bogus betrayal with a flickering eye. Harry bristled. He was wary of becoming too comfortable with either of them.

Hannah turned to Harry, apparently oblivious of any animosity.

"Do you know about the Midwinter rites?"

This is ridiculous, Harry. She's playing host, like she's offering sanctuary to lost travellers. Very Chaucerian; she's going to tell you a tale.

But Harry was interested.

He had already deduced from the candles and crude furnishings that the root cellar had been in recent generations a refuge for kids, probably Bernd and Skadi and their neighbours, the Olafssons. He also figured Skadi had tricked the inspector and her constable, telling them this is where Harry and Bernd were hiding, then bolted the door, leaving them to perish, before turning back to set the shed on fire. Not thinking through that a root cellar, by definition, maintains temperatures above freezing, not remembering there was a cache of candles, not knowing Sverdrup was an inveterate smoker, who would die before being caught without matches or a lighter.

"Quite cozy," said Harry. "I take it Skadi did this, locked you in here."

"She did. To protect Bernd, I suppose."

She doesn't know!

Or maybe she does.

"Harry, you smell like you've been through a fire. You both do. Well, we are glad you are here. It's the midwinter full moon tonight, Harry. The gods demanded propitiation. Skadi is a student of Nordic traditions, ancient and modern, apparently. And a practitioner."

She looked to Bernd, who had a grave expression on his wounded face, then back to Harry.

"Long ago, on every eighth year during the midwinter moon, the people who lived here, whose ancestors built this mound, would sacrifice a man and the males of seven kinds of domestic animal. They were mathematically very precise. One man, one stallion, one bull, one ram, one boar, one dog, one cat, and one cock. They did this for nine days. Very meticulous in their obsequies. The bodies were laid out to the elements in the branches of a holy tree, perhaps the old oak outside, and birds and rats would tear the frozen flesh from their bones. It was all quite gruesome, but you know, Harry, it worked."

"It worked?"

"Yes, for the next seven years the spring would come."

"As night follows day, so to speak."

"Yes, and on the eighth year, with the midwinter moon, they would do it all over again."

She seemed quite pleased with herself, then abruptly, she rose to her full height, so that the candlelight glistened from below, distorting her even features into a death mask like children assume when they shine a flashlight up from their chins. For a moment, Harry was transported into a world of pagan ritual and horrific rites. She was the embodiment of all about religion that defied logic, all that he hated, and feared, and desired.

"We will go now," she said, breaking the spell.

"No!" said Bernd emphatically.

The other three looked at him. Hannah Arnason sat down again on her crate and pulled her coat closer around her shoulders.

"We must talk," Bernd said. "When we go back to the house, Skadi's world will change, my world will change. Since Harry knows about her already, there is no way to hide."

Hannah and Sverdrup did not seem surprised by Bernd's apparent admission of Skadi's guilt, although even Harry was not sure which of the crimes he was assigning to her and which, if any, he took as his own.

"I would like to answer your questions now," said Bernd. "There is no mystery, only things you might not understand."

That, Karen whispered, *is the definition of mystery.*

Unlike Inspector Arnason and Constable Sverdrup, who leaned closer into the candlelight, anxious to hear what this man with the dark countenance and sorrowful voice would tell them, Harry sat back, edging into the flickering shadows. He gazed up at the darkest recesses of their cavern, tracing the lines of old beams with his eyes, beams that had been inserted in recent centuries to hold the space open for storing root vegetables and salted fish, for providing a sanctuary where children could hide from the ominous world outside. For all of them, the tall blonde, the man with a face like a satchel, the Italianate young man, the doleful young woman who dominated by her absence, and himself, Harry Lindstrom, this burrow into the arcane and terrifying past for such ordinary, practical purposes, this mound was their common heritage.

Bernd connected Skadi only to the earlier murders. He spoke with a kind of melancholy detachment. He became emotional only as he finished his account by declaring, "God knows, I tried to protect her the best I could."

And what about the women she murdered?

Bernd took a deep breath. "You have to understand, my mother loved her daughters. She believed it was my fault she lost them."

Brief thoughts about his own children flashed through Harry's mind. (Lucy, his feisty five-year-old who marvelled at being in the wilderness; Matt, excited about sleeping in a tent and listening to wolves.)

"All her daughters, Giovanna, Isabella, Sigrid, and her lovely lonely Skadi." Their names fell from Bernd's lips like a lament. "She believed she was losing her too."

"Unless she could shift the blame to you," said Harry.

"Oh, she already had, but she needed proof. So she framed you, an expert in murder. You would exonerate yourself by making me pay for the crimes she was certain I'd already committed."

"Killing your other three sisters."

The wind blowing at the door indicated it had shifted from onshore to the north. The door rattled and they could feel currents of cold air pressing on their exposed flesh. The candles flickered.

"When I was growing up, Birgitta would often cry in the night," said Bernd, "and in the morning sometimes she would come to my room and accuse me of destroying her life."

The root cellar door pushed shut in its frame, and for a moment Harry thought Skadi must be out there, locking them in again. The candle flames burnt straight in the still air. He listened for the bolt but heard only the wind skirling in the entryway, thrusting against wood. Skadi was back with her aunts.

Harry imagined Annie was already dead. After revealing secrets that changed everything, her heart might simply have stopped beating, and Lenke, silent and inconsolable on the sofa, would be holding her dead sister in her plump arms, waiting for her own heart to expire. People sometimes die like that, Harry thought. Old people who have been living on borrowed time. And Skadi would be seeing to them and not worried about the police she envisioned frozen to death in an ancient burial mound or the two men fighting the elements in a losing battle to save them.

Sverdrup spoke in Swedish. There was an awkward silence, then Hannah Arnason said, "Horatio, it would be a discourtesy to use our own language."

Sverdrup mumbled something indecipherable. Swedes are like Canadians, Harry thought, courteous to a fault.

Hannah Arnason ignored Sverdrup's grumbling and turned to Bernd. "Please continue," she said, as if he were in the mist of relating a rumour.

"My mother needed someone to blame to make sense of a senseless world. I think sending me here as a child was her way of taunting fate, flaunting her sorrow. She was certain Sweden would protect her surviving daughter. It never occurred to her Skadi might emulate the crimes she made no secret of assigning to me."

"Do you think Skadi was imitating you?" Harry asked. "Or was she getting back at your mother?"

"You knew it was her from the beginning," Hannah stated, shunting Harry's question aside. She was used to being at the centre of forensic procedures.

"Not the first one. It was near Tromso. That's in Norway," he added for Harry's benefit. "Skadi was at the university there on an Erasmus exchange. The next, as far as I know, was on Gotland, after Skadi returned home. I had just got back from Mauritania, very traumatized by what I had witnessed. Skadi met me at the airport. I was thoroughly depressed. When we got to Fårö, Skadi quite openly explained to me in front of Annie and Lenke what she had done. We spoke in English. She thought her confession would make me feel better; she thought it would comfort me to know she also was deeply involved with the suffering of women. She couldn't differentiate between causing misery and relieving it. I was horrified and frightened for her. I asked her to promise not to do it again. She didn't understand. She liked that we had a secret. When reports came out that the corpse had blackened fingers she didn't explain, but it never happened again. After that she cut the nails first. At that point, I had already signed up with my NGO to return to North Africa as a volunteer. But whenever I was able to spend time with Skadi on her field trips, I did."

"To keep her from getting caught," Harry observed.

"When your mother found out," said Hannah, "she only documented deaths on the trips where you were present, I'm sure. Never when Skadi was alone. She wasn't concerned with the murders themselves, was she?"

"No," said Bernd.

"And neither of you did anything at all to stop the rampage?"

Bernd looked thoughtful, his burns concealed by the glimmering light falling aslant across his face.

"It might have been much worse if I had not been with her."

Harry needed to make sense of his own sordid involvement.

"When did Birgitta first know about Skadi?"

"For sure? Not until after she went to you."

"To me?"

"A couple of weeks before Christmas. Birgitta had found the tea box full of fingernail clippings. She insisted she found it in this root cellar last summer. We used to play here, Skadi and I, Bjorn and Inge Olafsson. It was Skadi's sanctuary. My own refuge was the old boatshed and this was hers."

"She told me she confronted you when she found the tea box."

"Only to ask if I remembered a murder ten years ago in Visby. Did I recall reports of black paint on the victim's fingers? I told her I remembered, but she didn't pursue the matter, not until she found Skadi's manicure case. It was out in the open in the bathroom Skadi and I shared in the Toronto house. There were fresh fingernail parings inside. That's when she went to you."

"She still thought the nail collection was yours."

"Harry, who knows? She *needed* to think it was mine. She insisted the Icelandic kit was mine, as well."

"But it was Skadi's."

"So, I blew up, I went away. Birgitta tried to get the police to come after me, then Lindstrom and Malone. She was convinced I was a killer and that I had gone to Sweden. But Skadi was still in Toronto. She was staying in Sigrid's room. I couldn't leave her. I returned home the morning you and I met, Harry, when you came to the door. As you remember, I sent you away."

"And your mother sent me a cheque."

"Good. I hope she was generous."

"To a fault."

"And then there was another blow-up. An indigent young woman from Manitoba. Her body turned up, frozen dead in the trunk of Birgitta's car."

"Turned up!" Harry exclaimed. "I didn't see that one coming."

"Nor did I. Skadi had had the car all day and most of the night. Nevertheless, my mother blamed me, as you might expect. Not for the killing, which seemed to her of only passing interest, but for causing Skadi to be how she was. It was easier to accept her son was the devil's offspring than her only living daughter was a danger to anyone except herself."

"I thought she didn't learn about the Gimli girl until they got to Iceland," said Harry.

"It was hard to ignore a corpse in her car. She knew. That's why she wanted Skadi out of the country."

"But the car was Birgitta's. It could have been her?"

"Who? Birgitta killing the girl in the trunk? I doubt it."

"Then why would she tell me she'd done it?"

Asked and answered, Harry. To suck you into the vortex.

Bernd shook his head slowly in resigned frustration.

"I don't know," he said. "She did help dispose of the frozen body. She insisted we wrap it in a blanket."

"When she was in the trunk she was naked?"

"Yeah, when we found her."

"So that part is true. She was frozen to death in a sauna."

"Ironic, isn't it?"

"Your mother said the same thing."

"Did she?" He didn't seem surprised. "So, the three of us drove around Rosedale with the corpse in the trunk of the car until we found the cedar maze. We thought the body wouldn't be discovered until spring."

"Is it possible your mother killed the girl."

"No. Unless the body had been in the car longer than I thought—Skadi driving around with a corpse in the back? *That*, Harry, is ironic."

"The only irony is that you seem amused."

That's not irony, Harry. It's appropriately mordant, macabre, and morbid.

"Look, I assumed Skadi had killed her, I still think so, and Skadi seemed quite amenable to taking the credit."

"The credit?"

"The responsibility. She was confident Birgitta would not betray her, no more than I would have done."

"Then you broke into my condo, stole my things, so I'd take the fall for that one, at least. But why try to kill me? That would have defeated your purpose."

"We didn't. That was Skadi on her own initiative."

Harry hadn't seen that coming.

"Skadi listened to my mother and me conspiring. She wasn't exactly a conspirator herself, but when she heard how we intended to set you up, since you were already involved, she thought you must be our common enemy."

"The enemy. And I needed to be eliminated?"

"Skadi snuck into your apartment after I left."

"On Christmas Day? So she and her mother were still in Canada?"

"It's easy to hide when no one knows you exist. Skadi was virtually invisible. And Birgitta travelled with two passports and three names."

"Skadi locked me out on the balcony to die from exposure."

"She came back and told us. That's when we knew we had to get her back to Sweden as soon as possible."

"And the ceramic orange?"

"Skadi's inspiration, drawing you out into the cold with what she called *the forbidden fruit*."

"She was thinking ahead enough to steal the ring and the scarf."

"Ah, Harry, no. That was me. I broke into your place when you were in the hospital. I needed to unlock your balcony door, so your death would have seemed like an accident. But you survived."

"Barely."

"I took the scarf and buried it in the snow beside the girl in the maze. I kept your ring on a premonition."

"That Skadi would kill again?"

"Birgitta planted the ring under the corpse in Hagaparken."

"She was there!"

Bernd did not respond.

"So you were working together in Stockholm. What changed?"

"What do you mean, Harry?"

"What changed? Something did. Suddenly we were all in the middle of the Baltic, including Inspector Arnason and Constable Sverdrup."

"At your invitation, Harry," said Hannah.

"More specifically, at Birgitta Ghiberti's, in time for you to witness her ultimate sacrifice among the ruins of St. Clemens."

Bernd seemed annoyed to have lost control of his story. "Birgitta," he said. "Birgitta changed. She decided after watching the death in the park that I must be stopped!"

"You!" Harry exclaimed.

"If I were eliminated, she was certain Skadi wouldn't kill any more."

"If *you* were stopped!"

That's about as logical as you would expect.

Birgitta was not about logic.

I know, Harry.

Bernd sank back, despondent and exhausted.

Harry, I'm not sure I believe him.

About what.

Anything!

I think he's trying to be truthful. It's bloody difficult given the lies and malevolence he's lived with all his life.

"She actually saw Skadi kill the girl in the park, didn't she?"

"She followed her. She had rented a car in your name, Harry."

"Ah," said Harry. "So she could have saved the girl. If she followed Skadi, she must have got there before the girl died."

"She made Skadi leave. She was worried they'd get caught if the girl lived."

"And she coloured the girl's nails," said Harry. "She used Goth nail polish to replicate the corpse of the girl from Gimli. She just happened to have some with her."

"Apparently she did."

That macabre detail struck Harry as especially gruesome. He continued, "She stripped the girl naked—before the girl was dead, before she was stiffened from the cold or *rigor mortis* set in."

"It takes several hours," Bernd observed with peculiar detachment. "The girl in Toronto had been killed in a sauna. We had no clothes, she was in the trunk of the car, and she was frozen stiff. We would have had to cut her in pieces. Skadi was too gentle for that, mother was too fastidious, and I was stricken helpless. It was easier to change the pattern than to break up the body."

"But the girl in Hagaparken was still warm and pliable." Harry felt a surge of revulsion at the clear intimations of irredeemable, irremediable evil. He felt incredulous horror at the open display of moral degeneracy.

"Your mother was a fiend." The word seemed weak and empty, a vapid summation of unbearable malevolence.

Bernd looked downcast, as if a suspicion had just been confirmed.

"Please to continue," said Sverdrup.

Bernd squinted in the candlelight. His breathing was laboured. When he said nothing, Harry spoke up, "Bernd, even then, Birgitta was wrong, wasn't she? Skadi did kill again."

"Despite my mother's best intentions."

"Her intention to have you caught after having executed her in the church?"

"And or, Harry, and or—to have you take the blame. Either way, she would have died at peace."

A separate peace.

"But Skadi didn't come to get me like she was supposed to. Both Skadi and Birgitta knew you were watching, Harry. Skadi followed Birgitta and smashed in her skull with a rock."

Which must have been a satisfying expression of primal rage.

"And you only found out your mother was dead when Inspector Arnason came calling in the middle of the night?"

Bernd nodded in affirmation.

"Either that or Skadi did come to get you. And you killed Birgitta."

Bernd seemed stifled by remorse for having betrayed his sister.

"You talk about refuge and sanctuary, Mr. Ghiberti." Hannah's voice was soothing. "Do you mean from your mother?"

"From death," Bernd said, rousing himself. "As children we were haunted by the deaths of our sisters in ways it is hard to imagine. For years through my adolescence, I brooded about being a born killer. It thrilled me and scared me so much I would wake up from nightmares screaming. At home, Birgitta would get up and close her door. Here, Skadi would come down from her room and crawl into bed with me and hold me. She was so little and fearless. I know she believed my mother, that I was a killer. And she loved me more than anyone in the world, her natural-born killer, because she felt safe with me. Who better to protect her from death than Death himself? She would make up fantasies about death, about being dead, she would lay herself out right here in the ancestral grave on a bed of reeds and wildflowers, and wait, sometimes for hours, until finally I would find her, and then she would hold her breath until I declared her alive. Which I always did, of course, and she always survived."

"Death was power, play, affection, everything, then," said Hannah Arnason, sympathetically, before switching strategies. "Bernd, you were not in Iceland last summer with your sister, were you?"

"I was."

"No, you were not."

He took a long time answering. Sverdrup coughed phlegmatically and Harry struggled to quash his frustration at not being the one asking questions. But Arnason was in charge; Harry was an observer with vested interests.

"No," he admitted at last. "I was in Africa."

Records of travel between Nordic countries were scant to non-existent but to North Africa could be traced. He was probably telling the truth.

Hannah seemed satisfied, as if he had confirmed her suspicions. She exchanged a knowing glance with Sverdrup.

"That leaves Skadi and me," said Harry, leaning into the conversation. "We know she was in Iceland; her own research notes will prove it. And I've never denied it. So there you are."

"You take this lightly, Professor Lindstrom."

"I do not," he declared emphatically. "But you've made sure I'm involved. You and your henchman sent me to Fårö to flush out the killer. I assumed it was Bernd. You suspected it was his sister all along. You knew some of the murders were done when he wasn't around. You thought I could force him to betray her, which he did not do, even after she tried to kill him. She was actually quite open about it in an opaque sort of way. Whatever you think of Bernd's love for his sister, no one could ever doubt his commitment. You set me up."

"Did I? Well, it was very convincing, wasn't it? I think you broke Constable Sverdrup's nose."

"And I think he gave me a bloody concussion."

"But we did flush her out, didn't we, Harry?"

"At the cost of nearly getting us burnt to death. She was trying to protect him from you."

"By trying to kill you both, apparently. You'll have to tell me about that, some time. But you survived."

She could not have known about the boatshed fire but seemed unconcerned, even with the peeling skin on Harry and Bernd's faces as evidence.

Harry turned suddenly morose. "You knew I didn't push the girl into the crevasse. You never thought I did. She wasn't your sister, was she?"

"No, just a name. But real to the people who mourn her, real to herself until the end."

Her gaze had been fixed on Harry. She turned, trying to see across the candlelight into Bernd's eyes. He was wheezing; he had been through a lot and appeared on the verge of respiratory collapse.

When Harry began to talk again, she returned her attention to him.

"I'm assuming," he said, "you also made up that garbage about Miranda Quin. Whatever she told you, you manipulated the facts."

Facts and truth, Harry, they're never the same.

"She was worried about you, that part is accurate."

"And otherwise?"

Hannah shrugged. "Otherwise? Well, her usefulness has ended. Otherwise, she was certain it could *not* be you."

Harry felt a warm flood of relief course through his entire system. Miranda had not betrayed him. Of course, she wouldn't. She had entrusted him with her father's toque, which she had kept with her for over thirty years. Hannah Arnason had simply used Harry's doubts about himself, his lack of confidence in the good faith of others, to her strategic advantage.

"And you?" Harry asked.

"I doubted you were a killer from the beginning."

That makes what she did to you unconscionable, Harry.

But effective.

Bernd rallied from the margins.

"You counted on the rage of Harry's righteousness to bring me down," he declared, addressing Hannah with withering contempt.

"Whether I was guilty of murder or not. He was expendable. And my sister, if you suspected she was a serial killer, why didn't you stop her? Did you need my mother to do the work for you? Did you need me to betray her? Did you need Harry to catch her in the act? Perhaps for your own perverse reasons you needed her to kill again? Or were you waiting for Birgitta's murder, the only violent death of the lot."

"You don't think young women dying of exposure is violent?"

Harry did a double take. This was not Karen whispering in his head, and it was not Inspector Arnason. It was Horatio Sverdrup.

24 INSIDE THE BURIAL MOUND

THE PENETRATING CHILL HAD SEEPED THROUGH AND Harry began to shiver. When he had first come in out of the storm, he had been cold but dry and warmed quickly. But the root cellar was damp and the walls of piled stones glistened with moisture. The beams overhead gleamed with condensation from the bodies and breathing of four living people in a confined and airless crypt.

He reached for Sverdrup's hat and gloves, which rested on the rubble floor beside his crate. As he picked them up he caught a whiff of stale tobacco and looked over at his devious benefactor. The man was ashen and held his jaw stiff to fight the tremors coursing across the rough terrain of his face. Harry handed him his hat and gloves. The other man nodded and pulled them on. Almost immediately, he removed them again and without a word turned to Hannah Arnason, who was sitting close beside him. He took her hands, one at a time, and slipped the gloves over her fingers, securing them snuggly around her wrists, and then he placed the fur hat on her head and pulled the flaps down warmly over her ears. She accepted his ministrations without comment.

Harry, you've got competition.

Sverdrup rose to his feet, embarrassed. Hannah's eyes followed him into the shadows, and Harry thought he detected the hint of a smile. Then she returned her attention to Bernd.

"I can understand if you had wanted to murder your sister. Especially if you had killed the others."

Bernd didn't rise to the bait.

"But why would you want to kill your mother?"

Because she was a heartless bitch?

"I didn't," said Bernd. Exhaustion was creeping through his voice. "I am very fond of my sister."

In the extreme.

"And I loved my mother."

Ah, yes. Aristotle again. Sophocles. Oedipus.

"I killed no one."

Not directly.

"I would imagine you *wanted* to murder them both for a very long time." Hannah paused, as if enacting a courtroom revelation but she wasn't sure where her rhetoric was taking her.

Harry said, "Birgitta threatened to expose Skadi if you didn't cooperate. I doubt she'd have done that. In her own odd way she adored her. But you would have done anything to protect your sister as you had been for years. That was your mother's ultimate power over you, Skadi's vulnerability."

Bernd offered a fleeting enigmatic smile.

They were all suffering from the damp chill. Sverdrup lit the last three candles, so seven or eight were blazing on the decrepit table. No one suggested they leave. Not now, not when secrets were opening and mysteries were being resolved.

Bernd looked at Hannah quizzically and waited.

"We in fact know it wasn't Harry," she continued, having brought her rhetoric under control. "My constable and I observed him approaching the crime scene. We were there first. But in the few minutes between his leaving the hotel and our discovery of Birgitta's corpse, someone else had slipped into the ruins and killed her with a rock pried loose from the walls, possibly earlier. It was a carefully premeditated murder."

She pulled Sverdrup's hat from her head and rubbed her ears, indicating it prevented her from hearing. Then she did that thing that unnerved Harry with its impossibly subtle yet obvious sexuality: she ducked her head down, and, twisting so that she looked up at him through a veil of hair the colour of sunlight, she smiled.

"What do you think, Harry?"

"Whether she was killed by her surviving daughter or her only son, we know Birgitta arranged her own death. Bernd more or less admitted in the fishing shed that he killed her, and then, here, he offered up Skadi. What we've learned about the Ghibertis and the Sviars is that there are often profound gaps between what seems to be and what is."

"I did not *offer up* Skadi. I suggested there could be doubt as to who killed Birgitta."

"But if Skadi is going down as a serial killer, she might as well get nailed for killing her mother, as well. Bernd, you had every good reason to despise Birgitta, none to want her alive. She seems to have treated you and Skadi despicably, enough to send you chasing off after old bones and your sister after fresh bodies."

"I hadn't thought of my being a paleoanthropologist as therapy."

"Why did you go back to Africa?" Harry asked him. "If you found your experience there so traumatic, why not stay away?"

A match flared in the darkness behind Hannah. Sverdrup dragged deeply on his cigarette, hunched over, as if waiting for the wrath of his boss. His face appeared on fire as the tobacco embers glowed each time he sucked the smoke deep into his lungs. Hannah Arnason waved the drifting smoke away from her face but ignored him.

Bernd watched the man smoke, then shifted his attention back to Harry.

"Mauritania. Searching for atonement of some sort. For what Skadi was doing."

"You can't atone for your sister's sins. You can't redeem others."

"Jesus did."

"And you're not Jesus. You don't even believe in Jesus."

"Consolation, then. If I couldn't stop her and I couldn't make amends by balancing her acts of evil with acts of kindness, I could at least make myself feel better."

"You are an honest man," said Sverdrup, his features sinking into darkness as he took time off from inhaling to speak.

"Sometimes," Bernd responded.

"The *sometimes*-honest man is more dangerous than the liar," said Hannah Arnason. "At least when the liar says he's telling the truth, you know he's lying. Perhaps your work for women in Africa was to atone for your *own* sins. Could that be the truth of the matter?"

"Or he murdered African women as well," Sverdrup offered, proving his admiration for Bernd was ephemeral, at best.

"No," said Harry.

He was remembering Bernd's account of the *leblouh* encampment in the far country, where young girls were force fed to fatten them for prepubescent marriage to old men. Harry had nothing but contempt for cultural norms where men so feared women they coupled with children and kept adult women in virtual bondage. Bernd did not murder women in Africa—he did noble work there at great personal risk.

Harry could feel Karen balking inside. He knew she shared his sentiments about the pathological fear of women in Western religions, but she was wary of altruism in a man who shielded a serial killer from the law, even when the killer was his sister.

He might have saved lives, Harry countered.

Perhaps with the execution of his mother he did.

"I think it is time, now," said Hannah Arnason, rising to her feet. She looked even more imposing once she put Sverdrup's fur hat back on her head, holding the earflaps back to prevent them from impeding communication. "We need to interview Skadi Sviar. There is nothing more to do here."

She spoke as if their present location had been crucial to her inquiry. She seemed pleased with the progress they had made.

Sverdrup and Bernd were first to the door. They pushed on it firmly. It held fast, leaning open just enough along the top edge to admit a sliver of wind that threatened to extinguish the candles. Instinctively, Harry and Hannah closed ranks in front of the table to protect their only source of light and heat. The other two banged on the thick wood.

So it was Skadi, after all.

No, Harry, it was snow blowing into the entranceway. Listen, that's not the sound of a bolted door, it's frozen along the base. You know about frozen doors.

Harry relaxed, as if being held prisoner by an act of nature was somehow less deadly than by human volition.

He stepped closer to the door. Sverdrup and Bernd stood back. The flames behind them wavered timorously from their combined movement. He ran his hands over the old wood, feeling for flaws. Nothing. Oak planks, solid as stone. But the ancient bolts would be weathered. With the butt end of the flashlight he tapped on the bolts that fixed the crosspieces to the horizontal slabs. When the bulb flickered, he switched to a stone from the floor, searching for weaknesses with each tap, listening for the dull thud of rusted iron.

Sverdrup was suddenly beside him, a shovel in hand. He took over from what Harry was doing and jammed the blade under the head of a bolt. Harry stood back, shining the dull beam of the flashlight on each bolt as the other two men worked them loose. One oak crosspiece fell to the floor, then the other.

The upright boards held fast. They were bolted on the outside as well, Harry thought. Damn bloody hell.

But when they hammered on the door again with their fists, it sounded different. The candle flames guttered. In the blackness that engulfed them, they could see small cracks of light from the moonlit snow. In removing the bolts, they had broken the ice seal along the base of the door. In gradual increments, they pushed the door open so that Sverdrup, the smallest of them, could slip through after removing his coat. Hannah came forward and handed him his gloves and fur hat. Bernd passed his coat through, then the shovel, and the other man hammered and scraped outside until the passage was widened.

Setting the flashlight down, Harry dug Horatio Sverdrup's wallet out of his pocket and handed it to Bernd to give to Sverdrup. It seemed time to give the man back his identity, if not all of his money. Bernd shrugged, and took it with him as he squeezed out into the open.

Hannah turned to retrieve her own thin gloves from the table. Harry held the edge of her sleeve to guide her back. Suddenly, they heard the terrible unmistakable clang of metal on bone, followed immediately by blackness as the door slammed solidly into its frame. Harry lunged against it, but it was braced from the outside.

"Horatio!" Hannah called in a strong but tremulous voice, suggesting strength under duress that Harry found heroic, if futile. "Poor man," she murmured, letting her voice drop.

"He's not dead," said Harry with surprising conviction. "Bernd just wants to get back to the house before we do."

"I hope you're right," she said, speaking into the darkness. "I'm sure you are. Sverdrup will last until his lungs congeal, and then he will die. Not today."

The subject of her constable's mortality then seemed to have been swept from her mind. "You've developed a bond with this unusual Bernd Ghiberti," she observed. "You seem to know him quite well. So tell me, is he a cold-blooded psychopath? Or is he the victim of his family's misfortune? It is a very interesting family, yes?"

Interesting!

Not now, Karen, give her some room.

Killer and victim aren't mutually exclusive.

"We will see," said Hannah, seeming to agree with Karen.

"Meanwhile we sit and wait," said Harry. He retrieved the flashlight, but it had burnt out or the bulb had blown. "Do we have any matches?"

"Constable Sverdrup took them."

They eased their way to the crates and sat down, side by side for the warmth and reassurance. Harry felt certain it would not be long before Horatio Sverdrup regained consciousness. But just in case, he dug Sverdrup's grungy gritty chocolate bar from his pocket, and stripping away the wrapping as best he could, he offered Hannah a larger half, which she accepted without comment. In the dark it seemed quite palatable; even the unidentifiable furry textures were reassuring.

"If he has killed at all, perhaps he had no alternative." Harry was thinking of Birgitta's smashed cranium.

"There is always an alternative to murder."

"Think how much he has sacrificed."

"Do you also feel sorry for Skadi?"

Harry didn't respond. He stared into the darkness that had swallowed them whole. Only their voices and thoughts remained. And the intimations of body warmth hovering in the air between them.

"Harry," she said, tentatively.

"Yes." He was wary.

What was it about Hannah Arnason? She was enthralling, and not just because she was beautiful. She enchanted the way a *femme fatale* in early *film noir* was enchanting; she was seductive, intriguing, unpredictable, dangerous.

Don't forget intelligent. You always were a sucker for intelligent women, Bogie. She's devastatingly clever, and she carries herself like a goddess.

She makes the most of it, here among mortals.

Don't forget she's got Sverdrup, Harry. She doesn't need you.

Harry turned toward where the warmth in the darkness told him Hannah's face would be and spoke in a quiet voice, "Hannah, you are an unusual woman. I hope we get out of this alive, but if we don't—"

"No, Harry," she interrupted. "We do not have sex before we die."

Caught you off guard, didn't she?

"I was just going to give you a compliment," he responded sheepishly.

"So, you are such a good lover!"

"No, that's not what I mean." He could feel the contours of the air between them.

"We will wait," she said. "Possibly perhaps we will have sex. But only if we are not rescued."

Who decides when it's time?

She's not serious.

But Hannah Arnason was warming to the subject.

"I would like to have sex in the burial mound of our ancestors. That would be interesting. Very ironic."

You're two of a kind, Harry.

He heard a rustling in the dark. Suddenly a small-screen vision of the planet Earth burst into light, casting a glow on their faces. Instantly recognizable, entirely unexpected, and very disconcerting.

"My lovely iPhone will not make calls in our burial chamber."

"Root cellar," Harry clarified.

"Perhaps it is the same. And if Mr. Sverdrup is dead, then his cell phone will not work either. So then, perhaps, if you would like, we will have sexual relations before we join him. It would be interesting."

Just ignore me, Harry. Pretend I'm not here.

25 **THE DANGEROUS EDGE OF THINGS**

THE iPHONE SCREEN CAST AN EERIE SHEEN OVER THE rough walls of their prison, bleeding the colour from their faces, their clothes, and the rocks, wood beams, and rubble that surrounded them. If putrescence were a colour, this would be it. Then suddenly the screen burst into crackling flames.

"That's better," she said, laughing like a child.

Bright flames and no heat. That's one app too many.

But Harry liked it; he enjoyed the whimsy. He admired the defiance. This woman who stood six foot four in heels could play like a girl. Surrounded by death and in danger of dying herself, she could laugh. He liked her, and Harry Lindstrom did not like a lot of people, particularly after he got to know them.

The Stockholm Syndrome, Harry!

He was enthralled by Hannah Arnason but he was appalled by her as well. She had abducted him, stood back while he was abused by her henchman, and she hung him out as bait, but in spite of the contradictory impulses, he felt an unmistakable connection.

Lust, Harry.

No. What he felt was a curious kinship, as if they had been through similar experiences long before their worlds collided.

"You must have a story," he said. He wanted to know her.

"I have many." A heaviness in her voice displaced the brief interlude of their casual intimacy with something indefinable but much darker. She snapped off the iPhone to save the battery and the darkness engulfed them. "I'm sure you have many yourself. Perhaps you will tell me some time about you."

"Only one," he said. "There's only one story for each of us."

"Just one? How can that be?"

"I had a great aunt, a long time ago, and no one knew her but me. Everyone was afraid of her because she was old and very severe. But I always knew she had been young before she was old, and I guessed she had been bitterly disappointed in love. No one else would have dared to ask her, but I did and she told me. Between the wars she had been engaged to a doctor, and his housekeeper became pregnant. The doctor and the housekeeper moved away. My Aunt Beth never told anyone else but that one story shaped her whole life."

"It is not good to get close to people, Harry. Nothing good comes of it. I have my stories, too. Someday, perhaps, I will talk to you about me. But not here." She warmed as she talked, despite the cool message. "Do you know anyone who has not experienced tragedy? Sorrow? Only the very young and the very foolish. For us, Harry, it is enough to know that we have. The details are not important."

Curiously, Harry felt closer to this strange and beautiful woman than he had been to anyone since the accident in Algonquin Park.

"Have you ever read *Howards End*?" he asked into the darkness.

"When I was at Lund University, yes, perhaps."

Don't you love that, Harry? Perhaps. That's how I felt about most of the novels I knew, back then. I'm never sure whether I actually read them, but we talked about them as if we had. The great ones, anyway.

"'Only connect.'" Harry quoted, as much to Karen and himself as to Hannah.

"'Only connect the prose and the passion, and both will be exalted,'" said Hannah, continuing the quotation.

"'Live in fragments no longer,'" said Harry, leaving out the bit about love. "It's a good novel. E.M. Forster went to a college near mine at Cambridge. I suppose they all are, really. I was at Trinity. He was at King's. Perhaps that's where he learned to sum up the good and desperate life so succinctly, a bit like a prayer."

"Do you feel like praying, Harry?"

"Of course. I always feel like praying. Sometimes I pray for God to exist."

The silence between them was audible. The slight rustling of their clothing, the hush of their breath, shaped the darkness. She flicked on the fire app. Harry caught a brief glimpse of his silver wedding band before she clicked it off again. He turned the band with his thumb. It felt warm and cool at the same time. He thought he could hear Karen smile.

We live on the dangerous edge of things, Harry.

He wanted to object but he knew she was right. Only when he was grappling with death was he truly engaged.

Harry, turn away from death. It's too easy an out. Do an inventory: you're on the verge of hypothermia, your toes are hurting like hell, your cracked ribs ache, your knuckles are bruised, your lacerated wrist is throbbing, your arm is hurting, your face has been scorched raw, there's a suppurating cut on your forehead. You've had a concussion. What more do you need to remind you you're fully alive? And you're trapped in here with an uncommonly fine-looking woman whose name is a palindrome—which may, or may not, have symbolic significance.

I feel pain, therefore I am.

Descartes as an antidote to death! Forget the pain; try thinking, Harry. Try thought.

As a gesture to prove his vitality, seeking common ground, he asked Hannah what philosophers she had studied at university.

"The usual," she said. "The Greeks, the Germans—I remember liking Schopenhauer. Oneness with nature, I could appreciate that, nothingness in nature, not so much. I wasn't born to be an ascetic. But as a Swede, I liked the sublime; his notion that nature is awesome, the more beautiful, the more terrifying."

She could be describing herself.

"And Kierkegaard, I liked his thinking—God exceeds our grasp. Just not his conclusions, they seemed desperate. What about Nietzsche?" she asked. "You must have liked him?"

Why is she speaking in the past tense, Harry?

"There's no escaping Nietzsche," he said.

"You know about the graffiti, *God is Dead (signed) Nietzsche*?"

"*Nietzsche is dead (signed) God.* Yeah, it was scrawled on the walls in my college washrooms."

"Mine too."

"It's a very Nietzschean joke."

"There's no escaping Kafka either, is there?"

"That's what makes him so Kafkaesque," said Harry.

"There's something reassuring about shared awareness of mortality."

"Yes," said Harry, "there is."

He waited for a cheerful diatribe from Karen about Schopenhauer's pessimism, Nietzsche's gloom, Kafka's paranoia, German fatalism, one of her manic, ill-informed, inspired, provocative judgments. None came. Then Hannah spoke into the darkness, "Harry, the fingernails?"

Suddenly, they were back in the real world with its indefinable limits.

"They were Skadi's signature," she continued. "But why? You understand this family better than anyone."

"I don't know about that."

False modesty, Harry.

"I see the nail business as a grisly attempt to connect," he explained. "Love and deep hatred, virtually indistinguishable. I think Birgitta tormented Skadi for being alive when her legitimate daughters were dead. She loved her, I'm sure, but despised her. And Skadi loved and despised her mother. She desperately wanted to punish Birgitta for the abject loneliness of her childhood, and she needed to make her suffer for her cruelty to Bernd. But mostly, I think, Skadi was pathologically jealous of her dead sisters, enough to murder their surrogates. Blue-eyed blondes."

"The girl in Hagaparken had brown eyes."

"The exception that proves the rule. Even killers make mistakes."

"And why the nails in the first place?"

"That had to be the one image of her sisters that most stuck in Skadi's mind: the black soil under Sigrid's nails when she tried to claw her way out of her father's grave."

"How could she know that, Harry? How could she imagine it?"

"Just proves how wicked Birgitta really was, telling Skadi the horrific particulars of her sisters' deaths. Each detail was the lash of a whip, inscribed like a scar in a little girl's mind."

"Some of the nails were garish."

"No, just more appropriate to southern complexions. Skadi travelled to Italy and Athens, but death in a warm climate didn't suit her—however, she did it, if not by exposure."

"I can't imagine her being violent."

"Poison, maybe. Fire. Drowning. Random, unrelated and cruel but not brutal killings. She preferred more amiable murder. She needed to watch them die after sharing a few drinks with their new friend in the Nordic winter; girls who looked like her sisters, like her mother when she was young, venturing out for, for what, a good laugh, a long walk, removing their coats on some pretext or another, taking the girl's coat, settling into the snow, getting cold herself, watching the other girl lose control, watching her die; that was her story, again and again. They died and she didn't. Each incident proved she was a survivor."

And reinforced her sorry existence.

Karen, who knew something about ephemeral existence, was not going to be left out of this.

"I wonder if it started with an accident?" Harry said. "Perhaps she was rescued and a companion perished."

Killing for the first time is an overwhelming transition, Harry. She didn't tumble into an abyss, she was pushed. By her mother. And she caught an updraft, she liked soaring through darkness. It made her feel truly alive.

"It would be easy to check the records if there was an accident," said Hannah. "But I think each time she murdered a young woman, she killed her mother."

"Perhaps. Or she killed on her mother's behalf."

"No."

"Suppose the victims in Skadi's mind were seen as her mother's rivals. Young, attractive, female, most of them unmistakably Swedish. As Birgitta grew older, Skadi tried to exterminate them for being what her mother had lost."

"Her other daughters?"

"Her youth, her sense of immortality."

"How very banal," said Hannah.

No, Karen whispered. *Evil is never banal.*

"As a beautiful woman, I am not comfortable with that," said Hannah. "Age wouldn't drive me to Botox, never mind murder."

Isn't she smug.

Is she?

No, Harry, not really. She's been horribly isolated all her life. Boys wouldn't have dared ask her out, men wouldn't risk it. And women, well, who needs reminders of their own imperfections. Horatio Sverdrup is her only friend, Harry. No wonder they're renegades together.

Hannah flicked on the flames for a moment and gazed at Harry's highlighted profile. She reached into a pocket in her coat and pulled out a folded envelope furred at the edges, opened it and took out Karen's silver wedding band. She ran a finger over the dents and scratches, then handed it to Harry, who clutched it in the palm of his hand.

She turned off the fire again and the darkness of their dank crypt closed around them again, but Harry hardly noticed. He was distracted by the recurrent image in his mind of the bland young woman he had seen standing behind Bernd, talking to Birgitta that morning in Rosedale when Bernd had turned him away. She had seemed familiar, walking in the snow outside the restaurant, but only as a generic exemplar for what Birgitta might once have been.

He could not envision what Skadi and Bernd might now be saying to each other. She, shrouded in benighted innocence, and he, stricken by misplaced guilt. Was there anything they *could* say to each other now that Birgitta was gone?

"Harry," said Hannah, interjecting in his reverie. "We still need to sort out who killed Birgitta. It's more likely to have been Bernd."

"No," Harry responded. "Skadi killed her mother. She would have done anything to protect her brother. She loves him with absolute conviction. When she understood her mother's plot to expose Bernd, using me, she tried to save him the only way she knew how. Then when you came after him over here, on Fårö, she felt her mother had won. The best she could offer Bernd was a suitable death. The burning shed. And by getting rid of me at the same time, she saw him dying with his reputation for good works intact."

"But it could have been him. He admitted as much."

"It could have been. To protect his beloved sister. His mother's power over him was always the threat to expose Skadi, paradoxically, for the crimes for which she held him accountable. But I think there's a good chance Bernd only knew about Birgitta's death when you turned up at his hotel in the middle of the night, like he says. He would have known right off that it was his sister's work."

"How so?" She was letting Harry take the lead. "She hadn't been violent before."

"By a process of elimination it had to be Skadi—he is a logical man, trapped in an irrational world."

Aren't we all, Harry.

"You find him a tragic figure?"

"He's more victim than villain. But tragic? No, I think Birgitta is tragic."

"Birgitta?"

"She loved her daughters for what she saw of herself in each of them. They were meant to be her; she would never grow old. But three of them died. And the one who survived, the bastard outsider much like herself was despicable, because she stayed young, and she was monstrous, a killer. And serene, that was the worst part. In the midst of the maelstrom, Skadi remained untouched by the horrors around her."

"But it was you who turned their story from sordid to tragic, Harry."
Now that's a disturbing thought.

"In tragedy, the protagonist dies," Hannah continued. "It was you, stirring the devil's cauldron, who made Birgitta's death necessary."

"Necessary for whom?"

"All three of them, if you think about it. You were driven by righteous rage."

He waited. He could tell she had turned to face him in the darkness, but she was no more a physical presence than Karen. Perhaps less.

"I know more about you than you think, Harry. You know about rage. You know about fury and anger and shame." She paused, as if he might need time to catch up. "My own story is also about rage. In Scandinavia, we are not all blonde and blue-eyed, you know that. But I am. And these girls, they were chosen for death because we are alike."

Harry was moved by the resonance in her voice.

"My sisters, Harry. I did not even notice their death because as reports crossed my desk at random they all seemed the same. The same to me, as much as they had been to Skadi when she killed them. Can you imagine? When Birgitta first presented her list it seemed an affront. And then you came to Sweden as a catalyst."

She hesitated, she seemed uncertain how much she needed to explain, then proceeded.

"My story, Harry? I am those women. I am enraged by their deaths. I endure the pain and humiliation of their deaths. I am consumed by guilt for their deaths. Because? Because I am a woman, I am blonde, I am fiercely a Swede. I am the police. I can tell you in Swedish, *Jag är Sverige*. It does not sound so awkward. I cannot say the same words to a Swede, except perhaps in English, 'I am Sweden.' I mean it in all humility, Harry."

In the profound darkness, he heard a catch in her throat like she was stifling emotion. At the horror, at the loss. A crack in the armour through which the light of her hidden self radiated. But only for an instant. She turned away and he could feel the air move between them. Almost as a footnote, she added, "There are so many victims, so many killers, there is so much death. It is difficult to know who I am."

Harry stared into the darkness. He could hear their breathing. Images coalesced into memories. The woman beside him stirred but remained silent. Death seemed alluring, impersonal, deferential. He was fully awake and aware as he felt death as a companion transform into something terrible and the past once again was more real than the present.

AFTER A FLOATING LUNCH while they drifted down the centre channel through a broad marshy stretch, the Anishnabe narrowed. They approached a sweeping bend on river right. The soft shoreline gathered abruptly and rose up on either side into walls of broken rock impaled with cedars. A low rumbling rolled over them as they slid across the taut smooth surface with increasing speed. Looming shadows surging over beds of gravel flashed in the depths beneath them. Karen looked back to see if Matt and Lucy were secure. Harry slapped the gunnels with his paddle; she glanced up, he grinned. She grinned.

"Listen," he said.

He feathered his paddle to urge the stern away from the rocks. It seemed they were being drawn against the shore on river right, which meant Roll-Away was coming up. There was not a ripple on the fast-moving water, no sign of rapids.

Around the bend, the river's breathing turned to a sudden roar and the landscape tumbled into an abyss. Ten canoe-lengths ahead the water bent, broke, spewed turbulent clouds of spray above a maelstrom of sound and fury.

Having missed Roll-Away, they were on the wrong side of the river. Harry tried to force the canoe into the rocky shore. He yelled at Karen to pry, but the power of the current, which a moment before held the canoe too close, now thrust them away.

"River left," he shouted. "Pry right!"

As they swung out toward the portage sign on the far shore, the river caught the canoe full on the beam and swirled it around. It lurched precariously but did not capsize. They were now stern downriver, forcing against the current. With every fibre of his being bent to the paddle, Harry churned. Karen frantically thrashed at the flow, but the portage sign slipped gradually upstream.

Again and again, his left hand lifted high and plunged with each stroke, and the sun glinting off his silver wedding band flashed in his eyes, and once, as Karen strained to pry on his side against the force of the river, the sun caught her band as well, and the sunlight turned silver.

Karen suddenly stopped paddling and twisted around. Looking downriver past her husband, her straight nose and high cheekbones caught the light, and her eyes registered holy terror. Lucy and Matt were screaming. In Karen's eyes, the flicker of a smile. Her eyes gathered the family together, the four of them. The canoe shuddered. The noise was deafening; it was almost sublime, almost like silence. The water gave way and the river opened to receive them into its fury.

Plunging through air, through the shattered water, twisting over and over in the roiling depths, Harry somehow got hold of the kids. For a moment he dreamed everything would be all right. Karen's tortured body flailing above them swirled around and around. Matt twisted toward him, his eyes wide. He could see his father, the water streaked with blood between them, his eight-year-old face tormented with fear. He screamed water, his head exploded against rock. Lucy under her father's arm, his five-year-old feminist. Her body shattered inside her skin, her life jacket holding her together, her face for a moment thrust against his, cool and serene, then wrenched away. Shadows and all the colours of creation contorted and eddied into absolute blackness. Then life left him and he was rolled over and over inside the belly of the tumultuous backwash and suddenly disgorged, spewed forth gasping for breath, looking crazily around for his loved ones, losing awareness, tumbling downriver, crashing against remnants of their small expedition, clinging and bobbing, drifting, legs smashing rock, feet touching gravel, touching sand, hands on wet cedar, dry cedar, body crawling like a monstrous primeval mistake onto the shore.

Nothing, no light, no sound, not even pain, not even time.

Then a voice. "It's Virgil," said the voice. "We was worried so the wife and I come up in the kicker. You're the only one left, my son. The others is gone."

Karen. Matthew. Lucy.

In Karen's final vision, the three of them together.

Harry was missing.

26 FIRESTORM

RELIVING THE PAST WAS NOT LIKE REMEMBERING. THERE was no interval to protect from the raw immediacy of experience. Harry retreated into the present. Bernd was there, in his mind, waiting. Was it possible to feel anything but disgust for a serial killer? For a man who tolerated murder and was driven by the horrors of his family to protect his sister who spawned them. *Spawned*, an animalistic word. Reptilian. To drop offspring into the world without conscience, to reproduce with indifference to outcome.

Harry, you're maundering.

But Harry was listening. He could hear groaning and shuffling outside the door, then a clanking as the shovel that must have been used as a brace was kicked away.

The door burst open and their cramped catacomb flooded with silver light. The storm had swept the clouds away. When they stepped out into the night, the full moon shone brightly through the gnarled branches of the old oak, which, dead or dormant, stood proud against the sky. The moonlight cast blue shadows over the windswept landscape. Drifts curled like waves into deep blue furrows and patches of autumn stubble poked through where the ground had been stripped bare by the blizzard.

Sverdrup had backed out of the passageway and was leaning against a boulder slide. He was holding his head with the apparent conviction that if he removed his hands it might split in two. Evidently he had been floored from behind with the flat of the shovel. A trickle of blood had drained across his forehead and shimmered like a bolt of black lightening. He tried to smile and his yellowed teeth glistened.

Hannah squatted to retrieve Sverdrup's fur cap. She handed it to him and stood up, without offering further acknowledgement of his wounded condition.

The air was so still, when he lit a cigarette he didn't need to shield the match-flame.

"I did not expect him to hit so hard," he said in English, to include Harry.

Hannah said something abruptly in Swedish.

"You planned to let him go?" Harry was both incredulous and struck with admiration for the unlikely extent of their devious procedures.

"It was an option we had considered," she said. "Another was how to die with dignity. Mr. Sverdrup, ever the gentleman, decided he would allow me to go first."

Sverdrup coughed phlegmatically.

He's nearly dead, already. The poor bugger wanted Hannah Arnason to die in his arms. That's quite romantic, Harry.

"We'd better get moving," said Harry. "The temperature's falling."

"Yes, I suppose we should," Hannah agreed.

Harry was filled with begrudging respect. These two cops were renegades, the ice queen and the walking inferno puffing himself to oblivion. Their strategy had been to let Bernd get to Skadi before they did. Their moral imperative was to end the murders, no matter what.

Harry and Hannah and Horatio Sverdrup kicked their way through the drifted snow, past the ancient oak, which Harry envisioned with seventy-two cadavers draped from its branches in the light of the midwinter moon. He looked back at the mound.

In the clear still air it seemed diminished, simply a rock pile. Had it ever been a pagan burial site filled with the bones of warrior kings? Did the Sviar children play there for generations, embraced by the ghosts of their ancestors? Was this where Bernd discovered his calling to track down the dead? Was this where Skadi discovered her calling to become a serial killer?

So many questions, Harry.

And too many answers.

Harry still had Karen's ring clutched in his palm. He thrust his hand deep into his pants pocket and released the ring for safekeeping. He felt it rub against the silver band on his finger. It was only a twist of metal but it was good to have it back.

Once they reached the road, the walking was surprisingly easy. The final fury of the onshore wind before it died had swept the road nearly bare.

They could see the lighthouse at the very tip of the island, and halfway along, they could see the farmhouse. There were no lights in the windows.

Hannah nudged against Harry. She slowed her pace and reached out to him with an ungloved hand. He took his own gloves off and closed his fingers around hers. They resumed walking, catching up with Sverdrup who had stopped and was listening to the darkness.

Amidst the dissonant slapping of the sea against ice chunks and boulders along the shore, they heard a scraping of wood. Between the muted thunder of rolling waves and the splashing as they curled over on themselves, they heard voices.

Through a break in the shrubbery, they could see the heat signature of embers collapsed around the belly of the iron stove, all that remained of the wooden shed. And beyond that, they could make out the figures of Bernd and Skadi dragging the upturned dory into the surf.

Harry and Hannah and Sverdrup watched, silhouetted against the sky. The midwinter moon illuminated the boat as it surged into the deep while its occupants clambered over the gunwales and set the oars. They began rowing, side by side, like seafarers in an ancient saga.

There was a penetrating clatter when something metallic crashed against the floorboards as they crested the final big wave before breaking into the open water.

They stopped rowing and shipped the oars. They rose to their feet.

The moonlight glistened on the dark sea, highlighting floating chunks of ice that had broken from the shore in the storm, and magnified the scene so that the boat seemed closer than it was in reality.

One of the figures stooped, then stood upright, and slowly waved the gasoline container through the air. It was impossible to tell who it was. Planes of fuel arced against the night sky and stained the darkness. Emptied, the can clattered again to the bottom of the dory.

Time stopped, like heaven's held breath.

A red flare burst into flame in Bernd's hands. He held it high, casting a dazzling nimbus over the boat, illuminating Skadi's features and his own in a fiery glow as they balanced precariously, standing so close there was nothing between them.

Suddenly the air cracked open in billowing flames. A swirling inferno soared into the sky, briefly erasing the light of the moon. The two figures flickered dark and then dazzled bright, before flashing into pure luminescence as they turned into fire.

A roar of silence filled the air. There were no screams from the funeral pyre. The three on the shore were mute with horror. The ribs and the planks of the boat turned blistering red, then slowly subsided into the dark of the restless sea. After a while the moon emerged from the flames and the smoke in its fullest glory. The night chill settled into the bones of the survivors on shore.

MIRANDA QUIN MET Harry at Pearson Airport. She seemed distracted by the burnt skin and bruises on his face, the gash on his forehead, and his arm in a sling. She grinned when he took her father's black toque from his sheepskin pocket and pulled it on. She accepted with a strained smile his unwrapped gift from Arlanda Airport of a canister of tea that displayed a disgruntled woman on the label. She asked whether he planned in the future to work with no contract and no retainer. He mumbled something about filing a claim against the Ghiberti estate. She passed on the news that Horatio Sverdrup had been admitted to hospital in Stockholm. Hannah Arnason was under investigation by the Swedish authorities; she sent her warmest best wishes.

"Sweden in winter must be beautiful, but you look like hell," Miranda offered by way of an apology for her complicity in his wounded condition, which, as far as she knew, was simply to have inveigled him to take Birgitta's case in the first place.

He offered no explanation for Hannah's predicament. He loosened his coat and gazed out the car window at the snow gusting and swirling across sixteen lanes of pavement. Canada in winter could be beautiful too.

After she dropped him off, he checked his mail. There was a postcard from Hawaii, signed with a Happy Face. He stepped out of the elevator and walked through the door into his condo, leaving it unlocked behind him. He hung up his sheepskin, walked through, and looked out over the magnificent view of the harbour. He could detect the scent of lilacs.

We're home, Harry.

I love you, Karen Malone, wherever you are.

I love you too, Harry. I love you too.

He carried his bags into the bedroom and carefully unfolded his nubuck jacket, which had been retrieved from the Hotel St. Clemens in Visby. He'd forgotten to declare it at customs. He walked back out into the living room, drew the pewter-grey, slub-silk drapes against the midday sun, and settled onto the sofa for a nap. He didn't want to concede that he was bone-weary or that right now the bedroom in daylight would accentuate his loneliness. He gazed around at his Scandinavian furnishings. They made his antique Heriz carpet look new. The pain running up from his toes was curiously reassuring. His

Blackwood etchings warmed him with their raw emotion and sadly lyrical beauty. He closed his eyes and before long he could hear from a great distance the words of Psalm 22, the words of Christ's roaring from the cross, My God, my God, why hast thou forsaken me? *Perché me ne rimuneri cosi? Perché, perché, Signor?*

He drifted into a black sleep.

JOHN MOSS WRITES MYSTERIES BECAUSE NOTHING BRINGS life into focus like murder. Elected a Fellow of the Royal Society of Canada in 2006 in recognition of his career as a professor of Canadian literature with over a score of books in his field, John moved progressively away from literary criticism to creative writing and the mystery genre. He and his wife, Beverley Haun, whose book *Inventing Easter Island* grew out of her work as a cultural theorist, share a stone farmhouse with an Airedale and a Kerry Blue terrier and numerous ghosts in Peterborough, Ontario. He was a scuba instructor and an endurance athlete (Boston Marathon, eleven times; the original Ironman, once; Canadian Ski Marathon, gold bar; numerous treks in the barrenlands and many long-distance loppets closer to home). John is an amateur house builder, Bev is an inspired potter, and they still enjoy canoeing, cross-country skiing, and long hikes in interesting places around the world. In 2017 they did the Wainwright coast-to-coast walk across England and would like nothing better than to do it again.

www.johnmoss.ca

Other books by John Moss

The Jewel in the Cave
The Girl in a Coma
Blood Wine
The Dead Scholar
Reluctant Dead
Grave Doubts
Still Waters
Being Fiction
Invisible among the Ruins
The Paradox of Meaning
Enduring Dreams
A Readers Guide to the Canadian Novel
Bellrock
The Ancestral Present
Patterns of Isolation

Forthcoming in the Lindstrom Trilogy

LINDSTROM'S PROGRESS Responding to the unlikely invitation from a woman in Vienna to prove she murdered her lover, Harry Lindstrom is drawn into the threatening shadows surrounding Madalena Strauss, a striking detective who appears to have stepped out of a painting by Klimt. The comforting spectre of his dead wife, Karen, grows restless being his confidante as he becomes ensnared in the woman's story of unspeakable revelations she wants brought to light with his compliance. When Madalena disappears, Harry leaves the city of shadows, with its memories of historical atrocity and imperial grandeur, and returns to Toronto. As terrible perplexing events unfold closer to home, he returns to Austria for answers, first to Vienna, then Salzburg, then deep into salt mines near the ancient village of Hallstadtt where stories from the past and present come together with harrowing finality.

LINDSTROM UNBOUND In the third novel in the Lindstrom trilogy Harry has retreated to the idyllic Polynesian island of Bora Bora to savour and lament the lost past. He finds himself drawn into a strange relationship with a raven-haired, B-list movie actress and her invalid husband. Harry learns from the amiably grotesque Inspector Theophil Queequeg that they are leaders of a virulent religious movement, and the woman is far more dangerous than he could ever have imagined. Back in Toronto, she reappears as a university professor with a disturbing capacity to make Harry wonder about the moral justifications for murder. Separately, they travel to England where they challenge the horrific intentions of the cult, and the pitiless woman of many disguises resolves major issues connected with his own family tragedy. His deceased wife, Karen, recedes into memory, enabling him to move out of the shadow of death and into the light, to place the past in the past and move on.

CPSIA information can be obtained
at www.ICGtesting.com
Printed in the USA
LVHW03s1351180618
580825LV00001B/6/P